Trials

Trials

Anne Tolstoi Wallach

A DUTTON BOOK

DUTTON
Published by the Penguin Group
Penguin Books USA Inc., 375 Hudson Street, New York, New York 10014, U.S.A.
Penguin Books Ltd, 27 Wrights Lane, London W8 5TZ, England
Penguin Books Australia Ltd, Ringwood, Victoria, Australia
Penguin Books Canada Ltd, 10 Alcorn Avenue, Toronto, Ontario, Canada M4V 3B2
Penguin Books (N.Z.) Ltd, 182-190 Wairau Road, Auckland 10, New Zealand

Penguin Books Ltd, Registered Offices:
Harmondsworth, Middlesex, England

First published by Dutton, an imprint of Dutton Signet,
a division of Penguin Books USA Inc.
Distributed in Canada by McClelland & Stewart Inc.

First Printing, November, 1996
10 9 8 7 6 5 4 3 2 1

 REGISTERED TRADEMARK—MARCA REGISTRADA

LIBRARY OF CONGRESS CATALOGING-IN-PUBLICATION DATA:

Wallach, Anne Tolstoi.
    Trials / Anne Tolstoi Wallach.
        p.   cm.
    ISBN 0-525-94091-X
    I. Title.
    [PS3573.A4334T7   1996]
    813'.54—dc20   96-22023
                                                                  CIP

Printed in the United States of America
Set in New Baskerville
Designed by Jesse Cohen

PUBLISHER'S NOTE
This is a work of fiction. Names, characters, places, and incidents either are the products of the author's imagination or are used fictitiously, and any resemblance to actual persons, living or dead, events, or locales is entirely coincidental.

For Alison

Luck made her lovely, trials made her strong

The life of the law has not been logic: it has been experience.

—Oliver Wendell Holmes

Trials

1

PAX

Almost every judge celebrates being sworn in by giving a lavish party.

Pax Peyton Ford celebrated by going home to her penthouse terrace and planting a lavish cottage garden.

In the ten years since, digging, dividing, pruning, just thinking about the garden, had helped her cope with the worst horrors of her courtroom.

Right now, though, even the garden couldn't help.

Right now she had a small—and totally deaf—boy in her courtroom who'd crushed a hand in the trash compactor of his Park Avenue building's basement. A friendless child, he'd hung around the janitor, helped with chores. The garbage had proved one chore too many. His anguished parents were suing the building owners; the owners were suing the manufacturers of the disposal unit and, for good measure, the janitor. All the parties had lawyers, and all the lawyers wanted to talk at once. One look at Adam Ullman, six, terrified and wearing one empty black glove, and the jury had gone into shock. Half the women and both men had tears in their eyes.

Pax's heart had turned over, too. The child had lost more than a hand. He'd lost his chance at sign language as well.

And he was so tiny, so waiflike. Not at all the way her own sturdy, talkative Will had looked at the same age.

One lawyer was on his feet, scowling at the handkerchiefs in the jury box, shouting at his adversary, who immediately began shouting back. Pax made herself stop thinking about Will and raised both her hands, palms out. She hadn't made her reputation by losing control of her courtroom.

"If you two want to talk to each other, do it outside this courtroom," she said pleasantly. "If you want to *try* this case, you'll address me, and only me. You can think about it because we'll recess now, till tomorrow morning, nine o'clock."

She nodded quickly to the nearest court officer. He was up with her on the bench immediately, holding open the small door to her robing room. Pax went through, thinking that a rest would settle things down. Overnight the jurors would remember they'd sworn to leave sentiment out of their deliberations. They'd steel themselves against that sad, small face, that terrible empty glove, get their judgment back in place. And so would she.

Slipping out of her black silk robe, she could almost *see* her garden, fresh, beautiful, so different from her battlefield of a courtroom. If she went home this minute, she could forget that hideous glove, busy cutting the last chrysanthemums, the first Montauk daisies. And in an hour or so, admire her newest treasure, the greenhouse, catching the sunset, its glass glinting rose and gold.

You wouldn't dare, she warned herself, walking out toward the judges' elevator.

Plenty of paperwork upstairs on her big desk, letters, applications, motions. Plenty of time left in the day. She'd summon her law clerk, work down an inch or two.

But when she got out of the elevator, her secretary was waving urgently from the outer door to her chambers.

"I just phoned down to the courtroom; they said you were coming up," Selma called. "It's *Will*, Judge. He's here, he hoped he could catch you."

Will! Pax's step quickened, her pulse, too.

"And Judge Iapalucci's been calling," Selma was going on. "He needs to see you, soon as possible."

What else! Didn't it ever stop, the working mother's dilemma? The school play at six o'clock or the jury coming in with a verdict? The graduation exercises or the defendant suddenly ready to tell all? Even now when he was all grown up, Will waiting and Joe Iapalucci, her administrative judge, her boss, really, wanting her?

Will was in the doorway now, behind Selma. Pax forgot working mothers, forgot Iapalucci, forgot everything but her rush of delight in seeing him.

Not a handsome boy, *better* than handsome in his gray sweatshirt and khakis. Rugged, solid, with quick eyes and a wide smile. Dearest Will. Hers alone since his father had died, so that for ten years they'd been specially close, tuned in to each other. Anyway, hers alone until Will married Debo last year. Still, here he was, middle of the afternoon, even with a first-year law school schedule. Who cared if Joe Iapalucci fumed?

"Mom," Will said, in the clear, strong voice Pax hoped would someday fill a courtroom, "I need to talk to you."

As she reached up to give him a hug, she remembered. Tonight she had a half date with someone who'd surprise him. His own father-in-law, a defense lawyer so busy he only *made* half dates in case some sport hero or Mafia chief suddenly needed help. Or so he'd said last week after hearing her speak at the Bar Association, buying her a drink, vigorously contesting her point of view. It was the first time they'd been alone, without wedding guests, without Will and Debo. The best time, too. Leonard had talked to her as if she were his male law partner, looked at her as if she were the most entrancing woman he'd ever met. The combination was oddly stirring, especially since most men couldn't forget she was a judge for five minutes.

"Come inside," she said, taking Will's arm, pulling him into her inner chambers. Her son towered over her. Nearly everyone did, anyway. Leonard, on the steps of the Bar Association, had seemed huge, a great bear of a man. All of Pax's life she'd kept step stools in every closet, fat cushions on every chair, high heels on her feet even when they were out of fashion.

Now she waited, smiling, for Will to pull over a chair.

Like all gardeners Pax looked at seeds and saw bright flowers, at bulbs and saw tulips, lilies. Here, with a wall of law books behind him, Pax saw her son as a young prosecutor on his feet in court, a judge in a black robe like her own, perhaps even seated with eight other brilliant judges on the wide bench of the United States Supreme Court.

"What's happening?" she said.

Will felt shy, for once, with his mother.

He'd worked out the best way to tell her his news, even practiced what to say. He'd tell her straight out that law school wasn't for him. And then, fast, what he meant to do instead. And finally, that he knew she'd be disappointed, but she'd soon see he was aiming where he really wanted to go.

How small Mom was! He always forgot she was so small. It made her seem younger than her real age, forty-nine. She was still pretty, though, like the girl in the portrait over the fireplace at home, all long, fair hair and violet eyes.

Will realized he was sweating, rubbed a hand over his forehead. I've got to tell her, he thought. I've got to explain how little it means that I'm the son, grandson, great-grandson of judges, all called Pax, Latin for peace. Maybe studying law was peaceful for Mom. But even my first month hasn't been peaceful. It's been one messy nightmare. Last in the class in that quiz? Worse, clamming up when Zipnick shot me a question in the big lecture hall?

Oh, God, Mom had just asked *him* a question, and he'd missed it entirely.

He was clamming up here, now. But everything seemed suddenly wrong for his prepared speech, time, place, everything. Day's end, wrong. Mom's chambers, wrong. He'd do better talking to her at home, cozy, by the fire. Or better yet in the garden. Mom was always different in her garden, looser, easier, a little girl with dirty hands and a big smile.

Pax watched her son's mouth tighten, his shoulders become set. What *was* it? Surely not Debo. Surely not school, even though first-year law was tough, everyone knew that. But Will was bright, knew plenty of law just from growing up with her. Why had he gone so silent? Why was the only sound in her chambers the irritating buzz of the telephone?

Selma was at the door, clasping her hands.

"I hate interrupting you two. But it's Judge Iapalucci again, and he knows you came upstairs and he can't see why you haven't returned his call."

Pax smiled at Will, reached for the phone. She could imagine Joe Iapalucci. Frowning and pacing in his vast office, a small man with a small man's push and bustle, a small man's need to dominate. Especially the women judges, though he did it by treating them as if they were made of majolica. What else? It wasn't his fault. He was well over sixty, spoiled silly by a wife and four daughters who treated him like the king of Sicily.

"You quit early," he said, booming so the phone seemed to vibrate.

"Had to," Pax told him. "Things were getting out of hand. Plaintiff's lawyer had mistrial in his eyes. Tomorrow they'll all calm down and we can go on."

"Your girl quit early, too? Didn't she tell you I called? I need to see you, Pax. And it can't wait. Judicial emergency."

Someone should stop him calling the secretaries girls, Pax thought. I should. Maybe someday when he wants a favor, a citation, I can make him a trade.

"Joe, I'm with someone," she said. "Will it keep till tomorrow morning?"

"No, it won't," Iapalucci said, his voice gravelly. "Whatever you're doing, this is more important."

Damn that wife of his, those daughters! They let him

think women dropped everything the instant he wanted something.

No, not fair. He thought *everyone* should do that.

"Of course," she said. "I'll be right down."

"Good," Joe said, as if she'd finally come to her senses. And hung up.

Pax did the same, looked at her son.

"I can't believe it," she said. "The administrative judge. He leaves every single day about four, has his driver take him up to Yankee Stadium to play tennis. Now, just because you're here and you're special, he wants me in his office. I've got to say goodbye, Will."

She didn't miss the relief on her son's face, the relaxation in his shoulders. Whatever he wanted to tell her, it wasn't coming easily.

"Dinner," she said, touching his cheek. "The first night you two aren't studying, come eat and we'll talk."

But what did Iapalucci want to talk about?

She pictured him prowling his office, wearing one of his artfully tailored suits, padded shoulders, vertical pinstripes, all to look taller than he was. The man didn't look for meetings with women judges. He came from the days when judging was a boys' club, kept himself surrounded, bulwarked by men when he made announcements, ate in the lunchroom, came to judicial parties.

Suddenly Pax wondered if someone had complained to him about her new project, the committee to police the divorce lawyers. Aimed at disciplining the ones who preyed on women clients at their most vulnerable, took their jewelry, even their houses as security for their fat fees. She *was* the only judge on the committee. And there had been some frost from the matrimonial lawyers she ran into around the city. Too damn bad, and so she'd tell Joe.

Only five o'clock. But the vast lobby was almost empty, the air still. No one coming in through the new metal detectors, only a few people leaving, the huge rotunda echoing with their footsteps. Usually Pax had to dodge crowds here, make her way through knots of lawyers, jurors, clerks, school-children come to see the court system at work. Now she could tip back her head, take a leisurely look at the high rotunda, the vast murals decorating it. There they were, the great law-givers of history, Justinian, Charlemagne, Simon de Montfort, Washington, Lincoln, more.

Men, all men, Pax thought. For over a thousand years men did all the judging. We've only had about fifty years. No wonder they're still getting used to us.

She forgot the past, snapped quickly into the present, seeing the uniformed officer blocking the door to Iapalucci's chambers. Strange. Usually the floor was silent, all doors locked by this hour.

Stranger yet, Iapalucci's secretary was still at her desk, still busy, using a large, shiny scissors to cut out newspaper clippings. She glared, as if it was Pax's fault she was still hard at work.

A moment later Pax was in Iapalucci's private office, three times as large as her own, filled with the photographs and awards of his long judicial career. As she walked toward him, he bobbed up briefly from his huge throne of a chair.

"Pax," he said, jerking his chin at one of the six chairs on her side of the desk. "Sit down."

She chose one directly facing him. It gave her a clear view of the handsome leather tennis bag behind his desk, two racket handles protruding from its zipper top. Was it her fault, too, that he'd missed his tennis? What *was* this all about?

"You've heard the latest?" Iapalucci said. As if he expected a woman, any woman, to know all the courthouse gossip.

Pax shook her head. No, she wanted to say, I've been doing my job, thanks.

"The promotion?" he said, leaning forward. "One of our judges going up to the Appellate Division?"

Pax swallowed hard, wishing that, for once, she *had* been gossiping.

Promotion! What she wanted, what every judge wanted, a move up to the next highest court. Civil Court judges eyed vacancies in the Supreme Court. Supreme Court judges dreamed about the Appellate Division. Judges there jockeyed for the Court of Appeals in Albany, the Federal Court, even, God willing, the Supreme Court of the United States.

For Pax, promotion meant even more. Her father had been in the Appellate Division. His picture hung on the wall in the landmark courthouse on Madison Avenue. While she'd been growing up, he'd sat in its beautiful courtroom affirming or reversing other judges' decisions on the toughest, most controversial trials in the city. No woman had served in that courtroom till long after Pax was a judge herself. All she'd ever wanted in the law was to preside in her father's courtroom.

In the spring, along with more than fifty other judges, she'd applied for the latest vacancy. Submitted the elaborate résumés, questionnaires, recommendations. Faced the screening panels that asked tough questions about their education, experience, the smallest details of their personal lives.

By midsummer she'd been one of seven survivors, a triumph in itself. Ever since the whole courthouse had waited for the governor to choose just one. After that he'd throw away the list. Next vacancy the process would start from scratch.

Now Joe was telling her the governor *had* chosen.

And, since nobody'd called her with good news, he'd chosen someone else.

"Who is it?" she asked pleasantly, not feeling pleasant.

My God, was it Rosa, her friend, practically her little sister, whom she'd pushed, pulled through law school? She'd been on the list of seven, too. But Rosa was so young, only thirty-five. A darling, a great friend, yes. A beauty, high-spirited, strong, outspoken. But a high court judge? Surely not yet.

"It's Harry Silk," Joe said abruptly.

Pax realized she'd been holding her breath.

Not Rosa. Harry Silk. Sixty-five at least, bearded like an

Old Testament prophet. Nice man, good judge, loved getting in the newspapers, carried his clippings around to show anyone who'd read them. She could go to his swearing-in party and really wish him well.

"You know what a workhorse Harry is," Joe was saying. "Just this week I handed him a case that's a real piece of shit—pardon me, Pax. A challenge."

A challenge! Pax knew how Iapalucci used the word. It always meant a long, controversial trial sure to be appealed, probably reversed, with plenty of publicity along the way.

"A showcase," Iapalucci was saying. "More media attention, as much chance to make a big name as on O. J. Simpson."

Ah, Pax thought. You gave it to Harry and then he was promoted out of your clutches, so it's back in your lap. Do you think *I* want to make a name for myself? Because I applied for a promotion? Because I work on a committee that's making a lot of noise? I didn't do those things to get attention. I did them because they felt right. And the hell with media attention.

"I already have a name," Pax said. "And Joe, I also have a garden, and I should be in it right now, cleaning it up for winter. It's not like tennis, you know. It can't wait, or it's a big mess."

"Pax. You want to hear about a big mess, let me show you the newspapers, the kind of stuff that's going on already before the trial's even started. A freak show. You just wait a minute."

He watched her as he reached for the clippings, suddenly glowing about her garden, and just like a woman, distracted, when you were trying to say something serious.

It *was* some mess, this case coming in. Worse than that Kennedy kid, in many ways worse than O. J. Simpson, they made so much fuss about. Made you wish for a good, ordinary murder, a simple rape, the kind you tried by the book and stayed safe from the press and the public, from an Appellate Division reversal.

Pax took the clippings, wondering what could be worse

than what she had now. Divorce? Medical malpractice? Racial bias? Why a freak show? What kind of freaks?

"A custody battle," Joe said. "I'm sure you've read about it. When the reporters hear about Harry, they'll be all over me. They know they'll have a ball when it gets going. Cardinal O'Connor, bless him, has already taken a stand. So has Betty Friedan. Only hers is different from the cardinal's."

"What do you want from me, Joe?" Pax said. "Haven't I enough with a child whose hand got crushed? Six screaming lawyers? A jury that can't listen because they're crying?"

"Forget that, Pax. I'm talking about a groundbreaker here. A case with no precedent in the long history of the law."

Damn him, Pax thought. He knows all his judges love issues that haven't come up before, cases that make news. Voting rights for the homeless. Condoms in the high schools, textbooks on gays for grade-school children.

"You mean, nobody's *bothered* to find a precedent yet," she said. "In the long history of the law not much hasn't come up before."

"They've come close in a couple of places, Vermont, Florida. But that's been a real parent wanting custody, not some leftover companion, not when someone normal, heterosexual, wants the kid, too."

He looked straight at her.

"Above all, not when there's money involved. Real money, billions, they say."

He leaned closer.

"Take a look. It's that nutty artist who just died, left a little daughter. The one they're calling a mystery child because nobody's seen her. The boyfriend wants custody. So does the kid's aunt, a blood relation and as straight as they come."

Pax felt a stir of excitement. He meant the Johnny California case. But in spite of the publicity, what judge would want it? Custody cases *were* freak shows, held more emotion, more craziness than almost anything. Fathers killed their kids rather than let ex-wives have them. Mothers spent their last pennies on airline tickets to faraway places, spirited children illegally away.

Gay custody was worse, much worse. Couples couldn't adopt because the law didn't consider them couples. So children with two daddies or two mommies usually belonged legally to just one partner. Or were children nobody wanted to claim, HIV-positive, racially mixed, handicapped babies.

Johnny California's child, healthy, with billions of her own, *would* be something else.

"It'll be a zoo," Joe was saying, pushing back his chair, standing. "No jury, of course, it'll all be up to the judge. Harry Silk was tough enough to run it and old enough to retire afterward if he got crucified. I can't leave it to random selection, let it go to one of our weaker sisters. In my book you're a pretty tough judge, girl. So before the news about Harry gets out, before I start getting applications for special handling, I'm giving it to you."

Pax stared at him.

He thought she was tough, good.

He thought he could con her into taking on a mess, not good.

"Now, Joe," she said, widening her eyes, "I thought all judges were equal. All cases assigned in strict rotation."

"Oh, they are. Only somehow the tough ones usually end up with tough judges. The Central Park jogger, Tom Gallagan got that, hard-hearted Irishman that he is. The Bronx social hall fire, Judge Roberts had that, and he's a fire-eater. You, now, cool, a real little lady, why, you could make ice cream out of crap like this."

His teasing made her feel anything but cool. Good God, half the judges in the Supreme Court would be making a mess of the case she had right now. Little? Lady? She wouldn't be cajoled. She'd turn him down flat.

Then she realized Joe was watching her closely, starting to smile.

Smile!

"To be honest, Pax, it's worse than crap. It's a *rompicoglioni.*"

The word, the rich way it rolled from his tongue, somehow intrigued her.

"A what?"

"A ballbreaker, as we said in my old neighborhood. The demonstrations when this gets going, those gay groups, those hardhats, they'll make the anti-abortionists, the school screamers, look like peace marchers. All the nuts in the city will be out. Come on, Pax, wouldn't you like a little fame? Glory? Don't you want to prove yourself on something like this?"

Blarney, Pax thought. What's the Italian for blarney? I don't need to prove myself anymore.

Only wait a minute. Didn't she? After all, she hadn't been promoted. Harry Silk had said yes to this trial and he'd been promoted.

Besides, all the judges he'd called tough were men.

She looked at the clippings piled in front of her on Iapalucci's desk.

Pax had a special, blessed gift of memory. Closing her eyes, she could see pages of print, read them as if they were in front of her. A boon for a law student, a godsend for a judge.

Now she could almost see a list of all she'd read about the custody case, clear as if it were actually in her hand.

Johnny California, superrich, famous, collector, wild man. Private planes, houses in New York, Paris, London, Africa, the Caribbean, who knew where else. Armies of bodyguards, flotillas of pleasure boats, fleets of cars. Suddenly dead last month, in Italy? Switzerland? And his longtime lover almost as famous, ballet dance Tom D'Arcy. California's wife had died; his child would inherit millions. A mystery child, the tabloids called her, kept completely out of the public eye. The news people were clamoring for pictures of her. And D'Arcy was clamoring for custody.

Iapalucci was talking again.

"That's why the cardinal's making big speeches," he was

saying. "Why the gay organizations are getting hot. Why someone with genuine judicial temperament has to handle it."

Pax blinked away the list in her mind.

"Joe," she said, "you're right about one thing. It is a whatever-that-Italian-word was."

"Oh, you've only heard the half of it," he said, jaunty again. "You'll never guess who's on the other side."

"Mother Teresa," Pax said. "President Clinton. Who?"

"Almost as tough. The aunt, California's sister, is married to John Talcott Bishop, no less, publisher of our favorite newspaper, the *Bar Journal*."

My God, Pax thought. The legal profession's bible, what every lawyer and judge in New York reads every single working day. Bishop's a judge maker, he was on my screening panel. He can do what he wants, feature a judge's opinions on the front page or bury them in the back with the bail bondsmen's ads. What judge would want to take him on?

"Imagine deciding against Bishop," she said, shaking her head. "I could forget seeing my opinions in print. I could turn out to be a non-person in the law."

She stood up, gave him her best smile, to show she wasn't taking him seriously, not for a minute.

"You'd see your picture in every paper in the city," Joe said, eyes narrowing. "On every TV news program. You'd be famous in a week. You'd have the respect of every lawyer, every other judge. You'd be doing your job, Pax, doing it right. That is not nothing."

For one surprising moment he sounded like her father. Strange. Joseph Xavier Iapalucci wasn't a bit like her calm, stately father.

"And incidentally," Joe went on, softly, "next time there's a vacancy in the Appellate Division, you might well be first in line."

Pax felt her body stiffen.

"Even ahead of your buddy up in the Bronx," he said. "Even ahead of gorgeous, young, up-from-the-barrio Rosa Macario."

Bastard, Pax thought. Machiavelli.

Joe was pawing through the papers on his desk, picking up a newspaper, tossing it toward her.

"Cast your eye on the cast of characters. Here's today's paper, big pictures of them all."

Pax looked.

She'd seen dozens of pictures of Johnny California before, at parties, galleries, benefits, even the White House. But this picture was different. And horrible. California's death mask. A face, white, hard, cheeks sunken, eyes closed. It must have been made in Europe, wherever he'd died.

She shivered, looked at the rest.

A blurry shot of a uniformed nurse with a child. No wonder the papers were frantic for photographs of the little girl. If this was the best they had in their files, editors must be desperate.

Talcott Bishop, with his wife in what must be their living room. Looking heavy, important. Mrs. Bishop like any aging upper-class woman, pearls at her neck, simple pageboy, simple dress.

Then Pax looked at the photograph of Tom D'Arcy.

She'd seen him often, dancing at Lincoln Center, at Tanglewood. He'd been photographed almost as much as California a few years back when he'd launched a crusade to teach ballet to boys. This picture was old, taken for some performance, probably *Spectre de la Rose*. D'Arcy, in a rose petal tunic and tights, arms curved high, face extravagantly painted.

She stared down at the picture, feeling the room go dark, hearing the dissonant sounds of an orchestra tuning up for an overture.

"Today's *Times* has an op-ed piece," Joe was saying. "How this is going to be the biggest custody case since Gloria Vanderbilt's."

"Great," Pax managed, under the spell of D'Arcy's heavily made-up face. "Remember what happened to that judge? Broke down afterward, died in an institution."

Dizzy, choking, she hardly heard her own voice.

It's this picture, she thought. I can't look at it, I can't bear it.

Mind swirling, stomach churning, she felt herself slipping into another place, another time.

Eight years ago. A funeral. Her loving and loved husband suddenly gone, heart attack. Impossible. Because he'd been so alive. Alden couldn't die at fifty-one. He was in perfect shape, a runner, a squash player. But he had died.

Standing with the funeral guests, keeping an eye on her son, Pax believed nothing worse could happen.

Only then it had happened. Something to split her whole life into before and after, something she'd remember with all its force forever.

She'd been calm itself with the ghouls of the funeral world, undertaker, minister, obituary writer, flower people, food people. And poised with everyone else. Friends who'd come to say they loved Alden, loved her. Alden's partners at his architecture firm, her colleagues at the courthouse, men in Alden's clubs who knew him well, men with sad, serious faces.

Then, in front of her, a man she didn't know. Handsome as the day. Beautifully dressed, soft jacket, pale shirt, gleaming shoes, heavy signet ring. Not in a group with any other guest. Alone, in front of her, looking at her.

Her Willie, all wrists and ankles because there'd been no time for a new suit, had noticed the man, too, felt something ominous. He'd stepped closer to Pax, taken her hand.

"Do we know each other?" she'd said. "Are you a friend of Alden's? From the firm?"

He'd been silent. Willie had seen a cousin his own age, squeezed her hand, moved away.

Then the man spoke, looking into her eyes. "You don't know me. Maybe you won't want to know me. I'm Alden's best friend." That hadn't made sense. She knew Alden's friends, all of them, even though there were so many. She'd at least seen almost everyone else who was in her living room.

"I'm more," the man had said then. "I'm his lover. Was. Alden and I were lovers. We met at Yale, we've been together since. If you can stand to hear it, I miss him as much, maybe more than you."

Pax looked up at the beautiful face, the hard eyes, the thin, carved mouth, smelled the expensive cologne, and felt herself turning to pale, cold marble.

Because she was marble, his words seemed to glance off her hard surface.

"Is it a joke?" she'd said stupidly.

Because it was ridiculous that Alden could have a lover, when she was his lover. Alden was tough, strong, entirely male. He'd made love to her with zest, force. He'd adored her.

"Not funny," she'd said, too cold, hard to rail at anyone who would say such a thing at such a time.

"I didn't come to tell you," the man said. "Alden would never have told you. He loved you. But he loved me, too. Nobody knew, nobody at all, we turned handsprings so nobody would know. Nobody will mourn him with me. Alden said you were wise, strong, brilliant. I suppose I hoped we could mourn together. We'll miss him together."

Pax had dissolved, felt tears start, felt her insides turn to water.

This isn't real, she'd thought. I'm making it up out of grief and pain, I'm imagining it. Alden loved me. He made love to me once, twice a week, more in the summer when Willie was away at camp, when we were on vacation, when we were traveling.

The man had mistaken her silence for assent, because the next thing he said was still more terrible.

"There are things about Alden we're the only ones who know. How he liked memorizing Auden's poems. I even called him Auden as a joke. How he carried half a dozen handkerchiefs so he'd never have to use one that wasn't spotless."

He'd stood close to her, with his carved face, his beautiful clothes. Pax had thought wildly that he looked exactly like a homosexual in a cheap drama, looked just the way ignorant people think homosexuals look.

Can it possibly be true? she'd asked herself, frozen. Did Alden close his eyes, clench his teeth when he touched me? Did he think about this man when he reached for me? Did Alden make Will out of some perverted need to look normal, ordinary? Is my darling son a lie?

As if he could read her thoughts, the man had come closer still.

"I haven't told you my name," he'd said. "It's Will. Will Sheridan. Alden gave his son my name. For me. I've never seen Willie before, only pictures. He's a beautiful boy."

Memory stopped there, because she'd become so icy with rage she'd gone blank, never quite known what happened next, what she'd said, done. For all she knew, she had turned to marble.

She was marble now, in Iapalucci's office, cold, remembering.

She'd spent terrible months wondering if something about her attracted men who didn't need women. Then, because everyone gets over anything, slowly, gradually, she'd found peace. She hadn't failed Alden; he'd loved her as much as he could love a woman. When they were young he'd been all she needed, pleasant, caring, loving. Now she saw more, knew more. When Leonard Scholer had looked at her the other night, she'd known a man was looking, yes, and thinking a man's thoughts, feeling a man's feelings. Whatever might come next, she was sure of that much.

This case, now.

If she ran it right, Leonard Scholer would have to think she was extraordinary.

If she ran it right, she could bury that funeral scene, wipe out the memory of that nightmare of a man. She'd know she could be fair, impartial, everything a good judge should be. And when promotions were handed out, she'd be far out front of everyone else.

Suddenly she felt cold, hot, exhilarated, terrified, all at the same time.

She looked at Joe Iapalucci, drumming his heavy fingers on his desktop, frowning.

"Well, if you had to give up tennis," she said, taking the plunge, "if you had to waste a beautiful fall evening, I guess it's the least I can do. The California case has a new judge."

In the silence that followed, she could hear pigeons cooing on the window ledge, cars honking down in the street, the crash of a metal pail hitting the floor in the outer office as a cleaning woman began her nightly work.

"Easy as that?" Joe said, smiling, tossing his pen on the desk.

Easy? What easy? She was already a little sorry she'd said yes.

Joe was standing now, both hands on his desk, eyes on hers.

"Clear your decks, here, at home. Wind up the case you have as fast as you can. Yes, and get yourself off that feminist committee, let someone else scold divorce lawyers. The press will be on top of you the minute I announce it's your trial. We'll have amicus briefs from every side, the Lambda Legal Defense Fund, the Catholic Lawyers Guild, everyone else who knows already how this should come out. I did point out, didn't I, you have no jury, no one to share the blame. Custody cases don't have juries."

She wasn't getting off her committee for Joe or anyone else. Or letting him lecture her on the law, either.

"I know, Joe. I even know *why* they don't have juries. Custody cases come down from the English ecclesiastical courts. Juries only sat to advise. Judges decided alone."

"Yes, well, they're lousy, whatever they came down from," Iapalucci said. "We'll all feel this one, Pax. Remember when Judge Wilner closed the gay bathhouses? They picketed here, staked out his apartment building, burned his mail, tied up his phones, called out those Pink Angels who protect gays. Half the papers in town were calling for Wilner's blood."

"Don't unconvince me," Pax said.

"Pax, you're seeing Leonard Scholer, am I right?"

This courthouse *is* a village, she thought, stunned. A gossip factory. Sure, he's Will's father-in-law, everyone knows that. But I've hardly *begun* seeing him.

"Honey, there was this note," Iapalucci said, using a forbidden word, one the Gender Bias Committee of the Women's Bar would condemn. "Your girl called mine, said to tell you Mr. Scholer can't make it tonight, hopes you can make it tomorrow. Listen, Pax. He's a hell of a good lawyer, a hell of a good guy. He'll like getting the details of this case firsthand, not that you don't keep confidences, but we all know how it is. You better tell him I've handed you the trial of the decade."

As if, Pax thought, I'd walked in asking for it. He *is* a bastard. He *is* a Machiavelli.

"Come on," he said. "I'll walk you to the elevator."

She knew he was getting her out fast now, washing his hands, like that trend-setting judge Pontius Pilate. Last spring she'd seen Pilate's very own marble washbasin in a church in Bologna, or anyway, one the Bolognese claimed was his, a warning to indecisive judges everywhere.

"Watch your step," Iapalucci said as they walked, just as if she'd volunteered, demanded to run the trial herself. "Gay power, demonstrators, Act Up, big-deal lawyers, Bishop's clout, a mystery child, California's billions, you'll have a lot on your plate."

He looked at his watch, gold, worn enough to have been his father's.

"Harry Silk was an old-timer. He was ready to get right out, retire if things got hot. Take care. We wouldn't want this to be your last trial."

He turned, walked away, his words echoing in the empty corridor.

2

ROSA

ROSA SHOVED ASIDE THE SCREEN AROUND HER MOTHER'S HOS-
pital bed and ran for the nurses' station in the hall. Dodging
gurneys, mops, supply carts, she could feel her heart beating
double time.

The brightly lit glass cubicle was empty, its counters
cluttered with forms and files, its phones blinking.

Turning, she saw her face in the smudged glass.

She looked ready for a hospital herself, dark eyes glittering and feverish, skin sallow. Even her hair looked like a
patient's, untidy dark strands slipping from the knot at the
back of her head.

Nobody'd believe I'm a judge, Rosa thought, her heart
speeding further still. Let alone a judge the *New York Post*
called young and beautiful when I got elected just last year.

Of course, that was *before* these last months when everything outside her courtroom had gone so horribly wrong,
before this new agony over Mami.

Wheeling around, she saw a black woman in white pants
and shirt far down the hall. Within seconds she was pulling at
the woman's fat sausage of an arm.

"Listen," she said, "my mother's bleeding. A lot."

"Right with you," the nurse said, her slow Southern voice making her sound as if she'd been shaken out of a nap.

"Now," Rosa said, frantic. "I said, bleeding. Come right now."

The nurse sighed, making her double chin quiver. "She the one got shot? Came up from Emergency?"

"Yes," Rosa said, wincing, as if the stray pellets had pierced her cheek, as if Mami's pain and shock were her own. "Hurry."

They moved through the noise and bustle filling the corridor. Patients shuffling along with IV's trailing them, doctors who looked like teenagers, sweating orderlies, women in smocks with clipboards. The place reeked of sweat, urine, vomit, sharp disinfectant, the kind that was supposed to smell like pine but came nowhere near.

Frantic, Rosa felt her patience seeping away like Mami's blood.

"Who shot her?" the nurse was asking.

Was the woman a piece of ice? Why wasn't anyone here Puerto Rican? Someone who'd know how a daughter felt about a mother? Lots of hospital personnel were Puerterros. Where were they now when she needed them?

"Kids shot her," Rosa said, tightening her hold. "She was sitting on a park bench. The wrong park bench."

Hadn't she had enough with the project police, the real cops, ambulance men, those clowns in the emergency room? Why had she let them bring Mami here, to big, horrible, overcrowded Metropolitan Hospital? She'd wanted the best, New York, Mount Sinai. This was closer, they'd said. In case the wound was more than superficial, in case of shock. Now her mother was trapped in this rathole, bleeding, silent, and this lump of a woman could do nothing but act stupid.

Finally, the bed, Mami. Her face seemed half bandage, half mask, eye closed, mouth twitching. Blood, dark as wine, was spreading like ink on a blotter, wet on the white gauze.

Oh God, more blood than before! Rosa felt her throat thicken.

Suddenly she wanted to sink to her knees, put her hands together as if she were in church. *Ayudame,* she wanted to beg this nurse, help me, *por favor.*

But no, if she began thinking in Spanish she'd be lost. She'd be a terrified little girl again, dizzy from the big plane, scared of the tall buildings, shivering in her first New York cold.

Rosa swallowed, stepped back, allowed the nurse to get closer to her mother.

The years Mami had lived on 124th Street, the years Rosa, and Pax too, begged her to move near Rosa in Riverdale, move to the country, move anywhere. Pax's mother had been tall, cold, distant. Pax had adored Rosa's Mami, turned to her often, cared for her now. But Mami wouldn't go. Her friends from the island were nearby, Consuelo, Nita. The big A&P, the small *bodegas* and *botanicas* were all there. And Carlos, her adored grandson, just eighteen, had friends, too. Friends who till this moment had been Rosa's worst nightmare.

"No problem, honey," the nurse was saying. "Seeping a little, that's all. She had a shock, that's all. No problem."

Was she right? Could she be trusted? Did she know anything?

Ah, something was happening.

Mami's eyelid was fluttering, her eye opening. Her hand was moving, too, as if she was trying to touch her bandage.

"See?" the nurse said, shrugging. "She's okay. Don't get so excited. There's real sick people in those other beds."

Rosa hardly heard. Mami's mouth was moving.

"Que paso?" she said, voice weak but its tone critical, as if she were in her own tidy kitchen asking why Rosa had come later than she promised.

Rosa forgot the nurse, the shooting, Carlos, feeling a hot wave of joy, relief, love.

"Mami," she whispered. *"Esta okay, muy okay."*

Mami's eyebrow, still black, still full, was rising. There were questions in her dark eye.

I never could fool her, Rosa reminded herself. Not even when I became the *Señora Juez*, the judge. Carlos fools her, but I never could.

"Mami, it's a hospital. You got hurt. Boys in the park, shooting. You were in the way."

Surprised, she saw her mother's mouth go tight, the way it had been often during the year Rosa spent with her lover, Tony. Mami had never met him, even spoken about him, but she'd somehow known all about him, even that he was married. She'd known when Rosa ended it, too. Witchcraft? Intuition?

Under the bandage a frown wrinkled her mother's forehead.

Rosa stood up, seeing now over the white screen that was supposed to hide the other beds in the large room but didn't. Moving close to Mami, she took hold of the limp hand on the sheet. It was warm, dry, absolutely as always.

"Don't worry," she said. "Soon we'll get you to a better place, a hospital room of your own, a window. Just don't worry."

"Listen," the nurse was saying, "we get worse than this all the time. You wouldn't believe what we get every day."

Listen yourself, Rosa wanted to say. I could tell you stories. You should know what I hear in my courtroom, machete attacks, scalded babies, homosexual rape.

The nurse was leaning over, picking up the screen, straightening it.

Bronx Criminal Court, bottom of the barrel, worst of the worst. Not like Pax in a downtown courtroom, hearing civil cases, white-collar crimes.

Pax! Wasn't this Thursday? Pax's day to come up at lunchtime, visit Mami? The women in Mami's hall would be all over her, gabbling out the news, scaring her to death.

"Now, you calm yourself down," the nurse said, turning. "Don't need more patients around here."

No, Rosa thought. Pax is smart. She'll ask the building

guards, call the cops, find out where they took Esperanza Macario. And she'll come straight here.

She forced herself still, the way she did on the bench when she had to take control. Just the thought of Pax helped, anyway. Pax, who looked so delicate, but was made of stainless steel. She knew how to make things happen, had known even as a girl when Mami washed and ironed for her family. She'd taught Rosa how to make things happen for herself, too. Which it was high time she began doing.

"Is there a chair?" she said, turning to the fat nurse. "I want to sit with my mother a little. Till I'm sure she's as comfortable as you say. Then I'll need to use a phone. I want her moved, a private room, another hospital."

Surprise slowly came over the nurse's face like an image emerging on a Polaroid print.

"Over there, honey," she said, nodding toward the screen. "Between those two beds by the window."

"If you'd get it," Rosa said. "I don't want to let go of my mother's hand."

She felt a little rush of self-respect when the woman moved, fetching the battered wooden chair, then setting the screen back in place.

Rosa pulled the chair closer, sank into it.

Now she realized how drained she felt, how miserable. Dizzy, she closed her eyes.

She couldn't, though, close her ears. Sounds were everywhere, wheels grinding against the hard floors, patients behind other screens moaning, calling out in Spanish, English, other languages she couldn't identify, maybe weren't languages at all. This was worse than her zoo of a courtroom.

Before the cops had come for her, she'd been dealing with a bail application, routine, dull. Juan Rodriguez, twenty-one, handsome as a cigar box picture, jilted by his girlfriend, deciding to punish her. His way of doing that was to take a machete made for cutting sugarcane to the restaurant where she worked and start swinging at everyone in it. Happily, his swinging had been as wild as his reasoning, no awful harm done. Cuts, shocks, scares, screaming, but nothing like the massacre that could have been.

Rosa had sighed, set bail at the thirty thousand dollars she knew might as well have been thirty million for Juan Rodriguez.

But then the lawyer, an old man in a tight sharkskin suit, stepped closer, actually winked at her.

"I hardly need explain this to you, Your Honor," he'd said. "We deal here with a different standard, a different frame of mind, a cultural difference. We deal here with a mistake of passion. A dishonored man, heart wounded, masculinity threatened, sets out on a course which, while unfortunate, is understandable in the circumstances. You of all people will understand."

She'd felt just the kind of surprise and rage she could never show on the bench.

"Really? Why is that, Counselor?"

"Now, Judge. You will appreciate that this is not what we call a crime. A first offense, almost certainly a last. It will never, never happen again. My client is more than willing, eager, to apologize to everyone at the scene, the owner, the lady, to you, of course, most, to you."

Only the thought of Pax, who'd warned her over and over never to lose her temper on the bench, never to hold a lawyer in contempt because she'd have to explain herself to a judicial committee, kept her from taking the bastard apart. "Counselor," she said, "you've got that all wrong. You're talking about a crime, a felonious assault, to be precise. That is, of course, if a jury decides your client committed it. Bail remains as stated. And I suggest you find a better argument on your client's behalf before this comes up for trial in my courtroom or anyone else's."

You try enlisting me as a *compadre*, Counselor, she wanted to say, and I'll hold you in contempt no matter what my older and wiser friend says.

Remembering, she shivered, filled with cold misery.

Would she always be, not a judge, but a Hispanic judge?

Yes, unless she got lucky and got out of the trial courts. Unless she could capture a promotion, go up to the Appellate Division, the way she longed to do. Then nobody'd dare approach the bench with an oily smile, insinuate that she'd ever favor her own people.

"You okay, lady?" a man's voice said, loud, close.

Rosa opened her eyes.

A cop. Silver-haired, bulky, tall, peering from behind Mami's screen, already filling the small space with a cop smell, sweat and shoe leather.

"What is it, Officer?"

"You the judge?"

"Yes. Judge Macario."

He came all the way into the little space, smiling.

She couldn't seem to see him so well now, the noise around her somehow more distant, the room darker.

"Listen," she said, her tongue thick, "I've already talked to the cops."

She shut her eyes again, hoping he'd go away, disappear, *hola!*

The officer saw her eyes close, took his chance, gave her a good look, breasts, hips, what he could make out of her legs pressed against the bed. Even in that stiff suit, navy like his own uniform, there was plenty to see. Her spicy perfume seemed to fill his nostrils, sexy, stirring. It made him think of the dark beauties back in high school, the ones who were willing to screw in Prospect Park, then, strangely, of the Mexican burritos he loved so much.

So this was the spic judge the boys in the Bronx said was such a dish. Blue-black hair, straight, heavy. Skin like honey, eyes like big plums. Breasts a man could weigh in his hands. A beauty, even in that old-maid jacket, even with her hair scraped back tight.

Fighting a cloud of nausea, Rosa opened her eyes, saw the man smiling at her. He looked kind, even solicitous.

"I guess you're pretty tired," he said. "Takes a lot out of you, thing like this."

Rosa's stomach heaved. Jesus, she was going to throw up, here, now.

"Sorry to bother you, Judge. Must be there's nobody on the bench this afternoon. There's another lady judge downstairs wanting to come up here."

Pax, Rosa thought, her stomach steadying, nausea fading.

He was taking a piece of paper out of his pocket, consulting it. "Judge Ford. You know her?"

Energy seemed to shoot through Rosa, clearing her head, straightening her back. "Yes," she said, "she's my friend, my mother's friend. Please ask her to come up, Officer. Now."

Suddenly she couldn't wait another second for Pax, her friend, her defender. "Tell them right away," she said. "Please."

Now she felt well, safe, a little girl in the big laundry room on Fifth Avenue listening to the beautiful young lady who was Pax, while her own mother sprinkled linens the way the priest sprinkled holy water, pressed them smooth with her iron.

Rosa glanced down at Mami, who seemed to be sleeping, breathing evenly.

She got up, began pacing, hands clasped together.

Thank God for Pax, who even as a college girl had brought such calm with her, though she hadn't been much taller than Rosa in spite of the fourteen years between them. Back then Rosa would tell her what Sister Luz said in school, how Mami was having such trouble with her wicked sister, pregnant again. And Pax would listen, head tipped to one side, serene, still as a stone saint.

When Rosa was done, Pax would talk about her professors, her friends, of thrilling books she was reading, till Rosa's eyes went wide with wonder. Till she promised herself she'd read books, make friends of her own, do all Pax did.

And she had. But nowhere as easily, as smoothly. She'd had to type for a bilingual lawyer on Amsterdam Avenue, go tired to night school, join the Hispanic clubs, stand on the cold streets with petitions for other lawyers running for judgeships, then, later, for herself. She'd smiled at barrio storekeepers, canvassed the projects for votes, hung around the broken-down subway entrances, spoken at the schools, danced with other Latinos in uptown nightspots, politicked till she couldn't summon up one more smile.

Pax went to Harvard Law School, Rosa thought. I've never even seen Harvard Law School.

Suddenly, with a sharp pang, she remembered her nephew Carlos, the drug bust, the upcoming trial. The real horror, the one Mami might not recover from so easily, recover from at all.

Misery stabbed up from her chest into her throat, so she hardly knew where she was, forgetting Mami, hospital smells, noises, everything.

Then, from behind the screen, Pax.

Heart pumping, breath coming in bursts, Rosa moved to her, hugged her, tried to breathe her in.

Ah, she thought, feeling Pax stretch up to her. She's so *delicada*, so small. I always forget she's so small.

She looked down at her friend's face. Pax was still beautiful. Even with lines at the corners of her eyes, even with silver hair, beautiful. Now, in a silky silvery coat that seemed made to match her hair, especially beautiful.

"Traffic," Pax was saying. "It felt like forever, getting here. Rosa, they said she was doing well. *Is* she doing well?"

Her voice was beautiful, too, the voice Rosa had always wanted for herself, clear, somehow soft and strong at the same time.

"I think so," Rosa said. "Anyway, I am, now you're here."

"The police brought me. With sirens. They stop on every corner, so it's not all that fast."

Pax bent toward Mami, put a hand on her cheek, shook her head.

"They brought me, too," Rosa said. "Without sirens."

"Now, listen," Pax said, pushing back her sleeve, looking at her watch. "It's almost two o'clock. Obviously you're not going back to court. But I have to."

"Why? It's like the old joke, they can't start without you."

"That's just the trouble. They have to start. And I'm going on to something new, I have to wind this up. But I got the woman in Admissions downstairs to call the chief of this ward, explain who your mother is, who you are. We can move her in a few hours if we waive their responsibility. I think Mami should come with me for a few days. Flora's there, maybe a nurse for afternoons."

"No nurses," Mami said suddenly, her voice strong, clear. "And I go home."

Mami, wide awake, glaring with her one visible eye. While Rosa watched, the eye closed again, the face relaxed into sleep.

"Even with sedatives she's managing us," Pax said. "Let her sleep, Rosa. Go get some coffee in the cafeteria, get yourself together. I'll be back around six, we'll take her to my house."

"No, but I need you, Pax," Rosa said. "I've got something else to tell you, something serious. It's not just Mami. I have to talk to you."

She clutched Pax's arm. "This isn't my only trouble, Mami's either. Something horrible's happening, something with Carlos. I really need you."

Pax frowned. "Then let Mami sleep, come with me, downtown. We can talk in the cab, spend a little while in my chambers before I go back on the bench."

In a whirl they were out, in the elevator, feeling the wind from the river, waving down one of the cabs speeding across Ninety-sixth Street.

Pax told the driver to take the East River Drive, go uptown again for Centre Street. Then she sat back, turned toward Rosa.

"Now tell me. What about Carlos?"

In the light from the dirty windows she seemed to Rosa to

have a halo. Against the silvery coat her skin was pure ivory. Beneath the coat Rosa saw pale lace, the glow of pearls, the glint of a polished belt. Pax smelled wonderful, too, not of perfume but flowers.

"It's ghastly, Pax. I need you."

She watched Pax settle down, go completely still.

Only Pax listens like this, Rosa thought. With her head tipped sideways as if she were hearing music. As if there were no one in the world but me.

"I'm out of my mind," she began. "I didn't want you involved here, but I can't think of anything else. Talk to the judge, Pax, before he sentences my nephew and nobody can do anything at all."

"Rosa, begin at the beginning."

"There's no time. Right now Carlos is out at Riker's. In jail, Pax. Actually in jail."

"Rosa," Pax said.

"No, listen. When I finally got to see him, I can't tell you. It's been no time, and already he looks ten pounds thinner, ten years older. I've got to get him out. You've got to get him out."

But Pax was putting up a hand, palm out. "Calm down, Rosa. You're a judge. You send people to Riker's, and they're somebody's nephew, too."

"Don't joke, not now. It's the worst thing that's ever happened to us. Mami won't be able to stand it. Those crazy kids might as well have killed her."

"I'm joking, darling Rosa," Pax said. "To quiet you down. Get a little perspective here."

"Here's some perspective. Carlos was tried in Manhattan. His judge is a Manhattan judge, he works with you. Monroe Schiff. They call him Maximum Monroe, he's a heavy sentencer."

"Right," Pax said, frowning. "He likes saying he knows who's guilty just looking in their eyes. In the lunchroom we call it the Monroe Schiff optical test."

"Fine. So forget perspective. Ask him for a favor and say you'll owe him."

Pax was reaching into her pocket, taking something out, holding it toward her.

My God, a handkerchief. A cloth handkerchief, white, lacy. Upset, excited as she was, Rosa still felt a stab of fury. Who but Pax still used real handkerchiefs? Was she for real?

"Rosa, wipe your eyes. Yes, and blow your nose. Now tell me exactly what happened."

For a moment Rosa was a child again, in Pax's room overlooking the big museum, Central Park, books, banners, party invitations on her carved mantelpiece.

We could still be in that room, she thought, the difference between us. I'm a judge and she's a judge, but there it stops. No one will ever put her darling nephew into a holding pen. She knows the big judges, knows that sadist Schiff who's going to crucify Carlos. I'm not in the judges' club. If I call him he'll crucify me.

The cab came off the drive, whirled uptown, stopped with a screech in front of the Supreme Court building. Pax had money ready, waved it at the driver, pushed Rosa gently out the door. In a blur of motion they were up the endless flight of steps, in the elevator, walking the hall to Pax's chambers.

So clean, Rosa thought. I always forget it's so clean down here, so different from my courthouse.

She saw Selma, Pax's plain, plump secretary, and tried to muster a smile. And tried again for Tim Halloran, Pax's Irish law clerk, tall, dark, but definitely not handsome.

Tim was opening the door into Pax's large, beautiful inner office.

Immediately Rosa remembered she had always felt insignificant here, a second-class judge. So much space, such pretty things, fresh flowers, leather chairs, handsome books, so damned different from her own chambers.

Pax's desktop was empty, gleaming. Rosa watched her

reach into a drawer, pull out a pen, a pad. The pen was gold, with a gleaming blue jewel on top, the pad gilt-edged.

"Don't you do any work here?" she said, trying to smile. "It's all so neat."

Pax frowned. "I'm clearing the decks. There's a new case coming in. I'll tell you about it when we get through this. Now sit down, start again. Tell me from the beginning."

Where was the beginning? She needn't remind Pax that Carlos was her dead sister's child, rescued by Mami as an infant, raised, cosseted, by Mami all the years when there wasn't a cent to spare.

"Look," Rosa said, "you know Carlos is still just a kid. Nice. Sweet. I don't think you knew he's been working in a garage for a month or so. He's good with his hands, with cars. And after work he rides in cars with his friends."

"Carlos was arrested in a car?" Pax said.

"Pax, he doesn't understand the legal implications of being picked up in a car. He's eighteen, he thinks he knows everything, and he knows nothing at all."

"Eighteen. What happened to school, Rosa?"

"You know school was never for him, not since he was little. He's not like me."

Memories swirled into her mind then. She felt herself drifting into them, seeing herself as she had been the day Pax gave her the best present of all.

They'd stood in the quiet hallway of the Marymount school, Rosa in pigtails, Pax in her camel-hair coat, loafers, a gold barrette in her long, fair hair.

When Mother Marola looked out, Pax said politely that they must see her. Then, beneath the big crucifix in Mother's office, she talked about Rosa, how smart, how willing to work, how terrible if she was lost in a crowded school where nobody could learn.

Mother Marola seemed as stunned as if a burglar had burst in, snatched up the crucifix. But then Pax opened her shoulder bag, produced an envelope, counted out three hundred dollars. To help with the first month's tuition, she said, and more every month.

Later Rosa realized some guest at one of the family's pleasant dinners had given Pax the idea. He'd said Marymount wanted some scholarship girls to balance out the rich ones. So, thanks to Pax, they'd taken Rosa in with the society Catholic girls, taught her, cherished her. Soon she was fluent in three languages, Spanish, Nuyorican, and the proper English of the nuns. Later on colleges and law schools had needed balanced student bodies, too. She'd done all that part on her own. But it had started with her friend, with Pax.

"Go on," Pax was saying.

Rosa's mind jerked back to the present.

"So Carlos was in a car with a bunch of guys going for pizza. Do I have to tell you? They stopped to pick up some men. Carlos was in back, half asleep, hungry, only thinking about food. But he never got any food. The men were undercovers. It was a setup. They nailed all the kids. Including Carlos."

"And they're all liable," Pax said, pinpointing, of course, the important point. "Equally liable. Because they were all in the car. Including Carlos."

"Only here's what's horrible, Pax. The others got off, all of them. Not including Carlos."

"How did that happen?"

"You wouldn't believe. The ringleader, Cuban, a real cane breaker, he dealt, everyone knew it."

"Not including Carlos," Pax said.

"All right, the cops knew, they wanted him. And he knew what to do, spilled everything, turned in his suppliers, names, addresses, amounts. In exchange for a rap on the knuckles, lifetime probation. That means zip to kids like him. The cops know that, but they look good, they get information. He didn't even stand trial."

"That's one," Pax said.

"Yes, well, then there was a pair of aces. Twins. Irish,

handsome. Like two Mickey Rooneys from some old movie. Their mother sat in court crying, their priest swore they were altar boys. The jury took one look and brought in a good, loud not-guilty."

"I begin to see," Pax said.

"I knew you would. One more kid, retarded. A court shrink got him in some program. That left Carlos. He didn't have names to hand the police. He isn't anyone's idea of a cute bad boy. He's Hispanic, everyone's nightmare. And he's not *loco* enough for the shrinks. So he's facing a mandatory sentence, three to life, Pax. I don't think he'll make it. I don't think I'll make it. My mother's heart will break."

"Rosa," Pax said, looking away, out the big window with its view of the little triangular park below. "It's wrong. It's exactly what isn't supposed to happen in a courtroom. What we call a gross miscarriage of justice."

"There's more, just a little more. You see, one of the boys at Riker's is an old gang buddy of my nephew's. A few years ago he got a bunch of guys to drag Carlos under a tree and hammer a couple of nails in his heels."

"He did *what*?"

"You heard me. Revenge, something he thought Carlos did against the group. He never told anyone till Mami noticed he was limping, made him show her and practically flew him off to get medical help. Carlos made her swear not to tell anyone. I didn't even know till all this courtroom stuff started happening."

Pax's face was pale, absolutely still.

"Oh, Pax," Rosa said, wretched. "Now he's locked up with that charmer, along with everything else. You know about kids in jail. Rape, beatings from guards, who knows what? They don't tell the women judges all of it, either, you know that, too."

"I've seen pictures," Pax said quietly. "Heard stories."

"Bad enough if you're guilty," Rosa said, standing up, because she couldn't sit still one more minute. "If you're

Carlos, along for the ride, horrible. He's the least guilty one in that car, and the only one convicted. Please call Schiff. Now."

Pax looked at her again, tilting her head.

She looked so cool, so elegant, Rosa suddenly wanted to put out her hands, scratch her perfect face. Even the slight grip she'd had so far on her words, her body, left her completely.

"Damn it, call," she shouted. "Say you know me, know my family. Tell him if he does you a favor, you'll do him another. Carlos is like my child, I changed his diapers, put him to sleep, I taught him English, I was his mother while Mami worked. I'm thirty-five, Pax, I'm not married. He may be the only child I'll have. Rotten verdicts require rotten methods, Pax. Call!"

"To begin with," Pax said calmly, "the sentence would be unconstitutional."

Oh God, Rosa thought, she's going to be a scholar, get all judicious, when all she has to do is trade favors.

"You're going to tell Monroe Schiff that? What makes you think he ever read the Constitution? Get a straight trade. You back him for promotion, get him in one of your clubs, have him to a party, and he finds a way to lose Carlos."

"It *is* unconstitutional," Pax said. "I can make him see it."

"You can? Then do it. Call him."

"Rosa, that's the door to my bathroom. Go in and wash your face, fix your hair. There's a coffeepot, make us some coffee. *Bustelo.* Your mother got me used to the taste."

Suddenly Pax smiled, the wide, white, beautiful smile that took years away from her face.

"I love your mother, Rosa. I almost died this morning when they said she'd been shot. So come on, let's get going here."

"You promise to call Schiff?"

"I promise to do something, if you'll give me five minutes to decide what."

Limp, wrung out as the damp handkerchief in her hand, Rosa dared to feel a little hope.

She walked into the bathroom. And immediately felt as if she'd run smack into a line of cold, wet wash.

It was enormous. Nobody in the Bronx courthouse had one like it. Rosa had none at all in her own chambers, shared a rest room with the secretaries.

She saw herself in the big mirror, scowling, strands of hair straggling across her tear-streaked face.

Suddenly, without warning, Rosa was back in time, ten years old, waiting for Pax in her pretty room, looking into the mirror on Pax's dressing table.

She'd just touched a silver brush when she heard a footstep, felt a stinging slap on her cheek and turned to see one of the maids, Cathleen, scowling down at her.

"What are you doing? You can't be alone in here looking for things to steal. You shouldn't be in here at all, dirty little blackie like you. Be off to the pantry with your ma, tell her to keep an eye on you."

Blackie? But she wasn't black, not at all. Her skin wasn't black, she wasn't colored, so what was Cathleen saying?

Before she could open her mouth, she saw Pax behind Cathleen, in a creamy sweater and skirt, with an armful of books.

Had she heard? Would she get mad at Cathleen, tell her mother, fix the hurt?

But Pax had just put down the books, smiled hello at Cathleen and at her, exactly the same. Even when the maid left, she didn't say a word. Rosa's face burned then, burned again whenever she remembered.

Wasn't Pax a real friend? Did she agree with Cathleen that Rosa was a dirty little blackie? Why wasn't she cross with Cathleen? Rosa was too ashamed, too afraid of the wrong answer, to ask.

But she had never really forgotten, either. Lonely, sad, unable to sleep, she'd felt that slap again, heard Cathleen's furious voice.

Now Rosa shrugged, filled the shining coffeepot, waited

for the water to boil. When she came out of the pretty bathroom, a mug of inky coffee in each hand, Pax was at her
empty desk.

"Listen, Rosa," she said, looking up. "I can't trade favors. I
can't pressure another judge."

Rosa felt her hands go damp, making the mugs slip dan-
gerously. Trembling, she set them down on the desk.

"But I can try something else. We're getting Judge Schiff
on the phone now. Sit down. Listen."

Another moment, and a buzzer sounded. Rosa watched
Pax pick up the phone.

"Good morning, Judge," she said pleasantly. "I'm lucky
you're in your chambers. I'm in mine, with one of our colleagues, Judge Macario. She's a friend, a good friend. Did
you know you've just had a close relative of hers in your
courtroom?"

She stopped.

Rosa's breathing stopped, too.

"No reason why you should have put the names together,
of course. Carlos Macario. I've known him since he was
a baby. He's very young, actually even younger than my
own son."

She touched something on the telephone, and Judge
Schiff's voice boomed out.

Rosa shivered. She'd heard that voice at the trial. Hearing
it on a speaker phone seemed even worse.

"Judge," the voice was saying, "I don't suppose your son
sells drugs to undercovers. This boy did."

"I think we could say this boy was steamrolled. He didn't
sell. He was along for the ride. You've got kids, haven't you?
You know how kids go along for rides."

"Not rides that end in drug deals," Rosa heard.

"Yes, well, this puts you on the spot," Pax said. "You don't
want to sentence an innocent boy to three years in an upstate
prison."

"I don't know about innocent," Rosa heard. "Least guilty

of the bunch, maybe. And the sentence is out of my hands, as you know. Three to life, mandatory. Nothing I can do."

"You can declare the jury findings unconstitutional. They really are. The others didn't get punished at all."

"Now, Judge," Schiff's voice said, louder, "I don't go around declaring things unconstitutional. I don't need bad publicity. I leave all that to my younger colleagues, the ones with the beards, the ones who won't wear black robes. I sentence by the book. So if that's what you're asking, I can't help you."

"Far be it from me," Pax said. "Nobody needs ugly newspaper stories. I'm suggesting how to avoid some. There'll be an appeal, of course. Judge Macario will insist. And frankly, I don't think the Appellate Division will let one boy serve that tough a sentence when everyone else walked. Or the civil liberties groups, all the different kinds of court watchers." She paused. "After all, a Hispanic boy," she said.

Rosa's heart began to swell. She could feel it, a little balloon plumping up in her chest.

"But you don't have to defy the Constitution, Judge. You can uphold it, another part of it, that is."

What is she talking about? Rosa thought.

"Fourteenth amendment," Pax said crisply. "Equal protection under law. Turn that around, equal punishment for equal crimes. I think your mandatory sentence is unconstitutional here. The appellate court might well agree."

Rosa heard noises from the speaker. Coughing? Sputtering?

"No need to set aside the verdict. That would stand. The boy's guilty. But so were the others. And they didn't get hard time. If it were my trial, I'd say stiff probation, maybe five years. I'd look like a legal scholar. And a compassionate judge."

The balloon that was Rosa's heart blew up so fast she couldn't breathe.

"Of course you wanted a way out," Pax was saying. "The prosecutor's office probably wants one, too. They know what happens to kids in jail. I had a lawsuit last year, a boy dying, internal injuries, rectum torn to pieces."

Clouds of dizziness swirled inside Rosa's head; her heart skipped and raced, both at the same time. Dimly she heard Pax saying thank you, putting down the phone.

"All right, Rosa. He'll consider it. Which means he's telling his law clerk to check out what I said. Calling around to ask what other judges think. I'll drop in on him later, make sure he's got it right."

Rosa felt the balloon that was her heart burst, releasing so she could breathe, big, deep breaths of pure air.

"Oh, Pax," she said, "that's so smart."

"Not smart. Right. It's what you call justice."

Justice, Rosa thought, her happiness dwindling. My God, Pax. Without you Schiff would have creamed Carlos. This happened because he knows you, you know him. That's justice?

"Go see Carlos," Pax told her. "Tell him he's lucky. And that he might not be lucky twice."

Suddenly Rosa saw her face change.

She was smiling, smiling like a child with a secret, looking totally different, dreamy, as if her mind had drifted somewhere far away. And yes, good God, she was *blushing*.

"I have to get out of here," Pax said slowly, happily. "I'm meeting someone uptown."

Must be quite a someone, Rosa thought, to make her look like that.

"Who?" she asked.

"Just Debo's father. You know, Leonard Scholer. The one who's defending the Torcellos."

Rosa felt a stab of pain, as if a burning cigarette had lightly touched her heart.

Of course, she knew who Leonard Scholer was. Everyone in the law did, and plenty outside it. He was always defending hopeless people, getting them off in ways she would never allow in her courtroom.

Fat chance I have of anyone like him in my courtroom, Rosa thought. Unfair, it's so unfair. Pax has everything, looks, brains, money, a son. She gets celebrity cases, meets big lawyers. While I'm uptown with dealers, pimps, machete murderers, sleazebag lawyers, she's having dinner with a fascinating man. I haven't had any man at all since Tony.

She made herself give Pax a hug, turned to go.

Start on that road, she warned herself, and you'll make everything worse, you'll end up an envious bitch. You should be grateful to Pax, grateful to God she's your friend. You should be thrilled. You did what you came to do. You saved Carlos.

But it was Pax who'd saved Carlos.

Rosa realized she was rubbing her cheek.

Here, now, she was feeling again the force of Cathleen's slap long ago, hearing again the angry voice that was shaming her, sending her alone into the cold world.

3

LEONARD

THE LARGE, WINDOWLESS ROOM ON TIFFANY'S MEZZANINE was all gray velvet, walls, chairs, carpeting. The scent of Tiffany's own perfume filled the air, as if a rich, beautiful woman had just drifted by. It was so still, so different from the noisy courtroom Leonard had just left, he could feel his headache lifting, his shoulders finally relaxing.

He wondered if Miss Lester of the estate jewelry department, all gray hair, suit, shoes, had been chosen to match the room. Or better yet, to calm any heart attacks caused by revealing the prices of what she was showing.

On an afternoon like this, after the setbacks he'd had in court, he'd be near the ocean if he could. Lulling waves, soothingly repetitive, would settle him, remind him of who he was, the only lawyer who could defend the Torcellos the way he planned to defend them.

But the ocean was an hour away, Tiffany's a block from his office. At first he'd believed he was window shopping. Then, after loading Debo with pearls and old garnets, he realized he was doing something quite different. Reminding himself he could buy almost anything he chose and, since his divorce, *for* anyone he chose.

Without warning Pax flashed into his head, beautiful in lilac at Debo's wedding, riveting in conversation in Debo's living room, stunning across the small table at the Royalton, a brandy in her small hand. The glass had glinted in the low light. Pax's silver hair had lights in it, too.

He blinked, and saw Miss Lester pulling out a drawer, producing a small gray velvet box, turning it toward him.

An emerald, square as the box, green as the waters around Tortola. It was so large, so perfect, Leonard felt his breath catch.

Any woman's breathing would skip, too, he thought. Even a judge, even Pax. Strange, when he'd known her over a year, watching her debate at the Bar Association and suddenly discovering a totally new person. Of course, he hadn't seen her on a stage before, top to toe, small and straight. Or watched her obliterate an opponent quite as thoroughly with gentle questions as he could with temper and flair. He'd begun wanting fiercely to get her alone. And somehow wanting still more fiercely to get her into bed.

The gem blazed as Miss Lester took it out, put it on the counter. A ring, set in gold. Compelling anywhere. In the blandness of this place, mesmerizing.

"Eighteen carats," she said softly. "Flawless. That's rare. Emeralds are soft. Most of our estate stones, valuable though they are, show tiny chips, scratches. This one is perfect."

It certainly looked perfect. Magnificent, something from a maharajah's turban. He picked it up, feeling all the weight of his morning's frustrations lift.

Magic, impossibly large, impossibly green.

"Nice," he said, letting the ring roll from his hand onto the velvet.

Suddenly he was himself again. Leonard Scholer, with the riches of the world before him. Free of a marriage gray and bland as this room. Ready to engage with a woman as unusual as the jewel in front of him.

"Now I'd like to see the other stone," he told Miss Lester.

Poor woman. She didn't look as if any man had ever chosen a jewel for her. But when he'd called, for fun and games he'd asked to see two stones. Emerald, because Pax already wore a small one. And the jewel he thought she should have. Amethyst, the color of her eyes.

He expected Miss Lester to reach into the drawer again. Instead she put the emerald back in its box, clapped the top down.

The second ring was a vast purple oval surrounded by large, round diamonds that made the color even deeper, more mysterious.

"Thirty-four carats," Miss Lester breathed, as if uttering a prayer. "You said the lady is small, has small hands. This will look best on a small hand, even across a room. It's a thirties setting. Oval stones were all the rage then."

Looking at it, he could almost feel Pax's hand, fine-boned, delicate as a child's, cool in his own.

Staring into the amethyst, Leonard realized he couldn't remember the emerald.

"I'd like to see them both at the same time," he said.

"Oh, but you shouldn't. It's a hard decision, I know. But they're so different. One detracts from the other."

Hey, there, Miss Lester, Leonard wanted to say. Do it my way. I didn't even ask you about price, and I won't, either. You don't want me walking down to Cartier, or across Fifth Avenue to Harry Winston.

"I'd have to compare them," he said firmly. "It's the only way I could possibly decide."

Miss Lester was no fool. She had the emerald on the counter in seconds. Still, she hovered over the rings as if they were butterflies, might fly off if she wasn't alert.

All right, if he was *really* sure of his right to buy anything for Pax, which would she want?

Leonard picked up the emerald in one hand, the amethyst in the other.

Immediately he knew.

"The amethyst," he said. "It matches her eyes exactly."

"I see," Miss Lester murmured, nodding. "If you're sure."

Of course, he was sure.

"Any woman would be thrilled," Miss Lester said earnestly, leaning closer, as if she had a secret to share. "We think it was set for the Duchess of Windsor. The late duke, you know, spent hours choosing her jewels. He sat whole afternoons in the workrooms making sure everything was exactly as he wished."

The late duke, Leonard thought, fucked himself so badly he had nothing better to do afternoons. If he'd spent them studying his country's laws, he might have held on to his job.

"Interesting," he said, pushing back his chair. "I'll let you know, Miss Lester."

"Of course," she said, looking like the genteel WASP ladies who used to run the library out on Ocean Parkway when he was a kid, racing through five books every week. Should he feel sorry for her? Hell, these days he felt sorry for everyone who wasn't Leonard Scholer. He was so damned lucky, feeling great at fifty-seven, when his old man had *been* an old man at the same age. Playing tennis three times a week, wearing the same size belt he'd worn in law school—anyway, if he pulled in his middle. Loving his work, sure his proposed television series on defense law would be a smash hit, make him the talk of the legal town. And help him spread his gospel that trusting the law beat trusting anything else, God, humans, love, anything.

On top of all that, tonight he'd have dinner with Pax Peyton Ford! He could spare some feeling for Miss Lester.

"It's just what I wanted to see," he said with his best smile. "Now tell me the price."

"One hundred and forty thousand," Miss Lester said.

Leonard's heart leaped, gave him a single sharp pang of who-do-I-think-I-am guilt and what-the-hell delight, both at once.

The whole idea of buying it proved something, promised something wonderful.

All right, he thought. Sylvia's chinchilla was one thirty. And the only joy I ever got from it was watching her hike it up behind when she sat down. This ring? If I take this plunge, I'll feel terrific every time Pax moves her hand.

"Right," he said. "I'll take it along. Put a binder on it, will you, till I talk to my insurance people."

He put the jewel in its box, the box in his pocket. And looked up to see Miss Lester's eyes wide with panic.

"Oh, Mr. Scholer. In your suit pocket?"

"Don't worry," he said, smiling. "I've lost some coats, but hardly any suits. By the way, how much was the emerald?"

"A hundred and ten," Miss Lester said.

Good, he thought. I picked the more expensive one. Pax should have the more expensive one.

Moments later, he was bypassing Tiffany's stately elevators to run down the back stairs, moving fast across the main floor past hordes of buyers who all seemed to be Japanese. Spinning through the revolving door into the crisp fall air, he waited impatiently for his driver to come around the block he must have been circling for some time.

Tonight he'd take Pax to dinner at Bernadin. And if he felt like it, he'd damned well give her the amethyst. What the hell! She was Debo's mother-in-law, if he needed an excuse. She was a talented, clever, beautiful woman who'd been alone a long time.

Keyed up, buoyant, he raced into his office building, headed immediately for his partner.

But Jon Kistel wasn't in his corner office, filled with English antiques, Oriental rugs, and odd artifacts of the Royal Navy. He turned out to be in Leonard's corner office, filled with stainless steel and glass, pacing the thick gray carpeting.

Since they had started Kistel & Scholer in the mid-sixties, they'd tried to wind up workdays together. They'd both come out of Brooklyn Law, both tried being sole practitioners. And both jumped at the same time at the big firms that were finally hiring Jews. Leonard had gone on an interview at White & Case, found Kistel in the waiting room. That led to their joining forces, knowing that the discreet defense work in those firms, mostly white-collar stuff, corporate executives in trouble, wouldn't be the real kick they both craved. Long before they'd added Pressman, Trager and Rosenstein, Leonard grasped that Kistel's impetus was alarm, panic, while his was a joyous plunge into straightening out a mess. Yang and yin, salt and pepper, they made one hell of a team.

Tonight, one look at Kistel's agonized expression reminded Leonard how different they really were.

"Well, Leonard," Kistel said as he burst in his own door, "perhaps you should consider the stage."

Kistel always stepped close to people he talked to, cocked an ear. It suggested that secrets were safe with him, properly inviolate.

Leonard grinned at his partner, a small, neat figure in an expensive gray suit so undistinguished it might as well have been cheap. He liked his own clothes to look as costly as they were, rich tweeds, heavy broadcloths, patterns only the Italians could think up.

"What makes you say so?"

"If you need applause, retire. Pursue your hobby full-time. We're not in show business. We're here because everyone deserves a good defense whatever the accusation."

Christ, Leonard thought. He's worrying about the Torcellos, imagining them all doing hard time.

"I thought we were here to make money," he said. "Come on, Jon. What did you take out of this firm last year? Two million eight? The Torcellos alone must have covered that."

Kistel stepped closer. Leonard almost smelled dusty files, crumbling leather bindings.

"I'm not denying you do your share, Leonard. I only want you to keep at it. We're still out a great deal on the Palca case. And still suffering the loss of Toby Trager. You and Murray are the only litigating partners now. You should both be here, litigating."

The Palcas had declared bankruptcy, a disaster Trager must have known was coming, should have warned the firm about. When they'd failed to collect their fee, he'd slowly dwindled, retreated to Scottsdale. Great guy, a walking sports statistics expert. They missed him, just as they missed the money he'd brought in for so long.

"Murray lives for trial work," Leonard said. "I like getting out, taking on seminars and teaching stints when the law schools ask me. I like serving on the panels that pick judges. It's good for us having a handle on the judges. I like commenting on trials for CNN, Court TV, mixing it up with the experts, Fahringer, Dershowitz, Black, getting insights, sizing up my competition. What's wrong with that?"

"You've *got* plenty of insights," Kistel said crossly. "You've *seen* the competition."

He followed Leonard across the room.

"This fall alone you've gone off guest teaching at Harvard, Emory, Georgetown. Can't you stay put? Refuse one invitation? Give your best efforts to us?"

Leonard reached for the jewel box in his pocket, set it on one of the piles of paper on his desk.

"Am I getting through to you?" Kistel said. "Are you paying any attention?"

"Hey, Jon. You've made out fine with my teaching. Didn't we get the leading Irish litigator in New York City as co-counsel last month? Just before he was suspended for fighting dirty in a courtroom? Where did Pat Noonan find us, Jon? Did we meet in church? In the Emerald Society?"

He was enjoying himself now, playing to the invisible audience he often felt all around.

"Don't make speeches at me, Leonard. It's your ego that benefits, not our firm. What do I tell clients? No, you can't talk to Mr. Scholer. He's in Atlanta teaching black folks to sue white folks? He's learning from a fast-talking Irish drunk how to suborn a witness? He's at the Judicial College in Reno staying at a hotel full of casinos and playgirls?"

Leonard sat down. He was feeling too good for an argument, especially with a lifelong friend. Besides, he wanted to get to Pax. Should he show Kistel the ring, distract him? No, that might convince Jon he *was* going nuts. Why would the man worry about his teaching? For years the firm had practically printed money.

Kistel might sound agitated now, but in real trouble, when everyone else was screaming, he was a rock. Two years ago, when his beloved Jeanne had been in the hospital for an exploratory, he'd been in the office at least for an hour every single day. No speeches then. So why now?

"Some Torcello brother calls me every fifteen minutes, Leonard. Those boys *want* something for their retainer. And I want to transfer those calls to you, here, in this office, not some college town."

It is the Torcellos, Leonard thought.

He walked across the room, put an arm around Kistel's thin shoulders. "Jon, when I win this case, Joey Torcello will do a tarantella in the courtroom. Now, why don't you go back to your office and quit worrying?"

He stood up, started for the bathroom. But Kistel didn't move. What the hell was going on? Leonard had always taught, first to get away from Sylvia, then because he found he loved teaching. The new television series, God willing, would reach millions. He was an expert, and he wanted to share his expertise.

"If you're running from Sylvia, hide in the office, not outside," Jon said.

"I'm not running from Sylvia. Not that she isn't a thorn. Last week some bill came from Debo's wedding, seven months back, she says she forgot about it. But I don't run. In fact, I've just started seeing someone who makes me forget Sylvia ever existed. Oddly enough, Debo's mother-in-law, you know, the judge. Pax Ford."

Kistel walked to a chair but didn't sit in it. "That's none of my business. Judge Ford is an attractive woman. A fine judge. Her father was a fine judge, and her grandfather, in the old General Term."

He stopped, cleared his throat.

"Of course," he went on. "If it goes anywhere, it could be considered somewhat inappropriate. Was your father a judge, Leonard? Your grandfather? Do you have any idea how your grandfather made a living? Was he a rabbi? A ritual slaughterer? A milkman like Tevye?"

Leonard felt a sting, as if he'd ripped open a law book package from West Publishing and found in it a small, hissing snake.

"Jon," he said, "can it possibly bother you that Pax Ford is a WASP? You think at my age that means anything?"

Kistel came around the uncomfortable leather Mies chair that kept Leonard's visitors from staying too long, sat in it, somehow back stiff, legs neatly crossed.

"Leonard, you're our rainmaker. Nobody makes it rain business like you. But we never needed you more than now. And if your mind is on all these things, teaching, the judge, well . . ."

So it's not the television, Leonard thought, or he'd have said so.

He reached for a desk drawer, the bottle of Chivas inside, the paper cups. Across the room stood a fully equipped chromium bar with crystal glasses, fridge, liquor bottles. But he and Jon had started their working lives on paper cups, if not Chivas. He wanted to remind his partner of that.

"Jon," he said, pouring, welcoming the rich, warm smell of the liquor, "I'm a lucky man. Healthy. Wealthy. My kid married to Judge Ford's kid. I've been a good scout. Put myself through college, law school, my sister through college. Put my mother in a condo in Boca till she passed away. Handed Sylvia a fortune. Now I want to do what I want to do."

He drained his paper cup.

"I'm a bachelor again, this time with money. Hostesses can't get enough of me. I get more invitations than Maurice goddamn Templesman. Anywhere I could bring Pax, she'd dazzle everybody. She's stunning, smart, she understands what I do. She'd never ask why I'm defending some Arab terrorist, some child molester. She *knows* why. Come on, Jon. We'll survive if I teach. Or marry Pax Ford."

Why had he said that? Marry? He hadn't thought about marriage to anyone. Or Pax as a possible candidate for marriage. And yet the word had come out of his own mouth.

"Leonard," Kistel said, "I've never heard you make such a silly speech. We were all poor boys. We all did for our families. You want to be Clarence Darrow, fine. You have a new inamorata, fine. But at least get your head out of the clouds."

Suddenly Leonard felt tired, cross.

The clouds. His mother had said that. Almost. She'd said, you're not from the country, get your head out of the cows. She'd said it when he got lost in books, memorized the Gettysburg Address, saw every movie he could find with a courtroom scene. Get your head out of the cows, Leonard. Who will you marry, Bette Davis? Katharine Hepburn? You know Sylvia all your life. I know her mother all my life. Forget law school. Go in her father's printing office.

He'd compromised. Gotten engaged to Sylvia, gone to law school. When he'd begun making more money than Sylvia's father, his mother never admitted she'd been wrong, never volunteered she liked Florida, either. She'd just complained endlessly about heat, mildew, old people, Hispanics. This time, no compromise. He wanted Pax, a home, maybe a grandchild they could share. He wanted to talk legal theory so the dumbest television viewer understood it, so the brightest listener could catch fire, head for law school herself. And he didn't want anyone, even his best friend and partner, telling him where his head was.

"Hey, Jon," he said, "I know the direct approach bothers

you. Maybe it's unworthy of your negotiating skills. But something's bothering you. What?"

Kistel took a sip of Chivas. "My friend," he said quietly, "we have problems. We're not a big firm, we can't always absorb losses. When a client goes under, we feel it. When a partner is paid without contributing, we feel it, too."

He crunched the little cup between his fingers.

"One of my Washington friends called today, wanted to come up, lunch. I got some advance news. We're about to have tax problems. Evidently we've made our way onto some list. Perhaps because we're working for the Torcellos, perhaps because of that concentration camp fellow you got off. Hard to say. But we could lose money this year, Leonard, a lot of money."

Leonard felt impatience heat him. Jon was an old woman, a scriptwriter. The firm was rock solid. They could take a few losses, couldn't they? Pay a few taxes?

"I do not exaggerate, Leonard. A number of firms, small and large, have gone under lately. We are not invulnerable. I need you here, not in some college beer joint."

Who is it? Leonard wondered. Justice? IRS? Whose shitlist did I get us on?

"You should know," Jon was saying, "I had a more promising conversation this afternoon. With the possibility of a very lucrative case."

Leonard's impatience cooled. Jon didn't exaggerate. If he said lucrative, he meant it.

"Enough to bring this year up to par, certainly. But difficult, Leonard. Very difficult."

Leonard smiled. To Kistel all undecided cases were difficult. He'd panicked about the Borowik case. A sure loser, everyone said so. Leonard loved sure losers. Any limpdick lawyer could defend easy ones. It took balls to get acquittals for an accused serial killer, a girl the neighbors said had watched while her boyfriend beat up her baby.

Borowik had taken balls, brains, heart. A guard at Dachau.

Or so a lot of lovable, pitiable old people had said in statements that sent strong men rushing out of court to throw up in the toilet. He'd gotten it dismissed. Hammered out questions about eyesight and memory and age until the witnesses and the jury were so mixed up they had to drop deportation charges. Afterward he'd walked up to Borowik in an anteroom and punched him in the mouth, hard, just in case. He'd also made an anonymous gift of his vast fee to the United Jewish Appeal.

What could be worse than Borowik?

"You've read about it, of course," Kistel said. "It's been building up in the papers. John Talcott Bishop's suit for his niece. Versus California's boyfriend, the ballet dancer Tom D'Arcy."

Leonard felt anticipation tingle the skin at the back of his neck, as if a curtain were going up, a conductor raising his arms for an overture. *Bishop* v. *D'Arcy*! Real theater, a showcase!

"That's great," he told his partner. "But no surprise. Why wouldn't Bishop tap us?"

"Not Bishop. He's using his usual firm."

The phone rang. Leonard grabbed it up, heard Kistel's secretary, polite but tense, asking how much longer her boss would be; things were brewing up in his office. He gave Kistel the phone, waited while he gave instructions to hold everybody, then gave both the phone and his attention back to Leonard.

"I've talked with California's chief counsel, Buddy Barr. And with D'Arcy himself. I've been with them most of the afternoon."

Leonard wondered if he'd heard right, if he'd gulped the liquor too fast. "California's chief counsel? And D'Arcy? We're opposing Bishop?"

"Correct," Kistel said.

"You want me to get custody of a little girl for a gay ballet dancer? Jesus, Jon. It's the wrong side."

Kistel scowled. "Really, Leonard. There are no wrong sides. Of course we'll act for D'Arcy. This Barr fellow is a piece of work. Svengali, everything in the dark. He orchestrated all California's affairs, hires specialists for litigation, taxes, real estate, investments, here, Europe, everywhere. Bishop brought the suit here in New York. So jurisdiction is here, and he wants us."

"Did you discuss a retainer?"

"Yes."

Kistel stood up suddenly. "Two million now," he said. "A cap of four million, expecting most of it to come to us. Expenses, which will be considerable. California was a billionaire, perhaps a multibillionaire. Only Barr has any accurate estimate. When the man wanted another million, he simply painted another picture. I don't know how much of his estate goes to D'Arcy. I doubt D'Arcy knows. But Barr does. And he proposed the fee."

Kistel came a step closer.

"Our largest, Leonard. The largest single fee we have ever been offered."

Leonard began pacing as if he were Kistel. Four million! Cochran, Shapiro, he'd be right up there in the money!

"Too bad it's a bench trial," he realized he was saying. "I'm better with juries. Cochran had a jury to play to, not just that scared little judge. By the way, who is the judge, Jon?"

"Harry Silk."

"Good. Solid old guy. Runs a good courtroom. And he knows his law."

Kistel frowned. "I had the sense today that Barr is far less committed to this than D'Arcy. Might even have brought him here to lay out the problems, the difficulties for D'Arcy personally. Certainly he wanted to impress D'Arcy with the cost. He'd like D'Arcy to give up, spare California's reputation. There are still paintings to sell. I believe he may have admired Johnny California. But he has a genuine distaste for D'Arcy."

Leonard could almost hear a trumpet, a spirited call to arms. All right, he'd put on his armor, go into battle and win. Wait till he told Pax!

"Terrific news, Jon," he said, shrugging off his jacket, pulling at his tie. "Terrific case! All character building, character assassination. Bishop's not poor, he'll have top counsel. They'll dig for anyone, everyone willing to bad-mouth California and D'Arcy. A battle royal. Like the Kennedy kid. Woody and Mia. Worse. Better."

Leaving the door of his sleek bathroom cum dressing room open, he reached for his electric razor.

"So you see," Kistel said, "we have work to do. You have work to do. Don't get chatty with Judge Ford about it, either, she's a colleague of Harry Silk's. And a woman. Women talk, sooner or later. Leonard, you've lost a sleeve button. And I'll say good night."

"Night, Jon," Leonard said, looking at his sleeve, deciding to change his suit, watching Kistel turn, go. Calm, brisk, as if four million were all in a day's work.

Leonard stopped thinking, sloshed water on his face, grabbed a fresh shirt from the stack in the narrow closet, shucked his suit and chose another dark blue. Buttoned, tied, brushed, he picked up the box that held the ring, put it back in a pocket. Slamming out of his office, he called good-night to Evelyn, tore down the hall, tapped his foot till the elevator came.

Soon he was back in the Mercedes, license plate "Scholer 1," staring at the back of his ex-cop driver's neck. Grateful again for Dick's slithery driving, moving in a blur of speed and streetlights all the way across town to the Equitable building, the entrance to New York's handsomest restaurant, Bernadin.

He went quickly past the apples that perfumed the foyer, the sprays of pink and white flowers everywhere, the lavish lounge filled with tiny Japanese businessmen waiting for tables.

"Your lady is here," the headwaiter told him, smiling, taking his coat. "At the special table by the kitchen, as you asked."

Blessing fortune, blessing a world with Pax and Maguy

LeCoze and Tom D'Arcy in it, Leonard moved past black-clad waiters and diners far too dressed up to be real New Yorkers.

Pax. Looking up at the glassed-in kitchen behind her, hands folded on the pristine cloth, wearing something soft and dark, something lacy at her throat, something glittering at her wrist. Her hair glowed silvery in the artful light. He felt as if he'd forgotten everything he knew, remembered everything he knew, both at once.

She was turning toward him, looking up, smiling.

He leaned down to kiss her cheek, but found himself kissing her mouth. It made him think of roses, schnapps, the incredible softness of baby Debo's cheek. What was happening here?

"Madam Justice," he said, catching his breath, "you look beautiful."

She leaned toward him across the table, with its pottery mug of curly white flowers.

"If I look beautiful tonight, I'm a medical miracle."

"You are a medical miracle," he said. "And every other kind of miracle."

Immediately he felt foolish. He was jumping too fast, aiming too high, talking like an adolescent.

"Defense lawyers," Pax said, smiling. "Golden tongues, all of you."

All right, she hadn't told him to act his age. But she was saying something.

"Leonard, listen. I'm just too far gone tonight to do this place justice. Would you mind terribly if we had a drink and left?"

His heart shrank. She *was* telling him to act his age.

"If you're not starving, I could give you some supper at the house. Could you stand that? Bring me back here another time?"

He could actually feel his heart swell up with joy. Now he wanted to hurry her out to the car, go with her through her doorway and into adventure.

With a minimum of fuss Pax had her jacket on, her purse, briefcase, scarf collected from the bowing headwaiter. On the way out Leonard took her hand. It was like holding a small bird, fine-boned, warm. It surprised him to realize he wasn't hungry, wasn't thirsty. Except for Pax Ford.

Hunger and thirst grew in the car as they swept uptown. He knew he was making conversation, asking her what was keeping her so busy, hearing her mention some negligence case, Will, a visit from her friend, the Hispanic woman judge from the Bronx. He had just time to wonder why *they* were friends when the car reached her building.

The apartment was quiet. A few lights were on, so he saw himself and Pax reflected in the big windows of the living room, caught just a glimpse of the closest flowers on the terrace. In the glass they seemed to be walking through those flowers, Pax silver-haired, smiling, he, enormous, as if he could easily pick her up and sweep her into another room.

Which, after a moment or two, struck him as a fine idea.

Never had he borne a lighter burden, even Debo the last time he'd carried her, ages ago. Never had his mind seemed so separate from his body, arms tightening by themselves, legs moving surely, steadily up the marble stairs, as certain of his destination as if he'd been up those stairs before.

At the top, seeing a door, a bed, he stopped still, as if an objection had rung out in an echoing courtroom, cutting him off. Then he looked down and saw her smile, felt her arms reach around his neck and knew, *knew* he had leave to go on.

And then he no longer thought about courtrooms, because he was in new country.

As he set her carefully on the bed, she turned, touched out the bedside lamp. In the black dark, he had just a moment to think, worry, that he wasn't thirty, wasn't a movie star, that unlike the thirty-year-olds he hadn't loved a hundred women, hadn't moved this fast, this far before, ever.

But somehow he *was* thirty, *was* Bogart, feeling for the

buttons of her silky top with sure fingers, sweeping her clothes, his clothes, to the floor.

She makes me deft, he thought, with her shoulders like birds' wings, her small, soft breasts. She makes me feel tender, skillful, as if I've loved a million women.

Turning on his side, he nestled her close. Her skin was so smooth, soft. Her heartbeat seemed to tap urgently at his chest, inviting him on.

Effortlessly he swept her on top of him, felt her narrowness between his thighs, all weightless warmth. Then he was inside her, in, out, back, forth, amazed at the strength of her grip on him, delighting in the pleasure of that, the happiness of it, when he came, astonished and panting, with just enough consciousness left to feel her fingers tightening on his shoulder as she arched her back away from him, sighed a long sigh.

And then he was Leonard Scholer again, but a hundred feet tall, eighteen, hell, sixteen and strong, handsome as any movie star he'd ever admired. He lay back, cradled her silkiness in one arm, waited for his heartbeat to slow to a point where he could breathe, speak.

"I feel so foolish," he said finally. "Knowing you, smiling at you for, how long, a year? And all the time there was this. You."

He breathed her fresh flower scent as she shifted, reached for the lamp. Then, suddenly, she appeared, all ivory and silver hair, against the white pillow. Her hair wasn't smooth now. It was spun silver, glinting on her forehead, her cheek. He reached to smooth it away from her face, flushed, beautiful.

"If I told them in Federal Court," she said. "If they knew *you* were lost for words."

"Not lost. Found. Can I stay? Let me stay, I want to wake up with you, Pax."

But she was pulling away, sitting up, yes, and frowning!

"Leonard, listen. I'm sorry. Nothing would be better, nothing. But we can't. I wish I could."

Oh Christ, she was out of bed. He had just time to think how marvelous that was, that a naked woman was still a wonder to him, if not to the younger generation, when she reached for something, a robe, pale, lacy.

"I've got to be downtown long before the court even opens."

All his talent for opposition rose inside him, words crowding his throat, to persuade, coax, reason.

"I haven't had a chance to tell you," she said. "Because you moved so fast. We moved so fast."

Pain, sharp, alarming, shot through his left arm, his heart. She had a lover. Some bastard he'd have to out-argue, face down.

"Today I was given the Johnny California trial," Pax said.

Pain lifted, vanished.

Work. Only work. Work he understood, no problem.

And then her words reached him, bringing the pain, the pressure back into his body.

"Tell me again. You've got what?"

"*Bishop* v. *D'Arcy*. The custody case, the case everyone's talking about."

She wasn't frowning now. She looked elated, as joyous as he'd want to make her look. More joyous, more thrilled, eyes bright, flush deepening, than she'd looked a moment ago.

But *Bishop* v. *D'Arcy*. The custody case. His case. Not hers, his.

"More commotion," she said. "More attention, more chances to make a public fool of myself than I've ever had in all my life. At seven-thirty tomorrow I've called a meeting with the lawyers before me now to get them to finish up. That's just the first struggle."

"Well, you can't," Leonard said, louder than he intended. "You can't have that case."

Christ, he *was* an idiot. Relax, swallow, muster his forces. Lay out the arguments for her. No lack of them.

"For one thing, it's dangerous. I'd be hiring armed guards for you."

Harry Silk, he kept thinking. Jon said they'd given it to Harry Silk. What the hell happened?

"Who put you on it? Iapalucci? Of course, Iapalucci. What the hell did he have in mind? That the press would go easy on a woman judge? Things would look better for the judiciary?"

She was knotting the belt of her robe, pulling hard, jerking ugly creases into the soft fabric.

"Leonard, I'm not a woman judge. I'm a judge, remember?"

He leaned down, reached for his shirt, suddenly needing to be covered, craving the dignity of clothes.

His case. Wasn't that the first, the best argument? No, he'd sound like a shit. He'd have to explain Kistel, the firm's problems, the money. Better start with the problems she'd face. His fears for her. They were real enough.

"Pax, that trial will be a zoo. Gay custody is a nightmare today, violent opinion on either side, violent actions on either side. You could be derailed. Hell, you could be crucified."

Was that fraudulent? No, dead true.

Reaching for the rest of his things, he felt exhausted, felt his age. Sixty judges, more, in her court. Any of them could run it. Why her?

"Maybe we should talk about it in the morning," he said.

She was a still, pale figure on the far side of the bed. "I don't think so. I think we should keep right on talking about it."

Christ, Kistel would have a stroke. He'd see his fee vanishing, the firm vanishing.

"What happened to Harry Silk? Word was he had it."

"He got promoted. To the Appellate Division. Maybe because he was tough, willing to take on tough trials. At any rate, he got promoted. Not me."

Damn, he thought. That vacancy had existed for weeks;

the screening panels had finished asking their questions days ago. Why had the governor decided to fill it now?

"Okay, onward and upward for Judge Silk. That doesn't mean you have to take on the whole gay community. Or Talcott Bishop. This is Scylla and Charybdis, Pax. You'd be between two monsters. People get hurt between monsters. I couldn't stand you getting hurt."

Now he wanted to order, insist, forbid. Insane, the idea of this tiny woman presiding over the most punishing kind of a case a judge could have.

"Why aren't you pleased for me?" Pax said softly. "I know it'll be tough. But it'll be important."

"Important? A no-win case? A dangerous case? If the litigants don't get you, some nut in your courtroom will, guns, bombs, who knows? My God, we just had a judge shot dead in Texas on a custody case. It's always custody trials, feelings running high. You want poisoned candy in your mail like Judge Brieant? What about Daronco, some litigant shooting him at home while he mowed the lawn?"

"I don't have a lawn. Just a garden."

"It's not funny. Gay activists aren't funny. Neither are the tough bastards who go after them. Remember at the cathedral, St. Patrick's Day?"

"I can't believe you're saying all this. You're big on everyone being entitled to a good defense. Isn't everyone entitled to a good judge? Why couldn't I show everyone what a good judge is?"

Now he could feel a cramp taking hold of his gut, a painful waxing, a slow waning.

He had to tell her. Whatever he'd promised Kistel, whatever he owed the firm.

Bishop v. *D'Arcy* would showcase a defense lawyer. But it would ruin a judge. Not to mention that fee. Vital to the firm, to his partner, his friend.

Wait, though. Nothing as terrific as tonight had ever happened to him. Nothing as hideous as this case had ever happened to Pax. She'd never been in dirt. And this wasn't just dirt. It was shit, shit thrown at her in court, shit in boxes delivered to her chambers. The rest of her life she'd be the judge who fucked up the faggot case. Or the judge who gave an innocent child to a pervert. He knew. The Borowik case had brought him death threats. Toward the end he'd actually hired guards. Defending the Torcellos wasn't the world's safest work, either. But he knew shit, could handle it as well as anyone alive.

He walked around the bed, took her hand, soft, cool.

"Pax," he said gently, "there's another problem with this case, a special problem for a judge and a lawyer. A special problem for us. Let's hold this in abeyance for a while. Let's not spoil a marvelous start."

"Leonard, there are no problems. I accepted. It's done. I'm the judge in the case."

She paused for a heartbeat.

"And," she went on, "I'm the judge in this room. Period."

Now he felt as if she'd slapped him.

Furious, he wanted to slap back.

"You are," he said. "And you're certainly acting like one. A woman judge, at that. Arrogant. Self-involved. Power mad. You won't look at the down side. You won't acknowledge the cost."

Even in the low lamplight her amethyst eyes were blazing. "I didn't sign on just for the easy ones. To sentence Sirhan after everyone saw him shoot Bobby Kennedy. I'm not in a popularity contest. I take what Iapalucci gives me."

I know, sweetheart, I know, he wanted to say. You've got your grandfather's ideals, your father's, you're Portia, showing the world. I know because I think I love you. I love you because I think I know.

Looking at those eyes, he remembered the ring, wanted to feel in his pocket for the little jewel box, jam the ring on her finger, stop her mouth with a kiss.

"Pax, listen. I'm about to love you. Very much about to love you."

He cleared his thick throat.

"And I'm going to represent Tom D'Arcy."

She stared at him.

Now he ached for what he was doing to her, the crunch he was putting her in. But he had to go on.

"That's already trouble if the Bishop people use it. Want your doorman testifying that I came home with you tonight? Your friends dragged in to talk about our relationship? What about our kids? Suppose someone wants to subpoena Debo, Will?"

Her eyes went wide. She looked so like a statue he was almost surprised to see her mouth open again, hear her speak.

"Leonard, there are other litigators in your firm. Maybe you can't try it, not in front of me. But Pressman can. I've never met him socially, not once."

He can't try it like me, Leonard thought. Besides, she'd still be vulnerable. Murray and I are partners. At the least I'd have to stop seeing her during the trial. And who the hell wants to stop seeing her? I only just found her!

"Add it all up," he said. "Me, my firm, Bishop's power, organized gays, organized homophobes, real peril. You don't know what kind of peril. I mean, Pax, darling Pax, you don't know anything about gays."

This time a long silence.

"Leonard, it's done. Maybe we do have to stop this now. Or maybe your firm has to give it up. It's mine, and if you have any connection to it, we shouldn't be talking about it."

He was distracted by her hands, suddenly clasped together, tightening as he watched.

He couldn't bear it, wanted to reach out, take her hands in his, comfort her. Tom D'Arcy was trouble. And there couldn't be trouble between them. Not when he'd just discovered her, right as a legal principle, clever as any argument he'd ever made in court, beautiful as Justice with her scale in the pictures.

He wanted to shake her, say she should forget the damned case, love him, marry him. But words for once seemed to be failing him.

He reached into his pocket for the little box, opened it, put it on the pillow.

With a touch of hope he saw her look at the ring, saw her wide eyes grow wider still.

"My God," Pax said. "Leonard, it's beautiful. It's beyond words beautiful."

Hope bloomed in him. He began feeling suffused with hope.

"Your eyes," he said, groping for words, unused to groping for words. "It matches your eyes."

She looked up at him.

"But it's all wrong," she said, her voice forlorn. "The trial gets in the way. Of that ring. Of us."

"Don't be silly," he said impatiently. "You can have it, and me with it. It's that fucking trial you can't have."

He saw the quick frown, the narrowing of her eyes, heard her breath catch.

"What is it, a quid pro quo? I get the ring, you get the case that pays for it? A little present for a judge under the table, under the bed, maybe we should say?"

Shock struck him like a blow, making physical force, made him wince, close his eyes.

When he opened them to look at her again, he saw her face closing down, setting into pale marble.

"Oh, Pax," he said, searching for the right words, unused to searching for words.

"Goodbye, Leonard," she said. "At least, except with Will and Debo, goodbye."

He reached for the ring, feeling choked, suffocated. As if his head *were* in the clouds, threatening storm clouds, precisely the dark purple color of amethyst.

4

D'ARCY

USUALLY TOM D'ARCY FELT LIKE A YOUNG BARYSHNIKOV IN the room at the top of the town house.

A magic place, almost a stage set. Vast etched-glass ceiling, the red and gold leaves of the tall trees dancing behind it. Walls lined with shelves to hold John's fantastic collection of tableware and toys.

But not magic now.

Maybe never again, he thought, neck stiff, shoulders tight, as he began setting the breakfast table.

He wanted John in the doorway, arms wide for his little girl. And Caitlin hurling herself at him. That, of course, wouldn't happen again.

Stop it, he told himself, reaching into his jeans pocket for the keys to the cupboards. Caitlin's favorite things. Cups with little china feet. Forks and spoons that looked like small toy soldiers.

He had to be strong for Caitlin. Quickly he found the Mickey Mouse place mats she loved. The flower plates John had discovered at a jumble sale in a Welsh church, daffodil for him, rose for Caitlin. The creamer shaped like a cow. She always smiled holding its tail, pouring milk from its mouth into her glass.

He'd give it all to the Salvation Army if she'd smile today.

But when she came in, six, silent, small, gold hair rippling like the child in the Renoir downstairs, he knew there'd be no smile. Even the minute blue overalls, the tiny kidskin boots she loved, weren't pleasing her this morning.

Breakfast with Caitlin had been sacrosanct wherever he and John were the night before, no matter what went on. There were breakfast rooms in all the houses. The chalet in Zermatt, the Neuilly mansion, the beach house in Abidjan that hardly had rooms, just walls open to the palms, the sky.

The chalet. Where four burly men had come slowly through the door carrying John, neck bent oddly sideways, head lolling at a peculiar angle, laying him on the big painted chest in the hall.

Oh God, was he reliving that scene in daylight now? So far it had only haunted him nights, making him imagine the crash in slow motion, John on skis cartwheeling over and over. A man more alive, bursting with words and movement than anyone D'Arcy had ever known. Impossible, incredible that he was silent now, still.

Stretch, bend, reach! He needed to move. Pull open the door of the dumbwaiter, lift out the trays from the kitchen.

He'd told them crepes, Caitlin's delight. Neat rounds of them, lacy and golden, steamed under silver covers. Jelly, syrup, powdered sugar in crystal flasks. Oranges, tiny pears. Bananas in a bunch because Caitlin liked peeling them herself.

He pulled one off now, put it on her plate. And gave her a kiss. Her cheek was cool, her eyes down. The bloom of her early winter in Switzerland was gone. She'd been pale, quiet on the whole terrible trip here, shrinking into herself as reporters, photographers, battled one another for a look at Johnny California's child. At Kennedy, D'Arcy had picked her up, held her close, stayed well inside the clump of armed guards he'd ordered to meet them and get Caitlin safely home.

Hadn't he trained to lift grown women as if they weighed

nothing? He'd blessed all his ballerinas, with Caitlin a weightless bundle against his heart.

How he longed to do it again, sweep her up, run far from this city, this country. Impossible, of course. Till the trial was over. And then it might be impossible forever.

That fear was so strong it triggered every dancer's nightmare. Paralysis. Legs first, knees locking, calf muscles tight. Then spine aching, neck and shoulders stiff.

D'Arcy fought back, stretching across the table for Caitlin's hand, guiding it gently toward her fork. What would John do if he were here?

Grab a banana, be a chimpanzee for Caitlin.

Hop up, do a headstand, hold it till she ate.

Sing a bawdy song Caitlin couldn't possibly understand, would giggle at anyway.

But I'm not John, he thought. I can't be. I can only try to pick up the pieces, love her my way.

"Caitlin," he said, "eat something. Everybody eats something in the morning."

The child's mouth set in a line, her eyes dropped. Now she wouldn't look at him. Let alone smile.

D'Arcy poured his coffee, making big gestures to set an example, hoisting the cup high, sipping noisily. Like drinking warm, flat Coca-Cola. And Caitlin's head was down so far her face was almost hidden. Stricken, he turned, swept her out of the chair, held her in his arms, patting her frail back through the soft velvet.

"Caitlin," he said, "I know how you feel. I feel the same, just the same."

He felt her shudder.

And couldn't bear it.

"Listen, Caittie. He's gone. He's dead. This is what being dead is, we can't see him any more, talk to him. That means we have a job to do."

Was that wrong to say? No, couldn't be. She was lifting her head, looking right at him.

"We have to keep him in our heads. Eat breakfast, do what we always do, behave the way he'd want us to. Then we still have him, Caitlin. Then he's in our heads all the time."

Deep waters. But ah, she was relaxing a little.

"Did you ever see Daddy sad? Did you ever see him not eat?"

Caitlin frowned. "He ate a lot," she said. Finally.

A tap at the door.

Good thing, before he said something stupid, damaging. Talk about her father, the shrink he'd consulted had told him. Get her to talk. Easy to say. Tough to do.

Mademoiselle Claude at the door, Caitlin's nanny, teacher, almost mother, looking like a modern nun in her spotless white cotton blouse, her navy jumper. Maddie, ever since Caitlin had named her that when she first started talking.

D'Arcy smiled. The smile felt like a grimace, the leer of the magician in *Nutcracker*.

"*Bon jour*, Mr. D.," Maddie said. "They just telephoned from the door. Mr. Barr is here. He says it's urgent."

Startled, D'Arcy put his hands on his knees, kneaded, rubbed. Barr hadn't come here since John died. He'd had D'Arcy up to his bizarre office, a gigantic, echoing space empty except for his own enormous desk and chair, a single straight chair for a single visitor. Like having a meeting in a throne room, with a powerful king.

D'Arcy asked himself why he disliked Buddy Barr so much. Because the man made his contempt for John's lover so plain? Because Barr was so icy, impossible to read? He gave no clues to his past or present, to any companion he might have, man or woman, any interest apart from John. He dressed like a Mafioso, silk suits, ties that matched his handkerchiefs, pointed shoes, but spoke like a Boston banker, clipped, formal. Several times since John's death D'Arcy had wanted to knock him silly.

When I first moved in with John, he remembered, Paris.

Those bitchy letters from some boy, with snapshots. John tied to the bedposts, laughing. A man's hand stroking John's belly. Worse. John didn't show me, spared me, sent them to Barr in New York. And Barr flew over, shaking his head, fanning all the pictures out on John's Empire desk. Making sure I saw them all. Wanting to upset me, the bastard!

He stood up, moved toward the door.

Of course, Barr had scolded when John did something truly insane. Shipping crates of scrap metal from Berlin to New York, forgetting why. Buying a pony for Caitlin to keep at a house they used only once a year.

But Barr had got John everything he wanted. Higher prices for the paintings every year. Orders from the world's best galleries, museums. Thanks to Barr they had lived like royals, never carrying money, paying their own bills, keeping calendars. My God, he'd arranged for them to rollerblade through the huge stone underground of the Louvre! To sit down to an elaborate midnight banquet in the Taj, even when they'd officially closed it after dark because of the terrorists in Agra!

Barr had done the impossible. Now, let him do it again, for Caitlin, along with that Scholer fellow who'd be doing the actual work.

"Shall I call down, say you're coming?" Maddie asked.

Suddenly D'Arcy wanted to tense his muscles, take a deep breath, hurl himself high into the air. Who'd have dreamed John would die? Never see fifty? With the world in his hands, living more fully in a week than most people do in a lifetime.

"Yes, please," he said. "We'll have supper together, all of us. In the dining room, if Caitlin wants. What do you say, Caittie? Shall we eat under the chandelier, count the crystals?"

The child nodded, smiled.

Thrilled, he blew her as big a kiss as if she'd just danced Giselle to his Albrecht.

Pretend you're not worried, he told himself. Act. John used to act. He had fooled the world when he wanted the house on the Indian Ocean. Told everyone Bunschaft was building a place for him in Mustique, showed the plans in all the magazines. While Paul Rosenblatt's house was going up on a beach where Caitlin didn't need guards, played with the black kids all day long. John could fool everyone. I only have to fool Barr into thinking I'm not agonizing about this lawsuit, not sick with fear I'll lose Caitlin.

He reached the landing, looked down at the glorious room below. Glorious, without a piece of furniture, even a single ornament. Only light slanting in through the big stained-glass windows, sending colored shadows over the dozens of Persian rugs piled, layered on the floor the way they were in the great mosques of Islam.

John made this, D'Arcy told himself. Conceived it, designed the glass, studied the light, placed each rug. He made so many beautiful things. They're still here. But he's gone. And I'd gladly see all this priceless glass smashed to pieces if it would bring him back.

Taking the last steps, he walked to the double doors of the parlor. Great bronze handles, lion's heads. John found them in a junkshop on a wine-drenched afternoon in Assisi. Paid a few hundred lire for them, thousands to restore them. Now, in front of them, D'Arcy's feet seemed to hold him to the floor. His body felt rigid as a tree, his knees gnarled roots, his arms brittle branches.

What if Barr had bad news? Suppose Scholer's firm had reconsidered?

D'Arcy summoned up his favorite way to battle stage fright, inhaling deeply, holding his breath, letting it out in a rush. Today it only made his heartbeat quicken, his head spin.

My God, he was famous for grand entrances, thousands of incredible leaps onto hundreds of stages. And now he couldn't enter a room because bad news might be waiting for him in it.

Footsteps beyond the doors, a crack as they flew open.

Barr's heavy face, bulky shoulders, framed in the door-way. The scent of cologne, metallic, harsh.

"Twenty minutes," he said impatiently. "I've waited twenty, almost twenty-five minutes."

D'Arcy didn't think the man could speak without snarling. He followed Barr into the parlor.

The room enfolded him. John's favorite of all the rooms in all the houses. Not a bare inch anywhere, walls, floors, mantels, windowsills, tables, crowded with objects John had gathered. Dolls, rulers, fans. Surgical instruments, cookie jars, ivory ornaments, carpet balls, crystal animals. Game boards, slide rules, samplers. Clever things made by clever people.

And pictures of people, one wall covered with group photographs. Smocked chemists in a laboratory, Bremen, 1922. The 4-H Club, Wichita, 1943. Staff cartoonists at Disney, 1936. Collections on collections, like the rugs on rugs in the hall.

Even with so much, everything meant something to D'Arcy. The quilts from Kentucky the year John had owned the thoroughbred Sunshine Ray, which always loped in minutes after the other horses, gave John fits of laughter. The afghans John's grandmother had crocheted, hideous colors worked in perfect stitches.

D'Arcy waved at the couches. And got a sour look from Barr.

Of course, the man was telling him, if he'd wanted to sit down he wouldn't wait for Tom D'Arcy to invite him. And yet he'd told D'Arcy the house was his, with everything in it. No mention of the other houses. Maybe he'd never mention them; maybe they weren't D'Arcy's business.

He sat down. And regretted it. Now he had to look up at Barr. He regretted his informal clothes, too, next to Barr's sharkskin and heavy gold cuff links.

"Twenty minutes," Barr said again. "You can't imagine my office. We always have work on our hands, the paintings, the

houses, investments, legal problems, all the same things we
did for Johnny when he was alive."

I can imagine it, D'Arcy wanted to say. And all the money
it makes you, too. John never cared what you got, a piece of
everything he sold, probably everything he bought, too.

"Now," Barr went on, "it's worse. Some London tabloid is
making a big mystery of Johnny's death, claiming it wasn't an
accident. Yesterday someone slashed one of his paintings in a
Paris gallery. The insurance people want to pay original
prices, not current values. Some woman in Seattle is saying
she's Johnny's widow, has papers to prove it. Publishers want
rights to an authorized biography, museums want retrospec-
tives. There's even a child in Florida some idiot says is the real
Caitlin."

And you're loving it, D'Arcy thought. Yes, no, hold up on
this, pay that, sue her, send this one away, send that one in.

"Johnny's will alone is nearly eighty pages. With a
problem on every page. People we can't find. Bequests that
don't match inventories. Calls from half the countries in the
world, everyone wanting something."

D'Arcy clasped his hands to keep from punching the man.

Do you miss him? he wanted to ask. We're bleeding in this
house, Caitlin, Maddie, me. And you?

"I was having breakfast with Caitlin. We always had breakfast with her, you know, wherever we were."

His mind immediately produced a montage of those
breakfasts, on a terrace overlookng the green, milky Caribbean, a balcony over the manicured Paris garden, a glass villa
on stilts in Taormina. So many pretty tables, so much delicious food, so much love.

"Why can't she eat with her nurse?" Barr said. "Anyway,
not to waste more time. I wanted to make one more stab at
heading off a disaster."

We've had the disaster, D'Arcy wanted to say. John left
the chalet alive and came back dead. What else could be a
disaster?

"You should really give up this nonsense about the child," Barr said.

D'Arcy stared. Then, as the words bit into his brain, he felt as if he'd stepped through an open trapdoor on some stage, was falling into pain, maybe death.

"This custody business," Barr was going on. "If it had turned up later, the will probated, the property settled, when people got tired of gossiping. But now? The papers get worse every day. Johnny's death mask, for God's sake. Where the devil did anyone get a look at that?"

D'Arcy fought to relax, make himself limp, so he could get up and walk, dance again, after the crash.

"The Bishops are pressing, Tom. They've brought this habeas corpus action fast. They want Caitlin out of your hands. I've had a job keeping Caitlin out of foster care, keeping her with you till things are settled."

D'Arcy realized he wasn't breathing.

"I can field some of the requirements, fingerprinting, home studies, social workers. But I can't field the law. Nobody can."

D'Arcy felt his heart give one last beat. Stop.

Good God, Barr was standing over him. He was wearing one of his extraordinary suits, raw silk, the color of cappuccino. His steely hair seemed carved, his teeth gleamed. They made him look like a hyena.

Get hold of yourself, D'Arcy thought. Concentrate.

"We don't want a legal wrangle now, a lot of dirty linen. This trial could hurt you. And Caitlin. Cost her a lot of money in the end, too, if what we do lowers the values of the paintings, the properties."

Money. That was it for Barr, money.

"If we had a hope of winning. But we haven't. Leonard Scholer is a good defense man. But all defense men think they'll win. They get paid, too, whether or not they do."

He leaned closer, cleared his throat.

"Let's be frank. Homosexuals have trouble keeping legal

hold of their own children. When they adopt, it's usually outcast kids nobody wants. Caitlin is different. She's white, healthy. Rich, very rich. And she has a respectable, well-off aunt who wants her badly enough to sue you for custody."

Barr was finally sitting down. Not a touch of grace in the man's body. And not a shred of decency in his mind. He didn't give a damn for John's wishes. Or John's child. Or John's lover.

"Mr. Barr. John believed you could do anything. I believe it, too. I have to fight for Caitlin. You have to help me."

"Look, Johnny left you a fortune. Why throw it away? You're in a double bind here. You can only win convincing the judge you loved Johnny. And that's just what will turn everyone against you. We're dealing with New York state: gay adoption is some can of worms here. Hell, even a school textbook about gay parents is some can of worms here. You'll go through hell, and you'll still lose."

D'Arcy felt as if ropes were being knotted around him, one by one, making him immobile.

"I don't care if every cent John left me goes for this," he said slowly. "Maybe it's why he left it. It's certainly what he'd want me to spend it on."

"You don't know that. Johnny's will certainly keeps you far from her property. I control that till she's twenty-one no matter who becomes her guardian."

"But he'd want me to have her. He never considered anything else."

"You can't prove that. Johnny left you this house plus a life interest in one third of his estate. You're a rich man. Of course, you can't hand your money on if you form a new relationship. It reverts to Caitlin when you go, and she's got the rest anyway. She'll be a very rich woman. Not quite the queen of England, but well up there."

D'Arcy had a sudden vision. An airport shop. Caitlin sorting pennies, francs, lire, from her tiny purse, hoping she could afford a handheld electronic game. Frowning, counting slowly, her tiny pink tongue between her teeth.

"A child isn't a chair," Barr said. "There's no slavery any more. Johnny couldn't leave her to you if you're not fit to have her."

D'Arcy felt pure fury flare up inside his chest.

Yesterday he'd had a call from, of all places, the Board of Education. Someone asking if he'd consider teaching in the public schools. The dancing he'd taught in private schools had been his greatest joy before Johnny, his special crusade. Ballet for boys. Basis for sports, basis for strength, basis for a cultivated existence. He'd promoted it all, and successfully.

Of course, he'd said he couldn't discuss teaching now, he had Caitlin to think about. Should he tell Barr the Board of Education seemed to think he was fit to be around children?

"I'm trying to protect you, Tom. Johnny trusted my judgment. Why can't you?"

"I do trust your judgment. I trusted you to find me a top lawyer, I trust you to help me win. I even trust you to help me keep Caitlin from being hurt by my contesting this thing. I hate what's happening already. She's practically a prisoner with reporters climbing the gates."

"Your fault," Barr said. "If she wasn't the most notorious child in the world right now, she'd go to school, live normally. I've fought battles for Johnny, plenty of them. But this?"

D'Arcy saw the airport again. Caitlin smiling, taking his hand, trusting him to help buy her toy.

"Well," he said, "it's good it's not your battle. It's mine. You don't even have to show up in court. I have to fight for Caitlin. I'm all she has, aside from the money. But she'll have plenty even if I spend a fortune on lawyers."

Immediately he knew he'd said the wrong thing. Barr was staring at him with narrowed eyes.

"You can't throw your money into this and live on hers. Even if you won, I'd still control that. Unless, with your new zest for litigation, you've got some idea of removing me."

Removing him?

Just the idea calmed him, made his body looser.

Barr was up again, walking so heavily some of the crystal snowballs were shuddering, the dolls dancing in their stands.

I have a third of John's money, D'Arcy thought. When I die that goes to Caitlin. But till then I could have a new business manager. I don't have to use Barr.

"This isn't a ballet, Tom," Barr said gently. "Good people don't win the way they do on stage."

But D'Arcy was feeling warmer, stronger.

"The Bishops, Tom. They're related to Caitlin, even though John wouldn't let them see her. Somewhere, sometime, he quarreled with Barbara Bishop, cut her out of his life. We don't know why."

D'Arcy's heart took a little leap.

He knew why.

It's like my sister has a sickness, John had said. She's grabby. Possessive. Fanatically grabby, clutching, holding tight. We both are. But I collect things. She collects people. I don't want her near Caitlin.

He remembered John's face, contorted, furious, telling the story.

"Ba was disgusted by my life," he said. "She'd counted on a wife straightening me out. She never counted on Joanne bringing me problems of her own. When Caitlin was born, she showed up at the house. Went straight to the crib, grabbed the baby. Joanne yelled to hold her head: a newborn's neck can snap. And Ba went nuts, started shaking the baby, screaming she knew how to hold her niece. I pried Caitlin loose and I kicked Ba. I probably shouldn't have, but what could I do? My hands were full of baby. I haven't seen Ba since. And I made sure Caitlin didn't see her either."

Should he tell Barr that? But he'd heard it as a secret. Wasn't it what lawyers called hearsay?

John was creative, a storyteller. Sometimes he told things the way he wanted them to happen, as he painted things the way he wanted them to be. Maybe Mrs. Bishop had changed. Maybe she felt bound to get a baby away from a silly bitch like

Joanne, marrying John knowing he was gay, only wanting what she could get from him.

Joanne couldn't have wanted a baby. Luckily she cracked herself up in a fast car, wasn't grabbing for Caitlin now.

Barr was picking up something from a table, a pack of old G-Man cards. "My goodness," he said, his expression softening, "I had these when I was a kid."

Ugliest things in the room, D'Arcy thought. Of course he'd pick them to be sentimental about.

"Mrs. Bishop must have hated being linked to Johnny," Barr said slowly, staring down at the cards. "You couldn't read a paper without seeing something about him. She's the kind who thinks you're in the papers only when you're born, marry, or die. She hasn't the money Johnny had, of course. But enough so no one could claim she's after Caitlin's."

Money again, D'Arcy thought, contempt making him feel better, warmer, as if he'd been exercising at a barre.

"Look," Barr said, holding out one of the cards. "Machine Gun Kelly. Does anyone remember Machine Gun Kelly?"

Reluctantly he put down the pack.

"Tom, we should really reconsider."

"Buddy. What we? I'm a rich man, you said so. We're spending my money. Thanks to John you're rich, too. So do what he wanted. Get me Caitlin whatever it takes."

Barr gave him a sharp look, all business again.

"I'm a lawyer, not a magician. And you are, well, unusual. You don't look like a father. In fact, your looks will be against you in a courtroom. You're handsome, almost too handsome. You've got a movie star face, you walk like you own the earth. You look like a dancer."

And what else? D'Arcy wanted to ask. A faggot? A poufter? A fucking Mary?

"You look like a man who practices, we'll say, an alternative lifestyle. In the eyes of most judges, not a fit guardian for a little girl."

"I've been a fit guardian for six years. Ask her where she wants to live, she'll say with me."

"Oh, the judge will ask her," Barr said. "In an interview you'd want to spare Caitlin if you loved her. Psychiatrists, too. There will be plenty of asking."

"If Caitlin has to," D'Arcy said, "she'll do all that. Whatever has to be, we'll do. Just tell me the next step, we'll take it."

"Good Lord, Tom, you don't know what you're talking about. For one thing, we'll be getting amicus briefs."

"Buddy, talk English. I won't use ballet terms with you, don't use legal ones with me. What are amicus briefs?"

"Papers from special-interest groups to put pressure on a judge. Literally, *amicus curiae*, friend of the court. The number of them demonstrates public interest in the case. We'll have them from Lambda, maybe the archdiocese, the Christian Fellowship Fund, on the other side."

He paused, drew himself up. "And there's something else. They've assigned a new judge. A woman."

Easier for Caitlin? Not so scary as a man in a black robe? Though the women judges he'd seen in news broadcasts, in films, seemed to be harpies, old, schoolteacherish.

"I don't know yet why she's on it," Barr said. "Bishop knows judges. He's a permanent member of the panel that screens for the Appellate Division, decides if they're fit to promote. Maybe he pulled strings to get her. But it won't do you much good, you see that."

D'Arcy felt his stomach and heart do their own little pas de deux.

Stop it, he warned himself, standing up, walking over to the bell pull.

In a moment Garrison was opening the doors, looking at him.

"Coffee," D'Arcy said. "And the Armagnac, I think. Yes, Armagnac, please."

No, a woman wouldn't do him much good. He could see that.

Garrison was back quickly with a silver tray, balloon glasses, cups, a coffeepot. And the Armagnac. D'Arcy waved at him to put it all down, go.

He looked at Barr, who shook his head impatiently.

Then he poured the fragrant liquor into a cup, added steaming coffee, gulped. The rich mixture stung his tongue, warmed his gullet.

"Buddy," he said, "I love Caitlin. And I don't care if the judge is the wicked witch of the west."

"Actually," Barr interrupted, scowling at the bottle, "I'm told she's quite attractive. Though, they say, a piece of ice in court. So you see."

"No," D'Arcy said, "I don't see. Scholer can coach me. Rehearse me, I'm used to rehearsals. I'm used to acting. A little hard work and I'll come off a responsible, intelligent person with a long record of loving Caitlin."

He put down his glass, stood up.

Ah, now he was taller than Buddy Barr. He made the most of it, leaning aggressively toward the man, curling his fingers into fists.

"Buddy," he said, "it's my decision, my show, not yours. Curtain's going up, Buddy, old buddy. We're going to court."

He imagined a ramrod piercing the back of his neck, sliding between his shoulder blades, straightening his spine.

"And by the way," he went on, "Caitlin has a mother person. Mademoiselle, Maddie. Goes everywhere with us. A more loving lady you couldn't find. She'd never work for the Bishops, but she'll stay with me. Won't that mean something to a judge?"

Barr leaned forward. "By the time the social workers have checked her out, fingerprinted her, you may not have her any more. Listen, Tom. How old are you?"

D'Arcy reached for the bottle again, the coffeepot, poured another cup.

"Fifty-seven."

"I know you come from Richland, Michigan. I don't know what got you out. Another man?"

"Aren't you sweet to ask," D'Arcy said. "Actually, a lot of men. Sailors, all of them. I was in the navy, the Korean War, bet you didn't know that. It's funny to hear the talk about gays in the military. I knew quite a few who were rough, tough, and gay."

"If you don't like answering unpleasant questions, stay out of court. Now, where were you when Johnny died?"

Why, the bastard was trying to frighten him.

"With Caitlin," he shouted. "Dancing. We had a practice barre, I taught her afternoons. I've taught many, many children, you know. We were doing entrechats when they brought Johnny in."

"Suppose someone suggested you had something to do with his accident. Money, remember. You get a third of the money."

"Has anyone said that?"

"Not yet. But who benefits most? Did you have a dime before Johnny? What about your old boyfriends? Who are they? Are you ready to be an open book?"

"Fucking A."

Barr sighed, shrugged his heavy shoulders.

"If you won't listen," he said. "If even I, with the best advice in the world, expensive advice, can't convince you. If you must rush headlong into a mess, I'll prepare for the aftermath. I have to say, Leonard Scholer's won for a lot of impossible people."

"Thanks," D'Arcy said. So he was an impossible person. With an impossible mission. Damn and blast this bloated son of a bitch.

"The Bishops will have good lawyers, too," Barr was saying. "Make no mistake. They'll have investigators scaring up servants, doctors, suppliers, everyone who ever touched you or Johnny. They'll go to Richland, Michigan. Dig up everyone you ever made a pass at. You've picked a lost cause."

He wants to scare me, D'Arcy thought. But he's the one with the lost cause.

"You were a great dancer, nobody denies it. Your teaching was admirable, you made important friends. Enemies, too, no doubt. Other male dancers, parents whose kids you turned down. Drop this and you can sponsor ballets, commission them, choreograph, whatever you want. You won't be letting Caitlin down. You're not God, you don't know. It could be the best thing for her, being with her own family."

"I do know. She's six, she loves me, Maddie. She's loved us since she was born. We're the best thing."

Barr was getting up, looming over him again.

"Funny things happen in lawsuits, Tom. Take Oscar Wilde. He went to court to protect his reputation. Wound up in jail, died of being there."

In spite of his resolve, D'Arcy's stomach lurched.

"You're not suggesting I could wind up in jail."

"I don't know where you could wind up."

"Oscar Wilde! That was a hundred years ago. That couldn't happen now."

"Don't you believe it. Forget Wilde. Try Alger Hiss. He started defending his good name. With character witnesses that made even the judge stand up when they walked in, like Felix Frankfurter. Hiss went to jail. He didn't clear his name till he was ninety. It's not easy to defend your whole life when you're fifty-seven."

Suddenly he was smiling.

"One good thing, Tom. A small exit door. Leonard Scholer's daughter is married to our judge's son. There's a family connection. Things start looking bad, we say we just found out, move for a mistrial. Better to blacken the judge's reputation than ours."

You're a piece of work, Buddy, D'Arcy thought. You go every which way, your ass is covered no matter what.

"I'll call you," Barr was saying, smile broader than ever.

He's making the best of me, D'Arcy thought. Me and a bad situation. He'll come out ahead whatever happens.

"And I may say, Tom, you must really love that little girl."

"Buddy," D'Arcy said, "she's loving. Trusting. I don't think she's heard a harsh word, the world has always been wonderful to her. I've taught a lot of children, but never one like her."

Barr was listening, but his fingers were straying again toward the little colored cards.

"Would you like those?" D'Arcy asked. "To put on your desk? Maybe flip a few times, bring back the old days?"

He watched Barr stiffen, shake his head, start for the doors. "One last thing," he said, turning. "This trial will be a magnet for trouble. For people who march, yell, throw things. Maybe people with guns. People get shot in court-rooms. Gay men aren't everyone's favorites. You'll want to watch yourself, remember that."

But D'Arcy was already remembering.

The worst time, the first time, when he hadn't expected it, hadn't looked for trouble.

In the schoolyard. Guys from downtown, big guys who hung around selling cigarettes, liquor, a little glue. Even in peaceful Richland, Michigan. They'd jumped him, a skinny high school kid, too handsome, the way Barr said, too graceful. Too dumb to know what they'd do to him.

Bang, and three of them had him, two gripping his arms, one bending over him, all of them yelling, fairy, sissy, pansy.

He was athletic even then, strong even before dancing turned his muscles to steel. He'd made himself go limp. Sure of him, they'd relaxed. And he'd turned in a flash, gone for the nearest one, smashed a fist into his eye, tripped up another, sent him flying. The third disappeared, fast.

He couldn't smash guns, demonstrators, even with steel muscles.

But he'd smash the world, let it smash him, before he'd give up Caitlin.

"Whatever it takes," he said. "I'm not letting Caitlin down."

If he lost the trial, he'd run. Swoop up Caitlin and go,

Europe, Africa, Australia, anywhere. Fake a suicide, leave his whole life behind, get Caitlin somewhere safe.

He watched Barr gather himself up to go.

And even in the safety of this beloved room he could somehow hear the ugly words from that schoolyard, feel the meaty hands that held him, recall the heady mix of terror and delight he'd known sending his fist crashing into that stupid, brutish face.

5

BA

BA FINISHED POURING THE BREAKFAST TEA, CLEARED HER throat to speak. And heard the telephone buzz.

As her husband reached for the tiny portable, she felt like commanding him not to answer.

She looked around her pleasant breakfast alcove for comfort. How cozy she'd made it, a charming contrast to the formal dining room. Soft cushions and colors, sunlight filtering through sheer curtains, a small Queen Anne table that kept Tal close to her side. Though he always came down ready for the office in a Brooks Brothers suit, Ba liked wearing long, fluffy pastel robes. She always dealt with difficult things, upsetting things, at breakfast. Today she meant to deal with something that might upset him a good deal.

Just when I could have asked casually, Ba fretted. Now he'll be thinking about the office. Tonight's no good, either, guests till all hours.

Time was so short. Tomorrow morning she'd be in a courtroom trying to concentrate on all Scotty Wickham's coaching, all his advice.

She'd tried asking him the question. But he'd been so impatient this week, so determined to warn her about all the dangers ahead. Scotty was furious, probably, even though he was too well bred to show it. He loathed the whole idea of this custody suit, called it a tawdry matter involving tawdry people.

One of those people, she'd pointed out to him, was Caitlin.

Tal, of course, loathed the lawsuit even more than Scotty, and quite openly. He'd spent days arguing, cajoling, trying to dissuade her. She'd face disgusting publicity, ridicule. Risk her already imperfect health, rekindle her old, terrible migraines. Spend huge amounts of money battling a leading defense firm, money far better used for her beloved Huguenot Society, aiding old families down on their luck, educating their children. Tal had hammered at her about the terrible changes a child would make, in their schedules, their traveling, their social activities.

She'd fought both of them off, stood firm. She had to rescue that darling child. So while she didn't ask Scotty everything, she did listen carefully to all he said about her role in the courtroom.

"Keep it simple, Ba," he'd said. "Simple dress, manners, answers. Don't show temper whatever happens. You want to come off a decent, pleasant woman. After all, only a decent, pleasant woman would want this child. You must not let yourself get angry, annoyed. Leave that to Tom D'Arcy. You behave as if any judge couldn't help but want you to save a child from such an unhealthy situation."

She'd nodded. But Scotty had kept on.

"In a proper world she'd be yours without question. Today everyone claims rights: welfare takers, homeless people, even a creature like D'Arcy. Every problem in the whole country lands in some courtroom."

He'd frowned.

"And Ba. I don't want you looking angry, annoyed around Tal. He's doing this for you. Against my advice, which he's taken since we were boys at Andover. When you're upset, he's upset. Calm, steady, that's the ticket. Questions?"

Oh, she had questions. But all of them might show just how angry, worried she really felt. She'd temporized, asked something easy. Reporters. How should she deal with them?

"Don't," Scotty told her. "They won't pounce on you. You'll hardly be the most flamboyant person in that courtroom. Especially if you do what I say, wear navy blue, maroon, something quiet. Tom D'Arcy will get the press, the crowds. And, of course, the child."

Ba had wanted to kiss his cheek!

He'd told her one thing. Caitlin would be in court. And then she'd know so many things. Was Caitlin an attractive child? Did she look like Ba's mother or father? Perhaps like Ba herself? Did she seem healthy, well adjusted? Was she sweet, mannerly? Or sullen, shy, unwilling to talk? Would she cry?

If she cries, Ba thought, how can I contain myself? I'll have to run to her, hug her, carry her off with me no matter what Scotty Wickham says.

Scotty had left with a peck on her cheek, a pat on her shoulder. Then, too late, Ba had remembered her real question.

When would she get Caitlin?

Did the judge decide? Was there some rule? Was it possible Caitlin would simply come home with her when the trial ended?

If she called Scotty, she'd get another lecture. That left Tal. She'd determined to ask him at breakfast after he'd eaten his beloved Irish oatmeal, scanned all the papers.

Ba had tossed half the night, tried telling herself it didn't matter when Caitlin came. It would be so miraculous whenever it happened.

A child, she thought now. A girl. Six. Johnny's child, my very own niece. Small enough to sit on my lap. Young enough to teach, steer, shape. Someone to give my whole life real meaning, real value.

Suddenly she had to know. And Tal was still on the phone!

Ba felt her frustration swell up, tighten her throat. At least there weren't three phones on the table anymore. He had this one now, small as a pack of cards, with several lines, even a speaker. It was blaring now. Tal's managing editor, Sidney Steinman, booming away.

Ba pushed back her chair, picked up Tal's cup and placed it in front of him. He could eat a whole dinner talking to Steinman. Right now the man was running on in what sounded like a foreign language. *Res judicata. En banque.* Rosa Macario. The language of the law. And the *Bar Journal.*

Tal loved the newspaper his grandfather had founded, dedicated his whole heart to it. He loved the power it gave him, the knowledge, the prestige. He loved the presses, the people, the excitement of a daily paper. He even adored the scrapbooks Ba had made him, eighty-year-old front pages, yellowed clippings, pictures of stern and bearded judges.

Caitlin will love me more than anything, she thought. I'll make sure she does.

At least tomorrow she'd see the child, if only from a distance. Caitlin, of course, might not be pretty. Or healthy. The life she'd lived, she could be a little gypsy like her slut of a mother.

Ba knotted her hands together with impatience. She left Tal, went out through the dining room, with its mahogany table, its glassed-in cupboards filled with nineteenth-century English silver, walked quickly across the big foyer, past the marble staircase to the small room she'd made her office. Leaving the door wide so she could catch Tal when he finally emerged.

This room was perfect, too, chintz and wicker, masses of the flowers that came in twice each week from the greenhouse at their country place in Southampton, a chaise for her, a long table for Bonner, who was already making entries in a notebook. The flowers were, of course, mums, maroon, gold, some almost chocolate brown. Mums weren't supposed to smell, but these did, an acrid, bitter sort of smell, disquieting, faintly nauseating.

"Morning," Ba said.

A treasure, Billy Bonner. Pleasant, attractive, young, neat, even elegant in blazer and striped tie. A perfectionist, just like her. He did things before Ba asked, did them precisely the way she wanted.

Like the notebooks.

Unbidden, Bonner had bound each book in Italian marbled paper. Color-keyed each one to the large calendar on the wall, the one she kept herself. Red ink for parties, luncheons, teas, benefits, dinners. Blue for personal appointments, hairdressers, doctors, dressmakers, shoemakers. Green for anything that didn't fit either category, like the trial.

The calender was usually crammed with notes. Now, right in the middle, ten blank squares, starting tomorrow, covering two whole weeks.

"Maddening," Ba said. "Those blank days. If the trial lasts longer, we'll be cancelling things. And if it's over sooner, we'll waste time, which is worse."

"Mrs. Bishop," Bonner said, in the pleasant Tidewater voice that drawled sentences, made statements into questions. "Mr. Wickham said ten days was about right?"

"Mr. Wickham isn't taking on a child when it's over. I am. And I can't do it properly without knowing when she'll arrive."

Bonner frowned, as he did whenever she shared a concern.

"Such a little girl. She won't cause much fuss. You know how fast you do things? That luncheon last month? Entertainin' fifty people on a day's notice? Everyone thought you were amazin'."

True. Last minute, Lila Sherman bowing out of the Huguenot scholarship fund-raiser. Ba had stepped in, brought it off handsomely. Even Brooke Astor, Evvie Wechsler couldn't have done better.

"We'll get busy the minute we know," Bonner was saying.

"You don't know about New York children, Billy. Busy as their parents. Caitlin will need everything, all at once."

She began counting on her fingers. "A room here. Another in the country. Decorators, even I can't hurry them. A nanny. Agencies need time to screen, check references. A school, difficult even with all the people I know. Clothes. Toys, books."

She flung her hands wide.

"And more, Billy. Pediatricians, dentists, dancing school, tennis lessons, much, much more."

I know, Ba thought. I went through all that last year. Eloise, best cook we ever had, ruining dinners because she was panicked about her daughter in some hellish public school. How many schools did I have to badger before I got those fussbudgets at Chapin to take the child, find her some scholarship money as well?

"We could start," Bonner was saying. "I could make calls while you're in court."

No, he couldn't. She wasn't superstitious, of course. But it was tempting fate to pin things down before Caitlin really belonged to her.

"Or we'll work real fast when you do know," Bonner said. "We can do it. I look forward to doin' it."

Bonner always said the right thing. And they'd do the right thing. Ba knew how much New York City children were programmed, scheduled. But she knew, too, that there must be time for the two of them to be together. To read, play, talk. To take trips, museums, gardens, zoos, visit Washington, Colonial Williamsburg, the Liberty Bell in Philadelphia.

Where was Tal? How long could he listen to Steinman?

"You know, Mrs. Bishop?" Bonner said. "I could be settin' up books for the little girl, gettin' a head start."

Ba sat straight. Good heavens, the notebooks she'd need for Caitlin! Medical records. School records. Caitlin's friends. Scrapbooks of schoolwork, stories, art work. Photographs, perhaps swatches of her party dresses.

For a moment she felt joyous, fulfilled, as if she were actually expecting her own baby, as if the hopes she'd had of motherhood hadn't been denied for so long.

Caitlin would make up for so many disappointments, that was certain.

Bonner was handing her the newspapers. Her own newspapers, doubles of those Tal read in the dining room.

"I'm afraid," he was saying. "There's rather a lot about the trial."

Ba's heart plummeted. The life Caitlin's had, she told herself, I should be making lists of child psychiatrists.

"If it's just more gossip, I won't bother."

"Mrs. Bishop, don't upset yourself. You'll save that child, everyone says so. Then the papers will bother someone else."

Ba picked up the *Daily News*, hid behind it, let her thoughts wander.

She'd waited so long for a child.

Soon after she'd married, she'd been miserable each time her period returned. Again.

The doctors. So many office visits, fertility tests, so many embarrassing intimate examinations. So many questions, ovulation, frequency of intercourse, so much advice, temperature taking, relaxation, new positions for sex, all dreadful, all useless.

In the park, wanting to grab up every baby in every carriage, bitterly envying every pregnant woman she saw.

The touchy business of getting Tal to doctors, too. How he'd hated it, joked about producing semen on demand, masturbating in a cubicle full of porn magazines, sex videos.

Far, far from a joke to Ba. Because it had turned out the difficulty was Tal's. She could have had a dozen babies. He was infertile. She'd wanted to pick up the paper knife on the desk of the doctor who broke that news and stab it into someone, herself, Tal, the doctor!

And these days, with so much talk about fertility, drugs, surrogate mothers, her bitterness had grown worse.

Tal had simply thrown himself into the *Bar Journal* even harder than before. As if he'd decided that, failing at one thing, he'd be superb at another. He doubled, tripled the paper's circulation. Bought up small community newspapers, improved them beyond recognition. Became a judge maker, chairing the screening panels judges feared so much, featuring the opinions of judges he liked on his front pages, burying others in the back with the ads for bail bondsmen and process servers.

And Ba? She'd had a brief interval at Silver Hill, doing what she always referred to as resting. A frightening time of rage and depression, one she didn't care to think about, one she was determined would never be repeated.

Ba turned a page of the newspaper for Bonner's benefit. Anguished as she was, she'd still only had one open battle with Tal.

When Harriet Anthony called, wild with joy, to say she'd found a baby girl, bought her, really, from some clinic in Charleston.

Ba had ordered pancakes and those special Vermont sausages for breakfast, worn a pale violet robe Tal loved. Begged him to help her do the same thing. Let her emotions loose for once, cried, begged, pleaded, and kept right on even after his face darkened, his hands clenched. Felt ready to divorce him, slip away up the Merritt Parkway to Silver Hill again when he said he wasn't about to bring up someone's feebleminded bastard.

"Forget this, Ba. Plenty of happy people are childless. Plenty of parents are wretched. Listen to Steinman, his son marrying that manipulative little bitch, his wife trying to be nice. There's no pain like pain you get from children. You hear it everywhere. So just stop."

She'd wanted to fly at him, scratch his face there and then. But he'd turned and gone out of the room, left her seething, shaking.

Thank God, here he was at her door, at last. Poor Tal, so

good to her about everything else. How dreadful she was to feel so angry at him.

"Tal," she said. "We must talk."

Tactful Bonner was up, out the door.

"I need you, too, Ba. Listen, I want to do a cocktail party sometime in the next couple of weeks. A hundred people, maybe more. There's a woman judge in the Bronx, a Puerto Rican. I want to start getting her known downtown."

Ba stared at him. "With the trial starting tomorrow?"

"Now, Ba, we can't stop living because of this trial."

Remember Scotty Wickham's warning, she forced herself to relax.

"You've done so much," he went on. "For the paper, for me, with your parties. Everyone in New York worth cultivating, really. This Judge Macario is very much worth cultivating now, take my word."

Gracious, he was getting wound up. She couldn't bear a digression, not now.

"She's very young, very ambitious, like all the judges, but she's really got something. Up from the barrio, out of the projects, the whole story. We ran an interview with her last month, she made quite a speech about how the same qualities are perceived differently in male and female judges. A man is tough, a woman tyrannical. He's reserved, she's indecisive. A man gets to court late, they assume he's busy with other legal problems; a woman comes late and they think she was at Bloomingdale's. Everyone sees the woman first, and only then the judge. It caused a great deal of talk."

"Why are we doing favors for a judge? Aren't judges the ones who want favors from you?"

"Because," Tal said, "I'm about to launch something new." He leaned closer, smiled. "A special edition, Ba, in Spanish. Not just our own material translated. A completely Latino point of view, written, edited entirely by Hispanics. A board, advisers of their own people. Like Judge Macario."

"Tal, we're going to launch something new. We're going to have a child."

"I know. But even parents give parties. And this one needn't be special. Just a somewhat different guest list. Nothing to be worried about. You could do it with your eyes closed."

"You're sure it can't wait?"

"I don't think Rosa Macario will wait. A lot of politicians are watching her. She's unusual. Educated, extremely attractive, no castanets, no fruit on her head, not even an accent. Acceptable to a lot of groups, not just her own. Like Dinkins, when he first ran, able to mix with anyone and still represent his own people."

I don't care, Ba thought. Even if it's wrong of me, all I can think about now is Caitlin.

"Steinman thinks," Tal said, "this girl's going up to the Appellate Division soon. If we play her up, push her to the top of the list, she'll go owing us. We'll have a high court judge for a board member."

Ba felt her hands curling into fists.

"I've done my share for the paper," she said carefully. "Not just parties. Sorting years and years of old papers, making your handsome scrapbooks. Helping you make the *Journal* the first thing lawyers and judges read every morning."

And then, with a jump of her heart, she realized.

This party could be a godsend. An excuse, a reason for asking him her question without looking a bit angry, anxious.

"The thing is, when?" she said. "How long do you think the trial will take? When might we actually get Caitlin? We can't have a party the day she comes. So many eyes are on us, Tal. Shouldn't we look as if Caitlin is our first concern?"

Tal frowned. "Life doesn't stop when people go to court. Nobody knows how long we'll be there. Depends on how many witnesses, how much evidence, all that. Custody cases can take forever, Wickham says. Remember Woody Allen and

Mia Farrow. Judges hope people will settle, get them off the hook. They're always anecdotal, no real evidence, proof. Just stories about the fitness of each side. Did someone see D'Arcy kick a dog? Were you overheard scolding a volunteer? It's all in the judge's hands. She can delay. Or she can order Caitlin transferred forthwith."

Forthwith, Ba thought with a pang at her temples. Then I could bring her home from court. What power judges have!

"We should be giving our judge a party," she said, trying to lighten up a little.

"Good thing we never did. She'd have to recuse herself, get out of the trial. Believe me, Rosa Macario can do more for us in the end. I want to pin her down."

No judge can do more for me, Ba thought, than the one who gives me Caitlin. Forthwith.

"You can't imagine the strength, the growth among those people, Ba. In 1970 only sixteen percent of New York was Hispanic. By 1990, more than twenty-four percent. Puerto Ricans, Dominicans, Mexicans, Cubans, Salvadorans, they multiply like daffodils."

A string seemed to be twining itself around Ba's head, cutting into it.

"It's smart business to help one of them along. And your parties have been known to work wonders."

The string was tightening, hurting. Ignoring it, Ba leaned back, let her robe fall away from her legs. Tal had always liked her legs. Unlike faces, hair, hands, legs lasted, thank goodness.

"Don't worry," he said, patting her ankle. "Judge Ford will move this along because there's too much commotion about it. She's good. Wickham checked out her background."

"And?"

"She's one of us, really. Good family, good schools, good clubs. Loyal friends, many legal admirers. She gives small, quiet dinners, has schoolchildren into her courtroom for talks. She began with money, husband left her some as well.

He was an architect, no conflicts, no problems. You never
know with married women. Their husbands can make terrible trouble, like Geraldine Ferraro's. If you like, I'll have
someone make up a folder, our clips, Wickham's notes, bring
it home tonight."

Ba's eye went to the wall calender. Tonight, the Philhar-
monic, one of her little suppers later, just sandwiches, some
heavenly desserts. She could see other listings, too, but they
were in blue, personal.

She'd have to read about the judge late at night, after
people had gone. Hardly the best way to keep hold of herself
tomorrow, keep from looking angry, anxious.

Oh, God. Couldn't Tal see that all she cared about was
Caitlin! The string somehow cut into her forehead, releasing
a flood of fury at her own inadequacy.

"Tal, I can't think about it all now—guest lists, invitations,
caterers, service people, flowers, cleaners—I simply can't. I
want to get ready for Caitlin. I intend to get ready."

She knew her hands were in fists, her eyes slits.

Tal stood up quickly.

"Now, Ba, I know how you feel. I'm going into this custody suit with you, however reluctantly, because I do know.
If you're this upset, you should plan a party, distract yourself. We'll win. Vis-à-vis Tom D'Arcy it's almost impossible
not to win."

He always refused to recognize her loving nature, her
need to mother. He edited her, like his damned paper.

"You don't know how I feel," she said. "I know you hated
Johnny, hated all those stories about him."

"Even now," Tal said, shaking his head, "you'd think
nothing else was happening anywhere. Wars, recessions, elections all taking a backseat to that moron Johnny California.
And we haven't even started. But you'll handle it, as you
handle everything, straight arrow."

Straight arrow? She'd never told him how she'd learned
the truth about Johnny. Or how she'd battled over the baby.

And never would.

"Don't fret," Tal said, touching her cheek. "You'll have your little girl."

And was gone. Without the least understanding, the least real sympathy.

Once, for a photograph in the glossy program of some Huguenot ball, she'd had a makeup man come in to do her up. He'd hidden her wrinkles under pink and beige creams, her eyelids under mauve powder, her pale lashes under mascara. In the photograph she'd looked like someone else.

If only she could cover her feelings, her furies as easily. Or share them.

Ba looked across the room at her address book. Dozens of friends. But not one she'd trust with the truth.

"I was stunned Johnny California was your brother," Lydia Leeds had said on the phone, ready to wallow in gossip. "When I read in the *Times* you were starting a lawsuit, I couldn't believe it."

"Oh, I haven't seen him in years," Ba had said.

The *Times*, my foot, she'd thought. You read the *Daily News*, that's all you can read. Your father went to jail for insider trading. Who do you think you are, talking about my brother?

Ba realized she was perspiring. Which she almost never did.

She stood up, went to the window. Her office was at the back of the building, a maid's room, really. She'd made it pretty. But she couldn't change the ugly view over the low buildings next door, all water towers, broken parapets, asphalt roofing.

Johnny had been such a cunning baby. Cuddly, clever, laughing when she bathed him, dressed him, sang him to sleep. She could almost hear him, two years old to her nine, demanding from his bed, "Baba? Where you are?"

She'd pushed his stroller all over downtown Canton, showed him off to everyone. Later, when he was older, he trotted after her to her high school, Johnson's Drugstore,

Elsy's dress shop, the public library. Later still he was a perfect listener, an admirer. When she had afternoon dates, Johnny came along, even stole out nights to find her at the drugstore, the movie theater. Ba had made her dates admire his cleverness, his looks.

I was all he cared about, Ba thought. Anyway, besides his collections. He always had those, rocks, birds' nests, bottle caps, baseball cards.

Had her temperature suddenly dropped? She was shivering now in the light robe.

She always shivered when she remembered how they'd come apart. The most horrible moment of her life, worse than anything that followed, could ever follow. The moment she couldn't tell anyone about, even the nice Silver Hill psychiatrist, even a lawyer, even Tal.

Especially Tal.

Thirteen-year-old Johnny hadn't come to the library that afternoon. She'd missed him. Worried, rushing through her idiotic work sorting book returns, she'd gone home early.

Mama in the kitchen, fixing supper for the three of them. She hadn't seen Johnny, snapped that she hardly ever saw him, he was so busy following Ba.

Running upstairs to her room.

Opening the door, turning on the light.

And Johnny. In her bed. Wearing her best nightgown. Lipstick on his mouth, rouge, eye shadow, a ribbon around his blond hair.

And not alone. Pulling away from someone. At first Ba thought a girl. But when the two people in bed froze still, she'd seen.

Not a girl. Another boy. Ba even knew him, Jake Simkus from next door. Ba couldn't help herself. Shocked, stunned, she'd shut her eyes and screamed, screamed till Mama came rushing up and saw, too, till Jake jumped out of bed, tore past them to the stairs. Till Johnny climbed out of bed to laugh at them, pulling her nightgown down around his skinny legs.

And till her mother flew at him, raging harder than Ba had ever seen her rage before.

Ba never told Tal, either, about Johnny coming to see her here. Wearing an earring, something she'd never seen at that time on a man unless he was in a play, a pirate, a gypsy.

And makeup. Not much, but enough to frighten her. His blond, corn-fed Ohio look was still there, but masked. He was terribly thin. She said so, and he laughed.

"Coke doesn't exactly make you fat," he said.

She still blushed for not understanding, having some stupid idea that Coca-Cola did make you fat, what was he talking about?

"Johnny, is it money? Do you need money? Because I have lots. Tal has. I could write you a check for almost anything."

He threw back his head, then, laughed.

"Ba, baby," he said, "haven't you read about me? Are you so busy with your important husband you haven't heard of Johnny California? The paintings, Ba. The manhole covers."

She thought he'd lost his mind.

"Ask around," he said. "Talk to your arty friends, you must have some arty friends. The Wrightsmans? They paid twelve thousand dollars for one of my oils. Or the Hadleys? Fifteen thousand for two tiny gouaches."

Of course she'd heard of Johnny California. But she hadn't paid attention. Or dreamed he was her Johnny. A silly name. And what were gouaches, anyway?

Still, she was glad for him. Only why didn't he buy decent clothes? Look healthier? Should she send him to their doctor?

Even then she'd known better than to suggest sending him to Tal's tailor. He'd left without waiting for Tal. She'd exhaled with relief, then felt ashamed. But Tal wouldn't have understood. She wasn't sure she understood.

After that she followed Johnny's work, read about his fortunes, escapades, purchases, while he made a name for himself she did not want to share.

She'd seen him just once more. Tal didn't know about that, either.

When Caitlin was born. At his new town house set in a garden so large it was really a little park. So devastating, that visit, she'd put it absolutely out of her mind. Till she woke up to read about the accident in Switzerland. Till Johnny died and her heart yearned for the child he'd left behind.

Ba turned from the window because Bonner was back. The sun touched his fair hair as he sat down, picked up his pen.

Good heavens, Ba thought. He looks like Johnny. Uses his hands, holds his pen just the way Johnny did.

Was Bonner really like Johnny?

No. Ba was sure he wasn't. Bonner was perfectly normal. She was just angry, ready to see trouble everywhere.

"Dreadful about those marchers," Bonner was saying, smoothing one of the newspapers.

"Marchers?"

"Looky here, Mrs. Bishop. I honestly think it's better if you know what to expect, don't you?"

Ba looked at the paper.

ACT-UP VOWS COURTHOUSE DEMONSTRATION

Dear heaven, such horrible people. Carrying signs. Megaphones. Shaking fists. Would she face them tomorrow? With all she had to handle inside the courthouse, would people like this be outside?

Ba felt nauseous.

Bonner was looking concerned.

"I want to tell you about a party," she said firmly. She was not going to look angry, anxious for Bonner.

"Yes, Mrs. Bishop," he said agreeably.

"Mr. Bishop will send a list this morning. We'll plan for a hundred and twenty. Get the regular service people, not the expensive ones. It's a political party. Those people are always thirsty, ravenous, so plenty of hors d'oeuvres, not fancy, just solid."

"Right," Bonner said. "When do you think?"

Ba looked at the calender, felt all her irritation come back.

Two weeks from now? Bonner could manage that if the invitations went by messenger. But if Caitlin came earlier? Should she tell Bonner a month? But Tal said as soon as possible.

Two weeks. At worst, she wouldn't have to stay downstairs the whole time. She'd greet people, slip up to Caitlin. Come back down to say goodbye.

She told Bonner two weeks from tomorrow. Then she left him to get on with it.

She meant to dress for the day. Check on her clothes for the courtroom, make sure her suit, bag, shoes, were perfect. But the maids would be working upstairs. And she wanted to be by herself.

The library was spacious, peaceful. The cream silk shades were drawn to protect the books from sunlight. The smell of linseed oil on the leather bindings, of the pretty potpourri she made from her own roses, was calming, soothing.

Ba sank onto a velvet couch. Now she faced her wedding picture, framed in heavy silver, on one of the bookshelves.

A lovely picture. She had never looked prettier, felt more tranquil than on the day she married Tal in white organdie in the walled garden of his beautiful Southampton house.

How lucky she'd been. Coming to New York for the first time, a librarians' convention. Tal the main speaker, an important publisher of an important newspaper.

She felt his eyes on her while he was speaking. And knew, when he broke away from the honored guests, that he'd come over to speak to her. She hadn't dreamed he'd ask her to come out for a drink. Or that he'd just broken his engagement to some Biddle, was ripe for rebounding into her arms.

She'd been beautiful then, corn-fed like Johnny, blond, rosy.

She'd never gone home to Canton, never even sent for her clothes. Tal wanted to give her everything. Poor Mama was gone by then, and Ba certainly hadn't wanted Johnny giving her away.

Beneath her picture were the shelves that held her photograph albums. Dull green leather, gold-edged, each with a year's pictures, a date on its spine.

Soon she'd have albums with pictures of Caitlin. Soon, soon. When, damn it all, when?

Ba got up, walked to the shelves. Suddenly she loathed the albums filled with pictures of just the two of them, a childless couple, an empty couple.

Suddenly she was seething, rage heating her blood, burning on her skin. She reached for one of the albums, wrenched it out of place, tugged it to the floor.

Then she was on it, clawing the pages open, tearing them, ripping them into tatters.

And then she was spent, breathing hard, unnerved by the mess she'd left for the maids. And cold again, shivering, because she hadn't faced the real horror of testifying, not yet.

What would she say under oath if they asked how she had learned Johnny wasn't a normal man? Or when she'd seen him last? Or if she'd ever seen Caitlin?

She couldn't lie in a courtroom. But she couldn't tell the truth. Her own lawyer didn't know it. Her own husband didn't know it. She'd behaved more horribly than ever in her life, worse than most women could possibly behave! She'd made her own brother spurn her as if she were some raving hysteric, dangerous, dreadful!

Ba stared at her wedding picture. Such a sweet girl. Her eyes met the camera straight on. Her shoulders were relaxed, her smile bright, happy. I looked like that once, she thought. And I can still look like that. I try to be a nice woman, do a lot of good in this world. I'll be good for Caitlin, better than any leftover lover of Johnny's. Maybe no one will ask those questions. I've been lucky. Maybe I'll be lucky in that courtroom.

Ba straightened her shoulders.

And smiled the serene smile of the girl in the picture gliding smoothly in her white dress to marry Tal.

6

PAX

On Centre Street, a block south of her courthouse and an hour from the opening of the custody trial, Pax's cab slowed, then stopped dead.

She'd been lost in gray thoughts about Leonard. Sickening to lose him just when she'd discovered him. And it *had* been a discovery. She'd never, even with Alden, talked and loved at the same time the way she had the other night. A man she'd liked so long without realizing she could love him, loved so intensely for a little time that she knew she wanted more, much more. Did this trial have to mean forgetting about him? Could they start again once it was over? Or would it be too late?

Looking out, she realized she had a more immediate problem.

People, lots of people, massing, milling in the little park across the street from the courthouse, spilling over onto the sidewalk, about to block the street ahead.

Pax wound down the window to see better. A group of men, young, in jeans and leather jackets, clustering, hefting signs, obviously getting ready to march.

The closest sign she could read said ACT UP FOR GAY

ADOPTION. This cab would never move. She'd better get out, push through.

The prospect was daunting. With the window open, Pax realized how much noise surrounded her, a rhythmic chant from down the block, catcalls, shouts, furious, deafening car horns blaring.

She put her head out the window for a real look around, feeling the wind cold on her face, ruffling her hair. Just ahead, another group, altogether different. Men in hard hats, work shirts, standing in a tight knot.

Her heart contracted. What Leonard had predicted. A demonstration at the courthouse steps, maybe a riot. Gays, he'd said, and the people who loathe them.

More like a little war brewing.

Quickly, before she could lose her nerve, she rapped on the scratched plastic divider between her and the driver.

"I'll get out here," she called. He turned, shaking his head.

"No here," he said. "You can no get out here."

His name, she saw from the license on the dashboard, was Machado, Julio Machado.

Why could she no get out here? Latino chivalry? His fears for her safety?

"Too much people," he added.

"Esta okay," Pax found herself saying, as Mami used to say years ago. *"Muy okay."*

Wishing she believed it, she found a ten-dollar bill in her purse, crunched it into the little metal drawer in the shield. The shield was meant to protect the driver against dangerous people. But now those people were just outside.

She had to push hard just to open the door, get into the crowd, the harsh sunlight.

Among all the swinging arms and broad shoulders she felt panic strike her, heating her body, clutching at her stomach. Everyone seemed bulkier, far taller than she, all scowls and fists, crazily angry.

Not a hope of getting to the steps. She was being crowded, shoved, men's feet stamping perilously near her own size four.

My God, there must be a hundred, maybe two hundred people between her and the courthouse steps!

It's those newspapers, Pax thought dizzily. The television. I must keep that child out of court. I won't let a six-year-old near a mob like this. I can't give her to the right person if I can't keep her alive.

The noises were growing louder, the shouts more fierce and belligerent. Suddenly, startling her, the people in front of her stopped moving, then began pushing backward.

I could be crushed, Pax thought, terrified. Will I be able to keep myself alive?

An instant later she saw why the crowd's movement had changed. A fight had broken out just ahead. Burly men were charging a skinny boy wearing lipstick, eye shadow, holding a can of spray paint. An instant later Pax saw the boy shoot a splash of wet lavender at his attackers.

Then a man was swinging, knocking the boy down, kicking him. And people from the sides, from behind her, were zooming in to kick the inert body!

Shaken, Pax stood on tiptoe, looking around, desperate to find help, saw a dark blue wall across the courthouse steps. Cops, with masks, shields, riot sticks, standing together, arms linked, some only twenty feet away.

Hope shot through her.

Get to them, she ordered herself. Somehow get to those cops. Be glad for once you're small enough to slip through a crowd, duck past people, try it, go!

No good. The writhing mass of people were a wall, too. She'd never get anywhere alone.

Pax put her head back.

"I need you," she yelled to the cops, top of her lungs. "I belong in there. I'm the judge."

Then, she didn't quite know how, one officer was close,

huge, sweating, jerking her arm, hurting her shoulder, but helping, pulling her up the steps.

She leaned against his chest to catch her breath. For a moment the world turned navy blue, smelled of sweat.

"You all right?" he said. "You hurt, lady?"

"No," she managed to say. *"Esta okay."*

The officer looked so startled Pax actually found herself wanting to smile.

"I'm Judge Ford," she said, trying to sound calm, normal, as if he'd just escorted her smoothly out of an official car. "Thank you. Thank you very much."

And then turned, strode up the steps, keeping her back straight, her head high.

The courthouse seemed more like a cathedral than ever, only now she felt like a fugitive taking sanctuary inside it. Thank God the big rotunda absorbed sound, muffled the shouting outside. Even with flaking paint and scarred floors the building was beautiful, noble, a place meant for something higher than just eating and sleeping. People came here to find justice. Plenty of them today, normal, orderly people heading for courtrooms, jury rooms, judges' chambers.

Everything normal, orderly, in her own chambers, too.

Selma and Tim must have come in extra early, before the crowd built up in the street.

"Good morning to you," Tim said.

Pax managed to smile up at him. The perfect clerk, Tim Halloran. Irish, all pale blue eyes and jet hair, he'd been twenty years a cop, ending up investigating corruption in the force. His father and grandfather cops, too, but they'd retired at forty to spend their days catching bluefish off Montauk Point. Long before forty Tim started going nights to St. John's Law, took the bar exam when he retired, scored near the top, came to clerk in the Supreme Court pool.

Pax began noticing that the best case summaries, the tightest drafts of motions, the best memoranda, had Tim's initials at the bottom. She dug out the name behind the initials, called Tim in, warmed to him instantly when he saluted her as if she were his precinct captain. He told her she was the darling of the pool for doing her own final writing. And then announced he thought she'd ignored a very important point of law in a recent case. Pax laughed, promised to look again.

When her own law secretary left to care for her sick mother, Pax asked Iapalucci for Tim. He'd backed her up ever since, handling mountains of work, being unfailingly cheerful, singing "The Bard of Armagh" whenever he was particularly pleased with a case.

Right now he wasn't singing. In fact, he was looking stricken.

"You all right, Judge? We didn't hear the noise outside till just now. Tomorrow we'll be getting you a police escort, whatever Administration says."

Pax looked around when plump, motherly Selma came bustling out of her little office. Today she looked excited, the plucked eyebrows high on her forehead, the starched front of her white blouse quivering.

"Big morning, Judge. Oh, don't let me forget, you've got a visitor."

Leonard, Pax thought, her heart leaping. Worried about me today? Sorry about the other night?

"Judge Macario," Selma said, frowning. "She was here before me, even. With an escort, two officers from her courthouse. Waiting outside your door. How come she rates an escort and you don't?"

"How about that," Pax said.

Not Leonard. Only Rosa. Pax leaned for a moment against a bookcase, drained, exhausted. And miserable. Why Rosa? Now? Trouble with Mami? Carlos again? Judge Schiff?

I haven't time, Pax thought.

But she'd have to make time.

"Thank God," Rosa cried when Pax went into her chambers. "I just opened your window, leaned out. There's enough noise down there to start a revolution. I was beginning to be scared to death for you."

She looked as if she'd come from Elizabeth Arden, dark hair sleek in its knot, navy suit brushed, perfect.

Feeling unkempt, frazzled, Pax sank onto the nearest couch.

"Did you have trouble?" she asked.

"I had officers, with guns. Some man took us through a side door, ran us up in the judges' elevator."

"Some man had a key to the side door? The judges' elevator? A judge?"

"A court interpreter. Eastern European languages, he said, Czech, Latvian, those. In the Bronx all the interpreters speak my language. Anyway, he was nice. He said you're the best judge in the building."

That would be Stephan Haras. Gray face, gray hair, smile full of tobacco-stained teeth. Pax had gotten to know him when she sat in Criminal Court. Polite man, patient with the nervous people who came to testify.

Once, a stomach-turning trial, a gang of Estonian kids setting a homeless man on fire, Stephan came back from lunch with violets for her. He'd bowed, gazed into her eyes, said that their color reminded him there was still loveliness and that she must always remember that, too. Somehow after that she'd felt easier about examining the hideous photos of burns, hearing out the callous statements from the boys.

Still, what was he doing in the judges' elevator?

Pax forced herself to concentrate.

"What about your courtroom? How come you're here?"

"I took a day off to watch you work. I saw you lawyering the other day. Now I'd like to see you judging. Judges never get to watch each other. I except Judge Schiff, I had to watch him. But I thought you'd be more inspiring. And I have a lunch date here in Manhattan, anyway."

Oh Rosa, Pax thought. Here to support me, be a friend. I hope the lunch date is with a man. She's done so much, but now she needs a little romance, more, a husband, babies. Mami would adore Rosa's babies.

"Aren't you excited?" Rosa was saying. "We don't get reporters, demonstrations, all this, in the Bronx. Are you having TV cameras in the courtroom?"

"Absolutely not. That's all I need with a child, a circus like this."

"But you should," Rosa said, wide-eyed. "Think about it. That's how to get known, Pax, show everyone who you are."

When Rosa got emotional her accent came back just a touch. She was glowing now like a girl headed for a party, eyes shining, cheeks flushed.

Lovelier than ever. So lovely she made Pax feel bedraggled, tired. Yes, and old.

"After this trial I may not want anyone to know who I am," Pax said, moving to the closet for her robe. "Mami's all right, Rosa? No aftereffects?"

"She's fine, she said you called yesterday. So fine, I gather she scolded you about your garden. She hates it that you can't wear nail polish. She doesn't think a lady's hands should be in dirt."

"Don't worry, she told me," Pax said. "So I gathered she was feeling fine."

In the long mirror inside the door Pax saw Rosa standing just behind her, smiling, shaking her head no. For an instant their reflections were superimposed, looked strangely surreal.

She's almost a head taller, Pax thought. And almost fifteen years younger.

"You still wear a robe!" Rosa was saying.

"Don't you?"

"Never. I hate the whole idea."

"Rosa, it's not your choice. It's a symbol. Like everyone standing up when you come in. Not for you. For the job."

She thought suddenly about Wounded Knee, the judge who'd gone there to try Indians suspected of killing a

federal agent. They wouldn't stand up for the judge. He'd
fumed, shouted, held them in contempt; they stayed in their
chairs. Then he'd gotten sick and another judge had taken
over. When the clerk said for everyone to rise and
the Indians kept still, this judge simply got started, tried the
case. So well that when it was over, all the Indians stood up
as one to honor him.

Maybe she made too much of forms, traditions. Maybe
Rosa's way was more modest, modern.

"In my courtroom," Rosa said, smiling, "they rise for me.
Come on, Pax, even the holy sisters don't wear black down to
the ground anymore. And nobody exactly gives out judges'
robes. They're expensive."

All right, there were always judges who thought they
were making a big statement ignoring robes, mostly young
judges. Rosa was young even among young judges. Supreme
Court judges could work till they were seventy-six. Thirty-
five was a baby.

Pax stopped feeling tense, began feeling wretched.

"Come on, Rosa. I have a trial downstairs," she said.

And shut the closet door, making more noise than she'd
intended.

Rosa was thinking how dreadful Pax looked, how worried
and upset. Today there were new lines in her pale skin, dark
places under her eyes, a tightness to her mouth.

She looked overworked, unhappy. Old.

Mami's embroidering that gorgeous tablecloth for Pax's
big birthday, she thought. Fifty! When I'm fifty I won't be just
a trial judge. I'll be in an appeals court, maybe even in a Federal Court.

Not that it would be all that easy. Right now she was trying
small, stupid criminal cases, mostly drug busts, nothing to
write weighty opinions about, nothing with big news like this
custody case.

But things were happening. Lunch today with Talcott

Bishop's right-hand man, and at the Merchants Club, no less. Because Bishop, amazingly, wanted to give her a party. Who knew where that could lead? The Appellate Division? Pax was way ahead in the race, of course, deserved to be. But anything could happen to her in this trial.

She watched her friend smooth her gleaming hair, settle her robe.

At least, Rosa thought, when she put herself in danger it was for something important.

Like years ago, at Hunter College, leading the Hispanic kids in demands for more financial aid, help with money for books, supplies, once leading a demonstration! She'd been in the papers for that, even the *New York Times*!

Suddenly she felt impatient, as she'd often felt waiting for Pax to finish something, homework, a call from a friend her own age, so she could talk about her own day at school, her own troubles with the other girls.

How she'd waited around for Pax as a six-, seven-year-old, especially when boys were calling her for dates, when she'd taken so long on the phone in her room!

Stop, a voice said, from her heart. How much attention could you ask from a girl fifteen years older than you, in a whole different world, anyway? You wouldn't be here except for her. You wouldn't be anywhere at all.

But I would, Rosa thought. I got somewhere all by myself in college, in law school. Pax didn't make me a judge, I did that alone. I did plenty alone.

Especially for a child that ignorant maid could call a dirty little blackie.

Pax felt like a debutante again when Tim held out his arm to her, insisted on escorting her down to the courtroom with Rosa following.

He even waited in Pax's robing room to see her settled, pen, notebook, a sip of water from a paper cup. Then he ducked out to the courtroom, came quickly back.

"Not an empty seat," he said with satisfaction. "I'm having them add a chair for you, Judge Macario, up front, right next to the court illustrator."

He smiled.

"You get bored, you watch her draw."

"Bored? At this trial?"

"Rosa," Pax said, "he's joking."

Sometimes Rosa got serious at the wrong time. Did she work too hard to hang on to a sense of humor? Had she worried too much lately?

Better hang on to mine, she thought. Sounds like a million people out in that courtroom, all waiting for me to make a mess.

Tim saluted gravely, took Rosa's arm, let her out. Pax's court officer appeared, saluted, held open her door to the bench.

Poor Sean, sweating this morning, brow wrinkled. All this fuss in his courtroom, and he hadn't quite recovered from last month's worries about his wife, a lump in her breast, some uncommunicative second-string doctor in a big Queens hospital. Pax had spent an hour on the phone, got Mary Catherine an appointment at Strang, given Sean time off to be with her. Mary Catherine had called, actually blessed her. A blessing over the phone. Did that work? She could use a blessing now.

She paused in the doorway a moment, felt the smell of a lot of bodies reach her nostrils, looked out past Sean at her courtroom, dark wood, old. And far too bright, thanks to the long fluorescent bulbs that sent glare over all the faces, into all the eyes.

Good Lord, Joe Iapalucci, standing at the side of the room. Looking like a basketball coach, gesturing to the court officers, nervously checking out the clock.

She searched for Will, who'd insisted on coming down to cheer her on even in class time. Yes, there in the middle row, but on the aisle. He'd have to nip out, get back up to school.

But he'd come! And yes, Debo was with him, her dark hair glossy under the lights, her big eyes wide.

Rosa was right up front, near the flag, the gold letters that said, IN GOD WE TRUST, next to the court artist.

The best court artist, too. Caro Hansen did incredibly quick, accurate pastels for NBC. She could catch the crucial moment in a trial, skewer it like a butterfly. Her sketches showed up on television almost every week. She had the pale, blond beauty of her Danish heritage, the light blue eyes and tiny nose of the girls in Copenhagen. She looked as different from Rosa as another lovely woman could. But she was as competent as Rosa, as remarkable. Her presence proved that. Her network considered this one big-deal trial.

Once Caro had brought Pax a pastel sketch, a present. Pax had loved it, loved the way it made her look prettier than she was. And the way Caro had said, oh no, it doesn't, Judge. It's exactly how you look.

Smiling at the memory, ready to start, Pax caught sight of a familiar face at the back of the courtroom.

Suddenly she couldn't move.

Leonard.

Leaning against the wall, as if he'd just dropped in, had no intention of staying.

Oh, God, now he was looking straight at her. And scowling.

Don't think about him now, she cautioned herself. It's your trial, your triumph, or maybe he's right, your disaster.

She waited for her heart to stop rattling.

Leonard saw her catch sight of him, go pale.

He realized he was leaning forward, his body wanting to take him nearer. Jesus, if he'd surprised, upset her now, when she needed all her cool, he'd never forgive himself.

Cool, he thought ruefully. She was a piece of ice the other night.

Was that fair? She'd been assigned the trial. Still, judges

had ways of getting off trials they didn't want. She wanted
the fucking case. And he was positive she underestimated the
danger, to her career, to herself, in this courtroom.

Well, he had wanted it, too. And everything that came
with it, the chance to champion D'Arcy, tangle with that
tightass Scott Wickham, yes, and the glory.

Pale, she'd gone pale, seeing him.

What was he doing?

Leonard realized he was sweating, a little unsteady on
his feet.

Rosa turned her head, looked past the pretty girl in blue
jeans next to her, counting the house. People were even
standing at the back. And reporters were everywhere, filling
the front benches, holding their pads, chattering to each
other.

The noise settled a little as the lawyers came through the
side doors. Making a big deal, banging down briefcases, rustling
papers. A lot of lawyers. Three at one table, assistants behind
them in extra chairs. Two at the other, more assistants.

It's a big-money case, Rosa thought. That *maricon* Johnny
California made zillions with his paintings. The Bishops
aren't exactly poor, either.

Suddenly everyone went quiet.

Rosa looked at the door, saw why. The man coming in
had to be Tom D'Arcy.

Handsome. Better than handsome, fantastic! Carved forehead, narrow nose, wide, supersexy mouth. And eyes that
slanted, glinted green even this far across the room. And his
body! Wide at the shoulders, narrow everywhere else.

No wonder Johnny California had taken him to bed!

No wonder the little hippie artist was suddenly scratching
on her sketchpad.

Now there were whispers, shufflings, as everyone watched
for the next big entrance. The child, that's what they wanted
to see, the mystery child.

Another flap of the doors.

It seemed to Rosa that everyone in the courtroom leaned forward.

But it was only a middle-aged couple. Of course, the Bishops. Here in court Talcott Bishop seemed more patrician than ever, pinstripe suit, heavy glasses, gray hair brushed neatly back.

Quite different from Mrs. Bishop. She looked flushed, edgy. Obviously she'd been a pretty lady once, but she was lined now, gray. Hard for a woman like her to face that gauntlet outside, this crowd here.

Now the child? With a nurse? A guard?

But the doors remained closed. And the court officers were moving up front, turning their backs on the judge's bench, standing at attention.

No little girl? Rosa felt a rush of rage, as if she'd been cheated at cards by one of Mami's old lady friends. Had Pax kept the child out? Why hadn't she said so?

One officer was speaking, telling them all to rise, court was in session, the Honorable Pax Peyton Ford presiding.

And then Pax, on the bench. Beautiful again now that she was farther away, so the little lines around her eyes, her mouth, didn't show.

It's her hair that makes her always lovely, Rosa thought. That incredible color, really silver. And those eyes, my God, the color of orchids.

For a moment she was awed. Everyone else seemed awed, too. Only the artist kept on working away with her colored chalks. The motion, the scratching sound, was irritating, like a whisper in church.

One of the lawyers was up. Making a motion to dismiss the case. Pro forma, Rosa knew. Lawyers always did that. Judges always denied.

That would be Murray Pressman, the big downtown defense lawyer. He looked like one, dark, quick, sharp-featured, good suit, practically pasted along his back. A hotshot, everyone said.

There were no hotshots in Rosa's courtroom.

And there was no child in this one. Where the hell was Caitlin California?

Rosa was trying to suppress her annoyance when, with no warning at all, the courtroom seemed to explode.

Suddenly someone was yelling at top volume, a man.

"Fuck the gay bastard," he was screaming, once and then, without pause, over and over, his voice booming out in the big courtroom.

Frozen for an instant, Rosa quickly came to, turned her whole body to see what was happening.

Then, shocked, stunned, she saw something zip past her head toward the front of the room.

Whatever it was whizzed by her. Streaking through the air, heading straight for Tom D'Arcy. Stone? Grenade? Bomb?

Her heart seemed to be swelling up, pounding so hard it shook her whole body. *Dios*, if she got hurt in this courtroom! If she'd come all the way down here just to get herself killed!

Now the whole room was in motion, seething, people in back making for the closed doors, people in the front ducking, trying to get under their seats. Everyone was making some kind of noise, a man shouting, a woman screaming, the officers calling to one another.

Shoulders tight, hunched in her chair, Rosa clasped her hands to keep them still.

One officer was guarding Pax now, planting himself in front of the bench, stretching his arms wide. The court stenographer was half under his little tripod table. Half the lawyers were on their feet, the rest crouching on the floor. Only the Bishops sat frozen in place, Talcott Bishop still erect, Mrs. Bishop with one hand at her throat.

Rosa realized Pax was standing now, high above everyone, arms up, wide sleeves fanned out as if she were an angel come from heaven.

Somehow her face was calm, still.

That helped Rosa settle her own face, quiet her own

trembling heart. Now she was calm enough to see the girl artist at work, still drawing on her pad!

Smart, Rosa thought. This has to be the moment to draw, the one they'll show on television. The one we'll all see over and over, like the shuttle blowing up, like O.J. in the Bronco on the freeway.

She remembered D'Arcy. He was sitting still, too, like a *hidalgo,* tall, straight. But something about him had changed, making him look different. Something about him looked all wrong.

He seemed to be at the center of a star. A big star, a splash of something, dripping, slimy.

Blood?

Stupid, Rosa scolded herself. Not red. Something yellow, sticky.

Now the noise in the room was resolving into a single shout, a man's.

"Fucking cream puff," Rosa heard over screams and shouting. "You're nothing but a fucking cream puff."

But he'd thrown a cream puff at Tom D'Arcy! Everyone in the courtroom was in shock, hiding under the furniture, because of a cream puff!

Pax was taking a step forward, arms still wide.

"Sean," Rosa heard her say to the officer just beneath the bench, "use your buzzer, get help."

Tom D'Arcy was finally moving. Not dead, not hurt. Now Rosa found herself on her feet, too, trying to see better, her hands gripping each other tightly. She watched D'Arcy bend his elegant head, look down at his soiled jacket. Reach into his pocket, bring out a handkerchief, shake it open. Somehow he made the simple gesture look elegant, beautiful.

But Pax was speaking!

"Let's have some quiet," she was saying, her voice raised to reach even the back of the courtroom.

And now she was pointing. Rosa swiveled to see what Pax

was seeing. So did everyone else. Every head in the court-room seemed to move the same way, at the same time.

A man, on his feet, young, one hand in a fist, shaking, the other clutching a paper bag.

"That man. The leather jacket," Pax was saying. "Mike, Sean. Get him up here, please."

Rosa was too far front to see clearly what happened next. The officers seemed to rush the man, yank him forward. The bag dropped to the floor. One of the officers, still hanging onto the man, stooped for it, lifted it, holding it well away from his body.

"Up here," Pax was calling out. "Bring him up here, and everyone else, sit down."

Good, Rosa could see him perfectly as the officers hustled him up front. Big, crew cut, leather jacket, work pants.

As they struggled by her, she had a good look at his face, contorted, furious. Then she was looking at his back as they got him to the bench.

Rosa realized the courtroom had gone silent, everyone straining to see, to hear.

Still standing, Pax bent her head, looking down at the man pinned between the two officers.

"You threw that, right?"

"Fucking A, I threw it. And I want everyone here to know I'm a member of—"

But Pax was cutting him off.

"You're a member of the holding pen in this building," she said clearly. "And what's more, you're in contempt of court."

"Wait a minute—"

"You had your minute. Your only minute. Now you go with these officers. They'll take you where you can make a phone call, tell your lawyer the whole story. If you don't have a lawyer, they'll get you one from Legal Aid."

She was speaking for the whole room to hear, Rosa real-ized, not just the man. Who was making a try, scuffling, to shake off the hands that held him.

"Fuck you, lady," Rosa heard. "I'm here to see justice done. I'm here to protest—"

"We know why you're here. We saw. We get it. You protested. You assaulted someone in a court of law. There are consequences to that. You're about to learn what they are."

She turned, looked at the court stenographer, who was still crouched on the floor.

"Reporter," Pax said, just as if the man were properly at his seat, poking at his little machine, "I'm fixing a hearing in this matter for tomorrow, two o'clock, in this courtroom. Mark it down, please."

Then she looked back at the trio in front of her.

"That's it," she said. "Dismissed."

In seconds, all three men were gone. And Rosa found herself sighing, a long, deep sigh. *Brava*, she thought. *Brava* for Pax, my Pax.

She smiled at her friend, smiled even though Pax couldn't see, because she was turned, looking at Tom D'Arcy. She did look years younger when she smiled. She must have gone pale before, because now color was rushing to her face, making her cheeks much pinker than usual.

"I want to thank all of you for your good sense," she said, voice ringing.

She gestured toward D'Arcy, still with his head down, still staring at his splattered jacket.

"Mr. D'Arcy, gentlemen. I'm sure you'd like a brief recess. First, though, I want to say this. I will not let a small child face what you faced in this courtroom just now."

What we faced, Rosa noted. *Brava* again. Who knew that *pendejo*, that son of a bitch, didn't have a gun, wouldn't shoot her?

"Especially," Pax was going on, "a child like Caitlin California. She's only six years old. She's just lost her father. I think she's had enough upheaval in her brief life without our adding any more."

But what was Pax saying? No child? Caitlin wouldn't be in the courtroom at all?

"Mr. Pressman, Mr. Wickham. Caitlin California will not appear. I'll work out some way to see her privately, in a safer setting, a way I trust will be agreeable to you both. All right, everyone, fifteen minutes."

Pax turned and was gone, vanishing through the door in back of the bench.

Rosa saw D'Arcy lift his head, saw his shoulders relax. And then saw him smile. He's glad about that, she thought. Glad for the little girl.

At the opposite table Mrs. Bishop was still in her seat. But her head was down, she seemed to be glaring up at the bench.

She's not glad, Rosa thought. She looks upset, angry. Damn it, I'm upset, too. Coming all this way to get a close look. And the most important person, the one the whole trial is about, not here to be seen. The newspapers will be furious. Everyone will be furious.

The reporters were on their feet, and yes, she could see their red faces, hear them bitching, even across the big court-room. She'd lose their support, that was sure. Besides, they'd never let her get away with it, either. They'd haunt her, follow her, watch every move she made, her chambers, her apart-ment, evenings, weekends.

It's foolish, Rosa thought. She's making the child more of a mystery, more of a prize.

The artist, surprisingly, was still calmly working away, fin-ishing her drawing. Rosa leaned over, peered at it.

Pax standing, arms wide, sleeves falling gracefully, light gleaming on her silvery hair. Beautiful. And a little mad-dening. She'd see it again tonight on the news and yet again tomorrow on the morning shows. Over and over she'd see it.

Rosa felt tired, cold. She couldn't, wouldn't have done what Pax did. She could never act so calm, so imperious. She wasn't a chilly WASP. Her people were warm, emotional, they let their emotions loose, they did what their hearts told them. Anyway, nothing in the Judicial Conduct rules said a judge had to be cold, calm. Maybe rage, shouting, would have made a bigger statement. Certainly it would be more human.

She stood up, walked toward the doors.

In all her days she'd never be like Pax. Pax with her skin like ivory, her hair spun silver, Pax holding herself as if she were a queen.

Dirty little blackie like you, the voice said in her head, in her heart. You shouldn't be here at all, dirty little blackie like you.

Forget it, Rosa told herself. Those words are long gone.

But somehow they stung, sharp, hurtful, as if she'd just heard them for the very first time.

7

ROSA

ROSA SHUT THE BATTERED DOOR OF HER COLD CHAMBERS, murmured, *"Ayudame, Dios,"* to herself in prayer that the flimsy lock would hold.

Lucky Pax. Everything in her chambers solid, warm, in working order. If *she* wanted a moment alone, no one would bother her. Here? Any court officer could put his head in, ask when she was coming down. Any janitor could walk in and take a stab at fixing the radiator, the light switches, all the things that didn't work.

Pax, Pax! For two days the papers and television screens had been full of her and the wonderful way she'd handled the disruptive man at her trial. People spoke as if she wore shining armor, not just her dreary old black robe.

Face it, Rosa told herself. You're jealous, horribly jealous, which is disgusting, with all you owe her. Worse. You're ungrateful.

Knowing she was picking at a scab, Rosa opened the *Daily News,* reread today's article. Dreadful, the way the newspapers' computers called up all the previous stories, word for word, printed the same thing over and over. Like the gossipy stories about Chief Judge Wachtler blackmailing that rich mistress of his, run again and again. For weeks. Why hadn't the man simply divorced his wife and married that mistress? Saved everyone a lot of trouble?

Computers reprinted pictures, too. Pax's official photo kept popping out again and again. She'd evidently ducked new pictures, so the papers kept running this one. A far cry from Judge Ito in California, where they welcomed cameras in the courtroom, where a judge could be an instant movie star.

Every day, Rosa thought, there's some piece of craziness in my courtroom. Yesterday that old Dominican woman swinging her purse at her lawyer, attacking him with her fingernails. She looked a little like Mami till she went into that act; I couldn't make myself yell at her. And I stood up, bowed to her, spoke like a daughter asking her to take care, save her hardworking hands to go home, cook dinner for her men. Thank God, that struck her as sense, and she turned into a lamb for the rest of her testimony. I did that. But who puts *my* picture in the papers?

Last night's Fox News had opened with Pax, too. With a sketch that made her look like the picture of Justice herself, lacking only a blindfold, a scale.

Rosa crunched the newsprint into a ball, looked ruefully at her smudged palms. She didn't really begrudge Pax praise, she wasn't that kind of person. But Pax didn't sit in Bronx County, didn't know what danger was. And outside her courtroom what did Pax have to worry about? Did *her* mother get shot in a park? *Her* nephew get arrested for possession? Now she even seemed to have a new man, rich and important.

Rosa lifted her head, looked around her dreary chambers.

A battered desk for her law clerk. A worn rug. A lamp that worked only when it wanted to, a window so filthy it could have been a wall.

Why was she obsessing about Pax? Was it because of the new man? And because she was getting used to being all alone again? She'd felt pure love, pleasure in Pax's triumphs when she'd had Tony to love.

Anthony Giancarno practically ran the courthouse. Technically, Third Assistant Deputy Clerk. But with the chief an old man, the second an alcoholic, it was Tony who made things happen. Grubby as her chambers were, they were the biggest in the building. Unctuous as her clerk was, he was the smartest. Judicial seminars in New Orleans, Santa Fe, Reno, a weekend conference at the Concord? For a whole year Rosa had been at the head of the list because of Tony.

They'd met almost the moment she'd become a Supreme Court judge. All judges celebrated being sworn in by giving lavish parties. But hers was in the biggest conference room in the courthouse, two, maybe three hundred people. Her own Democratic club, local merchants' associations, Latino community groups all contributing, drinking, eating, dancing up a storm. Everyone in the courthouse came. Mostly they clumped with their own, Italians at the food, Irish at the bar, Jews arguing at the tables, Latinos up dancing.

But Tony cut a path through the dancers, took her out of the arms of a Puerto Rican assemblyman, slow-danced just as if they hadn't been playing a mambo. He'd literally swept her off her feet, pressing her close, touching her cheek and neck, electrifying her so it seemed right, wonderful to take him home to her apartment, let him make macho love to her, do all his bidding and love him back.

But Tony was married to Marisa. And had three kids. And a big family with brothers and in-laws who ran a restaurant in Queens that judges' associations somehow always booked for meetings.

They'd had nearly a year, a wild tarantella of a year, full of delicious secrets, shared glances in crowds, exciting daytime encounters, thrilling nights. Then, as Rosa began learning her judging, taking pleasure from doing it well, she'd started feeling ashamed. She deserved more, better. A man of her own.

So she'd given Tony a ruling, like a judge. Leave Marisa. Marry me. I'm not nobody. There aren't nineteen or twenty

Hispanic judges in the whole state, people who've accomplished what I've accomplished.

She fretted, suffered while Tony blew hot and cold. He loved her, she knew it, he said it, showed it with attention, adoration. But he couldn't give up a whole life, even for her. So Rosa had steeled herself. Cut him off, never looked his way again, even when he raged, called at all hours of the night, even as her chambers grew dirtier, her court officers less competent, her trial assignments drearier. And even when she felt more sickening loneliness, more misery than she'd thought any man could cause.

Though Rosa shared most things with her mother, she'd never mentioned Tony. A married man? She could imagine the head shaking, the predictions of doom. So there was no comfort from Mami. Or anyone else. She had nobody, nobody at all. And she was too young to have nobody, too old to wait much longer. Thirty-five was young to be a judge, but not to have babies. Couldn't life for once be unfair to someone else? To Marisa? To Pax?

The door banged open.

Rosa jumped, guilty as any defendant.

Her clerk, Larry Bernstein, glasses glittering, a stack of motion papers in his arms, his worn corduroy jacket smudged on the front, patched at the elbows.

A walking brain, Larry. Everyone wanted him. But Rosa had him. Tony had tried transferring him away. But Larry worshiped her, worked till all hours, even did errands for her, her shoes reheeled, a new watch battery, a new Elmore Leonard mystery from the public library. He'd risked Tony's wrath, refused to leave her.

Now he stood, hunched over, owlish, looking cross.

"They're waiting for you, Judge," he said. "And everyone is screaming at me."

Poor Larry.

Rosa sighed, smiled at him. Better get busy, stop in the rest room, smooth her hair, use her compact. But why? Her hair was neat enough in its knot, her makeup so light it didn't need patching. Besides, she wasn't Pax. No one of importance was going to watch her preside.

"Let's go," she told Larry, and moved to the door.

Leonard stood, restless, impatient, at the back of Judge Macario's courtroom. Still as noisy, crowded up in the Bronx as in his days as a young practitioner. More dark faces now, though. In fact, hard to see a face that wasn't dark.

He'd certainly spent a lot of time watching other lawyers work lately.

Couldn't be helped. He'd stood in Pax's courtroom to see if Pressman had things in hand.

No, that wasn't the reason. He wanted to see if Pax had things in hand, how she opened the trial, ran it. And then found himself, heart smashing against his chest, scrambling to get to her when trouble erupted.

She hadn't needed him.

But Debo needed him now, badly. She'd landed him in this zoo of a courtroom where some defendants and witnesses wore jail overalls and handcuffs. All scarred benches, ripped flags, graffiti on the wall behind him.

His daughter had been so hysterical he'd had trouble understanding what was wrong. He always felt a terrible clutch in his gut when Debo was unhappy. Since his first sight of her through the glass in the hospital nursery, he'd wanted to take all the heat for her, give her everything. He'd even stayed on with Sylvia years after he'd wanted out. Debo had been an adorable, confiding daughter, before Will and even after. But this story he'd had to pull out of her as she wept, a quarrel, Will slamming the door, calling hours later, arrested, Bronx Criminal Court, who knew why? If Daddy didn't bring him home, she'd die. If Will had done something awful, she'd kill him. And Leonard had said all the old words, hush, you calm down, sit tight, I'll take care of it.

Bronx Criminal Court? Judge Macario, he'd thought

immediately. Pax's friend. He'd go straight up, catch her on a recess.

He'd expected to feel edgy, impatient. After all, he hadn't sat listening to two-bit cases for quite some time.

Instead he found himself paying close attention. Any trial was better than no trial.

The clump of lawyers standing before Judge Macario was breaking up, the judge was lifting her head. Leonard saw her in the clear for the first time.

He found himself holding his breath. He'd heard Pax talk about her friend, read the *Journal* interview, looked at the picture with it. Carmen in a Peter Pan collar, he'd thought then, a preppy suit, a nurse's hairdo.

The picture hadn't done the judge justice. Rosa Macario was a true beauty. A Velasquez painting. Morgan Le Fay. The Dark Lady of the Sonnets.

Leonard exhaled, noted how much about her was all wrong, that hair, that mouse brown suit, worst color she could wear. In the interview she'd said she wouldn't wear a robe. But even a robe would do more for her than that dreary suit.

Still, what a fantastic face, what incredible black eyes! She looked like the Italian girls on his block when he was a kid, white teeth, sun-warmed skin, jiggling breasts their Catholic school jumpers didn't hide, girls who made a nice Jewish boy instantly horny.

For God's sake, he told himself, settling back against the dirty wall. Don't get nuts just because you let Pax get away, because you've been sleeping alone in that furnished apartment. Because you couldn't make yourself return that ring, even if you did shove it deep into the office safe.

But that wasn't the whole story. Rosa Macario was a knockout. And he didn't often see knockout girls in court, especially running the whole show.

This show, no surprise, featured a young D.A., a sullen Hispanic defendant, head hanging low. Why did they always hang their heads as if they were celebrities in hiding?

Leonard strained to hear through the noise.

"Your Honor, you can't dismiss the attempted murder charge. This defendant raped and sodomized Vesta Colon. Then he announced, 'Okay, bitch, I'm going to throw you off the roof,' dragged her upstairs at knife point. Only the fact that the door was locked kept him from doing it!"

"You don't know that," Judge Macario said. "You can't read his mind. The law doesn't read minds; that went out with the Spanish Inquisition. Your defendant was interrupted at a point too remote to complete the crime."

Spanish Inquisition? She sounded like Pax. Did anyone in Bronx Criminal know anything about the Spanish Inquisition?

"But, Judge! It's the classic definition of attempt. 'But for the intrusion of an outside person or force the crime would have been complete.' Well, but for the lock he'd have killed her."

"Counselor," Rosa said, "I give you back a classic case, the police following a car full of men with guns, driving around looking at banks. You may remember it. They were charged with attempted robbery. The trial judge who admitted the charge was reversed by the App Div. For attempted robbery to stick, they'd have had to walk in, point their guns. I don't like reversals from the Appellate Division. Your defendant would have had to get her on that roof and actually try throwing her off."

"But, Judge! He had a knife! She was in fear of her life!"

"That doesn't make any difference. If your man tried shooting someone who didn't even know he was being shot at, had no fear at all, that would be attempted murder. Fear has nothing to do with it. This count isn't going to the jury, Counselor. It would only confuse them, prejudice their decision."

She smiled, a beautiful smile.

"You have rape and sodomy. Be happy. And proceed."

Jesus Christ, Leonard thought. Who is this girl? Pax might

have said that more elegantly. But she couldn't have thought it through better. The law of attempts was always sticky. Appellate courts were often on both sides.

Even this far back, the rigid shoulders of the D.A. conveyed his outrage.

But now the judge, thank God, was calling a recess.

Leonard stepped forward, nabbed a court officer, and requested a few minutes of her time.

Rosa was furious when Larry banged into her chambers.

A recess was a recess. She'd wanted to hold that insistent kid in contempt. And forced herself to keep her temper, explain herself patiently. When she wasn't naturally patient, by any means.

"Yes, Larry. What?"

"Visitor, Judge."

Just behind him, a man, big and burly as Tony. But very different. Rosa saw bright brown eyes, a craggy face, a head of springy gray curls.

Another moment and she noted the expensive suit, silk tie, the dull gold wristwatch.

"This is Mr. Scholer, Judge, Mr. Leonard Scholer."

Leonard Scholer? A big lawyer, a famous lawyer, in her ratty chambers?

Before she could puzzle about it, Mr. Leonard Scholer was stepping in front of Larry, smiling.

"Judge Macario," he said warmly, as if he'd known her for years, was delighted to see her now.

A nice voice, deep, with power in it.

"I just heard you rule downstairs. Terrific. Not many judges would have been so succinct."

Had he come because of Talcott Bishop? The *Bar Journal*? Something about next week's party? Wait, wasn't he the man Pax had been having dinner with? Yes, of course.

"I haven't been up here for a lot of years," Mr. Leonard Scholer was saying.

Rosa had to smile. He seemed so genuinely pleased life had brought him back to the Bronx.

Larry was clearing his throat. Her silence was making him nervous.

"Thanks, Larry," Rosa said. And looked pointedly at the door.

Then she moved to her chair.

"Let me, Judge," Mr. Scholer said, reaching to pull it out.

Rosa suddenly found she wasn't breathing right. She swallowed, wondered why. Was it so long since a man had held a chair for her? Or that Mr. Leonard Scholer moved fast when Tony hadn't moved at all? That he smelled only of soap, no cologne, no aftershave, all the flowery fragrances Tony loved?

Rosa felt nervous suddenly, fluttery.

Why compare him to Tony? He wasn't nearly as young, as handsome. He wasn't after her, either, on the make the way Tony had been.

"Thank you," he was saying, taking a chair as smoothly if she'd actually invited him to sit. "Judge Macario, I'm here to ask your help. And presuming on a friendship of yours. With Judge Ford. Her son, William, is married to my daughter."

Of course, Rosa thought, feeling more curious than ever. Willie's your son-in-law.

"He's just been arrested," Mr. Scholer said flatly.

Rosa felt her whole body stiffen. "Arrested? What charge?"

"Possession. A party somewhere on Convent Avenue. A raid. Cops found glassine envelopes, booked everybody they saw."

Willie? Oh God, did he do drugs? Did Pax know? Willie was her darling. She'd be devastated. And she'd get hurt, especially now with so much attention focused on her. She'd be like Gerry Ferraro, with a kid caught selling drugs at school.

Gerry Ferraro's son had done time.

Here it comes again, Rosa thought, frightened. Those

dreadful mandatory drug sentences. Carlos had faced one, nearly broke my heart, Mami's heart.

"Here's where it stands," Mr. Scholer said. "They've printed him, done a NYSIS sheet. It's clean, no previous arrests, no dispositions. They could just ROR him."

Remand Will Ford on his own recognizance? Let him go?

Of course they wouldn't keep him, not like they'd kept Carlos.

"Then why are you here?" Rosa said.

"Record," Mr. Scholer said. "He's a law student, as of course you know. When he finishes, gets to the ethics exam, he won't need an arrest on his record."

No, Rosa thought. That, at least, hadn't bothered Carlos. He wasn't exactly pointed at law school.

"My daughter called me, caught me in my car on my way down to the Federal Courthouse. I sent somebody to ask for a postponement, turned around, and came straight up here."

He looked around. "You know," he said, "one of my first trials was right here, in front of Judge Naughts. Before your time, of course, but you've probably heard."

He paused, smiled again.

He's giving me time to breathe, Rosa thought. He's building up to what he wants.

"I have to say it's a lot better talking to you than Judge Naughts."

Naughts was a courthouse legend. Crazy as any psychiatric inmate. Endless trouble for lawyers and court personnel, wild rulings, temper tantrums. If Mr. Scholer had handled him, he knew what he was doing.

"My daughter was beside herself. She and Will had some sort of quarrel. Will slammed out, stayed out all night. This morning he called her from here. Feeling, of course, like a fool, asking her to forgive him. Deb got hold of me. I'd like to help. I'd like your help."

Now he was looking into her eyes. He was so intense, so

there. She felt almost compelled to do what he wanted, whatever it was.

"I'd like this off his record. The police may have an arrest, but they honestly don't have a case. Will didn't give the party, didn't handle a controlled substance. Nothing ties him to the drugs, nothing at all. I promise you, his character is unimpeachable."

He grinned suddenly.

"Why else would I let him marry my daughter?"

The grin was charming, took years off his looks. Now he seemed warm, boyish.

"Why else?" Rosa said, trying to keep from showing anything but polite concern.

"Of course, it's touchy. This kind of thing always is. And I don't want to make things worse, make it look like pressure, anything that could backfire. Or hurt Judge Ford."

Rosa tried to remember when she'd last seen Willie. Quite some time. She and Mami had been invited to the wedding, of course. But she'd been in Orlando with Tony, a seminar they could both, for once, justify for the administration, be at together.

Of course she'd help. She owed Pax for Carlos, for everything. And it would feel wonderful, marvelous, to do her a favor for a change.

"Judge Ford doesn't know about this," Mr. Scholer said. "And I'd be happy if she didn't have to deal with it for a while. You know what's on her hands downtown. So I thought of you, Judge. I know you're a friend of hers."

Are you saying you know what she did for Carlos? Are you asking me for a quid pro quo?

"I thought maybe you'd give me the lay of the land up here, what to say, what not to say. I don't know the arraignment man, Judge Weinberg. I've been out of this kind of case so long I hardly remember the procedures, the words."

Oh, I think you remember the procedures, Rosa wanted

to say. I think you remember the words. You're good with words.

"Do you know what Willie told them?" she asked. "What he's said so far?"

"No. It's a big worry. He could have been angry. Everybody does dumb things when they're angry."

"Everybody doesn't get picked up in drug raids," Rosa said.

Mr. Leonard Scholer leaned forward. "A surprising number of people do," he said, gravel in his voice. "People's sons, their sons-in-law, their nephews, a surprising number."

All right, he knew about Carlos.

"And you'd like good news for his mother, is that it?"

A frown appeared, wrinkling Mr. Scholer's face, somehow making it look older, wiser.

"I haven't seen Judge Ford in a while," he said. "But I'd certainly like some good news for my daughter. Better still, no news at all."

What was he suggesting? He wasn't really close to Pax?

"This courthouse," he said, looking around. "I started out here with a real nightmare. Rape. A two-year-old girl."

Rosa stared at him, her stomach contracting. Somehow, suddenly, the whole room seemed to go away. She wasn't an adult, wasn't in her chambers, wasn't even in America. She was back on the Island, a tiny girl, curled in bed with her brothers. Making herself into a little ball, hands over her ears, knees up to her chin. Papi was banging on the door. He'd been at the cockfights, where else? His footsteps and banging noise rolled around in the house like thunder. She felt the boys scramble out of bed, and then sensed him, smelled the night smell, rich and sharp, that came from the brown bottle of rum.

She was afraid to look, afraid not to look. Papi was coming for the bed, for her. She'd broken a jug that afternoon. Perhaps he knew, was angry about it.

But he didn't hit. He took her shoulders in his hot hands with a gentleness that scared her more than any way he'd ever touched her before.

Wet face on her face, huge hands pulling the ragged dress she wore days, nights, no difference.

Hands on her bony hips, holding her hard. And his mouth on her, down there.

And then his big thing was outside his shirt. He was touching her with it, spitting on his fingers again and again, making her wet down there.

And then pain worse than a blow, a burn, searing pain driving into her. Till she was wet, sticky, the bed beneath her wet, till he rolled off her, slept.

And in the morning nobody saying a word about Papi. She could have dreamed it all except that she couldn't walk without pain, that her bruises were blue, hideous.

Lady, you are gorgeous, Leonard was thinking. Even when something seems to be upsetting you a lot, like right now, you're gorgeous beyond belief.

And Pax's friend.

Well, Pax had been pretty cool, hadn't she? Her big-deal trial had meant more to her than he had.

Wait a minute, Leonard told himself. All that stuff you told yourself, you meant it. You could love Pax, you did love being with her.

But she hadn't exactly loved being with him. Not enough to ask off one rotten case. Certainly, he could buy this girl a drink, get to know her a little. She was going places in the judiciary; he ought to know her. And if she took care of Will for him, for Debo, he'd owe her. Buying her a drink would be no chore, either. He'd never in all his life been this close to someone as out-and-out sexy, as stirringly beautiful, as Rosa Macario.

Who was looking, at the moment, as if she was about to cry.

He damned well better do something for her.

Rosa came to because Mr. Leonard Scholer was looking so concerned.

"I'm sorry," he was saying. "I've upset you. I didn't mean to."

She shivered, made herself stop. Then she smiled at him, a smile for a nice man, simpatico.

Why had she remembered about Papi? In the daytime, in her chambers? When she felt, most of the time, as if she'd really been born after he died, born on the plane to New York?

"It wasn't you that upset me. What you said, the two-year-old. We have a lot of that here. It doesn't shock me anymore. But you, young, probably bookish, I'm sure you were shocked."

"Oh, I'm not all that bookish," Mr. Scholer said. "Or all that shockable. I get around one way or another."

Was he coming on to her? Could he be?

"Look," Rosa said, "the arraignment judge is a pistol. I don't think he'll react well to someone like you, a downtown lawyer, saying there's no case."

"Well," Leonard said, "I wasn't exactly planning to start with that. Or to put it to him that way. But I'm open. It's why I wanted to see you."

"I think this calls for my having a little chat with the judge."

"That," Mr. Scholer said, "will be his good luck."

"Ah," Rosa said, "he's not a lucky man. He's been in Criminal Court for some time, never got promoted."

"Well, we all know promotion isn't easy for some people. But you, now. I hear a lot of talk about you and the next App Div vacancy."

You do? Thank God for the *Bar Journal.* And Talcott Bishop. But there's plenty of talk about Pax, too. We were both on that last list. No reason we won't both be on the next one. Can you help, Mr. Scholer? Which of us would you help, Mr. Scholer?

"Let me see what I can do," she said. "If he's already been ROR'd, they'll probably just let him walk."

"Great," he said.

With emphasis, fervor in his voice, as if she were

indeed the world's best judge, the world's most wonderful woman.

Can he be fervent about other things, too? Rosa wondered. What would it be like to spend time with a man like this? Where could it lead? Was he perhaps invited to Talcott Bishop's party for her? Would he then see her as he should, honored, respected, dressed in her best black suit? Could he maybe escort her?

"Tell you what," Rosa said, taking the plunge. "Call me this afternoon, around five, when I get off the bench. I'll know then if the judge is willing to expunge the record."

Mr. Leonard Scholer stood up.

In her gloomy chambers he loomed over her, as big, as solid as Tony. But everything else, his rumpled hair, his beautifully shaped hands, the intelligence practically twinkling out of his eyes, a different story.

A new story.

Now he was leaning very close, startling her. And then backing off, surprising her still more.

"Extension 241, right?"

He'd only been looking at her phone dial.

"Around five, when you get off the bench."

Five o'clock, Rosa thought. When the courts close. When lawyers and judges relax, have a drink, a bite of dinner. When there's no hurry.

But hey, she wasn't a baby. She shouldn't play games. She should start straight, just in case he was in some way hungover about Pax.

"Mr. Scholer, I'm Pax's friend, her good friend."

"Oh, so am I," he said, unblinking. "A good friend, no more, no less."

He stretched out his hand.

Rosa found hers rising to meet it without effort.

His hand was hard, warm.

"Talk to you then," he added.

Then he was out the door, gone. He hadn't thanked her.

Because he'd do that later? Around five, when she got off the bench?

Rosa realized she felt warm, sun-touched, as if she'd been handed a glorious present. She stood up, blew a kiss at the empty chair across from her own, as if it still held Mr. Leonard Scholer in its rickety arms.

8

PAX

PAX FROZE AS TIM HALLORAN'S CAR SKIDDED IN THE SNOWY street a block from the courthouse, breathed again when he coaxed it into line.

All she needed this morning, a blizzard no one predicted. This visit to D'Arcy's had been hard enough to arrange, almost three days getting both Pressman and Wickham to approve. Pressman had accused her of being underhanded. Wickham, more courteous, simply had said he distrusted off-stage moves. She'd had to infuriate them both equally to get them to agree.

Now, exhausted, she felt like a disappointment to both sides. When she'd wanted so to be fresh, open to all Caitlin said and did.

"Sorry," Tim said. "Snow's getting worse."

"Yes, and we'll be late. Actually, we're late already. Go a little faster. No, forget that. Just be careful."

Pax shivered, watching her windshield wiper carve a fan out of the frosted windshield, pressing her wet shoes against the floor. Better not distract Tim with talk.

Trying for some peace, she tried to think about her garden. It didn't help. Snow now, when she hadn't yet cut down the last of the mums, tidied the rose beds. She'd meant to get out early this morning before she came downtown. But there'd been a summons to a special session of her divorce committee. A group of matrimonial lawyers protesting their suggested ethical guidelines, resenting the very idea that any divorce lawyer would take sexual advantage of confused, vulnerable women clients.

But she had to see Caitlin.

Pax closed her eyes. She'd known the trial would be tough. How could she have known so many other things would go awry, worst of all that Leonard would be involved?

Back to Leonard again.

Avoiding her, no doubt about it. Over the weekend she'd had brunch at Will and Debo's Upper West Side apartment. That happened often because Leonard wanted it to. Bagels and nova from Murray's made him happy; being with all of them made him happier still. Only this time he hadn't come.

Really, she scolded herself. If you must worry, worry about Caitlin. Suppose the child won't talk. Or gets hysterical. Or sounds like a little parrot coached by D'Arcy.

She couldn't help remembering a case years ago, a judge fuming at a rude five-year-old, ordering him into handcuffs. The handcuffs were too big. The child shook them off, screamed for his mother. And a judicial conduct commission shook the judge off the bench for good.

"I'm glad it's you with me," she told Tim. "Not just someone from the steno pool. How come you know steno?"

"Because long ago I got sore. In my cop days, we'd have suspects all ready to talk, camcorders set, assistant D.A. poised, and then sit around waiting for a CSR. So I learned."

"You'll have to use it today without scaring Caitlin. In a closet, behind a curtain, somewhere she can't see you."

"I drive you through a blizzard, take verbatims for you, and I don't get to meet the mystery child?"

"No," Pax said. "Not even you."

By now they'd both read every decision in New York law with any relevance. Pax was fascinated by one, from an appellate court. Two lesbians with a child conceived through artificial insemination, splitting up, the splitter petitioning for visitation. And the court denying, saying that only a parent could decide who visits a child. Though one woman judge dissented, saying that in the old days children might have been legal subpersons, but now were regarded as people with rights of their own.

So it still came back to Caitlin's best interests. Were they with D'Arcy? Or the Bishops?

At last, Eighteenth Street. A pretty block, wide town houses, shrubbery heavy with snow, walkways neatly cleared. Halfway along, a little park, an elaborate iron fence.

Then Pax realized it wasn't a park. More an enclosure, tall gates, driveway, even a gatehouse.

She meant to take deep breaths, relax, while Tim spoke to the guards. But, my God, they both wore holsters. With guns. Like the guards in her courtroom. She tried to look unconcerned. As if everyone's house was in a park with gatehouses, guards, guns.

But she had to stare as they began rolling on and saw the house set back among tall trees, like a Parisian mansion, entirely hidden from the street.

Now they were at the concave wooden door of the big house, watching it swing slowly back, a man in a white jacket coming out into the cold.

Of course, a phone in the gatehouse, a signal to open up for them.

"You wanted a closet," Tim said softly. "A hundred closets, at least, a house like this."

The man was offering her his arm. "Good morning," he said gravely.

No snow under her feet, none on the steps.

"Morning," Pax said. "I'm Judge Ford. My law secretary, Mr. Halloran."

He led them into a dazzle of light, a rainbow of color, took her bedraggled black coat, Tim's.

Thank God for Tim. Anyone else would have to gossip about this place.

"If you'll wait in the parlor," the man said, "I'll fetch Mr. D'Arcy."

Pax followed him through the massive doors, dark wood, with lion's head fittings. And immediately felt she'd stepped through Alice's looking glass into Wonderland. The room was like a magic antique shop. An enchanted attic!

"Please sit down," the man said, and disappeared.

"Holy shit," Tim whispered.

"Amen," Pax said.

"This settles it," he went on. "Give Caitlin to the Bishops. At least she won't grow up in a junkshop."

But Pax was under the spell of the room: log fires, flowers, pictures crowded on every wall, objects covering every surface.

Somehow it smelled like Christmas, evergreen branches, cookies hot from the oven, candy canes.

In one corner, dolls. A schoolroom full, all sitting in tiny chairs, a boy doll in a paper dunce cap facing the wall.

Not a junkshop, she thought. A museum, wonderful things made more wonderful by the way they were set out.

Turning, she saw a long row of pine hutches, each different, their shelves heaped with hundreds of alphabet blocks, wood, papier mâché, stone, glass. The blocks looked jumbled. But Pax soon saw they were arranged to spell one word again and again.

The word was "Caitlin."

Were all the rooms like this? And in all the other houses? My God, was there an inventory? Was some frantic paralegal struggling tearfully with lists, photographs, appraisals?

She turned and saw a collection that stopped her heart.

Snowstorms. Glass globes with tiny scenes inside. Hundreds, all sizes, filled with clear liquid and tiny snowflakes.

Ready for someone to shake, turn into snowscapes. Just like one she'd had as a child.

Pax couldn't help it. She picked one up in both hands, shook. It felt smaller than she remembered. Of course, her hands were bigger now. But the magic was exactly what she remembered. Little houses, tiny trees, a frosted lake with miniature skaters, all lost in swirling white, emerging again as the flakes settled.

A world, Pax thought. Beautiful, clean, safe. Like my world when I was Caitlin's age.

She shook it again, a twelve-year-old now, holding her own snowstorm, wishing she could live inside it. In the Bad Year, when she was afraid she'd never grow taller.

In school, a club. The Talls. Not for Pax. She was the smallest in her class. The Talls wrote notes in code. They giggled together, ate lunch together. Worse, they met at Sally Minot's Saturdays, and Sally lived in Pax's building. In the elevator, the lobby, the garden, the Talls would look over Pax's head and laugh.

She'd tried desperately to grow, stretching till she ached, stuffing handkerchiefs in her shoes. She'd lazed through her homework, sat silent in class, her white-blond hair unbrushed.

One day Sally called her a midget.

Pax walked out of school, heartsick. At home, her mother was out, the maids, Margaret and Cathleen, resting. But Esperanza Macario was in the pantry, ironing.

Mondays Esperanza took the family laundry down to the basement of the building, where there were washing machines, dryers. Tuesdays she sprinkled, pressed, folded. And sang soft Spanish songs that floated into Pax's dreams.

Safe at home, Pax had let herself cry.

In a minute Esperanza was on her knees, hugging, peeling a linen handkerchief, crisp and hot, from the ironing board. Another minute and she began hearing about the Talls.

She'd stood up then, frowning, fierce.

"Señorita Pax, tall is nothing. A tall heart is something. Your father's heart is tall, your mother's. Yours will be, too. And those girls have hearts that are small, like chicken hearts. Sing a song with me. No one can cry and sing at the same time."

Soon there was a Christmas party, boys from Buckley, Collegiate. Pax had a lavender dress, white gloves, red Mary Janes. And all the boys were short! The Talls stood in corners. Pax danced every dance. Two boys even asked her to the movies! She'd flown into the pantry next washday, hugged Esperanza, hard.

Later, when Pax was in her teens, Esperanza brought baby Rosa to work. Pax rocked, fed, adored the baby with her whole heart. Over and over she'd tell Rosa she'd be tall, beautiful.

Rosa was tall, beautiful.

And Pax, with her step stools, her custom-made clothes, wearing Will's boyhood jackets and sweaters in the garden, still hated being just under five feet.

"Judge," Tim was saying. "Don't get lost."

Pax put down the snowstorm, sat down.

"Maybe this just needs time."

"Time?"

"I mean, if I decide for D'Arcy, Caitlin stays here. If she goes to the Bishops, she gets used to them. It's not life or death. Custody, that's all. Some children have nobody. Caitlin has two people wanting her enough to fight it out in court."

Tim stared at her. "I don't agree, Judge. Her whole future depends on you."

"Tim, she's six years old. In twelve years she'll make the decisions. Find D'Arcy and live with him. Or ask the Bishops to take her in. At eighteen she'll have millions; she can buy any life she wants. I'm handing down a custody decision here, not a life sentence."

Tim was quiet for a moment.

"You can't mean that," he said finally. "Gloria Vanderbilt had millions. But a judge affected her whole life, gave her a childhood she never got over."

Pax leaned back. "Her custody trial was a circus," she said. "The judge was an alcoholic. He took her away from her mother, from the nurse she loved. No comparison."

"I've never heard you talk like this. There's more here, the whole business of gays and the law. If D'Arcy had a wife, nobody'd mind his raising Caitlin. I mean, why are those demonstrators demonstrating? Plenty of people think your decision matters."

Pax felt small. She hated disappointing Tim.

"I'm supposed to do what's right for Caitlin, not for whichever pressure group screams loudest."

"They're screaming because you could be making a land-mark decision here."

"Oh, Tim. Judges aren't supposed to remake the world. They're just supposed to apply the law. Sometimes they get creative, the way I did for Judge Macario. But the standard here is what's best for Caitlin. Do you want me to make gays happy and give Caitlin a rotten childhood?"

"Then it does matter," Tim pounced. "A rotten childhood or a happy one."

"Maybe it's getting to me. Those lawyers, everything an argument. They spent hours arguing about my bringing you today instead of a court stenographer."

"I know," Tim said. "Not the usual, lawyers who yell at each other in court and then play tennis together."

"Good morning," she heard from the doorway.

Tom D'Arcy. Wearing a tweed jacket that could have been woven of heather, a tie of silk so heavy it looked hard to knot.

Handsome, she thought. Better. Beautiful. He looks older close up. Creases at his eyes, his mouth. He's pale, too, edgy. Without his lover he's growing old.

Would that happen to her? Without a lover would she shrivel, grow smaller still, find new lines in her face every day?

"This room is marvelous," she said. "It dispels gloom, doesn't it?"

"Most of the time," D'Arcy said. "Lately, no."

Warning bells went off in Pax's mind. She'd asked for that, speaking like a friend. She wasn't a friend, she couldn't be.

"Caitlin knows a lady is coming to talk to her. That's all I told her. I couldn't think what else to tell her."

His voice seemed muffled, as if he was starting to have a cold.

"Fine," Pax said. "Is she used to this room? Will she be herself here?"

"It's really the top of the house that's hers. Her bedroom. A playroom, a little dining room. Down here her nanny is usually with her. Or we are. That is, I am."

He's broken, Pax thought. In mourning. Knowing I can take Caitlin, make him mourn her, too. And I can't even think about that, can't feel for him, just for Caitlin.

"I imagine you'd like to see where she lives, be with her up there. There's an elevator."

She felt a rush of childlike pleasure about seeing more, getting farther into this amazing house.

"Mr. D'Arcy," Pax said, "I want Caitlin feeling she's alone with me, that you're not listening, or her nanny. Mr. Wickham, you know, asked my permission to have a video-taped record of this interview. Mrs. Bishop is anxious for a look at Caitlin, even on tape. I've denied his application."

She noted his horror and then relief.

"I'm concerned about Caitlin's privacy, her safety. Videos can get into the wrong hands, turn up on television news. Mr. Halloran is my own law secretary, not just someone from the steno pool. What he hears will stay with him."

She saw D'Arcy turn to Tim, nod.

"Is there a place Mr. Halloran can listen without Caitlin knowing?"

"There's an alcove in her old nursery. A little place her baby nurse used to sleep. Now it's a dressing room. Do you want to look? If it's all right, then I'll fetch Caitlin."

"Good," Pax said. D'Arcy knew all about Caitlin's rooms, knew what they'd been like six years ago and now. And he'd fetch her. Nobody could call him uninvolved, say he didn't care about her. Unless, of course, he was acting. He knew about acting. She'd have to watch, listen. Tim would make a written record. But only she would see Caitlin's face, her gestures. Only she would weigh them, interpret them. She was the judge.

D'Arcy led them into the hall. Pax had only a moment to blink at its more-than-Oriental splendor.

Behind a Chinese screen, an elevator, a little gilded cage just large enough for the three of them.

"John never used this," D'Arcy told them. "He ran up the stairs. Good for his skiing, he said."

His skiing killed him, Pax thought. A rough slope in Switzerland? Snow slide? Nobody knew. A country doctor's autopsy hadn't helped. The Swiss police, embarrassed, hurrying to close the case, hadn't helped, either.

She watched the doors close, felt the elevator take them up slowly.

"I'll show you," D'Arcy said. "Caitlin is on the floor below, with Maddie. She won't see you till I get her."

Pax stepped out, felt another shock. She could have been in a different house. Or, yes, in a garden! The whole ceiling was glass, trees curving over it glittering with snow. The walls were covered with watercolor wildflowers. Trees, real trees grew in huge pots. And real flowers, hundreds of dollars worth, were massed in tall vases on the grass green carpet.

Pax stared at the carpet. There were mushrooms dotting it.

"They're not real," D'Arcy said, watching her. "John's little joke. He liked shaking people up, amusing them. He'd go to any trouble, any expense to produce a surprise, especially for Caitlin."

Now Pax saw the room was lined with narrow shelves, each crowded with objects. There had to be thousands of them!

How could I take Caitlin away from this? she wondered. Or should I get her away, fast?

Pax thought of Mrs. Bishop, impatient for six long years. And hoped for a sign from Caitlin, a word, a look, anything, to help her decide.

Tom D'Arcy pushed a button on the wall. After a few moments it brought the white-coated man who'd let them into the house. D'Arcy spoke to him, and he disappeared. Came back almost immediately with two men in dark uniforms carrying a screen covered with Victorian scrap pictures, stretching it across the small alcove.

"Will that do for Mr. Halloran? You can sit here with Caitlin. What do you think, Judge?"

"It's fine," Pax told him.

But was *she* fine? Could she concentrate, focus completely on Caitlin?

D'Arcy was gone, Tim hidden away. She was almost alone, the rich fragrance of the flowers dizzying her. Would she always, forever after, believe she'd met this child in a garden?

And Caitlin? Would she look back on this? Remember a silver-haired woman asking questions, making her uncomfortable? Would she blame that woman for every misery she might meet?

When Alden had died, Pax had put away her family photographs. Piled all the albums on a high shelf in a closet she seldom used. Pictures of him shattered her. She'd look and wonder, what was he thinking when this was taken? His arm is around me. Did he wish I was his lover? Did he cringe inside, touching me?

Later she calmed down, was able to put a picture of her handsome husband on her desk at home, scatter more in Will's room.

Last night, though, she'd climbed a step stool and stretched to take the albums down. Not to look at Alden. To look at snapshots of Willie at six, Caitlin's age. For a frame of reference, a precise image of a healthy, beloved six-year-old.

What had Will's expressions been at six? What toys, games, pets had absorbed him? Memory was tricky. She wanted all the help she could get in judging Caitlin.

Willie looked larger than she remembered. At six he came up to her waist, and he wasn't the tallest child in the world, either. But he was softer, more babyish at six than she remembered. Sweeter. Pax always thought of him as a precocious only child. But in the pictures he was a very little boy, head still a touch too big for the skinny body beneath it, eyes huge, expression grave.

In one snapshot Willie held his terrier awkwardly, proudly. Pax knew the terrier had been small, light. But Willie had obviously found him heavy. All right, six was young, six was small. She'd have to expect that.

So when the door opened and D'Arcy came in, hand in hand with the child, she was dumbstruck.

Caitlin: dainty as Pax had been, perhaps even daintier, a doll child.

Caitlin: far smaller than Willie at the same age, not tall enough to reach even to Pax's waist.

This child looked fragile as a marionette. Her neck was delicate, her hands and feet tiny. Pax hadn't dreamed she'd look so breakable.

After a moment Pax noted what Caitlin was wearing. Not a party dress, an outfit for an important interview. Play clothes, but special. Pale blue velvet overalls, a creamy silk shirt with puffed sleeves, dainty embroidery. Caitlin's hair belonged to a princess in a fairy tale, spun gold. Her eyes were the blue of the velvet, her nose tiny, her mouth, too.

Pax smiled. Should she take Caitlin's hand? She decided not to, looked down.

The little girl wore red Mary Janes exactly like the ones Pax remembered buckling up so long ago. Under one arm she clutched a battered cardboard box. She had to stoop a little to hold it, just as Willie in the picture had stooped holding his dog. Her other hand gripped D'Arcy's so tightly Pax felt as if it were squeezing her own heart.

"This is Caitlin," D'Arcy said. As if he were announcing the arrival of a duchess. "Caitlin, this lady is Judge Ford."

The child let go of his hand, stepped forward. Still holding tightly to her box, she managed to make a quick little curtsy. Then she reached again for D'Arcy's hand.

She must feel safe with him, Pax thought. She must love him.

Immediately she warned herself. Take care, now! Plenty of kids, victims of the most horrible abuse, physical and sexual, cling to their monster parents. Horrors they know are better than those they fear.

"Caitlin asked if I could stay," D'Arcy said. "Is that all right? Till she knows you better?"

Pax stared at him, dismayed.

Damn it, he'd agreed. She'd told him the rules, the reasons for them. She'd never learn anything useful while he was here. And she'd never justify this interview to Wickham or anyone else if D'Arcy had a clear advantage. Besides, if the press learned she'd seen Caitlin with D'Arcy, they'd howl.

Tim could hear, she remembered, almost expecting him to burst out of his hiding place and warn her. He wouldn't, of course. He had more sense. The trick would be to get D'Arcy out without upsetting Caitlin.

Pax took a breath, smiled at the child.

Tell the truth, she thought. Explain. Caitlin is small, but she doesn't look stupid.

"Caitlin," she said, "we have to be by ourselves. There's a reason."

The blue eyes wide, looking at her. Good. The child wasn't hanging her head, shutting down. She was listening.

"When I came, I talked to Tom downstairs. Without you. Now I need to talk to you without him. He had a turn. Now it's your turn."

She held her breath. Caitlin came a step nearer. Then, thank God, she let go D'Arcy's hand.

She has to, Pax thought. That box is slipping. She needs both hands to keep it from falling.

Caitlin put the box on the floor.

Over her head Pax scowled at D'Arcy.

Then Caitlin was on the floor, too. And D'Arcy was vanishing behind the screen.

Suddenly Pax thought of the Bible, King Solomon, the baby two women claimed as their own. World's first custody case. Solomon was wise. He listened to the claims, the tears. Told his court officers to cut the baby in half, give half to each claimant. One woman agreed. The other screamed, wept, begged the king to give the baby, whole and well, to the other woman rather than hurt it. And Solomon lifted the baby in his arms and gave it to the woman who screamed. He knew a real mother would never let her child be harmed.

So don't be angry at D'Arcy, she warned herself. He's not stupid. He risked your disapproval because he can't bear Caitlin being hurt.

Somehow she was on her knees, nearer Caitlin, able to look into her eyes.

"What's in the box?" she asked.

No answer.

"Would you open it? And show me?"

Again, nothing.

Should she get stricter? Like a teacher, a good teacher? Tell the child to put the box away, pay attention?

No. Pax remembered all the videotapes in court, psychiatrists with troubled children. Experts always let the children play with dolls, blocks, jacks. The wriggling, jittering, took them out of themselves, let them talk more easily. Fine, Caitlin could play, if she'd only tell Pax what she needed to know.

"I'll guess," she said. "Is it a doll?"

My God, was the child smiling?

Ah. She was taking the battered lid off the box, tilting it toward Pax. Not a doll. A plastic square with a little glass screen, with buttons, levers, switches. An electronic toy, of course.

She's a today child, Pax reminded herself. Willie didn't have toys like this. Now I suppose they all do.

"What does it do?" she asked.

"Pictures," Caitlin said.

She put a tiny finger on a button. The screen lit up. She touched another button. A line jumped onto the screen, began extending itself.

"Wonderful," Pax said, meaning it.

Caitlin touched something else. The line became a series of dots, a design forming on the little screen.

"Pictures," Pax said, risking another question, more significant. "Like your father's pictures?"

Caitlin nodded again. And went on making the design more elaborate.

"Did he give you that?"

"Tom," Caitlin said.

Her voice was a surprise. Deep, for a child, husky.

"That was nice," she said. "Does he do lots of nice things for you?"

"Certainly," Caitlin said reprovingly. As if any fool would know that.

And I worried about this child in court, Pax thought. She's got more poise than the lawyers.

"You must have nice toys," she said.

"Actually," Caitlin said, "my best ones are in this box. I take it when we go other places."

"I see. Do you go a lot of other places, Caitlin?"

"A lot," Caitlin said. "I have things in those places, too. Toys. My ballet barre. My dishes."

Pax found she was holding her breath.

"Are the same people in those places, too?"

"Yes. Daddy. Tom, Maddie."

Suddenly she looked stricken, eyes wide, tiny mouth tightening.

Pax felt her heart tighten, too.

"Actually, not Daddy. Not now," Caitlin said.

Don't ask any more, Pax thought. You've seen where she lives, how she lives. You've watched D'Arcy with her. He's obviously loving, deeply concerned. Why break something that doesn't need fixing? Why move this child anywhere else?

"Can you read books, Caitlin?" she asked.

"Of course. Big books."

I should ask her to show me, Pax thought. There's everything in this room except a book. But this isn't her playroom, that's downstairs.

"English and French," Caitlin said suddenly.

Pardonnez moi, Pax thought. But I believe you!

"Who teaches you about books?"

"About books, Maddie. And numbers, too. I have a teacher for drawing and a teacher for the piano. And Tom is my teacher for dancing."

But the Bishops will send her to school, Pax thought. Spence, Nightingale. Brearley, my school.

"Where's your mother, Caitlin?" she said, hating herself.

A short pause.

"Haven't got one."

"Would you like one?"

"I have Maddie."

"But Maddie isn't a mother."

"She's very nice," Caitlin said staunchly.

"Does Maddie make your supper?"

"No, Cook. And Garrison."

"Do Maddie and Garrison come with you when you go away?"

"Maddie comes. Garrison takes care of here."

"Who takes care of the places you go?"

Caitlin frowned. "Gudrun in the snow house. Arthur at the beach. In Paris there's a new someone, Maddie told me. Because François got old."

Her pronunciation of François was perfect, like a child from Neuilly.

I'll end this, Pax decided. Nobody can say Caitlin isn't responsive, bright. Nobody can claim she's badly treated.

"Would you like to go another new place?" she made herself ask. "Maybe just you, without Maddie and Tom? With some nice people to take care of you?"

Caitlin frowned, lowered her head.

Pax thought of Tim, listening behind his screen. Taking all this down word for word. Silence meant dots, empty spaces, on a transcript. Explanations. The Bishops would read it. So would Pressman and Wickham. Maybe someone would leak it to the press.

"Do you miss your daddy very much?" she asked, pushing her luck.

Again, no answer.

"I imagine Daddy was very busy. Had to leave you often, for his work, his friends. Wouldn't you like to live with people who'd never leave you? People who always stayed in one place?"

Caitlin lifted her chin, looked straight at her.

"We always had breakfast," she said clearly. "Every, every day. Tom and Daddy and me. Always."

Then her small face seemed to dissolve, melt. Her eyes shut tightly, her mouth became a flat line.

"I see," Pax said quickly.

A strangled sob, a tear sliding out of the corner of the child's eye.

Another second and Caitlin was wailing, the slow, hopeless crescendo cry of a child slapped hard, a child lost on a dark city street.

Everything seemed to speed up for Pax.

She saw Tim's face emerge from the screen, scowling, unhappy.

And before she could absorb that, saw D'Arcy plunge into the room, swoop Caitlin up as if she weighed nothing at all.

Dancer, Pax thought wildly. Lifts grown women effort-lessly. Why not a little girl?

The room rang with noise now, too. Caitlin sobbing. Tim saying something, D'Arcy talking, almost singing, to the child, saying her name over and over.

Soon he was setting her on her feet, reaching into a pocket for a handkerchief.

Caitlin stood trembling, hands over her face.

You cannot cry and sing at the same time, Pax thought, seeing Esperanza, hearing her speak.

She couldn't bear it anymore. She'd made this child cry. This baby.

Pax forgot she was a judge, forgot she was doing important work, forgot everything except that a little child was crying because of something she'd said.

And that the crying had to stop, that if it wasn't stopped she'd despise herself forever.

She reached out, pulled Caitlin close, knowing her own tears were starting, spilling over.

"Sing with me, Caitlin," she found herself saying, over and over, like Esperanza so long ago. "You cannot cry and sing at the same time."

Glancing up, she saw D'Arcy frowning, hands clasped together, Tim shaking his head.

And felt her heart turn cold.

9

BA

A SHOCK WAVE OF SOUND BROKE OVER BA AS THE GUARD HELD
open the courtroom door. Instantly she was in a fever of
hope. Now, day three of the trial, would she finally see
Caitlin?

Her face burned as she walked with Tal to their places at
what she now knew was the petitioner's table.

The courtroom smelled like a circus tent already, so many
bodies, so many musty clothes. Still, she could bear the
crowds better now than two, almost three weeks ago. Scotty
had been right. She was getting used to this. And once she
actually saw Caitlin she'd feel wonderful, she was sure of it.

Ba turned her head slightly to see if the audience was still
so large.

So many people! Did none of them work? Did they all
have hours to sit staring at her, at Tom D'Arcy? Did any of
them, all of them put together, long to see Caitlin as much
as she?

Tal was pulling out her chair.

This was the day she'd dreaded most. She'd have to get
up in front of everyone. Walk to the witness stand. And swear
an oath she had absolutely no intention of keeping. Her own

husband didn't know she'd ever seen Caitlin. Or her own lawyer. If they found out now, all her credibility, her respect from them, would vanish!

Still, Ba thought, the alternative is to commit perjury.

Perhaps no one would ask about that horrible day long ago. Johnny was dead, his vulgar little wife, too, Caitlin an infant. Nobody knew anything, nobody could, unless Johnny had told. And why would he? The story didn't make him look wonderful, either.

Scotty was in now, nodding to her. He went to bend over Tal, whisper.

Behind her, more noise. More people coming in, jostling for places.

And now Tom D'Arcy in the doorway.

The murmuring grew louder.

Ba turned her head slightly to peek at him, saw the elegant gray suit, the handsome, haggard face. If only that man had been willing to give up Caitlin. But he'd refused even to speak to Scotty, to Tal. They'd had to bring this custody petition.

All the extraordinary people she'd had to deal with lately! D'Arcy. That Puerto Rican judge, at the party night before last, large, noisy, full of Spanish people, quite as if she'd been entertaining Eva Peron.

It had gone well, actually, far better than Ba could have imagined. Of course, Bonner's arrangements had been impeccable, not foie gras, salmon, spinach pâté, but scads of cold cuts, cheeses, hearty breads, lots of liquor served up in large glasses. And the judge had been a surprise, modestly dressed, subdued. She hadn't talked with an accent, hadn't been pushy or strident. Everyone was fresh from having Veterans Day off, Ba curling her lip at the way judges took every holiday in the calendar.

Now she looked straight at D'Arcy, shuddered. Nothing modest or subdued about him. Every day he came here from Caitlin, went home to her. He had her. And he'd loved her brother, touched him.

Slept in his bed!

But she must not think about that, not now. If she did she'd be too angry to speak at all.

She stared at the witness chair. This morning, her chair.

Ah! The door behind the judge's bench was opening! The guards were straightening up, one of them droning the command for everyone to rise.

Ba obeyed.

Judge Ford was on the bench in a swirl of black silk. She'd handled things well so far. Admirable, her demeanor with the disorderly man. Brief, no nonsense with the whispered talks the lawyers seemed to require constantly, marching up to the bench together, turning their backs to everyone. Procedural, Scotty said, nothing to fret about.

"We're fortunate," he'd told her. "When they start rating judges, Pax Ford is always high on the list."

"We have friends in common," Ba had said. "But we've never met, I checked my party lists."

"Fortunate again. We don't want her recusing herself because she knows you. We don't need a new young judge who'd be only too proud to give a child to a pair of deviates. Judge Ford was at Harvard Law School. She's one of us, Ba. No Johnny California artwork in her drawing room."

Ba knew people who had her brother's paintings. Montel Morgan had one, a sort of gigantic Oreo cookie that resolved itself into a manhole cover if one looked long enough. Tal called it the Emperor's New Art.

"Essentially," Tal said, "she's our sort."

Your sort, Ba thought. I was just a girl from Nowhere, Ohio, before Tal.

Actually, this morning the judge didn't look so aristocratic. Tired, rather, like an ordinary woman, circles beneath her eyes, silver hair somehow tarnished. She was human. Surely she'd understand how terribly Ba wanted Caitlin, needed her.

*　　*　　*

Pax looked out at her courtroom, a blur of colors and shapes, a cacophony of sound.

Mrs. Bishop, neat in her navy suit, looking misplaced, as nice women often did in courtrooms.

Tom D'Arcy, handsomer than ever, handsomer at this distance than up close, when she'd seen the lines in his face.

And, my God, smiling at her.

Pax picked up her pen, stared at her notebook. He thinks I'm his, she told herself. Breaking down, hugging Caitlin. Needing Tim to rush out, stop me from blowing the whole trial. Tom D'Arcy doesn't understand that I have a big stake here, that I'm on trial, too.

She opened the notebook.

How could you cry? she asked herself for the thousandth time. Be motherly with Caitlin, of all the things you're not supposed to be? What if reporters knew? What if D'Arcy tells them? Or the other servants, that nanny who dashed in, that butler person?

Tim hadn't spoken five words coming back in the car. Worse, he'd vanished for the rest of the day. Tim, who till now thought her properly dispassionate. Like a man, people always said. So silly. She'd seen plenty of male judges show their feelings, especially when they began recounting their courtroom triumphs and troubles in the judges' lunchroom.

She'd fretted half the night, finally gone barefoot to check on her newest seedlings, get comfort from the warmth of the greenhouse. She'd even wondered what Rosa would do if she had this case. A new thought. She'd always considered herself so much more experienced than Rosa.

Pax nodded to Sean for silence.

"I want to inform counsel," Ba heard Judge Ford say, "that the court has an application from Mr. Saul Frolich on behalf of the American Media Group to compel the appearance of Caitlin California in this courtroom."

Ba felt herself jerk to attention.

"Her appearance is alleged to be in the public interest, based on the First Amendment of the United States Constitution."

Oh, yes, Ba thought. In the public interest, in my interest. Let Caitlin appear. Please. Now.

"The motion is denied. And now I'm ruling on the child's appearance."

Ba stopped breathing.

How much power did the woman have? Wasn't it enough she could give Caitlin away like a gift? Make Ba the happiest of women or the most wretched?

"I've talked with Caitlin California at her home. There's a stenographic record of our conversation. I'm not, however, making it available. It will be part of the sealed record of this trial pending any possible appeal."

Ba blinked.

What was she saying? A record? Did she expect Ba to take custody of a record? Anyway, her own records were her beautiful albums.

Ba thought of the album Bonner had made for Caitlin. Like the others but daintier, pale blue silk, smooth, beautiful. Ba had run her fingertips over it again and again. Blank, ready for the records she'd keep. Photographs of Caitlin on a pony, in a dinghy, the rose garden with her puppy. At a piano recital, her coming-out party, yes, and at her wedding.

"It's unusual in a custody case," the judge was saying. "But I've also issued an order of protection for Caitlin California. From now on anyone who invades her privacy will be guilty of contempt of this court."

Ba looked urgently at Scotty.

And was infuriated when he didn't look back.

Too much! She'd speak to Tal. If Scotty couldn't consider her wishes, she'd damned well hire someone else, even now, even in the middle of things!

"I'm confident counsel on both sides will concur, especially after the incident we've already had in this courtroom," the judge said.

Damn the judge. She'd seen Caitlin, spoken to her, spent all the time she wanted. But she wouldn't let anyone else have a glimpse!

Ba suddenly remembered she mustn't look angry. She was the normal one in this trial, the proper one.

She glanced again at Tom D'Arcy, the abnormal, artistic one. He didn't look angry. Why would he? He saw Caitlin whenever he liked.

"Mr. Wickham?" the judge said.

Ba felt her anger vanish, felt herself chill down as if she'd plunged into the freezing Atlantic in April.

"Yes, Your Honor," Scotty was saying in his clear, pleasant voice. And then the words she'd waited for, wanted, dreaded, insisted upon:

"I call the petitioner, Barbara Calvert Bishop."

Her turn. Nothing now between her and the witness stand. She would get up, walk forward, take the chair near the judge's bench.

Scotty was nodding at her.

And Tal's hand was patting her arm.

Ba rose, taking the handbag she'd meant to leave behind on her chair, somehow arriving where she was supposed to.

She raised her hand, kept it steady, repeated the clerk's words. Then she sat down, looked out at the faces. Dozens of people staring, hundreds. Standing at the back, jamming the benches, lining the sides of the courtroom.

But, immediately, Scotty was directly in front of her, blocking out everyone else.

Look at him, Ba cautioned herself. Ignore those people.

Somehow her hand was at her throat, fingering the lace trim on her blouse. A mistake, the blouse. She'd thought it ladylike, proper. But the lace prickled, almost scratched. If she wasn't careful she'd be fidgeting with it every minute. She put her hands together, set them firmly in her lap.

Why, Scotty was smiling!

He'd always had a nice smile, she remembered. As if he were asking a wallflower to dance, bestowing comfort, reassurance, a promise of fun.

Well, she knew what he was going to ask her. They'd discussed her testimony often enough. Like tennis, he said. He'd serve, she'd return.

"We've played this enough, Ba, so you know where I'll hit the ball. Just hit back, nice and easy. All there is to it."

Her right hand tightened, grasping an invisible racket.

"I've known you so long," Scotty said now, a little too loud for a simple conversation. "Would you mind if I called you what I always call you? Like everyone who knows and loves you? Ba?"

Startled, Ba seemed to see the tennis ball go slamming into a far corner of her court. Scotty never said he'd do that, call her Ba. But he must have a reason. To make her more comfortable? Actually, it did. Silly for him to call her anything else.

Ba found herself saying yes, certainly.

"Is this the first time you've testified in a trial?"

"Yes."

"Is it difficult for you? Uncomfortable?"

"Yes," she said.

But it wasn't so bad, really. His serves were within easy reach. He was anticipating possible lapses from her, making sure the judge would forgive them if they came.

"Ba," Scotty said gently, "not to worry. We'll tell the judge things you know because they happened, exactly the way you'll describe them."

Her audience had somehow vanished. She saw only Scotty in his quiet suit, his printed bow tie.

"How long have you and Tal been married?"

"Thirty-two years."

"No children, is that correct?"

"Yes."

She was feeling better and better, hitting the ball easily.

After all, she'd talked with Scotty all those thirty-two years at least once a month, often more.

"Did you want children?"

"Oh, yes."

"Where do you live, Ba?"

"We live at Sixty-Third and Park Avenue."

"An apartment building?"

"Yes."

"How long have you lived there?"

"Since we married. It was my husband's family home."

"Would you describe your apartment?"

Ba felt absolutely on top of her game. Anyone could answer questions about an apartment.

"Let me see," she said. "Six bedrooms upstairs. A living room, dining room, breakfast alcove, library, office, pantry, kitchen downstairs. Maid's rooms. The office is mine. There's a larger study for my husband."

"Would you say, then, enough room for a child?"

"Yes."

"And is that your only home?"

"No," Ba said. "We have a summer place in Southampton. And a small cottage in Bermuda."

"And is there room in those houses for a child as well?"

"Yes. Even in Bermuda, three bedrooms. The Southampton house is quite large."

"And how long had you been married, Ba, before you began to realize you weren't going to have children?"

"Oh," she said. "Five years? Perhaps seven?"

"And did that seem unfortunate to you?"

"Yes. Very unfortunate."

"Did you take steps to correct that misfortune? To have children of your own?"

Ba sat straighter. "A great many steps. We saw doctors."

"What sort of doctors?"

"Every sort," Ba said, smacking the ball. "Gynecologists. Obstetricians. Fertility experts."

"What does your husband do, Ba?"

"He's the owner and publisher of the *Bar Journal*. It's the more or less official newspaper of the legal profession. There's a New York edition and others, regional ones. He has other projects, too. It's a family business; my husband's grandfather was the founder."

"Would you say you're comfortably well off?"

"Yes," Ba said, pleased she could answer such a question in public so easily.

"And is your husband a busy man?"

"Yes, very. He keeps very long hours. Travels. He's almost never free of the office."

"What about when you're in the country? Or away?"

"My husband has all sorts of communication systems. Cellular phones, fax machines, computers that all work together. He's never out of touch."

"So you spend a good deal of time on your own?"

"Yes."

"Tell the court, please, how you spend it."

"I'm an active volunteer. I work on several boards of directors, committees. My main interest is the Huguenot Society."

"You spend a good deal of time working for the Society?"

"Yes. It's almost like a full-time job."

She realized suddenly that Scotty had been backing away all this time, was farther off now. My! She was really speaking out.

"Is the Society concerned with children?"

Ba found herself smiling! "Among many other things, yes. Scholarships, particularly. We offer full college scholarships for children who meet our requirements. We organize a volunteer network like the Junior League's for children's hospitals."

"Do you have help with this work?"

"A full-time secretary. And others, public relations people, entertaining help, that sort of thing."

"Then we're speaking of top-level organizing. Not rolling bandages or reading aloud at libraries?"

"Every sort of volunteer work is important," Ba said.

Easy lobs, high, soft balls she could put away.

"Are there experts on your board? People who know about children's welfare?"

"We call in a great many. Dr. Brazelton, when he has time. Dr. Herbert Spiegel. Many others."

"Are there other activities which involve your contact with children?"

"Many. My husband's family has always held summer programs for children at the Southampton house. Disadvantaged children, physically challenged children."

Why was she tugging at the lace again?

"Tell us, Ba. Does your work require travel?"

"No."

"Does it require personal publicity? Stories in the newspapers?"

"No."

"Does it require you to move about the world, take part in trend-setting activities?"

"Oh, no," Ba said.

"Do you have old friends?"

"I've known you since my marriage. Most of our friends are old friends."

"And your servants? Have they been with you long?"

"My housekeeper, twenty years. Others almost as long. We've been fortunate."

"Or you've been stable people, good employers."

"Objection," Ba heard from across the room.

She felt startled. Pressman's voice, unpleasant, nasal. She'd absolutely forgotten him.

"Sustained as to form," Judge Ford said.

"Ba," Scotty said without skipping a beat, "how are you related to Caitlin California?"

"She's my niece, my brother's child."

"Did you get along with your brother?"

She felt suddenly tense, realized her hand was at her throat again, plucking at the lace.

"No," she said. "That is, I did when he was young. We were great friends then. Later we lost touch."

"Why was that?"

"We led very different sorts of lives."

"We've heard about your life. What sort did your brother lead?"

"Well," Ba said, "he was an artist. Famous. Active, aggressive. He sought out new people all the time. New experiences, too. He had houses in many places."

"Your brother's wife died in an accident?"

"Yes. Soon after the child was born."

"Your brother also died in an accident?"

"Yes."

"Have you ever had a serious accident, Ba?"

"I've never had one at all."

"And did your brother marry again?"

"No. He was not the marrying sort."

"He was homosexual, is that correct?"

"Yes, he made no secret of it."

"How did you learn your brother was dead?"

"On television. The news."

"You weren't close enough for anyone to inform you he'd died?"

"I'm afraid not."

"And were you concerned about your niece?"

"Terribly concerned," Ba said, leaning forward. "My brother hadn't shared his child with me during his lifetime. I had to respect his wishes. But when he died, I thought only of her."

Scotty was closer, looking intently at her. "Is it that you want to do your duty by your niece, Ba? Now she's orphaned? Alone?"

"Objection," Ba heard.

"Rephrase, please," the judge said.

Ba had nearly forgotten the judge.

"Do you feel a sense of duty toward Caitlin?"

"Yes. But more, much more. I want to take care of the child. Give her everything I can. Love her."

Ba risked a look up at Judge Ford.

She was slumped, pen in hand, eyes down on the notebook in front of her.

"Very well. You've told us you live a stable life, do work that helps needy children. You want a child of your own, for the best, most selfless reasons. Thank you. That's all I want to ask."

Scotty turned, walked back to his chair.

Ba watched him go.

And watched Pressman stand up.

Suddenly she felt as if icy winds were blowing through the courtroom.

He seemed to grow larger every second. He wore a suit that was dark, somehow shiny. In his collar was a gold pin. Gold flashed all over him, wrist, tie, far too much gold. Not a gentleman, not a tennis partner, not at any club she knew.

Ba took her eyes away from him, looked up at Judge Ford. Annoying that the woman could relax while she had to sit straight. The judge's hair was silver, Ba's pewter, ordinary. The judge was slender, fragile, while Ba was tall, heavier than she'd used to be.

She couldn't blame Pressman. His job. He was paid to speak for Tom D'Arcy.

But Judge Ford was paid to listen. Yet she looked far away, almost bored.

Ba felt a rush of anger at this woman, so above the fray.

Pressman was standing, not in front of her, like Scotty, but to one side, leaving her open to the audience, the stares and whispers.

"Now, Mrs. Bishop," Pressman said.

He spoke harshly, like the men who set up her party tents, brought in cleaning people, supervised waiters.

"You won't mind if I call you Mrs. Bishop? Unlike my adversary, I haven't known you for years, right?"

"No," Ba said.

And realized immediately the word had come out more sharply than she'd intended.

And that her hands hurt because she'd clasped them so hard.

"And since I don't know all about you, you'll forgive me for asking some personal questions."

"Yes," Ba said.

"How old are you, Mrs. Bishop?"

"I'm fifty-six."

"Fifty years older than your niece, right? Six, fifty-six, half a century older?"

"Mr. Pressman," Judge Ford said from on high.

He didn't seem to hear her.

"How old were you when your brother was born?"

"I was seven."

"Then you weren't exactly a companion to your brother, right? A much older sister, more a caretaker?"

"You could say so."

"Well, what would you say, Mrs. Bishop? A seven-year-old girl, a newborn boy?"

"Very well, a caretaker."

"Now we've heard you've been married for thirty-two years. Without children, right?"

"So I said."

"So you said. You also said you wanted children, tried to have them, saw doctors, right?"

"Yes."

"Did you ever try adopting a child?"

Damn him, Ba thought, taking her hand away from her throat, where it seemed to have strayed all by itself.

"No," she said.

"Never? You never once tried adopting?"

"I thought a great deal about it," Ba said weakly.

"You thought about it. But did nothing?"

"No."

"Well, when you thought about it, was that with eagerness? Anticipation?"

"Of course," Ba said, heat in her voice.

"And your husband? Was he eager to adopt?"

"He was a little less enthusiastic. I think adoption is harder for men to accept."

"Do you? Isn't my client going to great lengths, great trouble to adopt a child?"

"I suppose."

"Oh, it's more than supposing. Isn't Mr. D'Arcy here because he wants to adopt Caitlin California?"

"I don't know. I don't know why he's here."

"Now, Mrs. Bishop," Pressman said, "you know why. Hasn't he lived with this child all her life? Isn't that why he's here?"

"Objection," Ba heard, thankfully.

"Sustained," the judge said. "Please, Mr. Pressman."

Pressman didn't even seem to take a breath.

"So you wanted to adopt, your husband didn't. Do you often disagree with your husband?"

"No," Ba said. "Almost never."

"But on this you had one of your rare disagreements?"

"You make it sound as if we quarreled," Ba said, wanting to set him straight. "And that's not so. We disagreed about adopting a strange child. We both want to adopt my niece, we don't disagree about that."

"How long did you discuss adoption?"

"We had many conversations."

"Conversations. You disposed of the idea of adopting a child in a number of conversations?"

"They were serious conversations," Ba said, warmer now, feeling herself blushing.

"I see. Serious conversations. Not frivolous, not offhand, not light. Serious."

The man was smiling! He looked like a small shark, whose open mouth might show rows and rows of sharp teeth.

"So you're not interested in children in general, as you've claimed. Your interest is just in a child who's related to you?"

Ba looked helplessly out at Scotty, miles away in his chair.

"But I'm very interested," she said with all the fervor she could call up. "Eager, very eager."

"Your brother's name was changed, I think. Calvert became California. Did he consult you when he changed it?"

"No."

"Did you get along well with him?"

"For years I did."

"As children. As adults, isn't it true you never saw each other?"

"I said we led different lives. In general, we weren't in agreement."

"You weren't in agreement. Well, did you disagree with the way he lived?"

"We simply grew apart," Ba said. "He lived one kind of life, I lived another."

"We've heard about the life you lead. But your brother was an artist, a very important artist. Would you expect him to live the way you did?"

"No. He was more flamboyant."

"Flamboyant," Pressman said, emphasizing the word.

Oh, God, Scotty said not to volunteer, just to answer questions.

"You mean he gave flamboyant parties?"

"Yes."

"Looked flamboyant, wore flamboyant clothes?"

"Yes."

"Do you own any of your brother's work, Mrs. Bishop?"

"No."

"Really? None? He's done so many different things, paintings, collages, sculptures. You have none?"

"No."

"Because it was flamboyant?"

Ba was feeling warm, dizzy.

"You might say that."

"Well, what would you say? Tell me, Mrs. Bishop, is that how you found his lifestyle, too?"

"Everyone knows my brother was unconventional," Ba said.

Now she felt really feverish.

"And everyone knows your brother was gay, isn't that so?"

"Objection," Ba heard from Scotty. "Let's stay with what the witness knows, Judge."

Pressman didn't wait for the judge to agree.

"You knew your brother was gay?"

"Yes."

"And did you approve?"

Ba touched her forehead, she had to. Tiny drops of perspiration were threatening to roll down her face.

"I loved my brother. I didn't want him to have a difficult life."

"You loved your brother? That surprises me, Mrs. Bishop. You went years without seeing him, right? How many years? When was the last time you saw him?"

Ba felt a great wave of heat come over her.

"Six years ago," she said.

"Six years? Six years exactly?"

"Perhaps not exactly."

"You said six years. Caitlin is six."

He's stalking my fight with Johnny as if he knows about it, she thought. And he's getting closer.

"You never saw your brother after Caitlin was born?"

"Yes," she said. "Yes, I did. Once."

She couldn't look at Tal.

"And when was that?"

Ba tried to appeal to Scotty with her eyes.

"I'm waiting, Mrs. Bishop."

"Just after Caitlin was born."

"Sorry, I didn't hear you."

"Just after the child was born."

"Did something happen between you and your brother at that time?"

What must she say? What could she say? She couldn't have Tal and Scotty knowing the truth, let alone all the crowds of people out there. That her own brother had shouted, actually kicked her, he'd wanted her out of his house so desperately! It made her family sound common— no, insane. It was humiliating! Degrading!

There were whispers, movements in the crowd. Pressman was looking up at the judge. And Judge Ford was raising both hands, palms out.

"Quiet, please," she said. "I don't want to have to clear this courtroom."

Something in her cool tone touched Ba like a hot coal, hurting.

Blast you, she thought. I'm burning. You're up there like an ice queen. I'm in danger. You're giving orders, you have men with guns to help you.

"Mrs. Bishop," the judge said, looking down at her.

Ba felt a shock. Her eyes were mauve. She'd never seen eyes that color. Perfect for an ice queen, like the mauve of a glacier top.

"You must answer the question," the judge told her.

"I can't remember the damned question," Ba said, knowing she sounded furious.

"I'll repeat it," Mr. Pressman said.

What if I never answer? she thought wildly. What if I say I'm ill? If I faint?

"When Caitlin was born, did something happen between you and your brother?"

Ba looked at Pressman.

And then at Tal, arms folded, frowning. He thought he knew all about her, thought she'd told him everything.

She moved her head, looked at D'Arcy, that leech, that thief, wanting her baby, the baby who'd felt so weightless in her arms.

"Mrs. Bishop, we can play guessing games. I could ask, did you quarrel with Mr. California? With his wife? Should I play guessing games, Mrs. Bishop, till we hear what happened between you and your brother?"

Heat seemed to flare up and overwhelm her, as if there were fire and smoke in the courtroom, as if she were choking, burning.

I did the best I could, Tal, she thought. Forgive me. I only meant to save you pain.

"Judge Ford," Pressman was saying, "will you instruct the witness to answer?"

Her throat was burning, each breath hurt.

And now sirens were whooping in her ears.

The piercing sound reached Ba, stiffened her, reminded her what she must do.

Why, we all know how to behave about sirens, she thought. We've known since kindergarten. We keep calm. No panic. We walk slowly, steadily to where we'll be safe, coughing perhaps, shoes scorched, but safe.

Ba cleared her throat. She wanted to sound precise, confident. The way she did at committee meetings, twenty people around a table.

The way Judge Ford sounded speaking from her throne.

"Six years ago I went to my brother's house to see his new baby. I said I was expected and walked into the elevator. I could hear the baby crying as I went up, louder as I reached the bedroom. My brother was lying in bed wearing his wife's negligee."

Mr. Pressman seemed to melt away.

"His wife was up mixing a pitcher of martinis. She was tipsy already, but she was making more. The baby was in a bassinet, screaming. Neither one of them seemed to hear."

It was cooler now in the courtroom. A little breeze seemed to blow around her.

"I went to the baby, picked her up, held her. If I could have taken her away, I would have. But my brother came straight to me and pulled the baby away. He wanted to strike me, I think, but he was holding the baby. So he kicked me, stood there holding the baby and kicking."

She took a deep breath, kept her eyes firmly away from the lawyers' table, from Tal, from Scotty.

Instead she looked up at Judge Ford.

The judge was sitting quite straight, looking down at Ba with those glorious eyes wide.

"Johnny's dead. But Caitlin is alive, young enough to bring up a better way, a normal way. I want to pick her up again and never let go."

To her astonishment Judge Ford smiled, her face softening into prettiness, her head tilting a little to one side.

As Ba watched, the judge nodded, as if she understood everything, approved everything. As if Ba had been a good witness, a star witness.

Ba smiled back. Then she folded her hands, sat back, enjoying the cool, green safety of the place she was sure she'd come to rest.

10

ROSA

Rosa stood at the entrance to the Palm Court, fascinated, as if she were watching a movie.

Creamy walls with curly gold trim, tall palms in enormous pots, expensively dressed people eating beautiful cakes and sandwiches, violins playing somewhere. The scent of a hundred perfumes, soft lights, discreet Thanksgiving decorations, gilded pumpkins, silvered ears of corn. Here, in the middle of raucous, bustling Manhattan, none of it seemed quite real.

I haven't seen linen so crisp, she marveled, since Mami starched, ironed for Pax's mother.

Did she fit in? She glanced at the nearest women. Fine, she'd worn her best navy suit, pearls, low heels. A bit severe maybe, but better than being overdressed. She did want to look right for Leonard, who must love lavish places if he'd asked her here for tea. And it was lavish. She wished Mami could see it, especially the display of glorious cakes and desserts on the large, round table nearby. Mami adored cakes and desserts. But she'd probably never let Rosa bring her down here, whatever the occasion.

When Leonard had left her chambers, Rosa had made Larry Bernstein look him right up in Martindale-Hubbell.

Top ratings, top clients, big-money clients. And a special note about his teaching. Obviously important, famous. The most important, famous lawyer she'd ever known. Busy, though. It had taken them almost a week to get together.

But here he came, headed straight for her.

"It's all right," he was saying to the headwaiter. "I'm already seated, we're all set."

Then his arm was around her, sweeping her through the sea of tables. Wrapping her in so much warmth, giving off such a charge of energy, Rosa felt charged up, too.

He was even larger than she remembered.

"This is nice," Rosa said.

And immediately, to herself, fool, can you do no better than that?

Thank God, the waiter, occupying him, giving her time to settle.

But it was nice. And he looked nice. Not like Tony, muscular in his carefully fitted suits. Leonard's suit was like her own, dark, plain. But his was rumpled. Tony brushed his clothes, hung them carefully on wooden hangers. Leonard apparently didn't know hangers existed.

"Let's see," he was saying, picking up the enormous menu.

Somehow his creased jacket went with the lines in his face, the every-which-way look of his hair.

Rosa realized her fingers had curved themselves as if she were about to smooth his curls.

"What do you think?" he said as she busied her hands with her menu. "Sandwiches? Cake? Or maybe a real drink, the kind of day you probably had?"

What would be easiest to manage?

Sandwich, no doubt.

Leonard looked capable of dealing with anything they brought him.

"Just tea," she said. "I'm not hungry. I'm what we call a *mistica* for food, not much of an appetite."

Instantly she was furious with herself. What was it about him that put Spanish in her mouth?

Was she so conscious, so wary of the differences between them? That he was old, Jewish, rich? What did it matter? If he liked her, if she liked him? And she did like him.

Pax had liked him, too. What had *she* ordered when she was with him? But he was telling the waiter sandwiches, pastries, tea.

"We say, eat, eat," he told her. "My mother never served food without saying it."

Leonard felt the sounds of people's chatter, the thud of waiters' footsteps die away as he watched her unbuttoning her jacket. He'd invited her because he owed her, hadn't he? But how to sit still while she undid buttons? Rosa had a way of smoothing her hands down her body that made him feel twenty. Sixteen. Was it unconscious? Or did she know what she was doing?

She was talking. He'd better listen. Or she might think he was deaf as well as old.

"All these people doing nothing afternoons," she was saying. "Don't they work?"

Were they going to discuss the Protestant ethic? Rosa Macario, dressed for mass, and Leonard Scholer, who'd insisted on a rabbi marrying his daughter even to Will Ford?

"For a lot of them this is work," he told her. "What they do all day long. Not like us."

"Weren't you in court this afternoon?"

"I am in court this afternoon. By proxy. One of my partners is taking over. Fascinating case."

"Lawyers. None of you ever have boring cases."

"I don't. The one now is the biter, the Attica man with AIDS who bit the guard. He's charged with intent to kill. I'm going to prove he was always a biter, long before he had AIDS. That's how he got to Attica, biting his wife's neck so she bled to death."

Rosa was laughing! That was better. He'd made her laugh! He felt terrific!

"You make me feel right at home," Rosa was saying. "That's the kind of case I get. And the kind of weirdo defendant that turns up in front of me."

"If I waited for non-weirdo defendants, we'd be eating in some luncheonette."

"I could handle that," she said. "Actually, it's more my speed."

He felt a vast rush of pleasure. She was herself, not one of those self-important judges.

She was also, beyond a reasonable doubt, the most beautiful woman in the whole room, probably the whole hotel. Only why did she make herself so drab? That stiff suit, that briefcase of a handbag? No wonder he wanted her to take off her clothes.

Ah, now he was thinking cant. Any man alive would want Rosa Macario to take off her clothes.

Rosa was fascinated by the way his smile erased the lines in his face.

"I wanted to bring you here," he was saying. "I'm really grateful to you. Will went home, made up with my daughter. Debo's like her mother, not easy to make up with. But it's done, thanks to you, Judge."

So he has a difficult wife, Rosa thought. Is she still his wife? I'd better make sure. I don't need another Marisa.

Besides, she had to get him to stop calling her "Judge."

"Not Judge."

"What would you prefer?"

"My name is Rosa," she said.

And gave him her best high-wattage smile, one she hadn't smiled lately for anyone but Mami.

It made magic. Leonard hitched his chair closer, looked straight into her eyes.

Wait!

"Are you still married to Debo's mother?"

"No," he said, sitting back again, smiling. "You're safe. I'm not married to Debo's mother or anyone else."

"Oh, I'm safe," Rosa said. "I've been making myself safe since I was about twelve."

"I'm sure you have. You know, it made *me* feel about twelve being in your courthouse. I had a case there when I was right out of law school."

Long ago, of course. He must be over fifty, maybe more. Old enough to be her father if he'd been Puerto Rican. Did Jews marry young?

"For a little while I was a sole practitioner," Leonard was saying. "Taking everything, anything. A friend in a big firm sent me a case, too puny for them. A woman, worked part-time for the phone company. Belonged to the union, paid dues. Had a long illness, a big hospital bill. And the union wouldn't pay, said their contract didn't cover part-timers, she should never have been union in the first place."

If I'd stayed in practice in the barrio, Rosa thought, I'd have had junk like that.

"I didn't know where to start. But my desk was empty. So, what the hell, I sued everybody in the phone company, union, insurance people. All big lawyers, WASP firms, fancy guys. And we land in your courthouse before the Honorable Washington Davis Mason."

Mason. A clubhouse hack. Lost without a smart clerk. Lawyers used to say he couldn't read the briefs.

"We're all hanging around your courthouse. Those lawyers look like they've only ever been in big federal court-houses. I've got a brief full of stuff on accountability, uncon-scionability. Mason calls a recess, gets us all in his chambers. I've never been in chambers before, and I'm nervous."

So you've been nervous, Rosa thought. You know how that feels.

"He says he can't concentrate, he's pondering a case from the week before. A complex case. Your court had marine jurisdiction then. This was a barge collision, bills of lading, letters of credit, insurance claims. Mason ends up asking us all for memos on that case, never mind ours."

Not dumb, Rosa thought. Free advice from downtown lawyers. Slightly unethical but not dumb.

"I could only think, next week new lawyers will tell him how to decide my case. But okay, I go back, do some research, write a memo. I never knew if the others even bothered. But I read in the *Bar Journal* that Mason's decided for my client, the union pays up, and I'm Clarence Darrow."

When Leonard got wound up, Rosa noticed, he seemed bigger, even more *there*.

"Was your client grateful?"

"No. She thought she should have gotten more money. A born fuckup. That's Scholer's rule, my rule. Fuckups fuck up. They make the same mistake over and over, that's why they're fuckups."

"Mason wasn't a fuckup. He had this week's lawyers working on last week's case. Smart."

"Only in the Bronx," Leonard said cheerfully. "My initiation on your turf. Here's a newer story. Huge commercial case, my firm works months, years. Finally there's a management shift, they want to settle, end it fast. Seventeen million dollars to my client."

What did your firm get? Rosa wondered. Two, three million? What did *you* get?

"Our judge has just gone up on circuit from Manhattan to the Bronx. So we all get in limos, their lawyers, our lawyers, drive up, wait for a recess. Like I waited for you. The whole scene, people eating, babies screaming, kids running around, what you see every day. And us, Wall Street types, looking like tourists."

Yes, Rosa thought, you would.

"I ask the bridge man for a conference in chambers. Judge says he's too busy, come up to the bench, we'll do it there. So we go up and I state we've agreed on a settlement, seventeen million dollars."

Rosa saw it, the crowd, the downtown lawyers looking as if they smelled bad smells.

"I've got a big voice and it's really up because of the noise. But after I say that number, the courtroom goes dead quiet. And then, from the back, comes a voice, loud and clear, saying, 'Seventeen million dollars. Shit!' "

She watched him put back his head, laugh. Oh, he was easy to be with, he was fun. And when had she had any fun lately?

"You must have stories, too," he said. "Still, things are changing for you now, aren't they? I hear Talcott Bishop gave you a party."

He'd seen that in the *Bar Journal*. But he'd noticed, remembered.

"He wants something from me," Rosa said. "I'm not sure what yet. Useful to be a Latina judge. When it's time to promote someone representing the downtrodden, I'm good on two counts. But I can't see why a whole party."

She hesitated. Should she try teasing, see what happened?

"I mean," she said, "if he wanted something from me, he could just have taken me to tea at the Plaza."

Leonard looked sharply at her.

Then he grinned.

"Tal Bishop's a complicated man. You'd never imagine him in a custody battle with a gay opponent. A quiet deal with D'Arcy would be more his style."

Ah, she'd teased, he'd reacted. And then gone right back to safe ground. But she could get a reaction.

"Gays," she said, leaning back. "If they want to be gay, fine. But give them kids to raise, create more gays? Not in my courtroom."

"That theory's in some doubt," Leonard said. "Nobody knows what makes gays. Born, made, no one's sure. D'Arcy is a talented man."

"Let him be talented away from a little girl. I know what men do to little girls, the wrong men."

"I bet you do," Leonard said. "I bet you do."

* * *

He caught the glint in her eyes, the set of her luscious mouth.

What was it? Puerto Rican born, barrio raised, abuse, incest, rape, could have been anything.

The waiter was there, teapots, cups, slices of lemon. Sandwiches so flat they looked as if the chef had stamped on them. Pastries like little bouquets.

He watched her drink, found himself wondering how her mouth would taste. She drank gratefully, even greedily. Appetites. She had them, healthy ones.

A pain struck at his chest, sharp, deep.

Pax. Not calling him. Not missing him. Not needing his help, advice, support. His love.

And Rosa, who could use him. Who didn't grasp her own strength, a Latina judge who should be making herself different from the establishment, not trying to join it.

Christ, what he could tell her about politics, promotions, what he could do for her! With his tutoring she'd sail into the Appellate Division. Maybe better, a federal judgeship. A year with Rosa and who knew? And what a year that could be!

What was she thinking about right now?

"Tell me about it," Rosa heard Leonard say suddenly.

She was startled.

"About what?"

"Men and little girls. What happened to you? Did it make you want authority, power? Did it make you want to be a judge? So you could take care of men who do things to little girls?"

"It wasn't any one thing. But I did start at the bottom. My mother was a laundress."

Should she tell him who her mother worked for? But maybe Pax had told him. He knew Pax had saved Carlos; he'd almost said so in her chambers.

"How did you get from there to here?"

She couldn't not tell. Anyway, she wanted to watch him react.

"Pax Ford. My mother worked for her family. Her father got interested in me because Pax made him interested. I've been following her around for a long time."

Am I following her with you? she wondered.

"You can't really follow her," Leonard was saying. "Pax didn't come out of Hunter, Fordham Law. You're totally different. Even though you try so hard not to be."

"Did you look up my résumé?"

"The moment I got back from your chambers. Obviously you knew that judging is a great escape, a great way up. Judges boss everyone, they've got all the marbles. What you haven't figured out yet is what to do with yours. You've got all the makings, but you're burying them."

"Burying them?"

"Rosa, you're putting yourself under wraps, trying to fade into the crowd. You're a Puerto Rican, a minority person. These days minority people ask, get. You could ask, get a lot more than a Bronx courtroom, a few crumbs from Talcott Bishop, if you made some changes."

"Like what?" she said.

Leonard leaned forward, eyes narrowed, hands flat on the table.

Was this how he looked at opponents in court? At clients who didn't pay bills? D.A.'s who wanted to indict a biter for murder?

"Take blacks," Leonard said.

Rosa felt dizzy. "Blacks?"

"Black men and women used to fade themselves out, dress like their white colleagues in court and everywhere else, talk like them, try to make people forget they were special, different. Not now. The whole act has changed. You're not with it."

"I'm not black."

"No, you're the color of honey. The honey my mother

drizzled into her glass of tea. And you're working to make yourself white sugar. Don't feel bad. For years the Jews did it, too, the immigrants. But that's over."

Honey, tea, mother. He certainly dealt in basics. Was he serious? Or was this his way of starting something?

"What should I be doing? According to you?"

"Not just according to me. You'll hear it from Bishop one of these days, I'm sure of that. White sugar's no good to him. He'll need you as Hispanic as salsa. Every way, clothes, speech, gestures, the works. I mean, does Jesse Jackson talk like Winston Churchill? Does Al Sharpton dress like Beau Brummell?"

"Who's Beau Brummell?" Rosa asked.

Leonard looked surprised. Then he began laughing, a nice, deep sound that made heads turn.

Rose felt hot, ridiculous.

"Sweetheart, I'm sorry. I forget what thirty-five is, a young thing, a new person. Listen. You can make big news for yourself as a Puerto Rican."

As a Puerto Rican! Was he putting her down? Telling her she didn't belong in Pax's league? Did he expect her to order rice and beans at the Plaza?

"Start with something simple. Right now you look like any woman lawyer, safe, underplayed. Your suit, your shoes, that blouse up to your chin. Even your purse looks like a briefcase. You blend yourself in, become just another girl in the crowd."

"A girl?" Rosa said, anger rising in her. "Don't remind me how old you are, a word like that. Not very p.c."

"Better," he said, smiling. "Much better."

Was this a come-on? Was he taking over as a schoolteacher? Why wasn't he saying she was beautiful, irresistible, the way Tony and every other man who made moves on her did?

"We all did it," he was saying, leaning closer. "Jewish boys took elocution at City College, manners lessons at the movies. We changed our names from long to short, bought Brooks

Brothers suits that faded us into our firms. Now WASPs talk
Yiddish in every law office, you hear it in every theater, movie,
network TV show. Even judges are letting Yiddish take
over from Latin, even our Arkansas president, a Japanese-
American like Lance Ito, use words like maven, megillah.
Rosa, you were ethnic as hell in college, all those groups,
petitions, sit-ins. Why not now?"

Rosa, stunned, nearly dropped her spoon.

He knew what she had done at Hunter? How? Who would
research that old stuff, her Esmeralda Club, the protest meetings, boyfriends who thought they were Che, thought she was
La Pasionara. Who'd dig all that up?

He was interested in her, he had to be. And he had to
have plenty of resources, researchers, probably detectives on
retainer. Talcott Bishop could help her, but he never got into
the truth, like this man. Talcott Bishop pretended her origins
didn't matter when he talked to her, like George Bush saying
Clarence Thomas's race didn't matter when he'd made the
man a Supreme Court justice, which was pure cant. Anyway,
Leonard was a lot more fascinating, sexier than Talcott
Bishop.

"Go on," she said. "And be specific, Counselor."

"Your suit."

"My suit? What about my suit?"

For a moment she felt sick, vulnerable. She hadn't
dressed right, after all. Pax was right: a black robe was a
blessing, everyone looked right wearing one.

"It looks like Peck and Peck," Leonard said.

"What's that?"

"My God, you *are* young. A shop where everything
matched, skirts, jackets, coats, hats, handbags. Used to be a
byword for preppy."

What was wrong with preppy? That was how she wanted to
look, like Pax, like the women lawyers from Harvard, Yale.

"Rosa," Leonard said.

His voice was suddenly different, caressing, fervent.

"You're young. You're beautiful. Things happen to men who look at you, men any age, happen in their heads, in their bodies, they'd happen to blind men. You give off steam, Rosa, a fragrance, like what rises from the earth in the islands, flowers, fruits, the sea, even a blind man, Rosa."

This was Leonard Scholer, famous, important? Rosa wanted to put out her hand, touch his unruly hair.

"I'm sorry," he was saying, looking away.

"Don't be," she said. "It sounds nice. Not much fragrance in the criminal courts. Just before I came downtown I had a woman on trial who put her baby in the refrigerator for an hour because she cried, that is, after having been hit awhile with a coat hanger. The child wasn't a year old, and incidentally, the mother couldn't exactly remember her name. Always used a term of endearment, her lawyer said."

"I'm glad she heard one term of endearment. That's what goes on, Rosa. You're right in it, not sitting on a cushion, sewing a fine seam."

"What?"

"It's a nursery rhyme," Leonard said. "I don't suppose you heard nursery rhymes as a child. I had to read them in English lit at college, myself."

What if? Rosa thought. If I told him what I saw, heard as a little kid? I never told Pax, she'd have been shocked to pieces. Or Tony. Poor, he knew. But he had a loving family, big dinners, relatives from Sicily coming and going, children the darlings of everybody. Ricans aren't like that, not from shacks in La Perla.

"Maybe we could all use a little endearment," he was saying.

Tony thought her career was sensational, loved her just as she was. He'd never understood her hunger for promotion, for getting out of his courthouse.

She was free of him, except, of course, for the misery of lonesome nights, the going everywhere by herself. She'd been miserable without his arm at the Bishop party, though that feeling got mixed up with some gratitude that he wasn't there being a drag. Leonard would never be a drag. She couldn't, mustn't take him away from Pax. But if he wasn't Pax's at all, as he seemed to suggest, well, then!

"More tea?" Leonard asked.

"Not really."

"I have an idea. Give me a minute. Don't move."

He waved for the waiter, got the check quickly, slapped down a credit card.

Alone, she peeked in the leather folder that held the check.

Forty-one dollars! And a tip still to add! For a little snack and a cup of watery tea!

Then he was back, picking up the card, pulling out her chair.

"Perfect timing," he said, sounding pleased. "The store will be closed. Let's go."

"Store?"

"You're a Latina, right? So let me be macho. Obey. You did something for me uptown. Let me do something for you."

Was he teasing? *Esta okay,* she'd see what the teasing involved. She could always walk away from him, get a taxi back to Riverdale.

Besides, she thought, I'm a judge. I could make trouble for him no matter how big a lawyer he is. Report him to the Bar Association, the court administration. I'm on top of this.

Guiding her through the lobby, touching her body with his as he held her arm, Leonard was in a fever.

What was wrong with him? Why had he said all that? She'd think he was nuts, she'd never go with him where he wanted to take her now. Maybe he *was* nuts. He was lonely enough, angry enough at Pax for cutting him off so damned fast, angry at himself, too.

Could Rosa really be interested in him? Older, so different? She'd never married, he knew that from his quick research. A rumor, yes, some guy in the Bronx courthouse, but she wasn't exactly hurrying home, either.

He steered her through the revolving door, out to the street.

Beautiful night, crisp, cold. Everything looked sharper, larger than life, the doorman in his glorious gold-braided uniform, the shining limos sweeping along the curb, the lights of Fifth Avenue across the little square and up near Central Park, the carriage horses stamping, the top-hatted drivers standing, talking to one another. Like a *New Yorker* cover! Like a movie about the magic of Manhattan by night!

She was so different from Pax. Not tiny like Pax, just up to his shoulder. Rosa was tall, much nearer his own height. He could kiss her just turning his head.

He could do a lot of things. Maybe sweep her off her sensibly shod feet. Jesus, marry her, honeymoon in Mexico, where the men would collapse just looking at her, only she'd be his, all his. Could he ever do that? Could he put her in a pretty house, maybe with a garden?

No. Not a garden. Why had he thought of a garden?

Leonard rallied himself, took Rosa's arm, hurried her past the tall, overly gilded statue of Sherman. Aha, he knew who the man in the statue was, William Tecumseh Sherman, and how many people knew that? He knew things, a thousand things this girl, no, this woman, could use.

And she knew some things he could certainly use, too. With that look in her eyes, he was sure of it.

Rosa felt as if she were on something, ganja, some kind of downer.

She moved obediently, dreamily along the dark street until Leonard stopped at a dark doorway, reached for a button, pressed it.

The door swung back, revealing a man.

Behind him, even in semidarkness, she glimpsed glass counters stretching far back, counters crowded with glass and gold and silver, with large pictures of impossibly beautiful women. A store, anyway a private doorway into one.

"What are we supposed to be doing?" she said.

But the man was bowing to them, closing the door behind them, locking it again. An ordinary man, in a neat gray suit that matched his neat gray hair, glasses that glinted in the low light.

Moving with Leonard, Rosa began seeing there were beautiful things everywhere, jewelry, scarves, hats, perfumes, things no woman needed and every woman wanted, nobody there to look at any of it. And on one white wall a sign, in gold: Bergdorf Goodman. Of course, practically next to the hotel.

"Great, Sidney," Leonard was saying. "Just what I wanted."

"Up to you, Leonard," Rosa heard.

Their voices echoed in the empty space. Rosa felt excitement stir inside her, felt the heady danger of being caught in an undertow, like the ones on some of her childhood beaches, plunged in swirling water, rushed toward depths she knew nothing about.

Who was Sidney? Why was he letting them in? Was Leonard buying her something now, at night? Was this what he was used to doing with girls, women? Did he perhaps own a piece of Bergdorf Goodman?

"I made some calls, someone will be right along," Sidney was saying.

He looked like a dummy in a men's shop suddenly down from his pedestal, stiff, wooden. Even his voice sounded somehow wooden, artificial.

He's learned to speak properly, she thought, even though he wasn't born to it. Like me. Only I was lucky, I learned as a child. This man didn't learn until much, much later.

"Rosa. Sidney Waxman. Sidney, this is Judge Macario. Rosa, you've heard of private viewings? We're about to have a private viewing."

Sidney looked serious. "What, exactly?" he asked.

"Business things," Leonard told him. "Then we'll see."

Business things, Rosa thought, disappointed. Clothes? But she had clothes.

"Armani," Rosa heard. "Klein, Lauren."

"No. Not what everybody wears. I want flashy, Sidney, bright. Here-I-am things."

"Versace," Sidney said, nodding. "Lagerfeld, Rena Lange. Follow me."

Leonard pulled her along to an elevator. Sidney produced a key, used it, pressed a button. They floated up into the silent store.

Rosa had questions, a million questions. And felt, even with her three languages, English, Spanish, Nuyorican, speechless.

The elevator stopped. Sidney Waxman led them into semidarkness, more silence. Then he clicked more switches, and brightness was everywhere, making the dummies, the clothes racks, the big spaces, even more dreamlike than downstairs. The carpets were soft, deep, the beiges and grays of the walls restful, lulling. Wherever she looked she saw beautiful clothes, clothes for the most beautiful women in the world. A far cry from Loehmann's in the Bronx, even from Bloomingdale's, where she bought her good suits.

Rosa realized she was walking on tiptoe.

"When I see," Leonard was saying, "I'll know."

He must bring other women here. Or witnesses, when he coaches them on what to wear.

Sidney was pulling up velvet chairs, holding one for her.

And then opening showcases, gathering dresses, suits, skirts, pants, as if they were stalks of sugarcane. And Leonard watching, shaking his head, yes, no.

Rosa realized he was picking colors, brilliant things going on a rack, pale things disappearing. Parrot green, tangerine, sharp blue, poinsettia red. For her? When she dressed to be taken seriously? Did he want her looking like a *puertorriquena*? And anyway, who knew her size, knew what would fit? Was this the way beautiful women bought beautiful clothes, just choosing, worrying about all that later on?

Sidney kept gathering more, shocking white, screaming yellow.

Now she heard a woman's heels clicking on the polished floor.

Leonard heard, too.

"Shoes," he said to Sidney Waxman. "High heels, spikes. I don't care what they're wearing, lumpy boots, ballet slippers, nonsense."

"Here we are," Sidney said. "Miss Harrison, our chief personal shopper. Judge Macario. And Mr. Scholer, who helped so much with our little legal problems. Anything he wants, Miss Harrison."

Rosa's brain was on fire.

Did he want her to wear clothes like this in public?

How could she? Everyone knew judges' salaries. She could never afford clothes like this. Was Leonard proposing to buy them? Impossible, dangerous. Judges couldn't take gifts, especially from lawyers. Independent women couldn't take expensive clothes, even if they longed for them.

But the woman was leading her to a spacious fitting room, and Rosa was looking at herself, tripled, in enormous mirrors.

Miss Harrison's hair was pulled back in a knot, almost the twin of her own. She wore a black dress, a blank expression. A servant, a saleswoman. Maybe Leonard was right. Maybe it was time she made some changes.

"We'll start with suits," Miss Harrison said, all business.

She plucked out a jacket, heavy silk, scarlet, ruffled around its edges. And a matching skirt, pleated, flirty as a flamenco dancer's costume, Spanish as an infanta.

In a dream, Rosa unzipped her skirt, let her jacket slip to the floor. Next to that suit her own looked like a cop's uniform.

She didn't look in the mirrors till she was in it, Miss

Harrison behind her fluffing the collar, pulling in fabric at the waist where the jacket was loose.

"A fitter," she said. "You have a beautiful shape, Judge. Slim enough so your bosom and hips make lovely curves. And perfect legs. We must make the most of them."

Staring at herself, Rosa was thinking that this was how she'd look in heaven. Thank God she hadn't asked stupid questions about sizes. Evidently for clothes like these, fitters took care of all that.

This was a color to make her dark skin glow, her jet hair gleam. Beautiful. But beautiful like a cigar box picture, a señorita in a bullfight poster?

Rosa frowned.

"Let's see what Mr. Scholer says," Miss Harrison said quickly, putting a hand on her arm.

Rosa let her lead the way out to Leonard, walking with a springy step, making the pleats put snap and dash in her walk.

Leonard's eyes widened with every step she took.

Glorious, he thought. In dreams I never saw anything so glorious.

"Rosa," he said, knowing his voice was husky, "we walk into the Bar Association with you in that, they'll all go into cardiac arrest. You've got it, Miss Harrison. That takes care of red. Keep going."

Christ, if she'd let him, he'd buy her something in every color, green, electric blue, brilliant yellow. Take her places in them one by one. At least, he could show her what she looked like, how stunning she was!

Miss Harrison moved away.

"Rosa," Leonard found himself saying, "give these clothes a break. Take your hair down. Now."

And felt like Clark Gable, Spencer Tracy, when her hands moved to the back of her head, pulled, tossed, shook. When the fall of glistening black spilled over the stunning red.

My God, he thought, I'm speechless. The great counselor, cross-examiner, speaker, speechless. He cleared his thick throat, tried again.

"Rosa," he said, in a voice he hardly recognized. "Yes. Oh, yes. When's your birthday? I don't think I can wait for Christmas."

A half hour later, Rosa hardly knew how, they were at the door of his apartment.

He was as keyed up as she was, she knew it. His hand shook a little as he turned the key. When he stood back to let her go first, she could almost feel the heat coming from his body.

She walked in, a little unsteadily, to face a room so beige, so empty of anything personal, it could have belonged to someone hiding out in the federal witness program. It even smelled dead, like an unused hotel room, airless, warm.

A small place, he'd said. Rented since his divorce. Okay till he found a bigger place.

But I could make it nicer, she thought. I could do things with this room.

She could do things with this man, so powerful, so commanding and yet as eager for her as any twenty-year-old who knew nothing, had nothing.

But she couldn't think, because his arms were around her. He was stroking her loose hair, taking great fistfuls of it in his hands.

Tony had never bothered with her hair.

It would look, feel different from Pax's hair, her helmet of smooth silver.

For a moment the thought of Pax made her feel sick, ashamed. But she needn't be ashamed. Leonard was through with Pax, if he'd ever been this close to her. He wanted her now, he was certainly making that clear.

Then, somehow, they were in his bedroom, he was releasing her only to unbutton her buttons, slide clothes off her shoulders, let them fall where they fell.

Holding her, arm's length, looking her over, top to toe.

She felt his hands tighten, heard the intake of his breath.

It's been so long, she thought. So long since anyone made love to me, let alone made love to me like this.

Leonard couldn't believe her, honey, cream, fragrance, desire.

So long, he thought. It's been so long since I touched a girl like this.

He sent a hand to stroke her bare back, silk, pure silk.

Then he was getting out of his own clothes, dropping them.

"If I'd known you were so ready," she said, "I might have hurried a lot faster in that store."

"Rosa," he said, "I've been ready for you for years."

And he had. He'd never seen a girl who looked like this, never such hair, such a ruby mouth, such ripe, beautiful breasts.

How long since he'd undressed a girl? Her body was seventeen, twenty!

Fifty-nine, thirty-five. What would Debo say about Rosa Macario? Jon Kistel?

What the hell did he care what anyone said?

What would Pax say?

Pax didn't want him. She hadn't made a single move to get near him.

Rosa needed him, and wanted him. Why else was she here, so close, so ready? She'd make him twenty again.

He took her as if he were twenty, breathlessly, speedily, feeling a hungry, boyish kind of triumphant joy he'd never known in all his years.

11

PAX

PAX LET HERSELF INTO HER APARTMENT, LONGING TO FLOAT in a hot bath, curl into bed with supper on a tray.

No chance.

Three frantic calls had come in to her chambers in the last hour she'd been in court. From Naomi Rosenbloom, secretary to her pro bono project, her divorce committee. An emergency, a sad one, a mess.

Naomi had told her about it crisply, in the manner of a lawyer detailing a case. A matrimonial attorney interviewing his client's thirteen-year-old daughter about her family. And getting her pregnant. The girl aborting herself with a #14 knitting needle in the bathroom at her school, Chapin, so her mother wouldn't know, so her friends could help. Friends, teachers, school nurse and frantic headmistress hurrying her to New York Hospital's emergency room. Police not far behind. Thus a committee meeting tonight, Pax urgently required.

In her taxi coming uptown Pax had thought, anyway, a change from my courtroom. Could a change of misery be called a vacation? What other kind of vacation was she likely to get these days?

Rocked by the cab moving in and out of traffic, she'd allowed herself to imagine a vacation with Leonard, London, Paris. No, Hayman Island on the Great Barrier Reef. She'd gone there last year, spent hours deep under the crystal water drifting in a glass bubble through rainbows of coral, flickers of fish. Such silence, such beauty: *there* was a change from her courtroom. Oh, to nestle into Leonard's arms and drift deep under the Coral Sea!

Lulled by imaginings, she reached home, rode the elevator upstairs, walked into her pretty foyer.

Tonight, however, her foyer wasn't pretty. It looked like a makeshift post office. Envelopes large, small. Telegrams. Packages on the marble table, overflowing the wicker basket Flora had set out when mail first began streaming in about the trial. Pax's address wasn't listed, but people unearthed it anyway, attacked with letters that were smudged, poorly typed or handwritten, ugly to look at, uglier to absorb.

Flora opened the pantry door, bringing the sound of a television program with her.

Dear Flora. To her all the new commotion was exciting, a marvel. She came from primitive Guyana, had worked at a ranch for tourists who fished, like her own Amerindian ancestors, for the huge *perai*, beautiful, silvery, lethal, capable of stripping the flesh from an animal long before it drowned.

Like reporters, Pax thought. Demonstrators. Letter writers. No wonder I feel all bones.

"You're on the news!" Flora was saying, breathless, thrilled. "Come see!"

Georgetown's Staebroek market in Guyana was the most sophisticated place Flora had known before New York. Television enchanted her. Catching Pax on the screen was pure magic.

But not for Pax.

"I couldn't look," she told Flora. "Listen, did all this mail come today? Just one day?"

Flora beamed.

"Yes, all, more every day now. You are famous, Judge! Shall I get one of the building men to put it in a sack? Send it downtown to Miss Selma?"

Pax shook her head. There were sackfuls of mail in her chambers, too.

She worried about the packages. Everyone had heard of letter bombs. But that wasn't the only nastiness. Last week the mail had brought a box with a rough little voodoo doll with her name on it, pins in its eyes, breasts, crotch. Ever since she'd been doing her own sorting, picking out recognizable notes from friends, piling up the garden catalogues. And dumping most of the rest unopened into the living room fire.

The phone, thank God, was screened. An operator intercepted everything, put through calls only from people whose names were on a list.

Top of the list, Leonard.

Just in case he missed her urgently, felt things had been cut too short, wanted to apologize.

But she was being ridiculous.

Pax picked up an armful for the fire, noted an envelope marked JUDGE, FAIRY TRIAL, 910 Park Avenue, New York 10022.

On impulse she opened it, suddenly remembering her mother's voice saying every letter must have an answer, however brief. Did her father, her grandfather, get letters like these? Surely not, in the old days when people respected judges. Today everyone had something to say and the vocabulary to say it, if not the grammar or spelling. "Equal justice" had figured prominently in several of the letters so far.

How would you answer a letter that said the writer wished to hang you by the feet and fuck you upside down?

Dear sir, Pax thought. Actually, I much prefer being fucked right side up.

Fucked.

Not lately. Let alone held, cuddled, cosseted. Loved.

She'd always had men when she wanted, attractive men,

for dinner, the theater, parties, a few romantic weekends in
Vermont, the Hamptons, once even Paris. She'd liked being
courted by an investment banker well enough, loved being
adored by an important landscape architect who knew every
famous garden in the world. Women judges met new men,
nice men, all the time at seminars, clubs, parties, political
associations. Besides, her friends had been working to marry
her off to nice men for years.

But Leonard was different, not just nice, not just successful, not just attractive. An equal. It seemed to Pax that
their brains had met as closely as their bodies.

Sighing again, she shuffled the pile of paper for any recognizable handwriting, bills, rescued a crushed reminder that
she was expected on the dais at next week's Women's Bar
dinner.

Underneath all that, a small box. Torn brown paper,
glossy blue cardboard showing through. Tiffany blue.

Pax's breath caught. Leonard practically lived in Tiffany.
The incredible ring she'd seen so briefly had come in just
such a box.

An apology? A peace offering? A reward for sticking to
her guns? Something to make her feel loved again?

She pulled the satin ribbon, scattered the tissue inside.

The smell struck her first.

Dirty, disgusting, the unforgettable stench of the old
wooden outhouses at summer camp.

Turds. Neatly wrapped. Unmistakable, appalling.

Pax sank onto the hall bench.

Someone's sent me turds, she thought, dizzy. Didn't Joe
Iapalucci say they would? Or Leonard? I can't remember.

But Flora was back, gasping, taking the box, vanishing
into the back of the house, to her own bathroom. Pax heard
the toilet flush, the sound of the kitchen windows being
thrown wide.

She got up, went through to the pantry sink, washed her
hands with strong soap. And washed them again. She'd only

touched the lid, the tissue paper. But her hands felt filthy, might always feel filthy.

"How *could* anyone?" Flora came back saying, furious. "Who would think of such a thing, trouble to do it?"

"Free country," Pax said, shuddering. "Everyone has a constitutional right to be a creep. Some days people exercise that right more than other days. This must be one. Flora, listen, I have to go out again. Would you run me a bath, please?"

As if nothing she wanted could ever work out, the house phone buzzed out in the kitchen. Someone from the committee to pick her up? Already?

Flora moved into the kitchen, back out again.

A gentleman coming up. She hadn't caught the name because the new doorman mumbled so.

Another moment and the doorbell was ringing, Flora opening the door.

Pax made herself stand straight, ready to smile at whoever had come to escort her wherever the committee was gathering. Howard Morse probably, the quiet, brilliant committee chairman, one of the nicest, most decent of the matrimonial experts eager to patrol their own murky legal waters.

But the door wasn't opening on Howard. Or any of her committee members.

It was opening on someone she'd never invited, would never have invited, above all, heaven forbid, not now, not in the middle of her trial.

John Talcott Bishop.

Large enough to crowd her, send her a step backward. Austere enough to dry her throat, make speech impossible, make her feel young, small, even somehow guilty.

Pax's skin went cold. Her hands flew up in front of her face.

But she *couldn't* be alone with this man, couldn't speak to him privately at all, not now, not in the middle of a trial.

Tell him? Even that would be to talk, to be involved.

Almost any conversation, any ex parte meeting *with* a litigant, *without* a record, wrong.

"Mr. Bishop," she said. Berating herself for girlishness, stupidity almost, before the words were out.

But *no* words would work. Talk was impossible. It was why she'd been so careful seeing Caitlin, bringing Tim along to note every word of their meeting. Anything less could bring questions from judicial committees, reporters, discipline, even dismissal from the bench. Bishop wasn't a legal igno-ramus. He was the publisher of the *Bar Journal.* He knew the rules as well as she.

Pax found her hands together, clutched tightly.

"You can't be here," she said quietly, her voice sounding weak, strained in her own ears. "You can't be in my house."

"Good evening," Bishop said in a tone so courtly, so pleasant, it snatched away her breath. The man was looming over her, closer than he'd ever been, larger than she'd real-ized. Till now Bishop had been a tall figure across a court-room, a head shot in a newspaper photograph. Suddenly, in her own apartment, he had dimension, weight, a scent, lemon soap, expensive tweed. She could see the elderly droop of the lids at the outer corners of his eyes, the look that seemed to threaten force nobody would want at such close quarters.

"Mr. Bishop, you must go. We haven't exchanged any words worth mentioning, so perhaps we can still ignore the fact of your coming here. If you go immediately."

"Don't be ridiculous," Bishop said in the same patron-izing tone. "There's no audience. You don't have to make a record here. But you ought to listen. It's important."

"Anything important happens out loud, in my courtroom, with court reporters present."

"Oh, you won't want to hear this in court. It might just be the last thing you ever heard in court, Judge."

What the hell was he talking about?

Suddenly Pax was on fire. He was a cliché, this big,

handsome, nicely dressed man with an educated voice, charming manners. He was every male judge who'd ever browbeaten her, every law school professor who'd demanded to know how she justified taking a job away from a man, everyone who'd ever turned to Tim instead of her assuming *he* was the judge and she the secretary.

Pax realized she'd backed against the table, ruffling the pile of mail that moments ago had seemed her worst problem.

She couldn't back off any farther. So now she'd better start making a move in the right direction.

After all, she was a Supreme Court judge. John Talcott Bishop was breaking the most basic rule of the system, enticing an elected judge into the most grievous possible error. He was in her house without warning or permission and, what's more, daring to call her ridiculous.

She'd show him ridiculous.

"Flora," she called out.

And to Bishop, "I'm telling my housekeeper to call downstairs, have the doorman send someone up to escort you out. And I'm telling you I'll announce the fact of this visit first thing tomorrow morning in court, for the record, from the bench."

"I don't think so," Bishop said.

He peered around, smiled at her pretty living room.

"Judge, I'm quite aware of the situation. Of course I'm out of order. Of course I'd be sorry if anyone learned I turned up on this basis. But I'm certain you'll want to hear what I have to say."

He looked at the kitchen door, smiled.

"And I don't believe you'd want your maid listening. After all, it won't help you to win a point on ethics and lose your whole reputation for good and all, now, will it?"

Lose her whole reputation? Because a litigant pushed his way into her house? Let him worry about *his* reputation.

"You must be loopy," Pax told him, Willie's favorite word

of the moment suddenly popping out of her mouth, which didn't seem to be quite her own, quite under her control. "*I'd* be loopy to spend another second with you. Besides, someone from the matrimonial bar is about to show up. And let me tell you, I'll get his help. I'll report exactly what's going on here, and Flora will corroborate."

"Oh, come off it, Judge," Bishop said crossly. "I don't worry about lawyers, I *make* lawyers. I make judges, too, in case you've forgotten."

"You didn't make me," Pax said, sounding girlish, feeble to herself.

"Ah, but I could next time, for the App Div. Or I could decide not to. We'll have to see. At any rate, Judge, my wife is your litigant technically, not I."

Pax felt her fingernails, short as she kept them, digging into her palms.

"You see," he said, stepping closer, "it's about your husband. About Alden Ford."

Pax's fingers went as slack as if he'd just shot her dead.

Alden was all over. Or was he? Hadn't she always known, rock bottom, that Alden's sexual choices would someday boomerang back at her? Like the curved wooden weapons on every shelf in every tourist shop in Australia? Wasn't the secret he'd kept even from her, especially from her, something that had haunted her days, her dreams?

"Alden has been dead for ten years," she heard herself saying.

"Of course," Bishop said. "And you make it sound like a very long time. It's not, you know. May we go in that pleasant room, please, and sit down?"

But Pax was rooted to the floor.

Hadn't she always felt she'd hidden away a tiny vial of poison, bubbling and seething, sure to explode one day, burn her, scar her, pit her skin?

Was this the day, a hideous replay of that terrible moment at Alden's funeral?

"I'm Alden's best friend. More. I'm his lover. Alden and I were lovers."

Somehow she was turning, leading Talcott Bishop into her living room.

"Thank you," he said, as if he were her guest, invited, welcome. "Judge, it's for everyone's good, you know, what I have to say."

Pax realized that Flora must have built a fire earlier. A strange one, with no warmth to it. The whole room was bitter cold, the chair she chose made of a block of ice.

"Good Lord," Bishop was saying, "you have a greenhouse out there. On your terrace. Clever."

Pax stared at him.

"Yes, well," he went on. "Never mind that. This case, Judge, has revived some old emotions for us all. Most sadly, of course, for Mrs. Bishop."

Pax shivered, watching Bishop settle himself on a sofa.

"She had, as you know, troubled relations with her brother. And as you've heard, she has always wanted a child. *This* child seemed to her to be dropped at our doorstep by angels. Who would have thought someone like Tom D'Arcy would want her?"

Alden, Pax was thinking, I always knew this would happen. I knew that friend of yours, that lover of yours, would never really go away.

"I must tell you," Bishop was saying. "I didn't feel the same need for Caitlin as my wife."

Pax was freezing. Bishop's voice seemed to be coming from far off, somewhere beyond tall mountains topped with snow.

"I could never abide Johnny California, support a connection with the fellow. Ba is a good woman, she doesn't see evil, doesn't know anything about it."

I was cold at the funeral, too, Pax thought. But I thought that over the years I'd warmed, thawed. Gotten over sadness, anger, my fear for Willie. Outlived the doubts about myself, the men who liked me. I stopped dreaming of Alden in bed with that man. I could go to a funeral again without terror. I moved on. Only somehow I always knew this would happen.

"Johnny California was an aberration, a lowlife, the worst sort of scum," Bishop's windy, echoing voice was saying.

Why did I ever accept this case? Pax was thinking. I'll be censured, thrown off the bench, disgraced, disbarred. Worse. Willie will hate me. Leonard will think I wanted the power to punish a gay man because I hated being married to one.

"Ba has been a superb wife," Bishop said. "I owe her a great deal. She's a perfectionist. And she'd make a perfect mother. You can rest easy on that score. Tom D'Arcy can buy himself a hundred distractions, a thousand. From what I've managed to learn about him, he may not live to raise a child. You'll hear about that soon. But my wife is sickening over this trial, Judge. And quite honestly, I can't allow that to happen."

Honestly! The man was suborning a judge and talking about doing things honestly! The word grated, scratched like a match against stone, sparking her, warming her.

"Look, Judge, everyone has a past. Everyone has things he'd like to conceal. Anyway, everyone of a certain age. You had a husband, a background, a career in the law. Judges make enemies all the time. Litigants who lose cases. Other judges who lose promotions. People who resent a judge's security, prestige."

Now her eyes seemed to be doing strange optical tricks, breaking up her vision into jagged, dizzying squares like one of those dragons' eye kaleidoscopes.

"Not everyone, of course, has the research tools I possess. A library of law, legal history, publicity second to none. Trained investigators already in place. It was simple for me to learn about your husband's sexual preferences."

He paused, cleared his throat.

"I could undoubtedly tell you things about your husband you may never have known."

The whole room was fragmented, Bishop's eyes somehow doubled and tripled, spinning, hurting her eyes.

"I don't like using unpleasant facts. But neither do I like allowing judges to run my life. Particularly when I know what judges are, how they're made, what they do to hold onto their jobs."

God, Pax thought. I'll be the judge who took a case to indulge her own prejudices. I'll be in public disgrace. I'll dishonor my father, my grandfather, my schools, my son, myself. I can forget the Appellate Division. I'd never survive the screening panel.

Bishop suddenly sat back, somehow managing to look as much on the attack as if he'd leaned forward.

"So I armed myself," he said.

Here it comes, Pax thought. Now he's going to tell me something I'll never forget all the rest of my days.

"Did you know your husband spent every Thursday night for eight years at a private club in the arms of the man he loved? A club with anonymous members? Partitioned into small rooms with high walls? Walls with panels just about big enough to copulate through without seeing who or what you were copulating with? I know it's not parlor talk, Judge, but he was your husband. Did he tell you that was where he went?"

Thursdays, Pax thought, trying desperately to think clearly in spite of her crazy vision. Alden played squash. On Vanderbilt Avenue. With the same group he'd had since Harvard School of Architecture, the group from the office that revolved, ten of them, he said, always enough for a game. Oh, my God.

"Well? Did he? Or can you remember some other Thursday activity he seemed busy with? Come on, Judge, you know it's true. I could prove it to you. I could prove it to anyone, the *Times*, Channel Four, Court TV, anyone."

Alden always came home with a bag of sweaty clothes, a racket or two, a glow. A glow!

A log fell in the fireplace.

It seemed to jog something deep inside her.

Bishop was trying to terrify her. And that wasn't acceptable. She was a judge. She was the daughter and granddaughter of judges.

"Now you know what I'm going to say," Bishop was smiling.

Yes, Pax thought, I know. What's more, I always knew this moment would come.

But her eyesight was swimming back to normal, Bishop's face taking its proper form, the room coming into view unbroken.

Because nothing is ever really a secret. The world finds out everything even if it takes years. Roosevelt's affair with pretty Lucy Mercer. Rock Hudson dying of AIDS. J. Edgar Hoover going home from the office and putting on a dress. Nothing stays secret. Alden got around, had friends; that funeral was jammed with them. How could I ever have thought no one would know? Besides, he wasn't an embezzler, a murderer. He was a good man with a different way of loving. He did his best for his wife, his son, the way he saw it.

"You're a clever woman," Bishop was saying now. "It's easy to go on from here."

All right, Pax was telling herself. Get yourself together. Deal with it.

"I want my wife to have Caitlin. You couldn't bring yourself to give the child to that pervert anyway. No real woman could do that. Half the world, the decent, worthwhile half, wants you to decide for us."

He reached into his briefcase, came up with a fat manila folder. Clippings peeked from the sides of it, yellowed, old, poisonous newspaper clippings.

"The day you make the correct decision all this is yours. Every photo, every report, every piece of information about that William person, that club, every statement ever made to my researchers by a witness."

Her eyes seemed clearer than ever, her hearing more

acute. The papers crunched loudly as he put them back, snapped them shut inside his briefcase.

"You really don't want all this getting out. Not that people might not feel sorry for you, married to a gay. Not that people care who's married to whom these days, all that same-sex marriage talk. But that you took on this case, with one litigant a well-known homo, without revealing *your* history, *your* bias? I think the world might well disapprove. And I'm certain you won't want this kind of publicity just as you're planning to try for higher office."

But Pax was hardly listening anymore. She was in the past, the far past, reliving something she hadn't consciously thought about from the day it happened till this moment.

She was twelve. At family dinner, her father talking. "Buffy," he was saying to her mother, "Frank Maridiana came to see me today. Swaggering, wearing one of his natty suits. Big district leaders don't usually emerge from their offices for mere judges. But this morning he walked right in."

"Dreadful little man," Pax's mother had said, frowning. "Those sunglasses he always wears. As if he's hiding something."

"He's hiding plenty," Pax's father said. "Swiss bank accounts, bearer bonds, dirty political secrets. He waited to make sure he had my attention. Then he pointed at a bum sleeping on a park bench across the street. And said, 'Judge, I'll tell you straight. You're aiming for the Appellate Division? Getting ready for the screening panels? Well, see that bum on that bench over there? I'd rather back him for a promotion than you. While you've got the friends you've got, reformers, liberals, bleeding hearts, you can forget about a high court judgeship.' "

"What did you do, Pax, darling?" her mother said, rapt.

"I thought about having been boxing captain at St. Paul's," her father said, smiling. "And then I thought how many years ago that was."

"And then?"

"Actually," her father said, "I believe I whistled. Yes. I think, 'Fair Harvard.' Anyway, it seemed to irritate him. I suppose now I'll be a trial judge for the rest of my days."

"Pax," her mother had said, "a trial judge is a splendid thing to be."

Now, for Pax, her father stood at her side. He could have been holding her hand.

Her father had been namesake, teacher, guide, answer. He'd been a great judge, he'd known right from wrong. Should she set a lesser example for Willie? And Bishop was a blackmailer. Blackmailers never stopped blackmailing. They had to be told what Wellington had once told a blackmailer, "Publish and be damned."

Pax stood up.

She walked forward, stood over Bishop's place on the sofa. Her head was only just above his.

Now Bishop was getting to his feet.

Tell him, she thought. Say it. Give in to you? Give a child to you, to be her father, her guide, her authority, her teacher? When hell freezes. When Jesus walks on earth. When Johnny California comes back from the grave and states what he wanted loud and clear.

In the foyer she stopped, stood tall as she could.

And opened her mouth to say it all, what you're saying is criminal, but if you go now, right now, I'll let *this* go because I took this case in good faith and I'm going to finish it the way the law intends. That's how I handle cases and how I got where I am *whoever* my husband was, and now you can leave my house.

The house phone was buzzing again out in the kitchen.

Her committee escort on his way up, of course. She'd have to greet him, go on to the meeting without showing one sign of battle, emotion, exhaustion.

"Judge," Bishop was saying, from his great height, "think about it. Think hard. It would be foolish to lose everything for a piece of nonsense like this. We're going to win it anyway."

Strange. She was hearing music.

Good Lord.

She was whistling!

For a long moment she seemed free, tall, marvelous.

Then, seeing his eyes narrow, his forehead crease, she felt her heart shrivel, her mouth go dry, heard her brave whistle fade into the air.

12

D'ARCY

D'ARCY SAT, TENSE, IN THE WITNESS CHAIR WATCHING Pressman turn his back and walk away. All the muscles in his legs, his back, strained to get him up, out, now he'd said what he wanted to say.

He couldn't go, of course.

Now it was Wickham's turn to cross-examine.

No help from the air in here. Stale, smelling of sweat after a long morning, like an extras' group dressing room in some crumbling theater.

Wickham was on his feet. Balanced, springy, as if he held a riding crop instead of a pad. But still at his table, not bounding toward the witness chair. Why? Ah, because the tall court officer, the handsome one, was whispering up to the judge.

D'Arcy leaned forward. So did most of the audience. By now everyone in the audience seemed to think it was *their* case. People got sullen during sidebars, recesses. As if Judge Ford had no right keeping things from them.

But the crowd wasn't with him on anything else.

At first a few people had smiled. That had stopped when the judge announced they couldn't see Caitlin. Now everyone glared. At Judge Ford. And at him. The two people who could see her.

The judge was beckoning the lawyers up. She looked worn today, hair dull, skin papery.

God, he was sweating. They'd bumped up the radiators to fight the late November cold outside, as they always did in this city of overheated interiors. Soon he'd be mopping his forehead. Well, dancers sweated easily, were forever swiping their faces with their forearms. Still, Pressman had warned him to look and keep cool. Cool! When he felt hotter, sweatier by the minute!

At least from here in the witness chair he could look at his adversary. Seated at the tables, he and Mrs. Bishop were parallel. If he turned to watch her, everyone in the courtroom would see.

Today the woman was again in a navy suit, perhaps the same one. And had the same air of being trapped among peasants. Since Pressman's cross-examination she'd been scowling like Giselle's mother. Pressman had said good, she'd ruin any impression she'd made earlier on the judge with that charity work shit.

And Caitlin could wind up with her for a mother!

D'Arcy looked away, saw the girl who drew for television. Ghastly pictures, like greeting cards, bad photographs. How John would have hated them!

Judge Ford was talking to the stenotypist. What a mixture she was. Strong, imperious, facing down a disorderly man in her courtroom. Melting over Caitlin, tender, motherly. At least she didn't stiffen up looking at him the way some women did. His own sister always stuck close to her sons when he was around.

"We'll recess," the judge said, surprising him. "I want to see counsel in chambers. Mr. D'Arcy, stand down."

Another wait? In the middle of his testimony?

The lawyers were following her out.

In giant steps D'Arcy was at his table, tugging at Pressman's assistant.

"What is it? What are they stopping for now?"

The young man shook his head. "Mr. Wickham has some request. Not to worry."

D'Arcy felt ignored, stung, as if another male dancer had suddenly been brought on stage to complete his variation. Pressman kept telling him not to worry, too. Pointless, he said, since D'Arcy didn't know what to worry about. "Waste your cool on shit, you'll blow when something tough turns up. Wickham's got to impeach your character, Johnny's. He can hit you with anything. Your childhood. Johnny's instability. Why he married a woman anyway, why he had a child."

The audience was talking, noise rising.

D'Arcy closed his eyes.

Joanne. One of Eileen Ford's finds. Tall, legs long as a dancer's, face angular, pure as a Botticelli angel. Just another lanky teenager till Eileen straightened her teeth, hair, shoulders, taught her how to seduce a camera.

Nobody thought about straightening her head.

He knew John had met her at an opening when he'd just begun getting close to the real money in the art world, Mellons, Bartoses, Klingensteins. Joanne was getting the top daily model rate in the world, even if she couldn't talk without revealing her nasal voice, her pea brain. But John above everything was visual, and Joanne had a flat chest, short hair, all the beauty of a golden adolescent boy. Someone convinced him marriage would help him with rich people, bring more invitations to houses, parties.

D'Arcy had raged, shouted. But John kept saying he could handle it. In no time Joanne was pregnant, John ecstatic about a baby, a whole new creative trip.

Bloated, idle, Joanne drugged even when the nurses were watching, made passes at those nurses for fun and games. She screwed every man around, claimed she did her obstetrician during examinations. When Caitlin was born, she lived on Demerol, in a cloud. Wouldn't nurse the baby, not for a minute. But once John caught the pediatrician suckling her dripping breasts.

John, basically innocent, ignorant about women, cracked then, for once in his life got touchy, hair-trigger tempered. His sister walked smack into that fierceness, that rage. Hearing the story from him, D'Arcy thought it lucky they hadn't dropped the baby, stepped on her tiny face.

A sudden hush alerted him to sit up, look around.

The lawyers were back, Wickham barely suppressing a smile. As if he'd just whipped the club champion at golf, wanted to grin, knew manners wouldn't permit it.

But Pressman!

D'Arcy took one look at his dark flush, his heavy eyelids, and felt alarms go off in his head.

Out of sight under the bench, Pax clenched her fists hard, working to make her face a blank.

Scotty Wickham was a bastard. Why not? His client was a bastard, and bastard clients had bastard lawyers, law school maxim. He'd fooled nobody with this new game, not Pressman, not Tim, certainly not her. Still, here in court, he'd just tied her hands, led her where he wanted, like a little silver pony he could easily control.

I suppose, she thought, I should feel honored that Bishop came to do his own dirty work. Maybe what he had done was so rotten he didn't even want his own lawyer to know.

She almost heard Leonard. "You'll get caught between two monsters, Pax."

And Joe Iapalucci. "This one's a *rompicoglioni!*"

She'd been doing so well till Bishop's visit, handled the protestor, protected Caitlin, danced away from the press, kept the trial moving.

But her slip at D'Arcy's had been a setback, letting herself get emotional over Caitlin. She'd wanted so to run this trial in the manner people said, insultingly, was just like a man.

And the visit from Bishop would live in her mind a long time, perhaps forever.

With all of it, today she could easily lose her temper. Wickham was introducing something really rotten. And legal, so she couldn't counter him.

Oh, Leonard, she thought. Where are you? Why weren't you there to punch Bishop in the nose? Why aren't you here instead of Pressman? I need you to laugh Wickham out of my chambers, find me some sound reason to block him. How can I keep steady in this mess without someone like you? And who's like you?

D'Arcy was watching carefully.

"We'll recess now, early," Judge Ford was saying. "When we resume, Mr. Wickham has a new witness for the plaintiff. He wants to postpone cross-examination until the witness testifies. He assures me this person has made a great effort to be here, and that his testimony will be both relevant and material. I won't refuse any testimony, however late, that could affect the whole future of a child. In fairness I must comply."

D'Arcy felt stung, shot at with arrows.

"And Mr. Wickham," Judge Ford added, narrowing her pretty eyes, "I'd better be satisfied this is in the interests of fairness."

"Stand," Pressman was hissing at him.

D'Arcy stood up while the judge left the bench, moved when the officers ushered them out, gave them a brief head start on the press, the crowd.

But there was a gantlet anyway, bodies, lights, shouts, questions. Didn't they ever give up? He'd always feel sorry for the Gottis, Simpsons, Woody Allens, the next lot of celebrities who had to claw their way in and out of courthouses, whatever they'd done.

Pressman was mustering his assistants, guarding D'Arcy like a president, a movie star.

Then they were in the car, the crowd receding as they pulled away.

For a moment he felt only relief.

Then, slowly, he realized Pressman was so enraged he was practically giving off heat.

"Who," he snarled. "Who, for Christ's sweet sake, is Kip Connor?"

Startled, D'Arcy put his mind to it.

Kip Connor.

Nobody. No one. He'd never even heard the name.

"Where to, Mr. D'Arcy?" Garrison asked, in his BBC accent, from the driver's seat. Suddenly tired of taking Pressman's orders, he told Garrison, the house.

"An hour and a half," he said to Pressman. "We're better off there than anywhere."

He was glad Pressman didn't object. Usually the man had something to say about everything, even lunch.

"Think," Pressman insisted.

So many people. Michigan, growing up. The service. Chicago, New York, Hollywood, on tour in big cities, not so big cities, everywhere in the world there were stages. Teaching, boys, parents. And with John everywhere in the world there *weren't* stages.

"I've never heard of him. Who is he supposed to be?"

They were at the gate, the house, the door. A glorious Christmas wreath on it, swathed with red velvet ribbon. D'Arcy's heart hadn't been in Christmas decorations. But there was Caitlin, and decorations there had to be.

"Tell them drinks, sandwiches, in the parlor," D'Arcy said to Garrison. "As fast as they can."

"Right-o," Garrison said.

God, how he wished he could throw himself on his bed, sleep.

Or surprise Caitlin, pick her up, bury his face in her soft hair.

Pressman was already on the phone.

"Muriel? I want a conference call, Leonard, Jon. In the next hour, at Tom D'Arcy's. Without fail. I don't give a flying fuck where they are, make it happen."

Garrison was back with a drink tray, followed by one of the maids with a larger one, sandwiches, raw vegetables. John would have approved. Hadn't he always insisted on drinks, great food, any hour?

"Leave everything," D'Arcy told them.

The doors closed again. Pressman slammed down the phone.

"Murray, what's going on?"

"Kip Connor is going on," Pressman snapped, scowling at the scotch, grabbing a Perrier. "Wickham just pulled him out of a hat. Dirty pool. Judge Ford was wild."

"Why? What does it mean?"

"It means a pig fuck. A surprise witness. The judge has a right to be furious. We both submitted lists, of course, stipulated who we'd call, what they'd say. And now Wickham springs this. Princeton boy. Opening a real crock of shit."

"Who does the witness say he is?"

Pressman reached for a sandwich, bit it in half, angrily.

"Your boyfriend," he said, eyes hard on D'Arcy's face.

D'Arcy felt a little fire begin burning inside his chest. "You think I have boyfriends with names I don't even recognize?"

"You tell me."

The burning spread, became anger.

"I am telling you. I've met a million people. I can't possibly remember them all."

"We're not talking about meeting," Pressman said. "We're talking about fucking. Or so this guy claims."

Without taking his eyes from D'Arcy's face he picked up sandwich two, finished it off, reached for sandwich three.

Now D'Arcy had hot coals inside him.

"It's a stage sort of name. An actor? Dancer?"

"Dancer. Ring a bell?"

"Beats me."

"It could," Pressman said heavily. "It just could."

D'Arcy folded his arms over his chest, hugged himself to ease the rage. "But he's not. It's a lie."

"It's a piece of shit, as I said. Especially now. I'll have to dig fast, find out when, where, our office has already started. God willing his dates are wrong, you were actually in Siberia when he says Pittsburgh. God willing I'll break him down. I'll handle it, that's what you pay for. I'm assuming you've told me the truth. Eat something, Tom. Long afternoon."

D'Arcy felt his hands go into fists, his face go crimson.

"Maybe when you see this guy something will come back. You'll watch, listen. You can even stare, like Gotti's boys stared at juries. You'll tell me then. The truth, remember. We can ask for recesses, too. But too many requests will annoy the judge. I'd rather leave that to Wickham. Eat."

Eat? His stomach was churning with hot acid, his mouth so dry he could be feverish.

He wanted a bathroom, cold water, towels, cool tile, quiet.

D'Arcy waved at Pressman, made for the door.

Five minutes later, outwardly tidy, fire still burning in his body, he was back watching Pressman on the telephone again.

Then everything seemed to happen like a film run backward. Garrison appeared to say the car was ready. The three of them swept from parlor to foyer, foyer to car, car to crowds, crowds to the courthouse steps. They ran the harrowing gantlet again, reached their table, chairs.

Suddenly all D'Arcy's heat, even his normal warmth, was gone.

What was he doing here? Why, when the Bishops wanted Caitlin, hadn't he let go? Barr had warned him. Pressman had warned him the day they met. He'd tried to do something impossible, like an entrechat vingt. With this new witness spewing lies, he'd look like a monster to everyone who watched television, read newspapers.

Where was this bloody man?

Forgetting what Pressman had said about looking at ease, D'Arcy turned around in his chair, watched the doors.

Immediately he saw the sea of faces, eyes shining with curiosity, some narrow with hostility, some blazing with contempt.

But nowhere a face he recognized. Not one. He turned back because the judge was speaking.

"Put your witness on, Mr. Wickham."

Behind him, the clatter of the doors opening.

D'Arcy looked again, saw people near the doors lean forward, heard murmurs rise. The movement, the noise, came rolling at him like a slow, dangerous ocean wave.

He stretched to see better.

But he could only see a young man moving slowly, arms extended in front of him. A gay young man. He knew immediately. He had always known.

Then he realized.

An attendant, pushing a wheelchair.

He saw feet extended, legs, torso. And a moment later, the man in the wheelchair.

D'Arcy looked carefully, felt himself grow chilly, stiff.

Thin, thin as someone in Dachau, made of bones. Pale, sick, white-skinned. Head lolling horribly as the wheelchair rolled forward, lesions on his face, neck, hands.

As the wheelchair reached the front, D'Arcy saw the man's legs. Swollen, freakish, ankles actually fatter than the emaciated calves.

D'Arcy's mind reeled. He knew the look. From hospital visits he and John had made, hospice bedsides they'd watched at. It wasn't a look anyone could forget.

AIDS, D'Arcy thought, his body immobile. That man has AIDS.

His eyes fixed on the sad face, the repulsive skin, the hot, heavy eyes, the thinning hair.

But somewhere inside him he felt relief, release, certainty.

I've never seen him, D'Arcy thought. Never, well or sick, dressed or naked. I've certainly never touched him. And thank God.

At his side Pressman seemed to be enlarging, puffing up with fury.

Wickham was up, solicitous, fussing, directing the placement of the wheelchair.

Through the hushed courtroom his voice came brisk, clear.

"Your Honor, I ask your indulgence in allowing the witness to speak from his own chair," he said.

Judge Ford, D'Arcy saw, looked almost as pale as the man in the wheelchair.

She's shocked, D'Arcy thought. She didn't know he'd be in a wheelchair, I'd bet anything. And she didn't know about the AIDS. Wickham hadn't said his witness would roll into her courtroom looking like grim death.

"Granted," the judge was saying.

"Son of a bitch," Pressman was muttering. "Son of a bitch, what a piece of shit trick."

"But I don't know him," he whispered to Pressman. "I don't know him at all."

He wasn't sure Pressman heard. The man's ears were scarlet, his neck raw beef.

Then everything seemed to move in double time, the witness raising a clawlike hand, being sworn, nodding the lolling head, speaking in a shaky voice. He looked only at Wickham, never at the judge, the crowd, never at D'Arcy. As if he had enough work to keep his eyes open, his head up. Giving his name, Kip Connor, occupation, dancer, address, some hospital, age, thirty-seven.

Thirty-seven, D'Arcy thought, horrified, pitying. And looking eighty. Surely this man couldn't hurt him.

He'd been watching rather than listening until Wickham asked the man how well he knew Tom D'Arcy.

"Very well," came like a stage whisper.

"Can you be more specific, Mr. Connor? I know this is hard, but it's important."

"Yes," he heard, in the weak voice. "You could say we were lovers."

Behind D'Arcy the courtroom audience seemed to gasp, one great sigh, in unison.

Judge Ford put her arms up, palms out to the crowd, asked for quiet, told Wickham to go on.

"You were lovers. When was that?"

"Say four years ago, five."

D'Arcy felt sick. Anyone who had loved that man five years ago was in terrible trouble.

"Five years," Wickham said sharply. "As recently as that? While Mr. D'Arcy was living with Johnny California?"

"I guess so."

"Tell the court how you two met, Mr. Connor."

"At a benefit rehearsal, in some studio. We were both dancers. We sparked to each other right away."

Pain was rising in D'Arcy's head, needles, icepicks jabbing behind his eyes. The sweat was starting again, too, rolling down his face, soaking his collar.

He'd never heard the voice, he'd never seen the man, he was certain of it.

"And you formed a relationship?"

"Not right away. We just saw each other a lot, had friends in common."

"This was where, Mr. Connor?"

"Here, New York. Summer of 1987, I think."

"Can you be sure?"

"I think that's right."

"We're talking about the gentleman over there, at that table, Tom D'Arcy. Is that correct?"

D'Arcy's eyes went so murky he didn't see if Connor looked at him or not.

"And did there come a day when you became more than friends?"

"We were all at a big party," Connor said wearily. "Tommy and Johnny had a fight. Yelling, screaming. Johnny stamped his foot, walked out, took some people with him. Tommy and I were almost alone. Soon we were alone. I said he was right to tell Johnny off. I meant it. I always liked him, and I wasn't wild about Johnny."

"And your relationship progressed from that point?"

"You could say that. Half an hour later we were in our host's bed."

"And you continued to see each other?"

"Whenever Tommy could get away. Johnny kept a tight hold on him."

Jesus Christ, D'Arcy thought. John never held on to me. More the other way. And we never fought, let alone at a party. People know that, they'll back me up. It's a lie, a lie. And besides, nobody ever called me Tommy, I wouldn't allow it from the time I was five years old.

He must have started to stand up, because Pressman's hand was on his arm, pushing him down.

"You are ill, Mr. Connor," Wickham was saying.

"I have leukemia," he heard.

"Leukemia? And something else?"

"I have an acquired immune deficiency," Connor said.

"Commonly known as AIDS?"

"Commonly known as AIDS."

"I'm so sorry, Mr. Connor. I know this is terribly hard for you. Thank you for coming so far to give testimony. You're a brave man. No further questions, Judge. And by the way, you'll agree that I've been very brief. In fairness perhaps you'd limit Mr. Pressman's cross-examination as well."

Silence.

D'Arcy looked up.

Judge Ford was no longer pale. She was flushed, eyes glittering, hands clenched.

"In fairness perhaps you'd allow me to run my own court-room, Mr. Wickham. Everyone has opinions about the way I should run this case, the press, the protestors, you. But I'm running it. I'm the judge. Mr. Pressman, your witness. Please take just as long as you need."

She is furious, D'Arcy thought. He got her furious. Wickham's done it, made her look angry. Now Pressman will come off looking like a bully whatever he asks.

"This witness was sprung on me, Judge, as you know," Pressman said. "Just before lunch. The desperate state of the witness seems to have been sprung on us as well, you included. I haven't had time to consult with my client, so I ask, for once, for a recess. No big deal. Ten minutes with my client, somewhere private."

Ten minutes? Pressman was no fool. He could grandstand, too.

Don't get excited, D'Arcy told himself. Or worse, cocky. This could be the most important ten minutes you'll ever spend.

Pressman motioned him up, out. An officer unlocked some small meeting room out in the hall, left them.

Pressman slammed the door, turned on him. "Talk," he said.

"It's still what I told you. I don't know him at all. Maybe he's danced with me somewhere. But bed? Never. I swear, Murray."

"You're sure?"

"Never. Not a friend. No love, no nothing."

That's a song, he thought, feeling silly. Some old song goes like that. Am I losing my mind?

It seemed no time at all till they were back in the courtroom, Pressman leaving his side.

Kip Connor should die, D'Arcy thought. A knife should fly in, pierce his groin, kill him dead. I'd like to kill him, anyway cut his feet off. Never mind, God is killing him right now. Dancer. Who ever heard of Kip Connor?

Pressman was talking. The caressing quality of his voice amazed D'Arcy. He hadn't realized the man could speak like that.

"Mr. Connor. You know why we're here, do you?"

"Yes, of course."

"Of course. Perhaps you'd just put it into words for us."

"I'm here to tell the truth," Mr. Connor said.

"Exactly. And you do know what you're telling the truth about, what the case is about?"

"Yes, Mr. Wickham told me."

"When was that, Mr. Connor? When did you meet him?"

"He came to the hospital."

"I see. What made him do that?"

"I wrote."

"Ah, of course. You wrote to Mr. Wickham. What did you say to get a busy attorney to come see you?"

"I wrote what's true. That I was Mr. D'Arcy's friend. That I knew things about him other people don't."

"You mean those things you said just now? Well now, Mr. Connor, some people know those things. Your host at the party. The guests there. People who could have seen you with Mr. D'Arcy that whole, long summer."

"I don't know about that."

"Do you know if Mr. Wickham found anyone else, any of those people, to back up your testimony?"

"I didn't ask."

"That's all right, I'll ask, you can count on it. Anyway, you wrote to Mr. Wickham, he came to see you in that hospital, and you told him your story. Why did you do that, Mr. Connor?"

"Listen, if you think I have anything to gain from this, you're talking to a dying man. They don't give me six months."

"I didn't bring up gain, Mr. Connor. But now that you did, have you gained anything?"

"There's nothing I could gain."

"Of course, because you've got six months. Are you telling the court then that there was no consideration, no payment from Mr. Wickham for your speaking out?"

"Expenses," Mr. Connor said. "He paid my expenses. Getting here, and that."

"Of course, your expenses. Tell me, Mr. Connor. The young man who pushed your chair in just now. Is he a friend?"

"An attendant."

"An attendant. What's his name?"

"I don't see," Mr. Connor said.

"Just tell us," Pressman said gently.

"Joel White."

"You have only a few months left, Mr. Connor. So I imagine you've done the prudent thing, written a will, is that so?"

"Yes."

"Tell us. Who benefits from your will?"

Silence.

"Mr. Connor?"

"Mr. White will get what little I have left. It's an expensive illness, months with home care, a nurse. Months at the hospital, drugs."

"I appreciate that. But Mr. White gets whatever you have left, you said. And did Mr. Wickham agree to increase that sum, what you'll have left?"

"He paid my expenses. Our expenses."

"For both of you. You and Mr. White. I see. Now, Mr. Connor, you're a dancer. Like Mr. D'Arcy. Were you as good? As well known?"

"I was as good. Maybe not as well known."

"There's some injustice, is there? You performed as well. But you didn't get the recognition, the world fame, Mr. D'Arcy enjoyed?"

"No."

Bravo, D'Arcy thought. Keep going, Murray.

"I know you're tired. There's just one more thing I'd like to take up, Mr. Connor. And don't misunderstand, I'm bound to ask, really. Your relationship with Mr. D'Arcy after you met at this party whenever that was, wherever it was. Was this your first relationship? Was he the first man you loved?"

"No."

"Not the first. And, since we know about Mr. White, not the last. Were there some other lovers, Mr. Connor?"

"A few."

"A few. Well now, Mr. Connor, we understand if you're not sure of your facts about Mr. D'Arcy. But we're talking now about your life. You must have some idea how many lovers you've had. Ballpark figure. You know what a ballpark figure is, don't you? When guys guess how many people came to the ballpark without getting an exact count? Give us one. About how many lovers in your thirty-seven years?"

"I don't really know."

"Estimate. Three lovers? Ten? Twenty-five?"

No answer.

"All right, Mr. Connor. We've learned a lot about you today. You'll be interested to hear my client says he doesn't know you, never set eyes on you that he remembers, never got near you in a bed. He'll repeat all that on oath, just as you're on oath, Mr. Connor, to tell the truth here. Anyway, no more questions. I wouldn't want to tire you. And I trust Mr. Wickham will show the same restraint in his redirect examination."

Oh, nice, Pax thought. I lost my temper, but you kept yours, Mr. Pressman. Four solid facts in no time. Connor was paid to testify. He needed the money he was paid for his new lover. He's jealous of the man he testified against. And he's had more lovers than he wants to admit. You also made it clear he's got opposition. D'Arcy will swear he doesn't know him. And you set Wickham up not to try a long rebuttal on redirect.

Leonard couldn't have done better.

But Caro Hansen was drawing Connor like a madwoman. And everyone in court was licking his lips.

Wickham may just have won this, she thought, her heart shrinking. He was out to shock me with an AIDS patient. I'm not shocked. AIDS doesn't shock anybody now, it just saddens them. But the one thing everybody knows is, people who have it have no future. I'm supposed to decide Caitlin's future. I can't give her to someone who's a potential AIDS victim, might not live to bring her up. Especially not with a healthy person wanting her.

Then, back of her mind, Pax somehow heard her father talking at dinner. "When in doubt," he loved saying, telling his stories of the courthouse, "call a recess. You can't be faulted for that. Always get off the bench and calm down."

"We'll take a recess, fifteen minutes," she said. And walked out through her door.

Pressman jerked his head at D'Arcy, walked out, too.

D'Arcy followed.

There was a man just outside. Waiting. Big, burly. In an obviously expensive but rumpled suit, a Phi Beta Kappa key twinkling at his middle.

Murray was pulling him into the little room they'd used before.

His partner, of course. The man he'd been supposed to hire in the first place, who couldn't run the case for some reason. Was it Kistel? Scholer? Murray had called his office at lunchtime. This man must have come to help.

Murray was slamming the door shut.

The sound was loud, too loud.

It seemed to jog something loose in his brain.

D'Arcy, suddenly devastated, clutched one of the two chairs.

"Murray," he said, "listen. This is terrible."

"You've got some lawyer," the man said, smiling. "I'm Leonard Scholer, Tom. Murray's partner. Unlike that liar on wheels in there, I can prove it. Murray said things were getting heavy. So I came down."

"Yes, but wait," D'Arcy said. "I do remember Connor. It just came back to me. It's a long time, lots longer than five years, but I remember him now."

Total silence.

As if someone had stuffed the whole room with cotton.

Then Pressman exploded.

"It's too fucking much. It's too fucking late. You remember him? Now?"

He seemed to be blowing up, up, like one of the balloons in the big Thanksgiving Day parade.

"You had to tell me. When I've just said in court you don't know him. If I let you change your story now, you look like an idiot, a sickie, certainly unfit to take on a child. If you don't change, I have to resign. I can't know my client's lying. It's unethical. It's shit. I could get disbarred."

Now Scholer was close, his hand on Murray's shoulder.

After a moment Murray seemed to pop, fizzle down to his usual size.

"Look, Tom," Scholer said, his voice easy, relaxed. "Think. Take your time and think. Your gut reaction was you never saw him. How many dancers have you known? In your life? Isn't it hard to be sure when one more turns up?"

D'Arcy swallowed.

"You're not a child, Tom. Do you remember how many people you've befriended? Every one? Their faces?"

Well, of course not, D'Arcy thought. What's he driving at?

"Couldn't a number of people claim they'd slept with you? Happens all the time with celebrities like you. You said Connor's name meant nothing. Face, voice, nothing. You're under a strain, your mind plays tricks, maybe you want to be nice to a dying man. But listen. For one thing, he's got an ordinary, forgettable face. For another, he's got AIDS. That changes faces. He's lost weight, his head wobbles. Do you know how far gone you are when you can't hold your head up? You learn that long before you can walk, say three, four months. When that goes, you go. Say he's even trying to tell the truth, maybe he still doesn't remember right. So how can you possibly be certain?"

D'Arcy's thoughts cycloned in his head.

Could he be certain? Everything Scholer said was true. He knew plenty of men who'd died of this plague, Alvin Ailey, Nureyev. There were many, many patches on the AIDS quilt that felt stitched into his own heart. What was he certain about in this world? His name. His feeling for Caitlin. Nothing else, not another thing.

"You know," Scholer was saying, reasonably, inexorably, "identification isn't fact. In the law it's opinion, something you think. This man's dying. He's saying why me, he'd like pulling someone down with him. He lies there reading about your case, thinks what lousy breaks he got with his dancing, what great ones you had, even before Johnny California. He wants one last chance for a blast of publicity, leave his friend some press clippings along with the money. He obviously doesn't have many clippings of his own."

He stopped, took a long breath.

"Now listen, Tom. Justice is a funny thing. When I was a kid, I was a camp counselor, fifty bucks for the summer. End of the summer, the owner stiffs me, no check. I go to college, law school, eight, nine years later I get my license. And first thing I do, I sue that owner for the fifty plus interest plus damages. Then he turns up, offers me the fifty. I tell him not a chance. That's not revenge, Tom. That's justice. Now, look. The lover part is a lie, right? You didn't often run out on Johnny California, did you? Especially for a zero like Kip Connor?"

That D'Arcy was sure about.

"No. Why would I? I loved John. He was the most incredible thing that ever happened to me, the most creative, fascinating, giving person anyone could love. I never got over that he loved me. I wouldn't ever have risked losing him, not for anyone."

"Well, then. Connor lied about one thing, why wouldn't he lie about another? That was how the defense made Furhman so big in the Simpson case, hinting that if he lied about using racial slurs, he'd lie about planting evidence. You don't want confusion, Tom, the need for rehabilitation after your testimony, not if Murray's going to win this case. Which he is. Help you keep Caitlin. Which you will."

I can't stand this, D'Arcy thought.

Into his head came a memory from a time when he was teaching little boys. A father had walked in and yanked his son away from the barre. "I don't want him dancing," he'd explained. "I don't want him being less than a man."

But these people were on his side. They were the best in the business, Buddy Barr said so. And maybe they were right, maybe memory did play tricks.

"The lover part is a lie," he heard himself say. "Maybe the rest is, too. John hated liars. Maybe I'm so angry I can't remember what I remember."

"Fucking A," Pressman said.

"Never mind," Scholer added. "This won't last forever, you know. Murray, she said fifteen minutes."

They were opening the door, guiding him through it, back to the courtroom.

Scholer lagged behind, remained in the doorway.

On the bench, Pax looked up to check the clock and felt a shiver of excitement shake her whole body.

Was she imagining things?

But it was, it *was* Leonard. Really and truly. At the side of the courtroom near the doorway. She only just managed to stop herself from smiling at him. He looked wonderful. Especially after that desperately sick man, big, strong, wonderful.

She must have dropped her eyes. Because when she looked again, the doorway was empty and Leonard had disappeared. Had she dreamed him up?

Be sensible, she told herself. He zipped downtown to help D'Arcy, Pressman. They must have had shock waves in that office. He couldn't come up to me, talk, even wave. We can't appear to be connected in any way at all.

I could recess again. Send Sean to find him. Tell him I miss, need, want him.

Terrible knowing he was so close!

Pax remembered where she was, who she was. And that Leonard was probably just as disconnected from her as he'd been before the night at Bernadin. The night in bed.

She swallowed, straightened her back.

And called on Wickham.

D'Arcy was in his chair, dizzy, almost ill.

Something dreadful was happening in his brain. He was remembering, reliving it, darkness, a party. Twenty, thirty men, smoke, clinking glasses, laughing. And a voice somewhere in a corner cutting through, a thin, whiny voice.

Kip Connor's voice.

D'Arcy could even remember almost exactly what the voice had said. Because it had disgusted him then, disgusted him now.

"Women! They're made all wrong. Soft where you want hard. Slick where you want rough, round where they should be flat. I wouldn't fuck a woman again if they'd star me in the Kirov."

Connor's voice. He knew it. He had no doubt at all.

But—just a voice. Not a face. Not a handshake. Certainly not anything more intimate, as Connor claimed.

All right, he was starting a performance. A tricky performance. He had to manage it, had to. Could he? It wouldn't take sinews, muscles. It would take words. He'd never been good at words.

"Now, Mr. D'Arcy," Wickham was saying, "you're acquainted with Kip Connor?"

"No," D'Arcy said.

"What? You've never met?"

"No."

"Frankly, I'm surprised. You heard Mr. Connor's testimony. It was quite explicit. Are you denying his claim to know you?"

D'Arcy caught a glimpse of Pressman, sweating now, wiping his face with a large handkerchief.

"Yes, I'm denying it," he said.

In the back of his mind D'Arcy began praying, asking for luck, just a touch of luck. It would be all he'd need.

"Mr. D'Arcy, you heard the testimony. Are you calling Mr. Connor a liar?"

"Objection!"

Pressman was on his feet, shouting.

And Judge Ford's hand was in the air.

"Sustained," she said.

"One moment, Judge. I'm simply asking—"

"Mr. Wickham," the judge said calmly, "the witness is not called upon to characterize the testimony of another witness. Go on, please."

"Mr. D'Arcy, you've never set eyes on Mr. Connor before today?"

"No, I haven't," D'Arcy returned.

Don't ask, he was praying frantically, don't for God's sweet sake ask if I've ever heard him speak, heard his voice, don't do it!

"If you're not calling him a liar, are you then suggesting his testimony was a lie?"

The judge's hand was up again.

"We are not going through the thesaurus on lying here. I've ruled. Proceed to something new."

"Lie is too good a word," D'Arcy found himself saying, on his feet. "I've never seen him before, I've never been his friend, I've never slept with him, Mr. Wickham."

"Strike that," Judge Ford said, leaning forward. "Mr. D'Arcy, you're here to answer questions, and that's all. Remember, please."

But when he looked up, she was smiling at him. Smiling!

A touch of luck! D'Arcy felt his heart flex, leap, soar, beyond the height of any theater, far up into blue sky.

13

PAX

PAX DRESSED QUICKLY, PALE GRAY SILK, HER GRANDMOTHER'S gray pearls, extravagant splashes of Cuir de Russie, her favorite fragrance.

At last, a happy event, a party!

Like taking a recess from real life, she thought, stepping on the closet stool to reach a silver scarf. Willie's birthday, the Cosmopolitan Club, soft-spoken, well-dressed people, a world away from the ugly things she'd been living through lately. And Leonard at last, even if only for a family dinner.

She put out the lights, watched the bones of the garden, hedges, pine trees, brick wall, loom up in shadow outside her windows.

My garden, she thought. My kingdom, my feast, my peace. Hurry, spring!

Fifteen minutes later, she was walking up the beautiful stairs to the Cosmopolitan Club's serene lounge.

Now she was in a blur of chintz couches in pretty pastels, Chinese vases bristling with dried flowers, beautiful, worn Oriental rugs, elegant people with modulated voices. The warm air was filled with the scent of burning logs, discreet colognes, potpourri. Here, at least, nobody was crowding her, looking up at her for rulings, shouting at her for comments. Nobody was handing her obscenity in a package, making obscene suggestions that she favor one party in a case.

Pausing in the doorway, she saw her family sitting by the fire over drinks, Will, Debo, Leonard.

Leonard! He looked wonderful, huge. He looked so solid, so safe! Pax's hand flew to smooth her hair, then to cool her flushed cheek. He'd promised to come, Debo had said so. Still, Pax hadn't been sure. He'd carefully avoided her in court, missed a brunch or two at Will's. She hadn't realized how tense she was till she actually saw him, relaxed, dwarfing the dainty chintz chair by the fireside.

Debo saw her first. Her dark eyes widened, her smooth, narrow face crinkled with relief. Debo didn't just dress, she became someone new every time she changed her clothes, a gypsy, a preppy, a cowgirl. Tonight she seemed to be a Russian folk dancer in dark pants, a smocklike top caught at the hip with a silver belt. Trust Debo to ignore the unspoken rule about skirts after dark in the club's formal dining room.

"Pax!" she said. "We were worried. You're so late!"

Debo was young, spoiled, Leonard's darling daughter. And mine now, Pax reminded herself. She makes Will happy, and so she should be making me happy, too.

Leonard and Will were on their feet.

"Of course she's late, Debo," Leonard was saying, smiling. "You too busy to read the newspapers? We're lucky she's here at all."

Will was kissing her, enveloping her in his nice soap-and-tweed smell, gathering her next to him on the sofa with Debo, who turned, gave her a kiss, too.

Debo smelled of lavender. We should trade, Pax thought. Cuir de Russie for the folk dancer. Lavender for a little old lady judge. Whom Leonard wasn't even pretending to kiss hello.

Misery swept over Pax in full force as she sank into the flowery softness. She straightened up, glanced around the big living room.

Quietly dressed matrons, substantial men, a few subdued children. With the Cos Club's polished chairs, carved tables, murky oil paintings, they could all have been in some drawing room, London, Surrey, Kent.

Better if I were in England, she thought, thousands of miles away.

No. It was Will's twenty-fourth birthday. And she'd never been apart from him on any one of the twenty-four.

"Of *course* I read the papers," Debo was saying. "I wish you were on television, though. Like Judge Ito. Then everyone would know you were busy. Though there's plenty about you anyway. On *Oprah* today they did a number on the trial. Had an audience vote. Everybody was dead against gay adoption."

"At least, we're not in California," Pax managed to say. "No cameras. Just artists."

Knowing her hands were trembling, she clasped them tightly in her lap. She was grateful when a black-uniformed maid stood in front of her, nodding when Pax said white wine, ice, and did anyone need another?

"How are you holding up?" Will said, patting her shoulder. "Today must have been fantastic in your courtroom. Outside it, too. On TV those reporters look ready to shake you for comments. That woman from Channel Five actually yanked your sleeve. I mean, everybody's losing it over your surprise witness."

"That's why we're having dinner here," Pax said. "The Cos Club, it's whatever's big in the London *Times*. And thank God for a little peace."

Now she found she could smile at Leonard.

He looked pleased, somehow more charged up than ever. As if he were likely to give her a small shock if she just touched his hand.

But Leonard always looked larger than life in this room. He made no bones about preferring his own clubs. The Friars was his favorite, teeming with show business people, sharp dressers, laughs, great food. When she'd first asked him here with the kids, he'd eaten in quick bites, still looked hungry. At the Friars Pax could never finish her steak or salmon, was always offered the rest, beautifully wrapped, to take home. Like Leonard, most Friars started poor, made money on their talent and brains. Few of them would ever waste food.

My God, a familiar voice, face. Lorna Green, with Lilyan Lewis in tow, plucking at her sleeve!

"Pax, dear," Lorna was saying. "Thank God they let you out of that courtroom once in a while! We're all glued to the news these days. In fact, Dick and I are over there with Lilyan and the Shermans, we were just talking about you. Join us for dinner, tell us all about the trial!"

So much for the polite, peaceful Cosmopolitan Club. Was there anywhere in New York, some religious retreat with vows of silence, where she could hide while the trial lasted?

Home, Pax thought. Better stay home, pull up the drawbridge.

She fobbed off Lorna and Lil with smiles, a mention of her son's birthday, the family she never got to see these days.

"Imagine asking you that," Debo said when Lorna had taken herself off. "But you can tell *us*, Pax. That sick witness. Is he for real? Do you believe him?"

They were all looking at her.

"Debo, darling," Pax made herself say, "he's dying. There are special laws, as two of you know, about dying declarations."

"Right," Will broke in. "From way back, in England, statements from dying people have counted more. The presumption is, why would you lie when you were about to meet your maker?"

The law student, Pax thought, feeling a touch of pride.

"Pax is no detective," Leonard said. "She can't know who's telling the truth. She works with evidence. Would anyone tell a lie like that for just money? Of course they would."

Inevitably, she and Leonard were talking about the case, shouldn't be.

Would anyone, she asked herself, collect turds, wrap them beautifully, spend time and money sending them through the mail? Someone just had. Would any litigant, feeling aggrieved, walk into a judge's apartment and ask her to slant the case? Someone just had.

Last year, Will's twenty-third birthday, he'd been engaged to Debo. Leonard had been joyous, all kisses, champagne, presents all around. He'd just gotten close to the Torcellos, been taken past the bodyguards to visit the old man at his infamous Dark Night social club. That night he'd talked excitedly about the endless gin game, the hero sandwiches, the shining cars with dark glass lined up outside.

Pax had felt happy, lucky. Loved.

Tonight he was acting as guarded as any of the Torcellos.

Leonard suddenly wanted to take her up in his arms, hold her, carry her out of this ridiculous, effete club to someplace warm, quiet, safe.

She looked so small! Whereas in court she'd seemed so vital, so absolutely in control of herself, of everyone else.

As if she used all her strength, heart, guts during the day, looked at night like a lost, overburdened little girl.

He realized he'd gathered himself up, shoulders tight, hands clasped.

What was the matter with him? He was behaving as if Rosa didn't exist. As if he'd checked his feeling for her in the stuffy downstairs coatroom.

He was on thin ice, wanting to touch Pax. But they were all on thin ice, talking about the trial. He knew a few things she didn't, too, would never know. Murray calling the office in a flaming rage over the surprise witness. Kistel hurling orders into the phone, telling the detective agency to check the man, names, dates. Their fee was safe, paid up front. But the next fee, and the next after that, could depend on what happened in the courtroom.

It could also depend on what happened *outside* the courtroom.

He relived his rush downtown this afternoon, pacing the little conference room outside waiting for Murray. With the door ajar. When the Bishops had come out into the hall, ready to have a war.

"I can't do this, Tal," Barbara Bishop had hissed. "I never dreamed it would be this, despicable people, terrible surprises."

"Get hold of yourself, Ba. For God's sake, we're spending fortunes to find people like him. Wickham's men were all over the country, Europe, too. It's how these cases are won."

"But, Tal. Caitlin was involved in that life. What did Johnny subject her to?"

Bishop had cleared his throat.

"You know more about that than I. You never told me you'd gone there, Ba. You never told Scotty, either."

"Oh, Tal. I simply came home, took a bath, a Librax, forgot the whole dreadful experience."

"You should have told me, Barbara. We might have done something earlier, put him in jail, ruined his reputation."

"No one could ruin his reputation. And he *was* in jail, a jail of drugs and craziness. That poor little wife. I hoped she'd help him over that affliction, that weakness. That day Johnny was wearing her robe! I think the poor thing wanted to die in that car crash."

Wearing her robe, Leonard had thought. That must have laid it on the line.

"Ba, you're not making sense. We began this. We can't just bow out. Connor's testimony helps us, however sordid. Scotty knows his stuff."

"But suppose we get Caitlin and something's wrong with her? Suppose she's sick, like that man?"

Ba Bishop had sounded like a true fruitcake. But why would she be a normal woman? Nobody ever had said her brother was normal.

Leonard had been almost ready to walk out and confront them both, tell them what to do next.

Get Wickham, now. Make him ask Pax for a conference, now. Move to give up your claim. You'll be out, fast. Pax won't have to decide the fucking case, ruin her judicial career. You'll even do a favor for my firm. We pull this off for D'Arcy, we'll look like legal magicians.

He couldn't stand the way Pax looked now, as if one more blow would send her fluttering to the threadbare rug this WASP club never repaired.

"Darling Will," Pax said. "It's not the night I'd pick for your birthday dinner. But I'm happy to be here, be with all of you."

Did Leonard hear? Did he know she meant him?

Not a sign.

She took a long sip of her wine. It tasted like perfume.

All right, it would help her behave as if things with him were normal, as if it hadn't been days and days since they'd talked.

The room would help, too. She'd come to the club as long as she could remember, dancing class as a little girl in organdie, her coming-out party in white and ribbons. The people tonight looked like guests at her parents' dinner table, the elderly Irish maids like their old Cathleen.

Remembering that, she sat straighter.

I'm at home here, she thought. I'm with my family. And I will not be unhappy because Leonard is being distant.

"Happy birthday, Willie," she said, meaning it, lifting her glass.

Through it she saw, not the man turned twenty-four, but the little boy he'd been, skinny, blond, grave, eyes too big for his face.

Suddenly she focused on him, realized he looked unusually tired, drawn. Nobody should look tired, drawn at twenty-four. Especially not her Will.

Pax forgot everything else, the trial, the witness with AIDS, Debo, even Leonard.

"Willie," she said, leaning closer, touching his cheek.

He was pale, thinner. By comparison to Leonard, big, so solid? No, he was. Why?

"It's a hell of a lot better birthday thanks to Leonard," Will said. "And your friend Judge Macario."

Judge Macario? Rosa? What did she have to do with Will's birthday?

"Now it can be told," Will said.

Spilling it all out like a law school case, the party, the arrest, the arraignment, Leonard's whirlwind enlistment of Judge Macario, who'd rescued Will, swept him off to her chambers, scolded, kissed him. And who he hadn't seen in ages, had forgotten was so smashing, so stunning.

Pax felt her brain whirl, her heart contract.

An arrest? Why hadn't he called her? Of course, he wanted to spare her. But Leonard? He could have told her. Damn it, he wasn't exactly a stranger, even if he'd been acting like one!

"Well!" Pax said to him, eyes narrowed, unsmiling. "Leonard, that was very good of you."

She took care to speak as if he were a stranger. And sent a quick blessing to Rosa, dearest, loyal Rosa, who obviously had wanted to spare her anguish.

"This trial's really taking it out of you," Debo said. "You've lost weight, Pax."

Pax wanted to glare at her, too. Would this girl ever call her Mom? Mother? Or was that reserved only for Sylvia Scholer?

"I think you look great," Will cut in. "Dad, doesn't Pax look great?"

Pax held her breath.

"Pax always looks great," Leonard said.

The words sounded so flat, so peremptory, even Debo noticed, looked confused.

"Judge Macario told me she could decide your trial in five minutes," Will said, trying to get to safer ground. "She said women should bring up kids, and that was that."

Not what the law says, Pax thought. And not sense, either, which is when you know the law is really right. Some mothers burn their kids with cigarettes, lock them in car trunks. Some fathers slave for them, move mountains for them. Rosa's talking about Esperanza, about her own background. Judges aren't supposed to do that. They're supposed to apply the law.

She must have fallen silent for too long, because Will was looking at her, then at Leonard.

"What is it with you two?" Will said. "Is it me? The shock of my stupidity? Is it the trial, Mom? More than the trial?"

Debo was breaking in. "Daddy was saying before you came, Pax, that you're really doing an excellent job."

Another silence.

"Well, we expect that," Leonard said, because now both Debo and Will were looking at him. "You and your mother come from a long line of excellent judges. God willing, you'll extend it."

Because she was sitting next to Will, Pax felt his body tense, his breath catch. Again, why? Will wasn't Alden. She knew when he was hiding something.

She realized, with a start, that people were drifting off to eat, that she'd ordered a festive dinner, a cake for Will, candles, his name on the frosting.

For God's sake, would this day last forever? Would she faint dead away, require the club doctor, the smelling salts he kept for tottering ladies?

They put down their drinks, moved to the dining room, a corner table, separate, quiet.

Leonard took the chair opposite, not next to her, where he might reach for her hand.

Suddenly Pax found herself trembling. Was it anger?

She shook her head no at the waitress bringing dainty menus, offering dainty rolls from a dainty basket.

To hell with him. If he put his firm ahead of her over this one tough trial, what would he do if she really needed him?

"Will is right," Debo said suddenly. "And I want to know, too, from either of you, Pax or Daddy. You two don't seem exactly on a wavelength right now."

Leonard was calmly breaking his roll in two, buttering the first half. "Well, who could be on Pax's wavelength right now? She's been living in the courthouse. Up to her neck in that trial."

"Maybe we'd all better talk," Debo said, biting her lip. "Birthday or not. Will and I aren't exactly on a wavelength either right now."

Ah, a family party, Pax thought. Where things really fall apart when you all sit down to dinner and look at one another. Where telling the horrible truth is supposed to be a virtue.

"Honestly, Debo," Will said, glaring the way Leonard had across her courtroom.

"No, tell them," Debo said, her eyes suddenly moist.

Before Pax could worry about why, Will was speaking.

"Mother, Leonard. I'm thinking about quitting law school."

Quitting law school? Columbia Law School, where people killed to get in? With his LSAT scores? His brains? Not to mention his great-grandfather, his grandfather, her? Why? For what?

"Why?" she said, pleased it was all she said.

"All right, since Debo's launched it. Maybe it's the right subject for a birthday dinner, at that."

He paused because the waitress was back again. Pax stared at her, picked up the pencil and pad at her place, dashed out an order for steak all around, waited edgily while everyone murmured about rare, medium.

"Thank you," the woman said, as if they'd given her a present. And was finally gone.

"Look, Mom. You're great. Dad was great, I loved him, I

always loved you both," Will said, looking away from her for just a moment, then straight at her again. "Nothing's wrong. Something is right. Deb isn't happy, obviously. That's because of you, Leonard. She wants me to be as great as she thinks you are. She wants me to be like you are. At least after I got busted, she started hearing me."

"I hear you," Debo said. "But I don't like what I'm hearing."

If she starts using her psychobabble, Pax thought, I will slap her. And then I'll slap Leonard for acting as if he only just met me.

Will frowned. "I think it's dumb to study law simply because everyone else in my family did. Because it's something to fall back on, a kind of higher education, all that stuff people say. It's too tough if you don't love it. I don't want to be a lawyer, Mother, or a judge."

"I see," Pax said.

Somehow she was back in the big lecture hall at Harvard, listening to Copley, aged, bald, wrinkled like a rhinoceros, terrifying, on torts. Next to her a boy, one of the radicals, George Allen, given to waving his hand and quoting from obscure books by underground lawyers, showing up the professor. Today, a scruffy paperbound book, a long polysyllabic quote. And Copley, so enraged he actually hobbled out from behind his podium, glaring down, saying, "That book, Mr. Allen, is a dream. And you, Mr. Allen, are a nightmare!"

Yes, tough. Unless you loved it.

She snapped to attention because Will was talking now as earnestly, fervently, as Allen.

"I want to try something, Mom. I've got a chance at a great job. J. Walter Thompson, with Harper Cummings and Paul Pitts, remember, from school? They're writing copy, having laughs, taking trips. Making money, Mom, not running up tuition bills. It's work, not just school. It's dealing with what's really happening, television, film, music. It's creative. And if I didn't study the law all night, maybe I could even do some writing of my own."

The waitress was there with their steaks, a silver platter of vegetables.

Pax hadn't had lunch. But the food could have been plastic for all she cared.

Will, after all, was a grown man, married. Alden had been creative, an architect. Children were the product of two parents, not just one. If he wanted advertising, all right.

The steak, small, slightly gristly, was soon replaced by salad, also dainty.

Maybe she should join the Friars. They had women members now, Liza Minelli, Jeanne Harrison, Joy Golden. There some big, expansive man like Leonard sitting at the next table would turn right around, say, kid, you crazy, quit law school for an ad agency where you'll worry all the time about getting fired, what are you, a schmuck?

Leonard must have been having the same thought.

"Will," Leonard said, frowning, "are you crazy? Quitting law school, Columbia Law School, to work in an ad agency? The law is in your bones."

"Leonard," Will said, "you're a great guy, and I really owe you for coming up all that way to the godforsaken Bronx and finding Judge Macario, springing me from a mess. But this one's my problem, okay? And thanks, Mom, for not having a fit. I do love you."

Pax put down her pristine fork.

"All right, *your* turn," she said. "I want to tell you some things. Important things. And I'll thank *you* for not having a fit, William."

She took a deep breath, sat straight.

"You should know that a man came up to me at your father's funeral," she said. "And told me he was your father's lover."

She watched their faces. Will's going blank. Leonard's creasing in a frown. Debo's eyes sharpening, the way they always did when she discussed anything to do with sex, clinically, relishing the formerly forbidden words.

Bother Debo.

"I didn't know whether to believe it or not to believe it," she said. "I wasn't thinking so straight right then. And it hasn't come up since. Until just now. Because it turns out I'm not the only one who heard that story."

She turned her head, looked at each of them. "I had an unexpected visitor at home. Talcott Bishop."

Leonard made an abrupt move, pushed back his chair, stood up suddenly. "What are you saying?" he demanded.

A few heads in the dining room turned, a waitress came to attention.

"Just what you heard. Please sit down, Leonard, Harriet Anthony's looking at us as if we were demented. Listen, Bishop would like to use his information to get me off the trial. To claim I'm biased. To make me look like a dishonest judge."

Leonard sat down, like a lawyer in a courtroom at the order of a judge. People nearby went politely back to their dinners.

Leonard, Pax implored silently, help me here. You can't do anything about Alden. You can't do anything about Bishop. But you can do something about my Will, sending his life off on a ridiculous tangent. Help me set an example, use my problem to solve his. Speak out.

But Leonard wasn't speaking at all. He was only glowering, subsiding into his chair. What was he thinking? He'd certainly come on full force with advice for her once. Why not now?

Well, Leonard was Leonard, Will was Will, hers no matter what.

"This isn't exactly how I meant your birthday party to be," she said. "But it's time you knew, especially if other people know. I hate secrets, anyway, I'm no good at them. There's right and there's wrong, Will. I've chosen, I've told Bishop to disappear. You choose. I won't waste time telling you not to be so dumb again about the company you keep, not to expect anyone to rescue you a second time."

God, how she wanted to put her arms on the table, her head on her arms, sleep.

"You love me, I love you," she went on, pushing herself. "So I won't watch you make irreversible errors without expressing myself. People love you, Will. Like Leonard, they tell you the truth."

Leonard winced.

Intent as she was, filled with turmoil as she felt, Pax noticed.

She also noticed Will's face setting into a stubborn, almost sullen look.

"They tell you until you listen," she went on, putting a chill in her voice.

Leonard felt as if Pax had thrown a dart at him, found a soft place in his heart for it to land.

Jesus, what she had on her head, Alden, that total prick Bishop, the trial, now Will.

If she thought he indulged Debo, she was right. He couldn't be tough with her, his only child. He adored every crazy outfit, idea, expression, she came up with. If she'd only forget the psychology and have a few fat babies, he'd be the happiest lawyer in town.

A son, of course, was different. Pax was strong, brave, she was right to take a stand with Will. She was a terrific woman, he'd been ready to love her, he didn't regret a moment, a present, a word, a move.

But Rosa was something else. She needed him, like Debo. And she offered so abundantly a kind of love he'd never had, a mix of amazing sex, buoyant pride, sheer masculine delight. Walking into a restaurant with Rosa made him feel as if he'd won the U.S. Open, was waving in victory to the crowd. Taking Rosa's firm breast in his hand, he felt like someone in a myth, able to change a statue into a girl, bursting to make love over and over like a very young man.

And Pax, brave, strong woman that she was, was talking like a judge, lecturing her son.

*   *   *

"Finish the year, Will. Five months or so the job can wait for you, or there'll be another. Get first-year law behind you, effectively enough so they'll take you back if you ever want to go. I know it's not what you want to hear from me. But it's what I want you to hear. I'd hate you having regrets. You're too young for regrets."

Will was still staring at her. Stunned by what she'd told him? Sorry he was stuck with a mother who said what she truly felt? Wondering God knew what about her driving Alden away?

"I'm pleased you told me about the funeral," he said finally. "It takes some thinking about, but I'm pleased you told me. But, Mom, whatever disappointment you felt for Dad, I'm me, I'm someone else."

"That's right," Debo broke in. "It's fascinating, Pax, you felt you wanted to tell Will that story tonight. At least, I think it's fascinating."

Pax knew her face must have darkened, because she watched Leonard quickly put a restraining hand on Debo's arm.

"I'll think about sticking a little longer," Will told her. "It would go down well with Debo, anyway."

"It certainly would," Debo said, smiling at Pax, yes, and reaching to pat her hand.

But Pax was looking at Leonard, wondering why he hadn't been more of a lawyer, more of a parent, more of a friend, why he was silent, staring at his plate the way Will had done.

Suddenly she was shivering, trembling so anyone could see.

Debo sat up in surprise. Will's eyes moved from his mother's face to her shaking hands.

Leonard was on his feet.

"Long ago stuff," he said. "You're not the first, you won't be the last. You're a brave woman, Pax. But I think you've had enough for one day, one night. Birthday or no birthday, there's court tomorrow morning. Kids, tell them to pack up the cake, the rest of the champagne, take it home, if they know how to do that here. I'm putting Pax in a cab."

They were all up now, fussing, kissing her good night, worrying aloud, apologizing for upsetting her.

Debo gave her the most fervent hug of her life.

Will gave her one of his many fervent hugs, told her to take it easy, not let the bastards get her.

In another moment Pax was walking down the stairs, Leonard holding her elbow politely. He waved off Edward, the doorman, helped her into the taxi himself, a model cavalier.

"Pax," he said, so her heart leaped up for an instant, "what did you tell Bishop?"

"To get lost," Pax said.

"You're a good mother. A good judge. You didn't need all that tonight. Give yourself some slack now, if you can, get some rest."

He paused.

"I hope you're not even thinking about going to the Women's Bar dinner tomorrow."

The Women's Bar dinner? Oh, yes, the letter, her place on the dais.

"No," she said.

She wasn't too exhausted to notice the relief on his face. Or to wonder why it was there.

A lot of whys. But no becauses at all.

A thought buzzed into her head like a flying insect, unnerving, dangerous. Rosa would be at the Women's Bar dinner. On the dais. Women judges always sat on the dais. Leonard would be there, too. Big law firms all took tables, filled them with associates, gave the best seats, the ones facing the dais, to partners like Leonard.

Could he want her out of the way when he saw Rosa again?

Don't invent things, she told herself. Rosa is your friend. Leonard was, for a minute, anyway, your lover. He might actually be again if you wanted him. Rosa is different from you, as different as two women could be. No one who ever loved you could love Rosa. No one who wanted her could have wanted you.

But Rosa was Rosa, beautiful, delectable. And thirty-five. What man would be immune to her? Especially a man with appetites?

Pax leaned back.

Enough, she decided.

She was Pax Peyton Ford.

"Good night, Leonard," she said, closing the door with a slam on her ex-lover, or whatever he was going to turn out to be.

14

LEONARD

By ten o'clock the courtroom seemed strangely quiet, the speakers' voices far away.

As Pressman droned on, Pax longed to call a recess. She knew of judges who got bored, some who even napped on the bench. Impossible in this trial, she'd thought.

But now, struggling to focus on Pressman's redirect examination of D'Arcy, she wasn't so sure. She'd tossed much of the night after the dinner party, risen early to tell the phone operator who screened her calls to take Leonard's name off the list of approved callers. He might never know. But she would know, feel better having taken action.

Only she didn't feel better. Just exhausted, especially after keeping alert through so many noisy exchanges.

Pressman was making D'Arcy repeat, in varying ways, that Kip Connor's testimony was false.

Useless, of course. If the faintest shadow of AIDS touched Tom D'Arcy, she must, must give Caitlin to the Bishops. A more pragmatic judge, like Rosa, might have decided to do that right from the start.

Dear Lord, now Pressman was declaiming. Tense, sharp, bullying. He was so different from Leonard, whose way was to speak gently, colloquially, make a jury love him, and then pounce.

"So you utterly and absolutely deny—"

A sound interrupted him, a sound she knew well from movies, television, a thud, an explosion: a gunshot.

Followed by another with precisely the same terrifying echo.

Pax stared, saw everyone in the courtroom freeze, then burst into frantic motion, some up, some running, some ducking to the floor.

And a man standing, pointing a gun, a gun, straight at her, shouting something in a language straight from hell.

Somehow she wasn't terror-stricken, because he seemed unreal, something from all those movies and TV shows. But a moment later, with screams and shouts assaulting her, she felt fear slice into her heart.

Not a cream puff, not this time. Pictures seemed to flash before her eyes, police sirens rang in her ears.

Los Angeles, Angela Davis poised in a courtroom to shoot a judge.

Arkansas, a tall, gray federal judge sprawled dead on the bench.

Texas, a man with a big shotgun in a small courtroom blasting his ex-wife after the judge gave her custody of their child.

New York had been lucky.

Now, in spite of the new metal detectors downstairs, the luck had vanished. She was unable to move, unable to think, silently, stupidly watching still another man aim still another gun.

Just below her, someone was moving. One of her court officers.

Sean.

He was slowly folding in two, arms across his middle, staying bent double for an endless, terrible moment.

Pax moved, faster than she'd thought she could move, found herself on her feet.

Somehow she felt tall, armored, invulnerable. And angry.
As if all the disappointment and turmoil of these past days
was boiling up in her veins, stirring her to action.

Leonard's defection. Will's folly. Rosa's mystery. A box of
turds. Bishop's treachery.

Who dared challenge her authority here? Who the hell
dared to fire a gun in her courtroom?

Sean remained still.

But everyone else in the courtroom seemed to be
exploding into complete chaos.

Halfway back in the crowd Will was up, burning to get to
his mother.

He wasn't sure if he was shouting or simply thinking the
words, Mom, Mother, down, get down.

He shoved some man aside, pushed, rammed. But the
noise was shattering, movement impossible, everyone heading at him, blocking his way. Hands pushed him back, frightened faces came at him.

She's going to die, he thought, his breath coming fast, his
heart congealing. She'll be as dead as Dad.

He put his head down, butted like a football player
through the sweating, scrambling people to get between his
mother and that gun.

Next to the witness chair D'Arcy was up too, knees flexed,
arms out.

The officer lay almost at his feet, crumpled, motionless.

The judge stood high over him, a black target for more
horror.

But of course he knew precisely what to do.

He'd done it so many times, saved so many fragile prima
ballerinas from so many wicked sorcerers with drawn bows
and pointed arrows, sweeping them to the safety of the wings.

He took position, leaped, soared, landed lightly in front
of the bench, reached up for her small, cold hand.

*   *   *

Ba shrank into her chair, feeling the first sharp migraine pain strike her temples.

I can't stand this, she thought. I won't endure this. That Ford woman can't keep order for ten minutes at a time.

She felt herself jerked to her feet, pulled, dragged. Tal. Holding her hand, wrenching her arm. How long since he held her hand, clutched it with his own palm sweating?

Pain flashed behind her eyes, pounded at her forehead. But the side door, their door, was just ahead.

Oh, God, now she was tripping, would fall! No, Tal had her fast, bless him.

Her fault, really. She'd brought them both into this terrible place. Idiotic. Because what could be worth this disorder, this racket?

Head throbbing, heart swelling, she decided it: she would never come back into this courtroom again, not for Caitlin, not for anything.

Mike O'Hare stood, arms wide, next to that dancer, between his judge and the gunman.

Little guy, shabby suit, gray hair, somehow familiar, someone who belonged here, who? He stopped staring, stopped thinking, as more officers came bursting through the doors, tackling the small man, wrestling him down.

As if released, he bent down to look at his partner, crumpled on the floor.

Holy Mother! Sean had only one eye, wide, staring. Where the other should be, blood bubbling, a mess, a nightmare.

Dead, dead as a doornail, whatever the hell a doornail was.

Could have been you, a voice in his head told him. That eye could have been your eye, those bright red gurgles of blood, yours.

Could have been the judge's, too, the judge he was sworn

to protect. Sean had been sworn, too. He'd done it, protected her.

Who would protect Mary Catherine, Sean's children?

As if that need could bring Sean back, he clutched the body, trying to shake some life into the man he'd worked with for such a long, long time.

Mrs. Busybody from next door was banging the screen door, pushing herself into Mary Catherine's kitchen, screaming, beyond speech.

Poor woman, Mary Catherine thought, putting down the feeding spoon, sliding the cereal dish out of the baby's reach. Another fight with that son? Drunk again, eleven-thirty in the morning?

"Your husband," Mrs. Busybody said.

Mary Catherine smiled, pushed her toward a chair, went for the tea kettle.

"No, listen, Mary Catherine, listen! It's your husband, in court."

She turned, stared at her elderly neighbor, face contorted, tears on her withered cheek.

Right off, Mary Catherine understood, saw the whole scene, Sean on a bench in the courtroom bleeding, saw it clear as if she were there cradling his head, holding him.

"Turn on the television, Mary Catherine. They stopped *The Price Is Right*, they're saying it now. An officer shot dead, a bullet meant for the judge. Someone who worked in the courthouse did it, someone who knew how to get around the guards, the security."

Mary Catherine scarcely heard her.

She was checking the clock, thinking that Pat was late from school for his lunch, that the one black dress she owned would need hemming up, that the older boys wouldn't be home till after three, that her head was hurting terribly, a nuisance with all she'd have to be doing.

"Are you listening, Mary Catherine?"

Through sickening pain Mary Catherine watched the baby reach for the feeding spoon, plunge it into the cereal, bring it straight up to her rosy mouth.

Wait till I tell Sean, she thought.

And felt the pain strike her to her knees.

Joe Iapalucci stood tall as he knew how at his desk, watching reporters pummel into his chambers, pressing past his secretary, sitting on the window seats, juggling their cameras.

Even his big office felt small, a crowd like this. A noisy crowd, everyone yelling at him. Statement, they were shouting, tell us about Stephen Haras, how do you spell it, what languages did he interpret, how'd he get past the metal detectors, what do you say, Judge!

He raised his arms high, stared them down.

Jesus H. Christ, he'd known from the start that fucking trial would blow up in someone's face, inevitably his face. He should have put a man on it. Woman judge, any nutcase decided he'd march in, start shooting.

No, not fair. Pax was as good as any of them, ran a tight ship. She couldn't be blamed for this, nor could he. It was the court system, the violence everyone learned from the media. And the failure of the administration to back him up with decent security, as he'd said time and again. He'd show these reporters, wave faxes of the requests he'd sent in for extra help, all tabled for budget reasons.

And then, like any smart judge, he'd take a recess and buy time. Suspend the trial temporarily till things settled down.

"All right, boys," he said. "And ladies. Calm down! Listen up!"

Caro sat slumped in the emptying courtroom, sketchpad on her lap, pencils in her left hand.

Some court artist she was! The most vital moment of her whole career and she'd muffed it. Sat motionless, staring, taking everything in, giving nothing back. When she was there to record events. Certainly an event as nifty as a court officer shot dead almost at her feet.

He didn't look like a court officer now.

He looked like a body. Inert, limp. Dead.

Judge Ford had been something else, getting straight up on her feet, trying to quell a storm.

While she'd sat still. Dumbstruck by the shouting, Polish probably, something Slavic, anyway. Missing the best sketch that would ever come her way.

Caro stretched, broke the spell she was under.

I'm lucky, she thought. I didn't get shot. I behaved myself, too, I didn't scream, stampede.

She began putting her stuff into her tote bag.

Anyway, she told herself, I can reconstruct it. Except for the judge, I had the best seat in the house. I saw it, everything.

And what she'd seen she could draw!

In the office of the district attorney, Morganthau's boys were making the calls.

To the mayor's office, sending a red alert as the press swarmed in for answers.

To the chief of police's command, send more troops, fortify the Supreme Court building from this minute on.

To the criminal justice coordinator in Albany, reports, notes thrust at sweating pages to put in the governor's hand whatever the hell meeting he was in.

The police had it all by now. Some court interpreter with a thing for the woman judge, like Hinckley's for Jodie Foster. A letter found on his desk, how her violet eyes shouldn't have to look at a hellish abomination like D'Arcy.

After all, New York. Where people snapped, shot up commuter trains, old ladies in parks, schoolyards. Needing harsher gun controls, less television violence. Because the best public servants in the world couldn't know when a man would lose it, gun people down.

*   *   *

Leonard sprang wide awake.

Next to him Rosa slept, curled like a child, beautiful as the day.

He reached for the bedside lamp, realized he didn't need it. His little bedroom was as full of light as it ever got.

Some night, he thought.

Shutting a door, even a cab door, on one woman, rushing to meet another.

Rosa's skin was incredible, tan, warm, smooth as the satins and silks he'd made her try on. Rosa's breasts were firm, her dark nipples made for his mouth. The burst of hair between her slim, smooth thighs was lush, springy. He could simply touch her and be eighteen again.

Rosa moved, jerked, threw her arms over her face. As if she were warding off a blow.

That's exactly it, he thought, head starting to ache. Who knows where Rosa goes when she dreams? How would I ever follow?

She was out of his orbit, his understanding, a girl who'd maybe been beaten by a father, a brother, yes, and maybe a lover, some man who'd taught her all too well what to do to rouse a man's body. For him she was all wrong.

And he was all wrong. Rosa was Pax's friend. So he was a shit.

Real pain throbbed in his head as he bent for the crumpled shirt on the floor, padded out with it to the living room.

Holy Christ, the kitchen clock said nearly noon.

He'd better get to the office. God only knew what he'd skipped this morning.

Leonard went into his small bathroom hoping there'd be soap, towels. Yes. His Evelyn came up from the office every so often to check on the maid she'd hired. If she noticed he hadn't slept there, she never said. Who knew more about discretion than a secretary who was used to stonewalling his clients about where he was? Who knew more about devotion than a woman

who ran out to buy him a shoelace, an aspirin, before he knew
he needed them, tucked an extra handkerchief in his pocket?

He got into the narrow shower.

One touch of wet soap on his body and he felt the smooth
touch of Rosa's fingertips coaxing him into power.

You, he said to himself, are out of your depth.

He wrenched the faucets shut, feeling shaken, off course.

What had he started here? He'd told Jon, big speech, how
he felt about Pax. Meant it. And here he was, like any straying
husband, lusting for Rosa, comparing her to Pax, thinking
about Pax.

Debo told him once something she'd learned in psych
class, why men left trails when they philandered, notes,
phone numbers for their wives to find. "They can't really love
two women at once," she'd said. "So they leave clues, let one
woman make a scene, force a choice."

Twenty years between them. What would Debo say about
Rosa? Or Will? Or anyone else? Not that he cared what
anyone said. Still, if Kistel had wondered how he came to Pax
Ford, what would he wonder about Rosa Macario?

What was wrong with him? How could he think about Pax
with Rosa still in his bed?

When he was with Pax he didn't think about Rosa.

So why, with Rosa, did he keep thinking about Pax?

Leonard found a plastic razor, shaving cream. Stared at
himself in the little mirror.

He looked fifty-nine, easy. Lines, deep ones, in his forehead. Pouches, puffy ones, under his eyes. And his hair, of
course, solid gray now, no longer even pepper-and-salt.

He began shaving, the familiar motions steadying him.

Finished, he moved to the tiny kitchen, found instant
coffee, powdered cream, sugar, saucepan, spoons, mugs.
Again, courtesy of Evelyn.

Now he heard footsteps in the bedroom. And the radio
clicking on, bursts of noise as Rosa switched stations, found a
band blaring Latin music.

"Leonard?" she called to him. "Is this ethnic enough for you?"

Rosa, in the doorway.

Naked, rosy, beautiful.

He considered fleeing back into the kitchenette. He considered grabbing her, rolling on the carpet, taking her right here.

He considered spending the rest of his life looking at a sight as beautiful as Rosa's breasts in the morning.

"Want some coffee?" he said, forcing himself to turn away from the incredible sight of her.

On the radio someone rattled out hard-edged Spanish. He couldn't understand it, except once or twice, Nueva York. Well, a quarter of Nueva York spoke only Spanish now. And got along in life just fine.

He realized Rosa wasn't in the kitchen with him, didn't seem to be making a move to join him, either.

He looked out.

And saw her standing stiff as a tree, rigid, silent.

"What, Rosa?" he said, surprised.

She raised a hand, palm out, for silence, suddenly the judge, imperious, quelling a crowd. Something on the radio? Something important?

Suddenly she was next to him, hands clenched beneath those gorgeous breasts, face like a stricken child's.

"Leonard," she said. "*Ay Dios,* Leonard, this morning, while we were sleeping."

She sounded like Debo as a child, terrified by a storm.

"Easy, sweetheart, tell me."

"Pax's courtroom," Rosa said. "A man, a *loco* in her courtroom, with a gun, Leonard."

He was turning cold, stinging dry-ice cold.

The floor was tilting. All his insides were draining away.

Leonard realized he was clutching Rosa's shoulders, shaking her.

Somehow he was there, in Pax's courtroom, remembering how she looked, a distant figure in black, a pale, lovely face.

"Where's your television?" Rosa said. "We'll find news, English. Pax wasn't hurt. But a court officer was killed, Leonard, with a bullet meant for her, for the *Señora Juez.*"

Now it was his turn to stand frozen.

No, Pax was all right, Rosa had said so.

But a court officer? Pax had a real affinity for her officers; they'd been with her a long time, adored her. Obviously, one of them had protected her when it counted. And at some cost.

And here I was, he thought, clouds of misery swirling around him. Protecting her from nothing.

Rosa was reaching for the damp towel he'd left on the floor, wrapping herself in it.

"No television here, I'm not around enough," he said, his voice sounding cracked, old. "Get it in English, 1010 WINS, some news station."

She was in the bedroom quickly, switching the dial again. He heard bursts of rock, rap, always maddening, the makings of total insanity now.

Naturally, everything but headline news. Traffic. Weather. Commercials.

You give us twenty-two minutes, Leonard thought, wild, furious. We give you fourteen minutes of shit.

Should he call Kistel? Pressman? Evelyn?

They'd waste time wanting to know where he was, where he'd been all morning. The Torcellos had probably sent dogs to sniff him out.

Finally, English, the top of the news.

Words poured over him.

Controversial trial in Manhattan's state supreme court ... another bizarre twist ... shortly after eleven this morning ... white male with a revolver ... obviously meant for Judge Ford ... a .38-caliber bullet through the eye of Officer Sean Thomas Hurley ... other officers overpowered ... the assailant dead ... panic ... administrative chief suspends trial indefinitely.

She's all right, Pax is all right, he thought. Even though I failed her, she's all right.

He felt an enormous wave of longing, desire to comfort her, hold her.

"Leonard," Rosa was saying. "Leonard!"

He stared at her, a skinny, naked girl in a towel, someone he didn't know.

"Leonard, *querido.* You look terrible," she said softly.

But of course I look terrible, he thought. Someone aimed a gun at Pax. I knew it would happen. Sean Somebody was there stopping the bullets. I was here fucking Rosa.

"We better go," he was able to say. "I've got to get to the office. You've got to get to court. We better go."

Oh, God, her eyes were filling with tears.

Immediately he felt sorry for her, guilty, ashamed, so sorry.

She knows, he thought. She's had the brains and guts to make herself a judge. She knows I'm wrong for her, wrong age, wrong background, wrong everything. I've let her think fairy tales. I've had my head in the cows, like Momma said.

Rosa couldn't keep her hands from shaking.

A judge, like herself, shot at? Not just any judge. Pax.

Bullets for Mami, for Pax. The bad guys were taking over, they were everywhere.

She looked at Leonard, hunched over, scowling, suddenly looking years older. Oh, God, was he remembering it was Pax he really loved?

But the dinner tonight! Her beautiful dress! That she'd chosen according to Leonard's words, ordered from the woman at Bergdorf's, closed out a savings account to pay for?

Rosa straightened up, began putting herself together properly.

Pax was always cool, strong in disaster. She could be, too. After all, nothing had really happened to her friend, Leonard's friend. Nothing had really changed. She'd make

Leonard come with her to the dinner. He'd promised. And Pax would never be there, not now.

She tackled the problem immediately.

"The Women's Bar, Leonard. Should we meet there? Drinks are at six-thirty, dinner at eight, Tavern on the Green."

She took note of his gray face, his lidded eyes.

He loves Pax, she thought, heart shriveling. He's ashamed, guilty because he was with me while that man was shooting at her.

No, he's just worried about her; he said so the day we met, she's finished with him. And I'm not taking him over, he's not a child to be given in custody to Pax, to me. He's a man, a strong, sexy man, we've made fantastic love together.

She looked into his eyes, smiled at him.

Leonard couldn't make himself smile back.

"I'll put you in a cab, Rosa. And I don't know about the dinner. My office must be crazy to get hold of me, I'll have to see."

He watched her face crumple, like a little girl's, her doll destroyed.

Christ, he'd led her on, admired and approved that dress, probably two months of her judge's salary.

If fuckups fucked up, he was becoming one, fucking up all over town.

He'd failed Pax.

Should he fail Rosa, too?

All right, he'd meet her at the damned dinner, take her in, that was all. She'd certainly sit on the dais with the other judges. He'd be at some table with Kistel, Pressman, a bunch of young associates, he could easily duck out. And he had the rest of his life to make it up to Pax.

"Six-thirty," he said. "At the restaurant. I may not stay the whole time, but I'll get you there."

Feeling like an automaton, he took her arm, took her

out. Downstairs, he waved at a cab, leaned over, gave her a little kiss.

When the cab moved off, he came alive, turned, ran for the elevator.

Key at the ready, he burst back into the apartment, grabbed the phone.

No answer in Pax's chambers.

Maybe too much commotion. Maybe she was already home. Of course, where else would you go when someone shot at you?

At her house the phone made peculiar sounds, clicked, buzzed.

"Who're you calling?" a voice said.

He remembered the phone was screened.

"Judge Ford," he said.

"Who is calling Judge Ford?"

"Leonard Scholer."

Wait. Click.

"Sorry," the voice said. "I am not able to put you through to Judge Ford."

"What are you talking about? Is she there?"

"I am not able to put you through."

"Listen, I'm a close friend, a relative. Check with her, I'll hold."

"I am not able to put you through."

Leonard saw red, the red of Rosa's scarlet dress.

"Stop saying that. Ask Judge Ford. If you want, I'll call back in three minutes, give you a chance to ask her."

"I am not able to take messages," he heard.

Jesus, she'd hung up.

Enraged, red filling his eyes now, he dialed again.

"Who're you calling?"

"It's Mr. Scholer again. Listen, it's extremely important for me to reach Judge Ford."

"Please hang up," the voice said. "We are able to trace your call. We will do so if you continue to tie up this line."

"What the fuck good is the line," Leonard shouted, "if nobody can get through?"

What was he doing? Arguing with a robot, a moron? Why, if this epsilon semi-moron operator had a list, wasn't he on it?

He tried again, couldn't help himself.

"Operator, this is urgent. Please check your list again, Scholer, s-c-h-o-l-e-r."

"I have checked. My instructions are that you are not to be put through."

Leonard felt his collar grow tight, damp. Suddenly he felt sympathy for the shooter in the courtroom. If he had a gun, had this woman in his sights, he'd easily pull the trigger.

He slammed down the phone, dialed Evelyn. And then hung up before she answered. What the hell, he'd get to the office, let her wrestle with the recalcitrant operator while he talked to his partners, gathered the shreds of this tattered trial together.

Maybe this was what he got for playing with Rosa.

He was more than old enough to know that flings today came with consequences. Never mind AIDS, any woman screaming sexual harassment could get a lawyer suspended while someone took months to check it out. Any ex-girlfriend, look at Wachtler, chief judge, the FBI all ready to jump in.

For a smart guy he'd been an idiot. Walked right through a series of events, not even coincidences, into one big mess. Will getting arrested. Rosa coming to the rescue. His pique, his loneliness and, yes, her beauty, pushing him at her, a lovely woman he could help, who needed him.

And his rage at Pax when she wouldn't take his precious advice, wouldn't let him help.

He looked around the ridiculous apartment.

Pax, he thought. We have to fix this. Whatever it takes. What we've got is too good. What you are is too valuable. I've been a fool. But I'll fix it. I'll do anything to fix it.

It seemed a first step to walk out the door, firmly closing the door of the apartment.

*   *   *

Pax clung to Will's arm all the way in the taxi, held tight as they finally reached home.

"I called Flora," he'd told her. "She's waiting, tea, all that. You stay there, Mom. I'm staying, too. Every reporter in town wants you right now. So you just stay put."

Darling Will. Whatever else, she had him.

But still somehow her little boy, so she had to be Mother, calm, brave, setting an example, something to remember when the time came when he needed calm, bravery.

With Leonard she could have let go, sobbed, carried on, been the mess she really was.

Sean. Gone in a split second.

He couldn't make up with anyone now, correct any error he'd made, repair any damage he'd done.

Life was so damned fragile, love was more so.

She couldn't let her life fragment, her love be lost in a moment, like Sean's.

Leonard, she thought. We have to fix this. Whatever it takes. What we've got is too good. What you are is too valuable. I've been an idiot. But I'll fix it. I'll do anything to fix it.

It seemed a first step to lean back against the greasy plastic of the taxicab and rest her head, close her heavy eyes.

15

PAX

Pax clung to the door handle as the cab driver shot lights, tilted at corners till her brain seemed tilted, too.

Maybe it *was* tilted. When she'd started dressing for the Women's Bar dinner, hell had burst loose. Will raging, how could she be so unfeeling, how would it look, her officer killed and a party! Even Flora fretting nervously, tears misting her huge brown eyes.

Of *course* she was sad, horror-stricken, Pax had said. But she was a judge. Guns in courtrooms were anarchy. Judges were meant to meet anarchy with law. She would *not* be afraid to do a judge's work, *not* be afraid to act like a judge. Hiding at home would be contemptible.

Besides, tonight's party was the first of the holiday gatherings of judges and lawyers, people she'd known for years. She had only to sit quietly on the dais while others made speeches, marked retirements, accepted awards. She had only to look calm and unruffled.

Calm and unruffled with Bishop there? And Leonard, who somehow didn't want her to go?

More reason than ever to go, remind them both she made her own rules.

The driver lurched to a stop at the restaurant in Central Park. She paid him, waited while he made change in slow motion, losing every second he'd gained by speeding.

From the cab window the Tavern on the Green looked like one of the glass snow scenes in D'Arcy's parlor. Tiny lights outlined every tree. Horse-drawn carriages with gaudy Christmas decorations waited at the entrance. A dusting of white lay on the courtyard. Why did the Women's Bar give parties here? This place was for tourists, prom couples, weddings.

Weddings.

Leonard.

Oh, God, tonight she had to stop thinking about him, about making up. Tonight she had to look as if she were still in good shape, on top of things.

And tomorrow, go to Sean's funeral, sit watching Mary Catherine weep, knowing she'd grieve not just now but every time she walked into her courtroom. Tomorrow she'd be listening to a priest but hearing the sounds of gunshots.

Pax took the change from the driver, dropped it into her bag, stepped out.

At least Rosa would be here for comfort. The women judges always sat on the dais, places of honor. Maybe they'd be seated together, maybe they could talk.

She squeezed into the crowded foyer. A thousand women taking off a thousand coats at the small checkroom, waving, calling to each other. Some in business suits, handing over briefcases. Most in festive clothes, the bright colors they couldn't wear in court, the beautiful fabrics they hid under judges' robes.

Pax had worn the first dark dress she'd touched in her closet, heavy silk, one line from shoulder to hem. Now she realized she might just as well have worn her robe. She *looked* as if she'd worn her robe.

She let herself drift with the crowd down the mirrored corridors, past the glitzy gift shop with its teddy bears and mugs, past the restaurant, all flowers and crystal chandeliers, to the enormous private room where cocktails were being served, gateway to the still more enormous room where the dinner would be.

She could hear the party noises from outside, saw from the doorway that the place was jammed.

Suddenly she felt overwhelmed. There was too much of everything, two bars, two buffet tables studded with hors d'oeuvres, a mass of people jostling for drinks and food, more in the background laughing, waving, calling to friends, pointing at the fantastic Christmas decorations, wreaths, mistletoe, pine swags, gold and silver baubles. She put a hand to her silky collar, pulled it. Already the air was heavy, filled with fragrances, perfumes, spicy foods, pine branches.

She'd been stupid to come.

No, she'd had to come. She couldn't fold under pressure, stay home with the vapors. Even after a shooting, a death, especially after, she had to act as if *Bishop* v. *D'Arcy* was just another trial.

A drink, Pax thought. I'll feel better with a drink in my hand.

She edged toward one of the bars, waited, finally could ask the sweating bartender for a scotch.

Mistake. The glass was sweating too, dripping onto her dress. Pax bent down, set it on the floor behind a scarlet poinsettia. Straightening, she saw herself in one of the many mirrors, small, insignificant, pale, even her hair looking dull, tarnished.

People kept murmuring hellos, moving by.

I'm the ghost at this feast, Pax thought. I'm embarrassing them. The shooting's been in every paper, on every news broadcast. It's like when I was first widowed, people looking embarrassed, dodging me, as if trouble were catching.

"She looks like a piece of shit," a woman said somewhere behind her. "Anyway, the Second Department's just declared homosexual adoption of partners illegal. So what's she fussing about?"

Pax turned, couldn't tell who'd spoken. What did the Second Department know? The child's best interests should count for something.

"Hello, Judge," another female voice said, softer, more pleasant.

Grateful for any connection to this party, Pax turned back. Caro Hansen, the little courtroom artist. Smiling, obviously eager to talk, she looked like a blessing.

Then, horrified, Pax realized the girl was holding a sketchpad, a pen.

"You won't mind?" Caro Hansen was saying. "I don't usually get this close to you, Judge."

Already she was drawing, looking at Pax, at the pad and back again. Somehow Pax was so surprised, so busy steadying herself for Caro, she found herself smiling back.

Caro had seen the judge come in, drink, hide her glass. And watched people moving around her, as if this one small woman were a rock in a river, diverting the natural flow.

What shits they are, she'd thought. Not Judge Ford's fault she got stuck with that impossible trial. Or that horrible things keep happening. Showing up here, she's a trouper, a real pro.

"You're great to come tonight," she said, looking down into the judge's eyes.

Gentian violet eyes, smudged with a touch of charcoal gray.

"Especially with everything happening," she went on, since the judge wasn't talking.

"Yes."

Great face, Caro thought. She'll never look ordinary, never really get lost in a crowd. Even when they're ignoring her they're all sneaking looks.

She turned, rudely asked someone who was moving on anyway to keep moving, told a couple who were standing back to stand farther back. How dare they dodge Pax Ford?

"But you look fine," she said, sketching extra fast in case the judge couldn't keep her composure, decided to split.

"*Bishop* v. *D'Arcy* must be good for you," Judge Ford said finally. "Your drawings are everywhere. Is that why you're here tonight? More sketches?"

"Actually," Caro said, "it's for Mr. Bishop. He wanted pen-and-ink drawings for the *Bar Journal*."

What the art director had actually said he wanted was a portrait of Judge Macario. But Caro hadn't found her yet. And Judge Ford needed a little help from her friends. All these people were successful, on top of their profession. Judge Ford had failed to prevent disaster in her courtroom, not her fault, of course, but still upsetting, a reminder that people did fail.

Caro made big gestures, squinted, sighted with her thumb, things she usually never did, but that everyone expected of an artist. They'd know that she, at least, considered the judge important.

Now her drawing was looking like the David sketch of Marie Antoinette being carted to the guillotine. Caro turned the page quickly, began again on fresh paper.

"It's great," she said. "When you talk. I get better expressions, likenesses. I mean, I can work anywhere, I usually have to. But it's great to have you posing."

"Yes," Judge Ford said. "Posing."

But she was looking pinker, more relaxed.

"I hate drawing outsides," Caro said. "I like trying to put down people's insides, what they're feeling."

"You draw what I'm feeling," the judge said, "you'll *never* sell this picture."

But now she was smiling, somehow smoothing out the lines in her face, taking away the years.

"My court officer," she said suddenly, wincing a little, as if she heard a loud noise in her head. "Do you have a drawing of him? One I could buy from you, give to his wife?"

Caro thought quickly.

One or two on the fringes of the room, maybe. Surely a sketch from the early days, holding onto the man who had thrown the cream puff.

Not good enough, not for the judge to give his widow.

"I'll do one from memory," she said. "Fast. I'll get it to you."

She'd do it tonight, approach the bench with it tomorrow like the lawyers. But wait. No trial tomorrow. Everyone said it would go into closed sessions. She wouldn't hear one more word of testimony, get one more drawing out of it, whatever happened to Caitlin. She'd never draw Caitlin.

Suddenly Caro felt cheated, as if she'd dropped her best sable paintbrush, forty-six dollars, into one of Johnny California's dumb manholes.

Did Judge Ford know one thing about gays like Johnny California? D'Arcy? Caro knew plenty. Half the guys in her art classes were gay and proud of it. Quite a few were HIV-positive, too; some even had AIDS like the man in court.

Could she possibly bring up the subject, get the judge to keep talking?

Pax watched the girl, flushed, frowning, eyes moving from subject to paper, hand hurrying over the pad. She realized people were starting to quiet down, turning toward the room where the dinner would be.

Finally. Was Caro finished? She'd stopped drawing, was staring, too.

Then I can look, Pax thought.

In the outer doorway, just arriving, a woman, a young, beautiful woman with great masses of black, beautiful hair.

In the most riveting dress Pax had ever seen outside a shop window. Scarlet, a color from a bullfight, a Goya. Soft silk cut low to show tawny skin, clinging at waist and hips, then bursting into ruffles that moved the way only expensive clothes move. Skirt very short, showing marvelous legs in stockings with a hint of red, shoes with heels almost too high to walk in.

Rosa.

Her lashes incredibly long, her mouth incredibly red, like something out of *Elle, Vogue.* And oddest of all, holding a fan. A black lace fan fluttering in her hand.

"Oh, wow!" she heard from Caro Hansen.

Wow again, Pax thought. She's stunning! Like a model, a movie star! A beautiful child, a beautiful girl, and now a knockout woman!

What was happening to her Rosa? Why was she wasting that dress on the Women's Bar?

The crowd headed for dinner seemed to change directions, aim toward Rosa. Quickly she was hidden, photographers moving on one side, people crowding in on the other, while the waiters at the opposite doorway tried vainly to get them in to eat.

"They talk about her for the Appellate Division," a man said behind Pax. "Promote her, those App Div judges won't concentrate on the cases."

Now Rosa was visible again. A man was following her, taking her arm.

Leonard. Leonard!

Pain, shock, shot through Pax as if she were back in her courtroom with Stephen Haras shooting at her.

What the hell was he doing with Rosa?

The group was closer. Someone was touching her shoulder. Caro. Wide-eyed, flushed.

I must have gone pale, Pax thought. I must have let the surprise show. She's a trained observer. She's observing.

The laughing, chattering people were coming close. Pax saw Rosa look up, the black eyes meet hers, Rosa's joyous expression change instantly to something like Caro's, concerned, afraid.

And she saw something else.

The little move Rosa made to put her hand on Leonard's arm. The gentle tug that turned him away, took his eyes from where Pax was standing, so he'd get by without seeing her at all.

Then Pax was looking at the back of their heads as they moved off.

And everyone was following them, waiters herding people, lights darkening in this room, blazing up in the room where the dinner would be.

I could leave, Pax thought. Get out, find a cab, go home. But there'd be an empty place on the dais with my name on it. I'd be more conspicuous missing than staying. Everyone in the audience would know I couldn't face the dinner, that I was only a weak woman judge after all.

For a moment she saw again the gooey splotch of the cream puff on D'Arcy's jacket, smelled the disgusting package in her mail.

"Judge," Caro was saying, "are you all right?"

"Dinner," Pax said.

She didn't try to be polite, wait to feel steadier. She simply did the best she could, turning, walking alone into the dining room.

Mira, Rosa was thinking, look at Pax, on her feet, dressed up, after that horrible day! But it's done something to her. She looks sick, awful. She should never have worn black.

And I, she thought, shouldn't be passing her by, leaving her to cope without my help. She's never seen me with Leonard, that could startle her. Who knows what she thought she meant to him? She could be shocked I'm so dressed up, so different from always. I could be making her look sick, awful.

But people kept coming up to greet her, exclaim about her beautiful gown, talk to Leonard, just behind her.

Some nerve, she thought then. Me feeling bad for Pax. She's a pro, she knows everyone here, and anyway, I can go straight to her when we go in to eat.

She forgot Pax as they moved on, because in the dining room, all the crystal, the silver, seemed to shine just for her. And because Leonard was stepping back, motioning her on. Of course, to the dais. Up front, up high, for everyone to see.

Pax would come now, too. Maybe they'd be together, maybe they could talk. She'd better think what to say in case her friend was upset, was wondering.

It wouldn't do Pax a favor to stand with her tonight, though. If anyone from the screening panels was in the room, and some were bound to be, they had only to compare the two of them. Not that looks meant anything. But the number of years someone could serve did. Tonight she certainly looked as if she had years longer than Pax.

Besides, representing your people was important, too. Judges couldn't be all white, all male anymore. Minority people should see minority judges, court personnel. Every court in the land was changing to meet that need, even the U.S. Supreme Court. *Esta okay.* She couldn't look more Latina tonight if she danced a fandango.

She smiled out at the crowd, feeling like a Spanish infanta.

Threading through the tables toward the dais was harder for Pax than anything since Alden's funeral. Her head seemed thick, her eyes clouded. She couldn't climb the steps without slowing, find her place card without bending like an old, old woman.

Thank God, somebody pointed at her seat. Just to the right of the podium. Almost center stage, visible from every table in the place. Visible to Leonard. Who'd turned away from her. To walk with Rosa.

Do what you did at Alden's funeral, she ordered herself. Act. Lift your chin, smile, talk to the woman next to you, eat your damned dinner. Pretend.

But Rosa! The dress! Her hair, flowing all down her back. And Leonard, turning away! Why? Because he hadn't wanted Pax to know he was with her? And how with her was he? How long had he been seeing her? How far had it gone? Were they, oh God, in love, sleeping together?

Pax looked with dismay at the crystal cup of cut fruit at

her place, turned to her neighbor. A judge in her eighties, Mary Frances Gunn, retired but still feisty, commanding. Wearing black, like Pax, hands covered with liver spots and diamonds, she was already telling one of her courtroom stories.

"First time the judge ever had two women lawyers," she was saying. "One each side. He just couldn't get our names straight, mixed us up all through the trial. Practically saying straight out, you women lawyers are all alike."

Pax tried to smile. At least the old lady was taking up the slack, letting her think her own thoughts. The thoughts were all questions, cross-examination.

How is Rosa in bed, Mr. Scholer? How does she compare to me? Are you just sitting there politely, impatiently, waiting to get her back into bed again? Tonight? The instant this damned dinner is over?

Hurting as if she'd tasted the fruit cup, swallowed a sharp little nail along with its orange slice, Pax remembered the enormous amethyst she'd seen for only a moment, handed back to him.

It matched her eyes, he'd said.

What was he giving Rosa? Ebony? Onyx? Jet?

A ripple of laughter, noise, on the far side of the podium. Rosa waving to the audience. Oh, God, and waving now at her.

Pax made a wrenching effort, smiled back.

Rosa glanced at the lineup of silverware at her place. Who knew what it was all for?

But who was hungry? She'd never need food again. Orchids and moonbeams would sustain her!

She looked around, two, maybe three hundred faces, to find Leonard's, saw him at a table full of men.

Good, she thought.

People were still standing, talking to friends at other tables, coming up to the dais in a steady stream, reaching up to shake hands, standing on tiptoe below her.

By the time waiters were taking away the fruit cup, coming with big soup tureens, the flurry was dying down.

But she hadn't dressed up like this to drink soup! She didn't want all those looks, that open admiration, to die down. She'd move, remind everyone they wanted to look at her, give them herself to look at!

Pushing back her chair, she stood up, walked along the back of the table toward Pax.

Let them all see her body move in this dress, see her hair gleam in the Christmas lights. Let Leonard see her with Pax, compare.

Rosa, Rosita, she said to herself, as Mami would say it. How can you be so? Be ungrateful to someone who helped you so much, so often.

No, not ungrateful. Realistic. She hadn't made Pax old. She'd done all she could for Pax, for her son. Leonard was a grown man. If he hadn't wanted to, he wouldn't have come with her tonight.

Rosa fluttered her fan, making her hair dance.

Maybe tonight would silence forever the harsh voice of Cathleen calling her a dirty little blackie.

Pax stiffened when Rosa leaned over her chair in a cloud of perfume, smiling, saying how brave she was to come after her terrible day, how shaken she must be, how well she looked.

Her spoon seemed heavy, enormous.

"Thanks," she said somehow. "You look beautiful, Rosa. The Women's Bar has never seen anything like that dress."

She watched Rosa smile, turn in a flurry of ruffles.

Mary Frances Gunn hadn't skipped a beat, was still running on. Caro was standing just below the dais with her pad. Of course, she was drawing Rosa. With her heavenly hair spilling over her shoulders. And with her fan.

Rosa couldn't believe it. An artist, drawing her! With everyone in the room watching!

A commissioned sketch for the *Bar Journal*, she'd said. For Mr. Bishop.

Which meant more good things would happen. The man was a permanent member of the screening panel for the Appellate Division. Two of the sitting judges were due for retirement soon, some others pretty old. If Mr. Bishop was giving her parties, commissioning portraits, surely he'd help her!

A familiar face was just below her, smiling. Eduardo Diaz, a district leader from the Bronx, her own territory, and some of his buddies with him.

Bueno, Rosa thought. Now she could really be herself.

She leaned down, smiled, began talking brightly in rapid Spanish, weren't they having a marvelous time, wasn't this a terrific place!

Eduardo was laughing, kidding around, saying how beautiful she looked. Leonard was right. It felt wonderful to speak her own language, speak her own heart. She needed Leonard, far more than Pax did.

Get up, Pax was telling herself. Get out.

A cough at her shoulder, someone leaning over her.

A waiter, sweating, harried, holding a wide, flat wooden box. Little brown sticks in a row. Candy? Cigars?

Cigars!

Good God, they were offering the women cigars along with the men. Like some sort of parody, some misguided declaration of equality. If men smoked cigars at fancy dinners, so could women.

"Oh, no, thank you," she heard herself say, in the voice of a woman she'd never met, prim, shocked. A voice she couldn't bear being her own.

Rosa turned, looked into the box the waiter was holding out to her.

Dios, cigars.

Good idea! If men got cigars at fancy dinners, why not women?

Pax watched Mary Frances Gunn take a cigar, put it in her worn alligator purse.

"For my doorman," she said.

Below them men were lighting up. In a moment the air seemed filled with clouds of heavy smoke.

Rosa was choosing a cigar, rolling it between her fingers, putting it to her ear. Ricans knew cigars, after all.

Leonard might think her foolish. But her compatriots, her *borinquenos*, they'd understand, they'd laugh.

She let the waiter clip it, light it for her, fluttered her lashes at him.

What a contrast to her feminine dress!

Evidently the photographers agreed. They were rushing in from both sides of the room. The girl artist was moving, too, turning over a page on her pad, finding a fresh one.

Rosa smiled at all of them, took an exaggerated puff, blew smoke into the heavy air.

Oh, my God, Pax thought. She's going to make a thing of it. Use it as a foil for that sexy dress. And what's wrong with Leonard? Why doesn't he come over? Didn't he see me?

She couldn't see him among the tables. But this was the perfect time. She was there on display. Wherever he was sitting he could certainly see her. And she wanted to look at him, know what was going on with him and Rosa. She'd know if she could only just talk to him a moment!

Inhaling the greasy cigar smoke around her, she grew dizzy, more miserable.

Damn him, why didn't he come?

God, she'd been ready to make up with him simply because she'd realized today, once again, that life was short.

But life meant endings, too. Sean's had ended. Hers with Leonard was ending in thick smoke, a blaze of scarlet!

Fury flamed inside her, hot as the tip of Rosa's cigar.

Enough!

She'd go before she showed her feelings, said something to Rosa she'd regret, made a display of herself to everyone in the room.

She went, feeling feverish, away from the dais, through the tables, into the foyer, for once glad she was small, quick.

She wouldn't even get her coat. Flora could come tomorrow, fetch it.

Then she was out in the cold air, heading for a cab, rage warming her, making her skin tingle, her face flush.

Rosa saw her go, dwindle away among the tables.

But she couldn't go alone! She could be sick. She could faint. The stress of the past days could strike her down!

Help was there, Leonard was there. He owed Pax, too, she was his family.

If something happens to her tonight, Rosa thought, I will never forgive myself.

She looked at Leonard's table, saw him deep in talk with the men around him. Oddly, from a distance he looked old, like them, gray and solid, a bunch of white men at a club.

Could she interrupt the white men at the club? Was she still an outsider to a group like that? Even if it included him?

For my friend, she told herself. For Pax.

She left her place, headed straight for him to say that Pax needed his help.

Pax was hot and cold in the taxi, in her elevator, going through her door, slamming her purse on the table in the hall.

Something was making a loud buzz in her kitchen.

Flora, in the doorway.

"House phone," she said. "Mr. Scholer is downstairs, Judge. He'll be right up."

Pax saw flames, crimson, vermilion, heard the elevator, footsteps, a key in the door.

Leonard. Right there!

Of course, he must have seen her leave, come after her. Good. But late, bloody late.

She had just enough sense left to see he looked worn, haggard.

"I had to make sure you were all right," he said quietly.

"Now?" Pax said. "After that whole, horrible evening? After how many days? After the other night, not helping me with Will and his ridiculous ideas about leaving school? You're no defender of mine, Leonard. You're no damned good to me at all. I was right to cut you off so fast. Go back to the party."

She knew Flora was fleeing, saw the kitchen door closing behind her.

"Come on, Pax," he said.

But the flames in her eyes were dancing wildly.

"Go back to Rosa. Since you seem to be judge shopping. I'm sure she's the real comer, the judge who'll do you the most good."

He looked paler still. "Don't make a mountain, Pax. Come on, sweetheart, you're supposed to be the one with the judicial temperament."

Is that so? she wanted to fling at him. Tonight I saw the kind of judicial temperament you like, and so did everyone else. Red dresses, fans, yes, and cigars.

"Wait," she said instead, in her best, cut-though-the-court-room voice. "Wait till we both show up at the screening panels. How will I top Rosa's dress? Do I wear nothing at all?"

"Pax, stop it."

"It's so obvious. I didn't take your expensive advice. So you found someone who'd take all your advice, do everything you say, someone young and stunning and new, right?"

He was moving into the living room, actually daring to sink into a couch.

Where Bishop had been, in the last horror she'd faced in her living room.

Beyond him Pax saw the greenhouse glittering on the terrace outside.

Moonlight glowed on it, frost whitened its glass, outlined its beauty. Behind its misted glass soft colors blended, shimmered to give her pleasure.

Leonard had given her pleasure. But how could someone who'd done that change so, hurt her so terribly? How could he make her feel old and ugly and, yes, small, tiny, insignificant? Did he think she couldn't get rid of anything that once gave her pleasure? What sentence could she pass on him for that?

Never mind talking, lawyers and judges talked too much. She'd *show* him, a side of her he hadn't seen before, one she'd hardly seen herself, but had always known was there. Did he think it was only Rosa who could change? Let him watch!

Moving into the living room, she kept on past Leonard through the French doors, out into the freezing air.

She went straight to the glimmering greenhouse, put out a hand, wrenched open the door. Inside, her breath caught with the sudden warmth, her eyes misted over in the thick air. All around, summer flowers seemed to be decaying, dying, finished.

On the bench, neatly ranged in a row, her tools. The largest, the heavy English trowel, squat, steely, with a wooden handle meant to last forever.

Pax reached for it, picked it up, pleased with the way it belonged in her hand, nestled into her fingers.

Behind her she heard Leonard's step.

She moved to the glass, jerked back her arm, swung the heavy tool.

Everyone else acts, she thought. They don't judge. They don't weigh and consider and worry about the law. They throw things. Shoot. Destroy. It's my turn. I can destroy, too. Watch me, Leonard.

She swung the trowel at the shining glass again and again, enjoying the crashes, the blasts of chilling air, thrilled at her power to make pots smash, seed trays crack, dirt fly, to stamp out summer beneath her own two feet.

16

BA

THE STAIRS WERE UNEVEN, TREACHEROUS, BUT BA KNEW SHE must get to the top.

Struggling for breath, she climbed, heels catching on the threadbare carpet, palm scraped by the worn banister. The higher she went, the more stairs there were. She grew warmer, till sweat ran down her face, dampened the back of her neck under her long blond hair. Soon her middy blouse clung to her back, stuck at her armpits.

Worst of all, she sensed that when she reached the top, touched her bedroom door, the sweat would sizzle on her skin, scald her past recognition.

Terrified, she lifted her hand and awakened, shaking, soaked.

Ba gulped air, waited till she was sure she was grown up, in New York, no longer a girl in Canton, Ohio. Good heavens, years since she'd dreamed of going upstairs at home to find Johnny in her bed with that boy.

Shuddering, Ba looked at the jeweled clock on the bedside table. Just past four. Worst possible time. Too early to get up, too late to sleep again. After yesterday's horrors she needed sleep.

She stretched her hand to Tal's side of the bed. Empty, sheets dry, cool. Where was he? On the couch in his dressing room? Downstairs in the library? After a shooting, after the worst day she'd ever known? Alan Foster, sweet man, had left patients sitting in his waiting room to rush over, stay with her till she felt calmer.

Alan had given her Librax, Halcion. But she'd still had the dream.

Pulling away from the clammy sheets, Ba went to the window. She looked out at the special New York darkness, black pierced with squares of light, dotted with the red and green of traffic signals, streaked with beams from the passing cars.

Usually the solid buildings seemed a bulwark against trouble, the wide street a protective moat. Now even ordinary night sounds seemed disturbing, a wailing siren, a tapping in the radiators, a low-flying plane.

She pulled off her nightgown, dropped it to the floor in a damp heap, wrapped herself in her warm wool robe. Then she went through to Tal's dressing room, turned on a lamp. He wasn't there, either. But he'd undressed. The contents of his pockets—wallet, change, keys, tiny pocket knife—lay on the table next to his couch, as usual.

And something else was there, not usual. Two plastic cylinders full of pills, with those dreadful childproof tops no adult could open without a struggle. Tal's pills? Tal didn't take pills, that was *her* province.

She picked one up, looked at the typed label. Not prescribed by Alan. A doctor she'd never heard of, Zelinsky, East Sixty-seventh Street. Who was that? Why was Tal seeing a doctor he had never mentioned? What did he have on *his* mind?

Confused, Ba squinted at the tiny print on the label. Pamelor. What was Pamelor? She put it down, looked at the second bottle. Trilofon?

New fears bored into Ba's heart. Dear Lord, Tal had some condition he hadn't told her about, requiring strange medications with strange names.

Four o'clock or not, she had to have answers. She had a right!

Ba went back to her bed, picked up the phone on the table next to it, dialed Alan. After just two rings he picked up the phone, as she'd been certain he would. It was one of the reasons she used him, his availability, his sympathy at any hour, even four o'clock.

"Alan? Ba Bishop. Alan, did you send Tal to a new doctor? I've just found pills with his things, pills I never heard about."

"Now, Ba. Aren't you taking the pills I gave you? What happened to your Halcion? Why are you awake?"

"Answer me, Alan. These are funny names, Pamelor, Trilofon. From a Dr. Zelinsky. Who's he?"

"He's a psychopharmacologist, Ba. The best. Of course I sent Tal to him, I'm no fan of antidepressants. Librax is as far as I go, as you know."

Ba felt her stomach twist, ache.

"Tal, depressed? Enough to need pills? Oh, Alan, he never said, he never mentioned anything."

"Then don't you mention it. I'm only telling you so you don't obsess any more than you've been doing lately. My God, Ba, getting this child is putting both of you through hell. You'll both be drug-dependent before you're through. Leave Tal alone, he's handling his end. Take care of yourself, take your Halcion and go to sleep."

But Ba could no more sleep now than she could have waltzed. A heavy lump of fear, remorse, lay in her stomach as if she'd eaten something sickening, Mexican food, spicy barbecue, worse.

Why had she insisted Tal start the lawsuit? Stirred her own worst memories? What longing for revenge had made her want to punish D'Arcy, take Caitlin away as he'd taken Johnny away from her, from a normal life?

The phone was dead in her hand, Alan gone.

What had she done to her husband? Every horrible thing that had happened in the trial was her fault. Even the death of that court officer, her fault. And it wasn't over. There could be more horrors.

Ba shivered, went into her own bathroom for her own pills, saw her face in the mirror, haggard, old.

My God, she thought, I look like Johnny. Same blond hair, same chin, same eyes. Caitlin probably looks like him, too. Is she like him? Could I come home and find her in bed with another girl?

She took two tranquilizers, went back to the bedroom, switched on her table lamp. It sent a beam of light toward her desk. On top was the new album Bonner had just got back from the bindery. Creamy leather, gold trim, each page with its own protective acetate cover, a name in gold on the front, CAITLIN.

My God, what would fill that album? Report cards covered with C's and D's? Notes from teachers complaining of Caitlin's behavior? Doctors' reports, positive test results for ghastly diseases? How could she have gone so wrong?

I can get rid of this album, she kept thinking. But I can't stop a process that brings Caitlin closer every day. I don't know how to stop it.

Ba picked up the album, left the room, went down the dark stairs. Tal wasn't in the library. He'd probably bedded down in a spare room. The maids were surely asleep in their own wing in back of the kitchen.

Head pounding, Ba moved through the pantry into the vast kitchen, its rows of copper pots gleaming even in semi-darkness, its pristine order calming her a little, so she could think, plan.

She'd been so hopeful ordering the album, shopping for everything Caitlin would need. The big storage bin in the basement was crammed with presents for Caitlin. Clothes, toys, books, even furniture, unopened, untouched. She'd collected enchanting toys, pretty dresses, the best books. Even scoured antique shops, found a beautiful German snow scene with flakes that whirled and tumbled around a tiny village inside. She'd shopped more these past weeks than ever before, every purchase making Caitlin more real, more her own.

Now the familiar migraine pain was beginning, little pinpricks in her temples. She put her hands to the pain, almost seeing the bin downstairs.

A wire cage, perhaps ten by ten. Somewhere in it was an antique bed, child-size, with carved and painted flowers. A rocking chair. A dollhouse, Victorian, towers, turrets, stained glass windows, a family of dolls to live in it. The whole bin must be filled.

Well, if those things had been chosen to bring Caitlin closer, perhaps getting rid of them would ward her off, keep her away! First thing tomorrow she'd have Bonner take care of it, clear out every package, send things to the Salvation Army, the Goodwill. Not her Huguenots, though, that would make talk among people she knew.

Ba felt the pains rise in her head, fan out through her cheekbones.

Hadn't she always tackled problems head on? Wasn't she proud of her ability, her efficiency? Now, she'd deal with the bin now.

She'd feel better when the job was done. Probably it was all that would make her better, able to sleep.

The back door was next to the large Garland stove. The maids put garbage outside for the building staff to collect. Ba's packages came to her unpacked, unwrapped, free of the cardboard and twine that required knives, chisels, rough strength to open.

Knives, chisels. She'd have to open the things downstairs.

Tools, then. A hammer with its claw to rip staples, wires. A knife to cut string, slash open brown paper.

Ba went back to the pantry, where the big toolbox was kept, each tool oiled, shining, in its own little belt, chose what she wanted, hammer, knife.

She even remembered to put the latch on the back door so she could get back in when she'd done the job. She put the album into the big garbage pail outside the back door, then rang for the service elevator. It would be in the basement. She couldn't hear its buzzer at all.

Then, because the building was so still, Ba heard the elevator gates crash open down in the basement, the grinding of machinery.

Good Lord, she realized suddenly. I have nothing under this robe. Or on my feet. Even my hair's not combed.

But only an elevator man would see her. A back elevator man, who never came up to the lobby or the front door. She was a stockholder, Tal served on the building's board of directors. Nobody would question her. Besides, she was only disposing of her own property.

She saw Cecil through the gates before he brought the elevator to a stop. A solid, young black man in a blue shirt and slacks, a bunch of keys at his belt. He'd been in service long enough so she'd seen him in emergencies, plumbing problems, broken faucets. He'd know who she was.

Yes, Cecil was smiling as he yanked open the door.

"Good evening," Ba said, stepping into the elevator, remembering not to clutch at her robe, draw attention to the fact that she had no nightgown under it.

"Trouble, Mrs. Bishop?" Cecil said, wrinkling his dark forehead.

"Not at all. I just want you to take me to the basement. I have to look over my bin."

Why, she could give Cecil some of the things. He might have a little girl of his own.

Cecil obediently closed the gates, took the elevator down. Ba smelled the basement before they reached it, dank, musty, even in the December cold. After all, garbage was collected here, men sweated over heavy work, walls were damp. Dark here, too. The windows were slits high under the ceiling, filtering the light even at noon. Now they were black.

Another woman might feel frightened, no clothes, a black

man so close. Of course, she wasn't frightened. But she did wish her headache would stop.

They went past the room where the men stored seasonal equipment, snow shovels, awnings, rubber matting for the lobby on rainy days. And past the room for the coin-operated washing machines, the super's office, the place with chairs, an old television set, where the men gathered on their breaks.

Ba tapped her bare foot on the icy floor while Cecil opened the door to the room with the bins. Hers was number twenty-two. No reason. Bins didn't go with apartments, there weren't enough. That always annoyed newcomers who thought storage space was their right. They had to wait for someone to give a bin up. Ba had had hers a long time, knew exactly where it was.

Cecil turned on a ceiling light. Her bin sprang into view, made, like the rest, of metal grating, everything in it visible from outside.

Her headache swelled into a nightmare of pain.

Even knowing how much she'd bought, she could hardly believe what she saw.

The bin could have been one enormous brown package. Jammed full, walls piled high with boxes and crates.

"Mrs. Bishop, are you all right?" Cecil said.

Ba knew she'd let her guard down, showed how she felt, overwhelmed, despairing.

"Certainly," she said. "But there's a lot to do."

With another step she realized there was more than she thought. The bin was padlocked. Where on earth was the key? Bonner must have it somewhere.

She was not going up to find it, not now she was here with this biddable young man.

"Cecil," Ba said. "Take this hammer and break that lock. I can't waste time. I'm going to empty the bin."

Cecil looked at her, wrinkled his brow. "Mrs. Bishop," he said, "you have an intention to empty this whole bin? Now?"

"That's right," Ba said crisply. "As soon as you take care of that lock."

He was, after all, an employee, a servant.

Cecil seemed to be remembering that, too.

He rapped the hammer sharply against the lock, wrenched at it with the claw end. In a moment it came apart. Ba gave him a smile, was startled to see sweat shining on his black face.

"Why don't I get the super, Mrs. Bishop? He could maybe give you a hand."

Ba just waved him off. She didn't need the super. She didn't want him asking questions. Cecil could go now, too. When she needed to go upstairs she'd ring again.

She forgot him, reaching for the nearest small box. F.A.O. SCHWARZ, the label read. Some toy, of course. Impossible to remember them all. She'd spent several afternoons shopping in the huge store. No need to open it, the toys could go right into the trash.

She used the knife to scratch off the address label with her name.

"I'm going now, ma'am," she heard Cecil say behind her.

But Ba was concentrating on the other small packages. She reached for something wrapped in brown paper. Ripping it open, she touched lavender tissue paper, ribbon. Dresses. Of course, the ones she'd had her dressmaker make up in size six, one pattern, four beautiful fabrics. Smocked, copies of the fantastic Loretta Caponi dresses from Florence that the little princesses used to wear, unhemmed, so they could be fitted to Caitlin when she came. Now they could be fitted to another little girl.

Ba dropped the dresses on the floor, looked for more packages that would be easy to open.

One box was small, pink. She tore at it, sure for once of what was inside. The baby doll she'd adored the moment she saw it, with a vast layette, bottles, diapers. The doll that said "Mama" when you patted it.

Beautiful, yes. But she didn't want it now. No one would call her "Mama" if she just got rid of everything here.

* * *

Cecil watched, sweating, frightened.

She looked strange, crazy, using a knife on those things. He'd seen nothing like her since he had begun working in the building when he came from Guyana. Except maybe some mad homeless woman in the streets.

If he fetched the super, things might be worse. Mr. Flaherty was not keen on his black employees, often mentioned the old days when all the staff was white. Get him up, middle of the night, who knew what could happen?

He waited quietly, ready to go to her, catch her, if she started swooning, anything like that.

Cecil had thought the ring from the ninth floor was a mistake, a joke. Nobody rode the back elevator at four in the morning. Even rushing to the hospital, dealing with a fire, they rang for the passenger car.

He had been foolish to answer. Mrs. Bishop might have given up. Or walked down the stairs, so the responsibility wasn't his. Another hour and he'd have finished his shift, started home. She would have been the day man's problem then.

Well, she was somebody's problem, hair every which way, face pale as paper. And her feet bare, so she looked like the ghosts at home country people left saucers of milk for, berries, bread.

Watching her shake out a little lace dress, Cecil realized he felt sorry for her. A real lady, like the old Englishwomen at home. Probably pretty when she was young. Everyone in the building knew about her court case. Piles of the *Daily News*, that pink paper, the *Observer*, had grown higher in the basement since the trial started.

Yesterday's big news, the terrible shooting, had been much discussed. In the room where the men took breaks, they had all shaken their heads, a man shooting near someone in their very own building.

Not what I came to the States for, Cecil thought. Enough

trouble in Guyana, people poorer every year, crime worse all the time.

He hadn't told the men he had a special interest in the trial. His own cousin working for Judge Ford a few blocks up Park Avenue! Flora adored that woman. She had so many wonderful gifts from the judge, best yet, help in going to school. There was nothing she would not do for Judge Ford, she said that often.

If only someone would help him go to school. Then he'd leave this work to the angry American blacks, the lowlife Puerto Ricans. Move up in life. Guyanans wanted to move up.

Cecil jumped, fear striking his heart.

Music was suddenly playing in his basement. Tinkling, echoing in the darkness. And over by the bin Mrs. Bishop was starting to dance in time to the tune!

Ba had forgotten the music box.

From Rita Ford's, a pretty painted sphere with little birds and flowers that turned when the music played.

"Cecil," she called as she dipped and swayed, "I need some help."

"Well, now, Mrs. Bishop," he said nervously, "what kind of help would that be?"

He looks alarmed, Ba thought. Wary. I'd better explain.

"I couldn't sleep, you see. I began thinking about all these things. I've been so busy there hasn't been time to go through them. So I came straight down."

"Good for you, Mrs. Bishop," Cecil said. "Certainly are a lot of things."

A thought struck Ba through her migraine pain.

"Do you have a little girl? Could you use them?"

"I do not myself," Cecil said. "But there are girls in my family. And back home in Guyana."

"Well, then," she said, standing still, "someone there will be glad for these clothes, these toys. I'd like them to go to deserving children, especially now, Christmas time. Don't worry about taking them, I'll speak to the superintendent in the morning."

"You surely do not want to be rid of all that," Cecil said, petrified.

"Oh, but I do. I can't take that child, I'm really not well enough. A child is such a responsibility."

"Well, Mrs. Bishop," Cecil said, "you're very kind."

No, Ba thought, I'm very fortunate. I stopped things just in time. I made a mistake and now I'll correct that mistake. Ever since Tal first saw me, I've been fortunate. How could I have thought I needed anyone else? Tomorrow morning, first thing, he can call Scotty, make him explain to the judge. The trial will stop. Then I'll be myself again; then he won't need those silly pills from that silly doctor. We'll both go back to normal.

Ba moved to the elevator, filled with peace, knowing that now, after such a long wandering in the wilderness, she was finally doing exactly the right thing.

17

BISHOP

BISHOP WAS PLEASED TO SEE THE LAW SCHOOL COMMON room uncommonly crowded.

He'd been focused on his competition, the other two speakers. Now, walking to the lectern, he realized that students lined the walls and windowsills, sprawled on the floor against every safety regulation.

Students! Baby faces, dressed for a beach party, smelling of dirty T-shirts, worn sneakers, spilled fruit drinks, worse. Still, there must be five or six he could use.

"Good afternoon," he said, launching the talk he'd made so often, so successfully. Officially, Career Paths in the Law. Unofficially, How to Get Out of Law School Now.

"I'm the last of the three wise men you've invited today," he went on.

Rustles, whispers. Today's kids had the attention spans of birds. And probably the brains.

"We're wise men here simply because we're lawyers. Long ago we earned the degrees you're working so hard to attain. But has it struck you this afternoon that none of us—not one—actually practices law?"

Ah, a ripple of movement, then a new stillness.

"None of us has used our law degree in ways our parents and professors would have dreamed possible."

Smiles, nods. Any failing of parents and professors, always a hit.

"What parent or professor twenty years ago would have imagined the law would have its own television network?"

More smiles for Court TV's genial, white-haired Fred Graham, whose face they all knew.

"What parent or professor could have foreseen the social changes, working women, black business, the momentous trends Newell Alford discussed today? Trends that have catapulted the large insurance companies like his own, Chubb, into rewarding new directions?"

How stuffy this room was, how thick the air. He'd get to the point now. Entertaining as Graham was, these kids knew TV jobs were scarce. As for Chubb, everyone suspected the big companies still hired for social standing, manners.

"Let me suggest a career path that would really shock parents and professors—perhaps even shock you—because it doesn't require a degree. It's the new world of legal publishing. The world of the *Bar Journal*."

To Will, sweating, pressed against the wall, the room seemed like the IRT subway he skated to avoid.

Bishop was a bastard. Tempting guys like him drowning in work who'd grab any reason to walk out past Minerva, her owl, the Columbia campus. Judging by the crowd, he wasn't the only one. But he *was* the only one who'd come, not to listen, but to act.

Beads of sweat were on his forehead, rolling down his burning cheek. Bad, because he *had* to keep cool. Even John Talcott Bishop couldn't talk forever.

But he hadn't felt cool since the other night when Mom told about Bishop's visit. She'd looked so upset. Poor Mom, for all she was a judge, a lady, protected from dirt her whole life. He'd wanted to rush out and find Bishop, fight at least one of her battles for her. He couldn't do anything about demonstrators, killers in her courtroom. But he could show Bishop she had a son backing her.

After that, Bishop had somehow taken him over, waking him at night, blurring his eyes when he studied. Bastard, smearing a dead man. Bastard, messing with Will's gentle, caring father. Bastard, standing here like Mr. Important, giving everyone the word.

A big man. And Mom so little. How *dare* he walk into her apartment? Threaten her, the judge in his case, a case on trial? Only what could a law student do about it? How could he get near Bishop, with his servants and secretaries?

Will tried to relax, leaning his weight against the paneled wall, gulping the stale air.

With Bishop living in his head, he'd been stunned to spot posters for this seminar. Prayers answered! Bishop coming here!

Right now Mr. Important was glorying in the history of the *Bar Journal,* his grandfather starting it in some print shop. Worse, everyone was in a trance. Thanks to Mom's trial, Bishop was a star. His face was on the front page, on TV news. And he was loving it, playing to all the starfuckers in the room, and to all the people who'd been behind in their work since October. The bastard was using the seminar to make a recruiting speech.

Will wiped his damp palms on his khakis. The only speech *he* cared about was the one he'd make when the seminar ended.

Hello, Mr. Bishop. I'm Pax Peyton Ford's son. My mother tells me you're big on blackmail.

Bishop knew he had his audience. One reedy boy against the side wall looked as if he was memorizing every word.

Quitters! In his day law students accepted everything, brutal teaching, ridicule, impossible hours. Now they whined, rushed for any exit. Well, let them rush for the *Journal.* It needed bodies, chewed them up quickly, worked them as hard as law school if they had any moxie.

Now he could do the needful without further attention, let his mind range while he finished up. He could think about Ba, suddenly in one of her moods, perhaps even one of her little depressions. About the child coming into his life. Yes, and about Pax Ford, who had more steel than he'd imagined. Still, she'd come around. No woman of her stature wanted public exposure. No woman of her breeding wanted lowlife innuendoes, jokes. Judges used to be beyond reproach. Now they were no more insulated than any other authority figure, priest, president, pope.

"Almost everyone on our staff has *some* work toward a law degree," Bishop said. "Almost everyone has *some* of the training you're enduring."

Enduring, that always got a chuckle.

People were fanning themselves with yellow pads, manila folders. The thin boy against the wall was perspiring, wiping his brow with his arm.

Enough. They'd seen him, heard him. They would figure out the next step. Résumés, heartfelt letters, would arrive on his desk. So much for Fred Graham, Newell Alford. *He* was the keeper of the keys.

Will was imagining he'd absorbed all the heat in the room, gathered it into his body the way that old Swiss hero Von Winkelsomething had pulled all the enemy's spears into his heart so his buddies could slaughter the Hapsburgs.

Bishop was telling them, heavily, that they needn't graduate to work for the *Journal.* Good news for first-year students. Half his friends wanted to quit, especially guys pressured by fathers with their own law degrees. Or worse, like him, mothers. What would his mother say about Bishop getting people to quit so they could work for his trade paper? She'd call that worse than blackmail.

"At my twenty-fifth Harvard Law School reunion," Bishop was saying, "I was astonished to learn that fewer than a quarter of my classmates actually practiced law. They did all manner of other things, insurance, politics, business, teaching. A law career doesn't have to mean courtrooms, dusty libraries, tax forms, and estate regulations. You've all heard that the house of law has many mansions."

What was the *matter* with everyone? They were lapping this crap up, hope blooming on their lumpy faces. Was he the only one here thinking, not about his future, but his present? The only one with a real reason to be here?

"I own and operate one mansion of the law, the *Bar Journal.* For the more creative of you, interested in communications, a career in legal publishing can use your highest talents. Nothing is stodgy or hidebound; everything moves with rapidity. We, for example, are exploring Spanish-language editions of our publications. Any of you who know the language, either by inheritance or study, could make real contributions."

Get me *out* of here, Will thought. Get me up on that platform. And then, God, if there is a God, get me out of this fucking school.

Now Bishop was stepping back to join the other two speakers behind him. The dean was on his feet, bowing to the speakers, smiling out at the audience.

Dizziness struck Will, clouding his eyes, ringing in his ears. His heart seemed to be battering its way out of his chest, as it had in Mom's courtroom when that guy shot at her, when he was shoving through people to get to her.

For Mom, he thought. Because I love her.

Through the applause he forced his head clear, flexed his Rollerblader's muscles so he could move fast.

"We'll let our distinguished guests go now," he heard. "And ponder their words. Our thanks to them for taking us behind the scenes of the important institutions they serve."

Will sprang as if he were shooting a basket, up, over, straight to his target.

Close up, Bishop seemed enormous, solid, a rock wall.

"Mr. Bishop," Will said, his voice weak, adolescent in his own ears, "I want to talk to you. My name is Will Ford."

He tilted his chin, looked up into cold blue eyes.

"I'm Judge Ford's son," he said.

Bishop's pulse quickened, as if a squash ball had ricocheted from an unexpected angle, straight at his face.

He took a step back.

My God, he'd just been through a shooting, through any number of crazies marching, shouting abuse. Judge Ford's son! Why?

Bishop looked for a weapon, saw none. Steadier, he frowned down at the boy.

Slight, fine-boned, like his mother. Only about a hundred and thirty-five, forty pounds. Not exactly the sort to attack on a public platform at Columbia. His eyes were his mother's, violet, a woman's color, out of place in a young man. But where Judge Ford conveyed stillness, control, this boy, eyes wide, mouth tight, looked all nerved up.

"Yes," Bishop said, as if addressed by some junior in his office.

I could break you in two if necessary, he wanted to say. No wonder, mother like yours, cold as dry ice, all brains, command. And a father, a sissy, a freak, a man of disgusting appetites.

"This isn't the place," he added.

How many people here knew this was the judge's son? One was too many. But a private conversation? Perhaps a second crack at the judge? He hadn't grown his grandfather's little legal sheet into a kingdom without recognizing second chances, grasping hot coals. And this boy was a coal, burning. Well, let *him* be consumed. Maybe he'd be more malleable than his mother. Maybe he'd help her do the right thing.

"My car and driver are outside, on Broadway," he said. "We'll be private there."

He'd had more important conversations in that car than

this boy could imagine. Besides, Johnson would be at the wheel. Not that he'd need much help dealing with a skinny kid like Will Ford.

The crowd seemed all backs and shoulders for Will, pushing behind Bishop down the halls, the steps. Soon he was aware of sunshine on his face, bricks beneath his sneakers, heart pounding as if he'd outskated a truck, head fogged as if engine fumes were all around.

Then he was in the car, a coffin of glass and plush.

"Drive, Johnson," Bishop was saying. "I'll tell you when to get back to the office."

Wow, he was huge, lanky legs filling the well of the car, bulky shoulders blocking the whole far window. Even his smell was overpowering, tweed and toilet water.

Will swallowed, tried to sit taller on the soft cushions.

"Well?" Bishop said, eyes turning to him.

Well. Did I ever think what I'd do if I actually got to him? What the hell was it? I can't punch him in the nose. I can't take out my sword and run him through. Well.

"You came to see my mother the other night," he began, putting as much heft as possible into his voice.

"Yes? And?"

"She told me—and some other people—what you had to say."

"Ah. Did they give her better advice than she gave herself?"

"They all agreed there's a word for what you did. Blackmail."

"Now, young man," Bishop said, sitting back. "You're in law school. Know anything about hearsay? Could you prove I said anything to your mother?"

"My mother may just be the most truthful person I know. If she told a story like that, I can bet it happened."

Maybe it was just getting out words, any words. But now he felt cooler, taller. Older. If all Bishop could do was deny the story, he wasn't smart, let alone scary. Anyway, he hadn't come to argue about whether or not Bishop said all that stuff. He'd come to tell him to leave Mom the hell alone.

"I came to tell you. Publish one word, one sleazy word about my mother, I'll go to the *Times*. Make sure everyone knows what you did. I don't think it would help your custody suit much. Or your paper. So now you know."

All right, he thought, I said it. Now I want to get out of here. I want to call Mom, tell her I got to him, warned him off. No, I don't, I can't. It'll just be more for her to worry about, and she's got enough.

Still, even sitting in this luxurious car, like the lair of the mountain king, he was feeling relaxed, easy. He'd done it, the best he could do.

They were passing Ninety-seventh Street now, the Wiz, then the old subway station, the lineup of crosstown buses. Impossible they were only a few blocks down from Columbia. This ride seemed to have lasted hours. They should have been all the way downtown at Battery Park.

Debo, Will thought, exhaling, feeling a great rush of relief. I'll tell it all to Debo. She's big on getting out feelings, being true to yourself. I've done something like her dad would do, like a defense lawyer. I can't wait to tell Debo. She'll think *I'm* the Wiz!

Foolish boy, Bishop thought. Never done anything like this before. It's too much for him, he's shaking. Not like his mother, that's for sure. Probably takes after the father.

"Young man," he said, "do you have any idea *what* I know about your father?"

"I know all about my father," the boy said, his voice quiet. "You think my mother keeps secrets from me? I'm her only child."

"Your mother," Bishop said, "keeps secrets from herself. She doesn't grasp the scope of your father's risk taking. Today there are places for people like him to go, socialize. In your father's day, in his class, it was different. Men like him were called perennial bachelors—real men steered clear of them, women didn't discuss them. My own wife had a brother whose behavior she knew nothing about. Why would your mother be different?"

"Come on," the boy said, "my mother is a high court judge. This is the twentieth century."

"Meaningless in this context. Your mother accepted the management of a trial involving a homosexual. Having been married to one, she's bound to have prejudices, feelings she should have disclosed. Or she should have refused the case."

"My father wasn't a homosexual," Will said.

"Bisexual, then, whatever you like to call it. It's all too true, I'm afraid. Public figures like your mother have to be Caesar's wife, above suspicion. Or how did Cardozo put it, they require the punctilio of an honor the most sensitive. Judges have been in trouble for less than bisexual husbands, believe me."

"I'll get out now," Will Ford said.

"You'll get out when I'm finished. Now, you're a law student. You probably still think a trial is a search for truth. Whereas it's a search for *provable* truth, quite a different thing. It isn't what I know about your father, or even what I care about. It's what I can prove, document. The *Bar Journal*'s legal-research facilities are as good as those of the *Times*, better. My picture files are vast. I could show you photographs that would shake the judiciary, the public, make your mother a figure of ridicule and pity in very short order."

Now the young man was looking very young indeed. Realizing he'd bit off more than he could chew. He wouldn't want those pictures out and around himself, a boy on the threshold of his own legal career. He *was* softer clay than his mother, could be shaped to get her to behave herself.

"If you want to help your mother, tell her to get through the trial quickly. It can only tarnish her career. It's a circus like the Simpson trial, more salacious and possibly more lethal now AIDS is involved. And there's no issue. Any decent psychologist, teacher, normal human being, could decide this case in an hour. I care about my wife as much as you care about your mother. But deciding in our favor won't just help your mother. It helps that child. It harms no one except a man likely to die of disease. And there's another thing you should consider."

Will Ford was hunched over, looking smaller than ever.

"Your mother wants to be on the Appellate court. I'm a member of the screening committee for that court. I can reward her as well as bring her down. Mention that, if she hasn't realized it yet."

"You *are* a son of a bitch," the boy said quietly, suddenly looking straight at him.

"Don't get out of your league, sonny. How will you feel when the *Daily News* runs a picture of your father, shall we say, copulating, through a hole in a board?"

Silence.

Good, Bishop thought. Let's drive this one home.

"I'm probably more than twice your age. I daresay I know more about homosexuals than you, more about most things than you. I was at boys' schools, I saw homosexual behavior from first form on. It disgusted me then, it disgusts me now. It's not an alternative lifestyle, it's a sickness. I'm with Edward VII, who thought men like that should shoot themselves. I'm not about to give up anything I want to one of them. If you love your mother, tell her so."

Who knew about *this* boy's lifestyle? Right now he looked womanish himself.

"I do love my mother," Will Ford said. His intensity made him seem dangerous for the first time. His arm on the door handle showed muscles that made Bishop glad Johnson was close by. "And I'm not telling her anything. I wouldn't want her to know I got my hands this dirty. Now, tell that man to stop your fucking car."

Bishop smiled, tapped on the glass.

Johnson responded immediately, pulling over to the crowded curb.

Crash, slam, and he was alone in the backseat. The sudden exit unnerved him a little, sent a flutter into his chest.

But after a moment he could settle himself, lean back on the soft cushions.

Judge Ford's son was nothing. At his age, he'd have rounded on any man who threatened his mother. Just as he was about to round on anyone who threatened Ba. Wasn't that what this was all about? Wasn't that his duty to his position, to his wife?

He told Johnson to get downtown quickly, suddenly highly satisfied with *both* his lectures, all his afternoon's work.

Will stood weak-kneed on the curb with cars, buses, cabs speeding around him.

One thing to see a movie where someone strong-armed a villain. Another thing to do it, feeling like a fool, a kid. Was there any bastard like a man who looked terrific in public, made speeches at Ivy League schools, worked on judicial screening committees, and talked blackmail?

He's rich, Will thought. Insulated. What could I really do to him? The *Times* would probably throw me out on my ass.

Copulating through a hole in a board, Bishop had said.

A memory for Mom to treasure.

Poor Mom, what did she know, anyway? Almost fifty and a sheltered life, Radcliffe, Harvard Law. What would she know about fucking through boards?

Debo. Debo was a graduate student in psychology. He'd share it all with Debo the instant he walked through his door.

He moved inside fast, words half out of his mouth, and stopped short.

Damn. Debo wasn't alone. Leonard, squashed comfortably in their softest chair, a glass in his hand.

Will remembered with a rush of despair. God, Mom and Leonard both coming tonight. Debo was going to order Szechuan. He'd lost track of the calender, everything, revving himself up for Bishop.

"Hi," he managed to say. "Leonard. Debo. Where's Mom?"

"Not coming," Debo said. She was in her favorite outfit, some kind of flimsy Egyptian caftan. It looked nice with her dark hair, her big black eyes. It clung to all her curves. "She called, she has a terrible cold. Took home a pile of motions to read in bed. All her other cases are getting stale, she said, with the custody thing taking her over."

Will suddenly longed to go to bed, too.

"You know how Pax is about getting work out," Debo was saying to her father. "She doesn't want to be one of those judges who keep cases three, four years."

Poor Mom. She wanted to be the best. And here was this shitload of trouble about to descend on her.

Some help I am, he thought. I've probably made Bishop really sore, made everything worse.

He turned to dump his books, skates, realized with a flush of misery that he didn't have them. He'd never planned to leave with Bishop, so his stuff was still in his school locker. Books he'd need tonight, too. He'd have to go back up after dinner on the subway, find his knapsack, stay up half the night. So much for a talk with Debo.

"Will," Leonard said, "you look awful. Not another party, I hope."

Oh, God, was he going to hear about that forever?

Will sank into a chair, looked at Debo, then back at Leonard.

"Not another party. What about Mom? She never has colds. Or leftover motions. I'll call her, I guess."

Unaccountably, Leonard frowned, looked away. But Will couldn't puzzle that out now. He needed to get out what was bothering him. Debo and Leonard both knew about Bishop. Nothing to stop him telling them both.

"I just had a weird experience," he said. "I went to hear John Talcott Bishop speak at a seminar. And I talked to him afterward."

Now both of them were staring at him.

"*That* bastard," Leonard said.

"More than you know. I meant to tell him to lay off Mom. I got into his car to tell him."

"His car!" Debo said. "Will!"

"He's something else. Pure Teflon. He was glad to have the chance to drive his point home, via me. He said he has stuff on my dad even Mom doesn't know."

Leonard seemed to be changing, head lowering like a fighting bull, eyes narrowing. "What, exactly, did he say?"

"That he had pictures of Dad. I'll spare you doing what."

Leonard was on his feet. "Par for the course, a bully, a blackmailer. Now, listen. First of all, Will, it was a hell of a thing to do, take him on. I have to congratulate you."

Debo was up, too, coming to give him a hug. She smelled delicious, felt soft, warm. For a moment he wanted only to bury his face in her large, beautiful breasts.

But Leonard was talking.

"Look, you don't need this, you've got enough on your hands. I'm the defense attorney around here. And I've been thinking about Bishop, thinking hard. After all, it's my trial he's fucking with. I'll take my turn. Will, do what I tell clients, forget all about it. Your worries are over. I'll handle this."

"How? What'll you do?"

"I don't know yet," Leonard said, frowning. "But I will. Now, listen. I'll take a raincheck on dinner till nobody has a cold, books to crack. I'll let you know when I get somewhere."

But Debo was pulling back, clasping her hands.

"But, Dad," she was saying, "you can't go. Remember, we were all going to the movies? Will and I haven't been to the movies in ages."

She was turning back to him, wide-eyed, a little girl cheated.

"Will, we promised ourselves. We negotiated, we need a piece of our own time, remember? There's been enough of everything else."

Leonard was turning his whole body, his huge bulk, toward his daughter.

"Debo," he said, "you married a law student. Law students study law. Anyway, they do if they want to be lawyers, not gas station attendants, copywriters at J. Walter Thompson, here today, gone tomorrow. Let your husband run his own life, okay?"

Will saw Debo flush, saw moisture come to her eyes. Her dad never criticized. Now he was criticizing. He must feel strongly about this trial.

Leonard was putting a large hand on his shoulder.

"You did a good job, Will, taking him on alone. Now do something even smarter, give the problem to a gun hand. Nobody could have stood taller for his mother. Or his father. Now leave it to me."

Will looked at him, suddenly a rock, a wall, a vast comforting presence.

Something new, Leonard putting Debo down, praising him.

Suddenly he felt galvanized, shot through with energy, yes, and more than energy, a wave of craving for this new, contrite Debo.

"Thanks," he said, reaching out, pulling his wife close, putting an arm tightly around her.

In the tiny, dark restaurant, smelling of garlic, basil, simmering tomatoes, Leonard was lighting the largest cigar he'd been able to find.

Marco paid no attention to city ordinances. The Torcellos' cigars were part of them. Therefore, all Marco's waiters cupped cigarettes, patrons flourished Havanas. Leonard would have preferred brandishing a stiletto. Still, the cigar was something to point, stab aggressively at Bishop. He couldn't kill the man. But he could blow smoke at those cold blue eyes.

For Pax, he thought. For my girl. Because I've got to get her back, take care of her. I can handle Bishop. This is my territory, my field. If I can't put him away, I'm a rotten lawyer, a rotten lover.

He was pleased to see there was almost nobody in the little restaurant. He hadn't requested privacy from Joey Torcello, just said he needed a place to talk. Joey had made a single phone call. He was naturally attuned, you could say, to privacy.

Even without a lot of customers, though, the smells from the kitchen were mouthwatering. And Bishop was coming down the steps from the street, big, broad, straight-backed, an owner of the earth.

Leonard was up, his whole body aching to spring, his fists tight to smash the pale WASP face, the face of so many men who'd had no job for him at their firms, who played all the smooth games men like Bishop expected from birth to win.

I haven't felt this hot since that Nazi Borowik, Leonard thought. I'd better go easy.

Bishop was holding out his hand, the hand that was threatening Pax, his Pax.

Thank Christ for the restaurant. He wouldn't have wanted to risk meeting Bishop anywhere else, not even the time-honored park bench. Dangerous, a private talk with someone involved in his firm's trial, something a careful lawyer would never do. Unless he was ready to take risks, big ones, for his lady love. And, oh, was he ready!

At least they were the same height, eye to eye across the red-checked tablecloth. And oddly, dressed alike, Brooks Brothers suits, rep ties, plain shirts. Did Harvard Law prescribe clothing for its graduates, whatever stratum of society they came from?

"Tal," Leonard said, "I'm glad you saw your way clear to coming. I take it Scotty Wickham approves?"

Did Wickham know his client was here? Would he make hay out of it at some future date?

A glance at Marco and glasses were on the table, a bottle of wine. It would be superb wine, Tuscany's best. The food would be equally excellent. Bless the Torcellos, never settling for less.

"I don't clear everything with Scotty," Bishop said. "He knows we're on an important screening committee together. Quite natural for us to meet."

"Well, not exactly kosher for a lawyer to lunch with a litigant on the other side. You went to law school, Harvard, wasn't it? So did I. They taught me that. I imagine you, too."

"They taught me a great deal," Bishop said, unfolding his starched napkin, waving it as if he were blowing Leonard away. "They taught me it's a lot easier to disbar a practicing lawyer than one who doesn't need the bar membership."

"Oh, I don't think anyone's going to be disbarred. That's why we're in this place."

Murdered, he wanted to say. That's a possibility. But not disbarred.

"Always glad to have a good ethnic lunch," Bishop said. "But why? Something you need to discuss in the privacy of your own Italian restaurant?"

"You could say that."

Leonard's blood seemed to be turning the consistency of the wine, cool, thin, with a touch of vinegar.

He knew what would make it heat, boil. Telling this prick what he thought of him. Only that solution wasn't available right now.

"I'm a great admirer of your *Journal*, you know. Always subscribed, even when I was young and penniless, even at four bucks a copy."

"Did we meet to discuss the *Journal*?"

"In a way," Leonard said easily. "In a way."

Food appeared, pasta, creamy, steaming, smelling of Naples and cream and heaven.

Bishop picked up his fork, tasted. Smiled. Dug in.

"What way?"

"Well, now," Leonard said, "did you know Will Ford was married to my daughter?"

"Of course," Bishop said. "Young, isn't he? For a husband?"

"Young," Leonard said. "But very determined."

"Good. Then you may know I gave him a piece of advice the other day. To have a talk with his mother, get her to see straight."

"Oh, I don't think she has much trouble seeing straight. She knows her job. And a shit when she sees one."

"Plenty of those in this case," Bishop said, putting down his fork. "A tough case to live with, you know. The papers, the publicity, pressure, dreadful. Particularly for my wife. All she wanted was to rescue her niece. Now she finds herself in a nightmare. The sooner it's over, the better. I expressed my feelings to the judge on that score."

"So she told us."

"Then you might add your counsel to mine. Perhaps she'd listen to you."

"Oh, she'll do what I advise," Leonard said. "As a lawyer, of course. After all, she'll be turning up soon in front of both of us at the screening panel. That's a public forum, for all intents and purposes. Anything that's revealed there in the way of pressures resisted, strong-arm tactics faced down, all to her credit."

"Yes, the panel," Bishop said. "I think when Pax Ford's in a higher court, she'll be happy, too happy to fret about a simple issue like this."

"Could be," Leonard said, draining his wineglass, reaching for the bottle. "You bring up just what I'm interested in, keeping everybody happy. Personally, I know how things are when my clients are happy, how they can go wrong when clients worry. Take the Torcellos."

"The Torcellos," Bishop said.

"Nice guys, you know, contrary to popular impression. They don't trouble to correct impressions, especially when those impressions serve their purposes. Emotional, of course. Headstrong. But loyal? They invented the word. Their loyalty to people who've been helpful to them is extraordinary. People like me."

"Commendable," Bishop said.

He looked up as Marco put fresh plates in front of them, arugula, radicchio, chopped, beautiful, fresh as if he'd just picked it somewhere outside the back door.

"I'm not saying there isn't an old godfather type somewhere, back in Palermo. But the Torcellos I know have been around for some time, had money for some time. Their kids are at Yale, Princeton, all the best places. They don't break knees anymore, if that's what you thought."

"It makes little difference to me what they break, Leonard. I don't have to defend them."

"It might make a difference under certain circumstances. You see, the Torcellos love me. I've never asked for favors, never needed them. So I've got quite a few markers. They want me happy, concentrating on them and their affairs. They worry when I get distracted, concerned about someone more or less in my family. Like Judge Ford. They understand being concerned about women, it's in their culture."

"Leonard," Bishop said, putting down his fork, "get to the point. If you have a point."

"I have a point. I don't imagine you get too close to your delivery operations, Tal. But you may know that Torcello people deliver your paper. The teamsters' local may be working out a contract. They've been mulling one over for some time, I gather. But meanwhile, your circulation director is coasting along with a working arrangement."

"What of it?"

"It works because your man, Johnny Russo, asks his friends about dependable people, and on their advice gives his business, your business, to nonunion truckers he can count on. No contract, just an agreement. You haven't signed a contract in some years. You see, I have research capabilities, too."

He saw Bishop's lip curl. "Sitting here," he said, "I can believe it."

"Why, Tal," Leonard said, "something wrong with your salad?"

"There's a lot wrong," Bishop said.

"Sorry. Because I sincerely feel you run a great news-paper. You have tremendous subscription commitments, you face them every single weekday. There's not a lawyer, a judge in the city, who doesn't subscribe to your *Journal,* the big firms, by the dozens. It would be too bad if your papers didn't get where you wanted them to go."

"Oh, for God's sake," Bishop said, pushing back his chair.

"Not for God's sake," Leonard said. "For your own sake. I happen to be a defense lawyer on retainer with a bunch of men who run a number of enterprises in this city, restaurants like this one, nightclubs, supermarkets, dry cleaners, linen supply, and more. Like newspaper delivery."

"Aren't you being a bit dramatic?"

"Not at all. You spoke to a woman and a boy. Now you're talking to me. Somehow you didn't fully grasp the kind of friends I have. I don't make threats, I'm not foolish. I'm only suggesting what could happen if my friends don't like my being distracted."

He watched Bishop toss his napkin on the table.

But he was seeing Pax, his Pax, small, fine-boned, beau-tiful, smelling her fresh flower scent.

And feeling invisible armor closing itself all around him, greaves, clasps, breast plate, a sword heavy in his hand, its scabbard weighty at his side.

"After all, Tal, you don't want anybody confusing news delivery with garbage disposal."

He saw Bishop's face flush. The bully bullied. It never failed. They crumbled.

"Think about it," he said softly. "It isn't really your style, blackmail. I don't think your heart was in it. I think talking to Judge Ford was just an impulse of the moment. I know you're worried about your wife. I know how your judgment fails when you're worried. Why don't you forget the whole thing and let the judge try the case?"

He followed Bishop up the steps to the street.

They walked together toward the two large black cars parked at the hydrant, smack in front of the restaurant, drivers alert at the wheels.

Something about letting this bastard out of his hands, seeing him safely to his car, seared Leonard's soul.

"I just want to tell you," he said, "if anything funny finds its way into print about Pax Ford, I won't need the Torcellos. If there's even a hint, a reference, a joke, I'll take care of you all by myself."

He watched the car slide smoothly away from the curb, realized that though he was shaking with red fury, he was still somehow eleven feet tall.

18

ROSA

THE LAWYER ON HIS FEET BEFORE ROSA HAD A COMMANDING voice, but Larry's cut through it as he shouted from far back in her courtroom.

"Judge! Recess! Call a recess now!"

Shocked, she looked up. He waved wildly at her, red-faced, sweating, corduroy jacket buttoned wrong.

"Tomorrow, nine o'clock," she said to the lawyer, hoping her law clerk hadn't lost his mind.

Her officer was up, repeating her order, starting to clear the courtroom. Now Larry was just below her, catching his breath.

"Your nephew," he said, coughing. "Your nephew, Carlos."

Rosa stared at him, eyes widening as if the courtroom had suddenly gone dark.

"Waiting outside. It's your mother. He took her to the hospital, Judge, in an ambulance. Now he's out there, in a cab. He says come right away!"

Another emergency room?

"Take your purse, Judge, go. I'll get the rest of your stuff, bring it to the hospital."

And when she still stared, feeling punched in the chest, he reached up, took her arm, tugged her.

"He was afraid to come in for you, the driver wouldn't wait. Come on, I'll show you where."

Rosa's eyes cleared. A Puerto Rican boy in a taxi. Of course the driver wouldn't wait. Anger released her, sent her following Larry up the aisle, into the big lobby, out the front door.

Carlos, beckoning from a cab window, slender body tense, face strangely old with fear, worry.

"Hola!" he called. "Here, Rosita."

"There you go," she heard Larry say.

Then she was in the cab, taking off in a screech of tires.

Carlos took her hand. "Just calm down," he said.

Calm down! She hadn't said a word. But there was plenty to say. What was happening? What was wrong with her mother?

Now there were tears in his eyes!

"She never told me, never said one word," he said in Spanish. "The wound, Rosa, from the shots that time, the boys in the park."

The wound? But that was old. Healed, anyway healing. They said if her mother kept up the antibiotics, went back to have the dressing changed, she'd be fine.

Rosa seemed to hear a deep minor chord.

Had Mami taken the pills? Walked back to the hospital to let them look at her wound? Had Rosa ever asked her? Made sure?

"Infection," Carlos was saying. "She had no idea, paid no attention. She had headaches, slept a lot. Yesterday morning it must have blown up."

"Mira," Rosa said, automatically speaking Spanish, too. "Why an emergency?"

"Rosa, she fell. On the floor in the kitchen. She must have been there half the night, all the morning. Now she has a big fever and a big wound, badly infected. The doctor said they

worry about the brain; head wound infections can spread to
the brain."

Mami? Rosa had talked to her early this morning.

No, yesterday morning. They hadn't spoken for a day,
more. Guilt, shame made her head throb, as if she too had a
big fever and a big wound.

The taxi swooped into the hospital driveway. Metropolitan Hospital again. Decorated with Christmas lights now, only
half of them working, it seemed. At least they'd have Mami's
records. If they kept records in this place.

"Can you pay?" Carlos was saying. "I do not have enough."

She reached blindly for her change purse, handed it to
him, mustered the strength to get out.

In a flurry they were through the crowded lobby, in an
elevator, running down a corridor. A different floor, a different corridor from before.

But they're all the same, Rosa kept thinking. They're all
too noisy, too busy, dirty, jammed, all the same.

Finally, a bed, two men in hospital green bent over it. And
Mami, in a bed again, her head swathed in white again.

"*Mira*, Mami," Carlos said. "I have brought Rosa. Now you
will feel better, you will be fine."

Rosa tried to speak in any language, couldn't. Fear and
terror were taking away all power to talk, think. She only
wanted to cry out, wail in misery and terror.

Mami's face was a red, moist mask, eyes glittering, feverish,
lips dry and cracked. One of the doctors turned, frowned. An
Indian, dark as Carlos, small, with tiny, glittering eyeglasses.

"Everything is under control. First we have to get the fever
down. Then we can deal with what may be a kidney involve-
ment. Has she complained of urinary problems?"

Carlos looked embarrassed, turned away.

When had Mami ever complained?

"Well, we'll get her right. But she needs rest, a chance to
let the antibiotics take over. A night on the kitchen floor does
no good for anyone."

Rosa felt tears come to her eyes, spill down her cheeks.

"Carlos," Mami said suddenly, her voice very small. "Go. Work. You will be late."

Carlos stood straighter, looked at Rosa, grinned.

"She can't be so bad," he said. "They must be right, she'll be fine."

"*Esta okay*, Mami," he said. "I go, Rosa is here."

Even going to the job Pax helped find him in a midtown parking garage, a job he didn't like, Rosa sensed his relief at getting away. With one jaunty look he was gone, hands shoved in his pockets.

Rosa dried her eyes, started to sit back and then jolted upright.

His pockets! Her change purse was in those pockets! She tried to remember how much money was there, couldn't. Well, she wasn't going anywhere. Larry would come, lend her cab fare home. She turned her whole mind to her mother, glad to be close, able to watch over her.

Mami looked small as a child. Her face was coral, like one of Rosa's new dresses. Rosa longed to take her mother in her arms, kiss her wrinkled cheek, smooth her thinning hair.

More, she wanted to get a bowl of soft, delicious food, maybe rice and beans, feed Mami spoonful by spoonful, give her sips of rich, black Bustelo, make her strong again.

She stared at the plastic bag, the tube dripping something yellow and thick into her mother's arm.

She'd have to be Mami's mother, watch everything for her. Keep Carlos in hand, too. Who knew what would be next with him?

Forget Carlos, she told herself. Mami needs you now.

And she needed Mami. There were so many things to tell, to talk about.

"I'm sorry, so sorry I didn't call," Rosa said softly. "I was saving things to tell you. I went to a party, Mami, a big, elegant party. In the most beautiful dress I ever had. They took my picture for the newspapers. Wait till you see!"

"Beautiful dress now," Mami whispered, her eyes moving down Rosa's tangerine suit, silky, short, clinging.

Rosa could feel herself take on the color of the suit.

She'd wanted so to tell Mami about Leonard. "I bought it to be pretty for a new friend, Mami. A wonderful man."

Mami had hated her boyfriend, met him once, never stopped nagging Rosa to be rid of him. Because he was married. How Mami knew that Rosa wasn't sure, but she knew.

"Leonard Scholer," Rosa said, savoring the sound of it on her tongue.

"Not *Puerterro*," Mami said, without emphasis, so Rosa couldn't tell whether that displeased her or not.

"Jewish," Rosa said. "A big lawyer, very important, always in the newspapers. He came to me for help with Pax's Willie."

"If he is important, why does he need your help?"

"He wanted something only a judge could do," Rosa told her, thinking, no wonder I'm not married, there was never anyone to please her, never.

"He's been a big help to me," she said, smiling. "He knows a great deal, how I should dress, behave, to be an important judge, maybe more important than now."

Mami was frowning.

"*Señora* Pax can teach you those things, too," she said, obviously making a great effort.

Pax, always Pax, Rosa thought, annoyed.

A doctor, putting his head around the screen at the end of Mami's bed.

"Try to keep her quiet. They're getting a bed ready. Soon we can move her."

"Who is this man?" Mami said to Rosa, as if the doctor didn't exist.

She'd never lied to her mother. Why try? She'd never have gotten away with it.

"He is a friend of Pax's."

Mami was moving, my God, trying to sit up!

"Lie still," Rosa said, alarmed. "Or they will make me go."

"What kind of friend?"

"He is Willie's wife's father. That is why he came to me for help when the boy was in trouble."

Her mother's eyes were closing. "It burns," she said. "It bites, Rosita."

Indian doctors. Couldn't they give Mami something to keep her from pain?

"I'll get someone," Rosa said, starting to stand up.

"Stay. He is married?"

"He was married, to a nasty lady, the way it sounds."

"As he makes it sound."

"Mami, he's decent, honorable. He takes me beautiful places, teaches me things a judge should know. He thinks I'm young and pretty and smart."

"You are young and pretty," Mami said, as if she didn't think much of any man for discovering those things. "Not always smart."

Why had she ever thought Mami was the child, she the grown-up?

"He was proud to take me to the party, be seen with me," she said, patting her mother's hand.

Though not so happy when Pax saw us together, she thought. She left, upset. And I helped her, sent Leonard after her. And went home alone in a taxi, with a driver who whined all the way about the long ride up to Riverdale.

Leonard hadn't called this morning, either.

All right, if mothers could criticize you, they could also comfort you. Suddenly Rosa desperately needed comfort from somewhere.

"Mami," she began, the soft Spanish syllables coating her tongue with honey, "I'm lonely, you know it. Not every man can love a judge, a woman with power. This man understands the work, understands me. He can love me, help me. I deserve such a man. I've waited so long. I've never had a wedding, babies."

"You surely had no wedding, no babies, from that Italian," Mami said.

Suddenly Rosa felt feverish herself, raging.

Why can't she just listen? Why do her old-country ideas get into everything? Was it a hard life that made her so fearful? Is it my having it easier that makes me feel so guilty, so eager to please her?

No, that wasn't the reason.

She loved, valued her mother. Mami had been everything when Rosa was small. She'd been Mami and Papi both, earned the money, cooked the food, made the rules, enforced them, sang the children to sleep. She adored Carmen and Mickey, so far away, the only children left to her out of so many borne, so many dead. But she blazed with pride for her Rosa, simply shone with pride.

Rosa let her shoulders slump, tired, her stomach twisting a little from the smells around her, the unceasing bustle of the huge ward.

Esperanza Macario looked at her prize, her beautiful, brilliant daughter. Right now Rosita looked smudged, blurred, as if seen through dirty eyeglasses.

She looks so tired, Esperanza thought. And why not? A sick mother making trouble. A nephew making trouble. Sister and brother far away, no help at all.

Ay, how her head hurt. Her scalp was burning, pain spreading to her forehead, her cheekbones. If only she had a poultice, cucumber, pineapple, cool, healing. In her own kitchen she could peel, chop, fold up a clean dishtowel, soothe this pain.

But she must not rest yet. Not till she told Rosa the truth about Señora Pax. So she would know her rich friend was never to be envied, had troubles of her own, hard troubles.

I can't do it, Esperanza thought, burning. I have no strength. I love them both, Pax and Rosa, Rosa and Pax.

I must tell.

"Querida," Rosa heard.

"Sí, Mami. Yo estoy aquí."

"You do not know what happens behind people's doors," Mami said, lifting her head. "Pax has carried trouble in silence for many years."

What was Mami talking about?

Rosa wanted to stand up, walk away from this relentless little person in the bed.

"Listen, Rosa. Alone I got you away from a *papi* with big fists, worse things, as we know. I brought you on the plane weeping with fear, and I no less afraid than you children. I made a home in a place where boys had knives, girls went in the streets with men even before they became women."

Here it is, Rosa thought. The old song, the island song every Puerto Rican mother sings over and over.

Then, quickly, she was ashamed. It was all true. Thanks to her mother *she* hadn't had to wash clothes, be someone's servant.

"You have only been poor," Mami said. "Poor is nothing, poor can be fixed. Pax's trouble can never be fixed."

What was Mami talking about? What did she know?

Rosa's irritation faded, uncovering a little dagger of curiosity, sharp and pointed, honed by Mami's words into something bright, lethal.

"What trouble, Mami? What are you telling me?"

Mami turned her head on the pillow slowly, as if she wasn't sure no one was listening.

"I tell you as my daughter, as a judge. Never tell any other."

"Yes, but what?"

"Señora Pax's husband was one who loved other men."

Delirious, Rosa thought. Sicker than I thought, probably sicker than that Indian knows. I'm going out and get him, make him give her something.

"Mami," she said, leaning forward, "don't talk anymore. Just rest."

"Listen, Pax's husband was not for women. In her mother's kitchen they all knew. That Cathleen, she knew."

"But Pax was married for years. They had a son. They had Willie."

Now her mother was sending her a pitying look.

"Oh, Rosa," she said.

Wait, but her mother was no fool. She knew things. Servants always knew things. How many times had Mami said there were no secrets from a laundress? One who took stains out of sheets, lipstick off shirts, blood off a woman's panties every month? A laundress knew all the secrets of a household! And Mami had stayed there long after Pax married, until Pax's mother died, left Mami a little money of her own.

Can it be? Rosa thought, blood stirring, brain starting to spin. Was Alden really a *maricon*? Pax never said. Did she know from the beginning? Or did she find out later?

"For a while," Mami said, "the maids talked of nothing else. But they loved the family, they kept quiet. When he died I was glad, Rosa. Señora Pax would never have the shame, or Willie."

Rosa's head swirled. My God, if she had found out her husband was a *maricon*, she'd be beside herself! Some women might not mind, though. *Yanqui* women might not feel the same. Especially if there was an arrangement, an understanding. Many men loved both women and other men; perhaps Alden was one of those.

Rosa's head was whirling, spinning.

Out of the many little thoughts, one came clear. Pax's trial! She was presiding over a case that was all about being gay. One litigant was gay. One witness was dying of being gay.

But she hadn't recused herself. Revealed any prejudicial interest. Yet how could she be fair? If she hated gays because of Alden, she'd be prejudiced. If she was sympathetic because of him, she would be prejudiced the other way. She couldn't be an impartial judge. If the story got out, she'd look terrible. If the screening panel people knew she'd withheld information, they'd never put her name on an approved list!

Rosa stared at the dirty wall.

Did Leonard know? And what would he think if he did know? If she told Leonard, what then? That his perfect Pax had been married to a homosexual, lived a lie? It would have to make her less in Leonard's eyes, even if it had been long ago.

And if Rosa hinted the news to Talcott Bishop? To reporters? One word to the gay organizations, those Lambda people, the Gay and Lesbian Coalition, and Pax's reputation would be shredded past even Leonard's help!

She came to, realized her mother hadn't spoken in some time.

Mami's eyes were closed now. And something was wrong with her breathing.

There wasn't any.

Mami wasn't breathing. Not at all.

Rosa felt cold terror touch her heart. She laid her palm on her mother's cheek.

Cold, her mother was frozen cold.

Terrified, knowing what she didn't want to know, losing all balance, sense, control, Rosa put back her head and screamed from deep down in her throat for someone to come.

All through the funeral in the church on 125th Street, Rosa tried to fix the ceremony in her mind, terrified she'd never remember a single detail.

But she could only stand, kneel, pray in a kind of ugly dream while it all became one dark blur: priest, church, her sister and brother, so many faces, so many mourners, men, women, old, young, children, babies.

We could be on the island, she'd thought, seeing how the faces ranged from her own honey color to deep black.

She sat in front with Carmen, Mickey, Carlos, all the family that was left. But felt only that she didn't belong with them or anyone here, that she should be set apart, high over everyone, as if she were in her courtroom.

She tried to think about Mami, stared at the white casket.

But she couldn't focus, her mind kept popping off. Had every woman in her mother's project shown up? Every Rican in the neighborhood? Was anyone left in the sweatshops, luncheonettes, *bodegas*? Would they all press into her mother's small apartment to eat, drink, talk?

Later, she wasn't sure how much later, she stood dishing up rice in the tiny kitchen, feeling nothing.

Thank God for her plump sister, a teacher in Portland, Oregon, and as *yanqui* now as anyone, kind, sweet to the weeping neighborhood women who'd brought so much food, wept so many tears.

Thank God, too, for her older brother, an engineer from Texas, filling glasses, making talk, telling how Mami had never clung to him, tried to keep him close, urged him to go out West and make his own way.

More people kept coming, crowding the little rooms, knocking the crucifix on the wall crooked, putting their coats on Mami's beautiful crocheted bedspread.

If she were still here she'd be cross, Rosa thought. Chase them all away, call them freeloaders. She'd vanished so quickly Rosa still felt she could return, walk into the kitchen at any moment. So Rosa couldn't really mourn. She could only dish up great platters of rice and beans, stewed pork, chopped tomatoes and peppers, sticky cakes, make sure the rum bottles were replaced as fast as they emptied.

She looked at her wavering reflection in the damp kitchen window.

Terrible, she looked terrible. Wearing one of her own dresses, black, a far cry from any of Leonard's rainbow choices. Like a *jibara* woman, sallow, ugly, old.

But nobody here cared how she looked. She was just another woman reheating beans in a big pot so the rich chocolate smell grew thick in the rooms, rolled up against the windows. Her compatriots didn't like open windows in New York winters.

Someone was with her now, standing just behind her.

Rosa turned, surprised to see a pale face, a *yanqui* face.

Pax. Smaller than ever somehow. Coming close, looking up at her, putting up a hand to touch Rosa's shoulder.

"Rosa," she said, "I'm so sorry. You know I'll miss her, too. I loved her, too."

Having Pax actually standing next to her woke Rosa up. Her emotions began simmering like the food bubbling on the stove. She felt a rush of all the different things she wanted to say, many things all at once.

Where were you, why didn't you come before?

I missed you so. I need you. And I have things to ask you. Mami says Alden was gay, is that true? Do I like you, Pax? Love you? Or hate you, am I burning with envy of you?

Had Mami's death sent her off her head?

"I didn't see you," she made herself say. "Not here, not at the church."

She watched Pax bite her lip, saw her eyes flash just a touch. "You were in front," Pax said. "You never once looked around."

"You might have spoken to me."

Pax was frowning now, as if she were arguing with herself.

"Let's say I'm getting used to it, Rosa. You didn't see me so fast at the Women's Bar dinner, either."

Ah, she was angry.

"I'm sorry," Pax said, putting her hand on Rosa's arm. "I shouldn't have said that. I didn't come to say that. I came to say I'll miss your mother, Rosa. Very much. She showed me how to keep going when bad things happened. She came and stayed with me when Alden died. I learned from her, I loved her, and I feel for you."

"Pax," Rosa said, "if I've hurt you, I'm sorry. If I've stepped on your toes, I'm sorry. It's not my fault if things happen. Mistakes are made on both sides. A man changes his mind. A screening panel chooses a judge. Whatever happens, Pax, let's be friends, the way we've always been."

*   *   *

Pax felt the words like an assault.

There was a small cut on her hand, from the glass of the greenhouse. Now it stung, sharply.

Did Rosa dare suggest she hadn't gone after Leonard? The way she'd flirted at the dinner? And didn't she know which of them was the better judge? Was she retreating into Latino fatalism, pretending that chance governed everything, that she herself wasn't responsible for anything? Hadn't she learned yet that everyone makes his own troubles?

Suddenly her cut hand was tingling, wanting to slap, shock Rosa out of this ridiculous act, this talking cant, that black dress, that look of lines cut in her face, the sound of hysteria in her voice.

Easy, she told herself, mustering a lifetime of governing herself. *Esta okay*. Rosa has a point. Leonard is his own person, he goes where he wants. The screening panel makes its own decisions, they do what they want. All I can manage is myself. I've done it before, I'll do it now.

No need to lose Rosa, too, after such a long, long time.

Tell her, she thought.

She opened her mouth to begin. But then she heard steps, knew someone had come into the kitchen, turned.

Leonard, filling the doorway. Filling her with joy, relief, like a rescuer with a bright lamp after long, terrified hours in a black cave.

Then she remembered. He hadn't brought comfort for her. His lamp was for Rosa.

A sense of loss as great as her loss of Esperanza Macario filled her heart.

She walked past him, through the crowd, out the door of the little apartment.

To Rosa, Leonard looked strange, alien among all those small, dark men.

He was too big. His suit was too beautiful, his tie too

elegant, his whole demeanor too somber among all the noisy, chattering people.

Worse, he looked shocked, punished, as if Pax had slapped him before she'd gone.

"Rosa," he said, "I didn't know about your mother till I read the *Bar Journal.* When I knew, I came."

The way he said it made her want to cry, cry hard for the first time since the hospital.

Leonard's face crumpled. He put an arm around her shoulder, handed her his pristine linen handkerchief. Was she the only one in this world who didn't carry beautiful linen handkerchiefs? Maybe she should buy some. The way she was crying now she might never stop.

Leonard was turning his head, searching the group in Mami's parlor. Looking after Pax? Frowning when he couldn't see her? Or because he felt so alien among these noisy people, tearing into platefuls of spicy food, tossing down tumblers full of dark, rich rum?

She's gone, Rosa wanted to say. She's wise. She knows where she doesn't fit in, a lady, white like you, quietly dressed like you, speaking English in her college voice like you. Pax knew these people would be awed. They've all seen her pictures on television. She was sensitive to that, wouldn't intrude, and so she left.

A vast sadness seemed to fill her heart.

What am I telling myself? she thought. He doesn't fit in with me. I don't fit in with him. He came to my house looking for Pax. He should be in her house, with her.

She made an enormous effort, stopped crying, wiped her tears away with his handkerchief.

Mami knew, she thought.

She put his handkerchief in her pocket, the way Carlos had done with her change purse. If she acted like a friend instead of a lover, if she did right, it could be the only thing she'd have of his.

"Leonard," she said, "you were kind to come. Now go.

This is no place for you. This is my place. You don't belong, you wouldn't understand what happens here. We have our own way with death. There will be a big party, everyone will laugh, cry, eat and drink. You wouldn't like it, you wouldn't even like the food, Leonard."

Leonard's forehead was wrinkling, he was staring at her in puzzlement.

"What is it, Rosa? What are you trying to say?"

Ay, Dios, she'd spoken to him in Spanish.

Spanish!

Since he'd appeared, she'd been thinking, speaking entirely in Spanish.

Rosa took a long breath, began saying it all again, English.

But she seemed to be speaking to empty air. Leonard was becoming invisible, his face fading, disappearing from her sight. Because he was a foreigner, one who would never, could never, however hard he tried, speak the language of her heart.

19

LEONARD

THE ELEVATORS AT THE WORLD TRADE CENTER SHOT UP LIKE guided missiles. Nevertheless, Leonard remembered, they'd stopped cold when terrorists got busy with bombs.

Near the fortieth floor his ears sealed themselves tight. Getting out on the sixty-fifth, he could hardly hear his own footsteps as he walked toward the meeting room. The sudden small handicap was maddening. He'd need all his senses, all his sense for this meeting of the screening panel.

By rights he'd have had months before the panel convened, near next year's elections. Months to make up with Pax, let Bishop see sense, let Rosa find someone better for herself than he'd ever be. Now, because an App Div judge who'd lingered so long in a hospital had suddenly died, left a vacancy in the overworked court, here he was. In an office tarted up for Christmas in plastic and tinsel with both women coming, both at the big conference table.

Pax and Rosa.

Rosa and Pax.

Leonard fought an impulse to get back in the elevator, let whatever was going to happen, happen without him.

Seeing Rosa, he'd feel like a shit. But seeing Pax, he'd feel like a fool, and that was worse in his book.

All right, he'd made up his mind to be here, not to push openly for Pax, which he couldn't appear to do, but to cream the competition.

He went through double doors into a conference room. Empty. He was early. Proof positive he wasn't himself. When was he ever early?

He walked to one of the vast windows, stared down at the ribbon of river, the toy boats in the harbor.

That night with Pax made me feel sky high, he thought. With my head, not in the cows but the clouds, like the white ones out there.

Pax and Rosa, Rosa and Pax. What the hell would he do when they came in? Act as if they were just two more candidates? Sit like a potato latke while others asked questions? Recuse himself, go slump in the reception room while they answered questions?

Already he felt hot, sweaty. And winded, as if he'd run one of Bishop's well-publicized *Bar Journal* marathons in Central Park.

It didn't help being in this room, this monument to foolishness. The Trade Center had been blueprinted in boom times. By the time it was finished, Manhattan offices were going begging. The state had foolishly taken over the space for a law library nobody used, a vast conference room no committee filled. And some state official foolishly had helped his girl by letting her decorate. She'd OD'd on fake Chippendale, gold draperies, big flags. And bad portraits of old judges nobody remembered.

Looking up at them, Leonard realized, for the first time, that all the old judges were men.

Whoever picked them had it easy. Nobody'd fallen in love with a candidate, or fallen in lust, either. Different now that women had half the places in law schools, now Judith Kaye was the chief judge up in Albany. Still, Sandra Day O'Connor and Ruthie Ginsberg were the only women on the U.S. Supreme Court, Betty Ellerin and Angela Mazzarelli the lone stars on the court they'd be discussing today. Things weren't exactly equal for women in the law yet.

Still, he could remember a professor in his own law school who refused to say "Miss" to any woman, called the few female students there were "Mr." just as he'd always done.

He jumped when the doors banged, flew inward. Dan Heller, a buddy, a mensch. One of the three trial lawyers on the panel. Men who practically lived in court, really knew one judge from another. Handsome as ever today, big, salt-and-pepper hair perfectly cut, suit a model of tailoring.

"All right, the working stiffs are here," Dan said, slinging his tennis bag behind one of the chairs.

Wait, Leonard thought. Wait till you see how much work I do today.

"So where are the pols?" Dan was going on.

They both knew that once Whit Saltonstall walked over from his Wall Street firm, the real horse-trading would start. Everyone else represented some group. Women lawyers. The black community. Gays and lesbians. Hispanics, the quarter of the city's population that provided jobs for interpreters in every New York courtroom. They'd battle till they could agree on seven or eight names to present to the governor. Then the man would choose one judge to fill the vacancy in the Appellate Court, First Department, serving the Bronx and Manhattan, one of the busiest courts in the country.

The panel's own three lawyers were coming in now, bustling around the table like waiters, arms filled with papers.

Leonard sat, almost grabbed his copies out of the lawyer's hands. Fat questionnaires, filled out by each candidate, education, experience, publications, teaching, health, finances, judicial successes and reversals. The panel could, and would, question everything. The questionnaires would be arranged in the order of the judges' appearances.

Dan was thumbing his pile. He'd have a favorite, of

course. Everyone would. But Dan's could well be Pax. Whit's too.

"Saw you on Court TV, Leonard," Dan said without lifting his head. "That year-end review. For the Borowik case. You deserve an Academy award, defending that Nazi asshole."

Ordinarily Leonard would be pleased. Dan was no flatterer, didn't need to be. He was big in the negligence bar, winning multimillion-dollar awards for mothers who found ants in cereal boxes, children who cut themselves on toys, patients whose surgeons removed the wrong eye.

The third questionnaire in the pile was Rosa's, the fifth, Pax's.

"Your friend Kistel's not big on pro bono. Doesn't he scream about your serving on this panel?"

"Only a little," Leonard said. "He likes knowing one judge from another. Today there's a lot to know."

"I hear we have our orders. The governor's let it be known he wants a broad."

I want one, too, Leonard thought. A particular broad. Pax Peyton Ford, who'll grace the high court with her presence.

"Be nice for Judge Ford," Dan went on. "Wasn't her old man in the App Div?"

"His picture's right outside the courtroom, next to Roy Cohn's father's," Leonard told him. "Glares at me whenever I go down to argue an appeal."

"He's glaring at what's happening to the judiciary," Dan said. "Women, gays, blacks, those stuffy old guys would die all over again."

He stopped short because the doors were opening again, a woman coming in.

Marion Esdras King. Big as a man, smart as two men, wearing a suit as tailored as Dan's, first vice-president of the Manhattan Women's Bar.

Marion had been at the dinner smoking one of the cigars. Had she seen him with Rosa? Just like her to say something.

Others were drifting in, clustering at the end of the table, all talking at once, puffed up with behind-the-scenes power. Being a judge still meant being able to ruin or repair people's lives. The App Div was top lawyers arguing top cases. The power to discipline lawyers, swear in the new kids who passed the bar exam. Even a higher salary, not that judges cared much about money. If they did, they'd all be lawyers, especially now that starting law associates made almost as much as they did. So it still meant something to pick judges, too.

Leonard looked up, saw Talcott Bishop coming through the door carrying a briefcase so scarred only a rich man who didn't put on a show for anyone would touch it.

Immediately he felt his shoulders tighten, seemed to taste garlic, tomatoes. Bishop would surely have to sit out for Pax, too; she was running his trial. Why hadn't he stayed away? What did the son of a bitch have in mind? A blackmailer wouldn't hesitate to pull some other dirty trick.

Bishop was heading for Raoul Garcia, a wheel in the Hispanic Bar Association, young, earnest, wearing a tight, dark suit. The bastard had courted Rosa; he was running pieces on the Puerto Rican Legal Defense and Education Fund, the National Congress for Puerto Rican Rights. Was Rosa his candidate? Did his new Spanish-language stuff mean bad news for Pax? But that was stupid. Bishop would clobber Pax anyway, if he could.

For a moment Leonard felt queasy, as if he were still in the elevator.

What was he supposed to do? Pax was far from his. She didn't have a clue that he'd talked to Bishop, and she'd never hear it from him. She'd been a wild thing smashing her greenhouse, a cool little person at Rosa's mother's house, while Rosa turned into a foreigner from a Spanish-speaking country. Maybe he'd only ever see Pax in family gatherings, or in court. If she won this promotion, he'd have to make a specialty of arguing appeals. And why was he making jokes, even to himself? He'd probably blown his best chance for happiness.

Easy, now, he told himself. It's not life or death. Just love, where all's supposed to be fair.

He looked around the table, counted heads.

Alton Taylor, editor of the *Harlem News,* a battler, a power-house in the black community. Alton looked like a Baptist minister, vests, gold pocket watch, the serene expression of a man who talks regularly to God.

Maria Torres, big deal in the teachers' union. An ugly woman, skin pitted, body shapeless, heavy in a lumpy dark suit. How would she feel about Rosa? Jealous? Sisterly?

William Chase Carson, head of the Gay Lawyers Association, HIV-positive and proud of it. Leonard thought of the witness in Pax's courtroom, emaciated, desperately ill. Would Chase ever look like that?

The thought died with the entrance of Barry Scott Williams, managing partner of Lubbers, Henshaw. A big entrance, handshakes, asides, whispers, making his presence felt. The panel chairman, looking like a wise old owl, beak-nosed, neckless, turning his head quickly to check out the other arrivals. Chairperson, Leonard reminded himself. Chair. Whatever the hell they call it now so women won't fuss.

Manny Rose, the elderly labor lawyer, a founder of the Jewish Lawyers Guild, five feet tall in built-up shoes, worth a million a foot.

Martha Voice Bartos, one of the rare women in the Inner Circle of Advocates, big-money lawyers. Not much taller than Pax, blond, tough. Her suit was expensive, fussy, funny little frills all along its lapels. Lately she'd been giving Dan Heller a run for his fees.

Twelve people. A jury for judges. For his lady love, his girl, his Pax.

Not that they filled the table even when committee counsel took their places. Everyone was still crowded at one end, like a Christmas dinner where half the family hadn't showed.

The chairman, chairperson, chair, called for order.

"Ladies, gentlemen," Barry Scott Williams intoned, hooking his wire spectacles on one ear at a time, looking around at everyone in turn. "We're about to undertake the not unimportant business of selecting a high court judge. Our method, like democracy, is probably the worst in the world, except for all the others."

Leonard shifted in his hard chair. Williams liked to come on like a dotty British judge. Disarming, it cloaked his sharp brilliance, his nastiness. He wouldn't hesitate to comment on members of his panel who took judges to parties.

Or slept with them.

"A number of us believe judges should represent the different elements of our population, be a visible reminder of democracy in the courts. Others here believe judges should be elevated on merit alone, even if it means a court is composed of, say, all women."

He chuckled at the absurdity of the idea, making little bows to the ladies.

Get on with it, Leonard wanted to say.

"I'm certain that today, after spirited give-and-take among our own diverse group, we will honorably discharge our responsibility to the governor."

Everyone looked solemn.

The questionnaire on top of Leonard's pile was Joe Iapalucci's. He'd be easy. Joe knew everyone, everyone knew him. Tough, outgoing, shrewd, a solid administrator. Not so big on the law. But very big with people.

He was in the room already, waving at everyone, a dapper figure in a double-breasted suit, a big grin.

"How the hell do you guys breathe up here?" Joe said, yanking out the empty chair at the end of the table. "Jesus H. Christ, sixty-fifth floor."

"Good afternoon, Judge," Williams said gravely.

Doesn't like jokes, Leonard thought. Italians, either, probably. Where would he ever have met one? Not at his schools, his clubs, his church, in that WASP firm. By his standards Iapalucci's just off the boat from Naples.

Joe made the opening statement Leonard expected. His administrative soundness. Practical sense. Ability to move cases along, get dispositions. Knack for staying within a budget, keeping the Office of Court Administration happy. His constant surveillance and care for his judges, the many demands he'd made for increased safety, protection in these terrible times.

Pax's boss, so to speak. Who threw her to the wolves in the custody trial.

When Joe finished, people nodded, sat back.

Only Garcia leaned forward, tapping his pen on the gap between his front teeth.

"Judge, you've been in administration for some time. The Appellate Division means lengthy discussion, long, complex writings. How would you handle that? Would you look to your law clerk? Would you plan to bring your own law clerk up to the App Div with you?"

Maria Torres chimed in before Joe could tackle that one.

"That's right," she said primly, like the grade school teacher she'd been before her rise in the union. "And more important, you've worked with all the judges in the lower courts, you've formed opinions. You may have some bias against those judges who made problems for you, who are difficult, unusual. Could you review their decisions fairly? Aren't there preconceptions you've formed through the years?"

In spite of his worries, Leonard wanted to grin. Everyone knew Joe's law clerk did every stroke of writing that came his way. And that he had favorites among the judges. Some always got a little more vacation time, more spacious chambers, extra cleaning help, better furniture. Who'd tipped off Maria? Had Joe stepped on one of her pals, some Latino judge?

"I don't have problem judges," Joe was announcing to the group. "All my judges are solid citizens. And about the law, let me say this. It's not in books as far as I'm concerned. It's in my bones. Rules of evidence, the law of hearsay, I don't even pretend to know that stuff. But right from wrong, that I know. I feel it here."

He thumped his chest, somehow managing to look everyone in the eye at once.

After a bit more bluster he was gone, replaced by one of the oldest black judges in Criminal Court, Tom Watson. Dignified, spectacled, on his fourth try for the high court and desperate to please.

Leonard sensed the impatience around the table. Nobody was going to recommend Judge Watson. He knew zilch about civil cases, not much more about criminal ones. A courtroom character, he quoted poems, gave juries flowery speeches. Lawyers labored to switch assignments out of his courtroom.

One or two people threw out puffball questions; everyone smiled when the man stood up to leave.

"God bless you in your heavy task," Watson said, true to form.

Amen, Leonard thought. Only now he was starting to panic, throat suddenly as clogged as his ears, hands too wooden to turn the pages in front of him.

Next up was Rosa. He hadn't seen her since that hot little uptown apartment with its crucifix on the wall. He'd never said words, shaken hands, done anything to mark their breakup. Just accepted what she'd said, and gratefully. They didn't belong together. They'd had a wild, exciting trip, but a short one. Or was he kidding himself? Was he ashamed? Would he have a panic attack whenever he met her with Pax? What was the *matter* with him, anyway?

Leonard wanted to wipe his face. He wanted to drop his pen at his feet, lean down to pick it up, remain under the table.

"Sitting this one out," he said to nobody special, shoving back his chair, sitting well back from the table, not looking to see how that grabbed anybody, just doing it. Then, of course, he felt worse, more conspicuous, back there all by himself.

He had to look up when she came in. And he had to stare. So did everyone else.

Rosa stood framed in the doorway wearing the yellow suit he'd insisted on her buying.

Her glossy hair was loose, tumbling down her back, more thick, glorious hair than any one girl had a right to have. Her waist seemed impossibly small, her legs impossibly long in, Jesus, the sheerest of black stockings.

Judge? She looked like the star of one of those movies uptown, or on the Spanish television channels. It seemed to Leonard he could even smell her perfume, something sexy, tropical, wafting across the room.

He felt warm, knew he was blushing as she began to speak, her hands going a mile a minute, very Latina, just the way he'd told her.

Miss Puerto Rico herself, he thought, wanting to mop his face. She only needs a white swimsuit, a ribbon diagonally across that luscious bosom.

And Christ, now he was responding with his body, starting a hard-on, like a kid. A hard-on in a panel screening? Debo would say midlife crisis, he told himself, changing position. But, Jesus, Rosa's wasted in clothes, even the right clothes.

He turned his head, watched the other men watching Rosa. And the women? She was having quite an effect in that department. Martha's eyebrows were high on her forehead, her lips pursed. Marion King's arms were folded tightly across her chest, her face sour.

Their big chance to judge judges. Lawyers could make up for every ruling against them, every courtroom error they'd suffered through. Women could feel like the first female astronauts, thrilled to crack one more male preserve, as if they were there for the history books. The blacks, Hispanics, were paving their own roads into the future.

Right now Rosa wasn't connecting with any of them. The panel members looked stunned, as if they were wondering why someone who looked like Rosa would want to be a judge.

His Rosa—no, not his, but at least in the Versace suit he'd chosen, or whoever the hell designed it—was turning everyone against her just being there.

"You know who I am," Rosa was saying. "You know what I do. It's all in those papers in front of you."

Her voice was strong, challenging, different from the conciliatory tones the panel usually heard.

"If details impress you, fine," she went on. "But I think the big picture is more important. I'm a woman, I know women's problems. Incest, rape, sexual abuse, all of them. I'm Puerto Rican. We were the lowest of the low when I was growing up, I know about that, too. My mother was a washerwoman. If this city needs judges who come from the people, well, you'll never do better."

They were listening, that was sure. All eyes were on her, fixed, all the mouths were either open or pressed together tightly.

Here was one place, Rosa thought, where the island song rang true, sounded right.

In the law you could start with nothing, worse than nothing, the liabilities of race and poverty, and rise high. Look at Clarence Thomas! A U.S. Supreme Court judge!

There sat Leonard, sweating. He looked ancient today, deep lines in his face, a tightness in his mouth. For a moment she longed for him, wished with all her heart he was here on her behalf, urging her on. She hated seeing him look like that, worried, weary. Old.

Don't get distracted, she warned herself. Forget Leonard. He didn't leave you, you turned him out. When you're in the Appellate Division, there will be many rich lawyers to court you. Some will be younger, with less baggage than Leonard. Some could even speak your language, read your heart.

"And we do need such judges," Rosa said to her audience. "It's wrong for a man to come handcuffed into court and see a white judge on the bench, white court officers wherever he looks. It's wrong for a terrified, hopeless woman whose husband has beaten her child to see only men, elderly men, who are judges. It's wrong for a youthful offender who's never had a role model, never known a man who was decent. New judges should come from new people."

Jesus, Leonard thought. Only Rosa would make this speech in a six-thousand-dollar suit.

"I'm a new person," Rosa said, leaning forward. "I sit in a tough court among tough people. But they're my people, Ricans, Cubans, Dominicans, Colombians, Mexicans. We share a language, we're *simpatico*. We know the *bodegas*, the uptown social clubs, the *mercados*. I believe from my heart that judging isn't about intellect, it's about people. That's why I believe you couldn't find a better appellate judge for this time, this city."

What did I launch? Leonard thought, dazed.

Barry Scott Williams looked as if he were facing a large, coiled snake.

Garcia, Maria Torres seemed ready to applaud.

Bishop, for some reason, looked delighted, smiling, nodding.

Suddenly Leonard understood.

He hadn't been her only coach. Bishop had advised her, too. Helped her fix it so they asked her no picky questions, had to put her on the short list, had to pass her on to the governor.

Another idea struck him.

Pax must be outside. Now. Her papers weren't far down the pile from Rosa's. The interviews were closely scheduled so the judges would wait, not the panel members. She could be twenty, thirty steps away!

Leonard coughed, thumped his chest, stood up, fled.

Barreling through the doors, he almost crashed into her.

His heart simply stopped. Pax looked so beautiful. Her suit seemed to have been dipped in *café latte*, a creamy brown that darkened the violet of her eyes, emphasized the brown lashes around them.

Those eyes were fixed on his face.

And she was smiling at him, the smile widening as he watched, as if she couldn't help herself greet him!

He stepped close, ready to adore, encourage. But the big double doors banged and Rosa was there too, breathless, eyes shining.

She stopped, looked at them both, then smiled like a grown-up watching two awkward adolescents.

"Hello, Pax," she said. "Leonard, they asked me about you. Just now, after you left. Imagine!"

He stared at her.

"I said I have many friends, I go where I like with people I like, as men judges do. Then I left. They weren't finished, but I left."

Holy shit!

Years of brainwork, years of control in public, kept him steady.

"Then I better get back," he said. "Calm them down. Rosa, Pax. Good luck."

He swiveled, walked through the doors. Now every head was turned toward him. Probably they were still staring after Rosa.

He tried to look unconcerned, businesslike, walked around to his chair. But he felt better, free of unpredictable Rosa, waiting for cool, steady Pax. Nothing the panel could ask her that she couldn't handle. Nothing any lawyer could ask her she couldn't top.

"We'll break for a few minutes," Barry was saying.

Leonard was up as if he were an athlete, moving to Dan's side.

"After I left," he said into Dan's ear. "What?"

"She's got some set, that Rosa Macario. She tangled with Alton. He asked if Judge Macario had a relationship with a member of the bar or what, because he thought a woman judge should be beyond reproach. Macario gave it right back, said that the other women should join her in resenting the question as demeaning, prejudiced, even racist. I thought Williams would expire."

But Barry Williams, when he called the meeting back to order, seemed intent on taking care of Rosa his own way.

"I'd like to remind you," he began. "We all know and respect John Carro. He was born in a Puerto Rican village. He worked up, policeman on the beat, parole officer, law school, the judiciary for many years, and, of course, a former member of the Appellate Division. Quite a different story from Judge Macario."

Maria was on him in an instant.

"Carro is a man," she said, as if that was something disgusting, repulsive. "Macario isn't just Hispanic. She's a Hispanic woman. It's different. You'd have to be one to know."

"Maria's right, Barry," John Bishop said suddenly. "Judge Macario is a double-header here, Hispanic and female. Maybe we can't afford to shrug her off."

"Yes, well, perhaps we should save the discussion for our executive session later on," Williams said.

Leonard let his mind coast through the next interview.

Marvin Gerstner was a tough, smart judge who spoke his mind, wrote opinionated letters to the *Times*. In one he'd said judges weren't underpaid, they were vastly overpaid for the amount of work they did. Naturally he had few friends among the judges, fewer still on the panel. No one would go to bat for him, though he could end up a compromise candidate if his luck was good.

When Gerstner walked out, Pax would walk in.

Leonard didn't want to hurry that moment.

No, wrong. He didn't want to slow it down.

What was happening to him?

He could feel himself lean toward her as she came through the door, stood a moment at the end of the table.

Whenever he saw Pax at a distance, he remembered how fragile she seemed. Now she looked almost breakable.

Tiny, delicate, the pretty color she wore making her look delectable, precious. Somewhere near her throat, a touch of lace. Like foam on cappuccino, delicate, sippable.

Leonard's breathing stopped as abruptly as if he'd plunged underwater.

I love you, he told her silently, breathlessly. Only you. I miss you, the scared, desperate way I missed my mother when I lost her on Rockaway Beach as a little kid, when I thought the waves would get me, when I blamed myself, promised myself I'd never go off alone again.

He was surprised to find himself on his feet, walking again toward the door.

And totally surprised to realize Bishop was up, too, coming along just behind him.

But naturally Bishop would have to leave. His case was *sub judice* right now.

"That woman," Bishop said, looking at him as coolly as if their lunch had never taken place. "Piece of ice. Inflated opinion of herself. No lady."

Leonard felt a fierce desire to make his threat good, take care of the bastard then and there.

Hey, he thought. I could get in more trouble outside that room than in.

He moved toward a window, turned his back. A brief time had made a magic change in the view. Lights speckled the scene now, twinkling in the buildings, gliding along the black river.

Why wasn't he at Pax's side instead of out here with a man he loathed in a darkening room?

As soon as he asked the question, he was moving again.

If he couldn't speak in there, he could smile in encouragement at her, frown when she faltered, if she faltered. He could be with her.

In fewer steps than he would have thought possible he was through the doors, back at the table.

Pax was speaking.

Her low, beautiful voice seemed to sharpen his hearing, melt his tension. The very sound of it filled him with pleasure. He could look full at her, feel his heart leap.

She was talking to Martha. What had the question been? Something about the custody trial? But that was supposed to be out of bounds here. Had Rosa unsettled them all?

"I can't comment on that," Pax was saying. "As you know, the case is adjourned *sine die.* We had, after all, a death in the courtroom."

Oh, Pax, he thought wildly, show them who you are. Show them why I love you so.

Carson was leaning forward now, almost spitting words.

"It's not out of bounds to discuss the demonstrations you've allowed outside your courtroom," he said. "Every significant gay rights group has been watching your case, Judge. How do you feel about those demonstrators? Will they affect your decision? Intimidate you? Arouse your anger?"

"Mr. Carson," Pax said, "you just heard me say I can't discuss *Bishop* v. *D'Arcy.* That means I won't discuss anything that's gone on inside my courtroom or that's related to it outside my courthouse. If it helps, let me remind you I care about the Constitution. It guarantees the right to demonstrate. It doesn't guarantee the right to throw things or start shooting. I've tolerated the first and come down hard on the second."

Pax tensed in her hard chair, waiting for the next question, head brimming with odd little memories.

She was a little girl at a family dinner, hearing her father say that Gladstone, whoever he was, considered the American Constitution the most remarkable work produced by human intellect at a single stroke.

In her grandfather's study, sprawled on the soft rug, trying to puzzle out the fancy picture over his big desk titled, oddly, the Bill of Rights.

At a beer party in Cambridge, some law student relaying a trick for remembering the amendments. Wine, women, and song, he'd said. Eighteenth, repeal of Prohibition. Nineteenth, women's suffrage. Twentieth, swan song, cutting the tenure of lame-duck congressmen, changing the inauguration from March back to January. Nobody could catch her out on the Constitution. With her picture memory she could close her eyes and read it aloud, page after page.

No screening panel member could say she didn't know what she was talking about.

Leonard had looked so stricken when he saw her outside this room, then so happy when she'd smiled.

Maybe they'd be happy again. If she could only get through this, get her lifetime wish, be in the Appellate Division, maybe they'd be happy together.

Leonard was thinking, the Constitution, always good for discussion. We don't get to hear much about it in this room.

"Judge," Dan Heller was saying, "without getting into the merits of the case, I think we could agree you've been running the noisiest trial we've had for some time. I'd like to know how you got it. Was it the usual random distribution?"

What was with Dan? Everyone knew the random distribution of trials wasn't always random. Everyone knew Judge Ito had landed the Simpson case because he was neither white nor black, but a Japanese American. Was Dan trying to make Pax look greedy, like a publicity seeker?

"Custody cases aren't judges' favorites," Pax said. "As you know, they're lengthy, difficult, emotional. They rarely get settled. Women aren't often assigned to them. I think that's wrong, deciding ahead of time what we can and can't handle. I work against that kind of thinking whenever I can."

Her chin was up, her beautiful eyes narrowed a little. Leonard fought a great urge to get up, go to her, put his arms around her.

"So of course I agreed to take the assignment, Mr. Heller."

"Would you do it again? Considering the mess it's in?"

"It's proceeding. No demonstrator has stopped it yet. Not even a gunman has done that. Of course I'd do it again."

"I guess you'd have to say that, Judge. But are you satisfied with your part in it? What about the death of a court officer? Would that have happened if a tough, strong man had been on the bench, if Judge Iapalucci, for example, had tried the case himself?"

"I can't bar bullets, Mr. Heller. Or rule on gunshots. Even Judge Iapalucci can't do that. But of course, you ask an impossible question, you know that."

Leonard could actually feel his blood begin to heat, run hot through his veins.

"You're begging the question, Judge," Dan said, his face darkening.

"I'm trying to explain, Mr. Heller, that most judges care about the judiciary as a whole. They want judges to be good, they want the institution to look good. They sorrow when a chief judge winds up in federal prison. They fume when an incompetent judge runs a double murder case for all the world to see. They believe in the work they do, the system they administer. I'm no exception."

Leonard kept himself from applauding.

"You may not know I have a peculiar gift," Pax said quietly, so quietly he had to lean forward to hear. "I have the kind of memory people call photographic. I can recite from a page I've read as if it were in front of me. Useful in law school, useful in judging, too. The Constitution is in my head. Uncanny how it covers things that come up every day, amazing how a few men a few centuries ago made something that stands every test lawyers throw at it. Sometimes judges go off at tangents when all they really have to do is read it."

"Very noble," Dan said.

Had he deliberately given Pax a platform? Was he for her or against her? Had something gone wrong for Dan in her courtroom, some big verdict gone awry?

"Judge Ford," Manny Rose said, as if he were waking up for the first time today, "your father was in the Appellate Division, isn't that right?"

Pax smiled. "Yes, he was, Mr. Rose."

"Does that give you a special reason to want this nomination?"

"I don't feel it gives me an edge, if that's what you mean. It would be a proud link to the past, a proud link for my family. My son's in law school, it might inspire him. I'm not suggesting, of course, that it's any reason to prefer me over anyone else."

Manny's trying to help, Leonard thought. Good old guy. Buy him a drink one of these days, trade war stories. He probably has great ones.

"Since we're speaking about women judges," Martha said, in her clear, high voice, "Judge Macario told us she saw no reason her personal life should come into our discussions, any more than a man's might. How do you feel about that statement, Judge Ford?"

Leonard felt his stomach shrink.

It was her chance to blast Rosa. Or kill her with kindness.

"Judge Macario is an old friend," Pax said. "She's alert to insult, to condescension, as you can readily understand. She's seen more of it than most of us. I don't think women have a special duty to set standards, I think judges do. Men or women."

Nice, Leonard thought. Very nice.

Williams was clearing his throat, making a big deal of looking at his pocket watch.

"I think we have your position clear, Judge. We must move on, I fear. There are still others to see."

Pax was up, smiling. Leonard knew he couldn't watch her go away, he simply couldn't. He was up, too, standing with her at the end of the table, taking her arm, walking her to the doors.

In the reception room he took her chin in one hand, tipped her face up to his.

Being close to her felt wonderful, like a total fulfillment, a rest for all his senses.

"You were terrific," he said. "And there's nothing I'd rather do in this world than leave here with you. But I can't. Better for both of us if I'm here for the executive session. Not that you need help. You were great in there."

Oh, God, she was looking at him, listening, at last.

"We'll be at Debo's together on Christmas. Let me come back with you afterward, let me stay, Pax. We can't be apart anymore. It's simply not possible. Please."

She was very still, very solemn.

But when her smile finally began, began just where his hand was touching her face, Leonard felt wonderful, as if all the Christmas lights the world held were blazing out, as if his whole body were smiling, too.

20

PAX

FACING HER FRONT DOOR AFTER A LONG, STORMY AFTERNOON with Wickham and Pressman in her chambers, Pax steeled herself for the ruin on her terrace.

Almost all her windows overlooked the wrecked greenhouse. So she'd shuttered them, trying to concentrate on Leonard's return, on the holiday. Christmas Day, concentrating had been easy. Will and Debo had worked hard to make it wonderful. Pax had happily gone through drinks, presents, the turkey Will cooked, mashed potatoes Debo made out of a box, turkey and potatoes tasting much the same. Leonard had touched her arm, her hair, her shoulder, to the obvious delight of the kids. He'd eaten joyously, joked, talked about the Library of Congress backing his television series, given Will what was evidently an enormous check.

But he'd left before evening, driving to Washington, he said. And she'd gone home soon after, claiming exhaustion.

This morning, weary of shutters and darkness, Pax finally made herself look through her bedroom window.

A landscape after a battle. Glass everywhere, twisted metal, shards of terra cotta, tattered plants, pages from books and catalogues fluttering in the blasts of icy wind. A big carton filled with trash showed that Flora had tried to do some cleaning up. But for Pax it made the whole scene only more forlorn.

Flora hadn't made a comment, asked a question.

Nice of her, Pax thought. I'll get a cleaning service, hire someone. Maybe Carlos, for extra money. No, not Carlos. I don't need to explain to Rosa. In the new year, when the trial's over, then I'll take care of it.

How she wanted the trial over! She'd put so much aside for it, things she'd have to struggle with, like the greenhouse, before she could find some peace. Willie's problems, his poor grades at midterms. The pile-up of motions and applications in her chambers. The mountains of legitimate mail waiting to be answered. There'd be a new case, with problems of its own. And where was she, really, with Leonard? Would they have a new year together? New years?

She'd done her best to set all the problems aside while she heard out Pressman and Wickham, absorbed the last testimony of the trial.

Medical testimony all morning, Pressman with affidavits from an array of doctors, proving D'Arcy's health was superb, no hint of trouble. Wickham, exhaustively, boringly, querying the credentials of every doctor, objecting to every claim, every sentence.

Pax had ordered sandwiches so they could keep going, get done. By three, when her head was aching, her heart sick at the legal games they were playing, she'd asked for summations.

And then Pressman had played a trump card, made a sudden, daring attempt to nail down his case.

Speaking forcefully, excitedly, he'd revealed the existence of what Johnny California had called his time capsules.

At some point California had decided that everything a great artist like him did was important. Everything. He'd had special cardboard cartons made, begun a nightly habit of filling a single carton with the documents of his day.

Calendars, gum wrappers, prescription labels, theater tickets, notes, sketches, letters, postcards, blueprints, bills, photographs, leftover small change from a dozen countries, used condoms, seashells, everything.

More than that, he'd started keeping a tape recorder on his body. Each of the cartons he called his time capsules held five or six mini-cassettes of his day's conversations, even those he had only with himself. Miles and miles of audiotape, never replayed, never catalogued or indexed, were in those hundreds of cartons.

D'Arcy had told his lawyer about them by chance during some pretrial conference. Indefatigable Pressman asked to examine some, broken seals, dug into cartons at random. And realized how many precious nuggets were buried among the junk. Tapes of talks with presidents and princes, artists and celebrities. Sketches worth a fortune, more money every day since California's death. Priceless material for a museum of California's work, books about him, enough to keep researchers busy for years. And most important, material that would make Johnny California's intentions about Caitlin absolutely clear. What was more, he planned a press conference to tell the world about the time capsules.

Pax knew if she stopped him, she'd look as if she'd ignored vital evidence. Shocked, head pounding, she'd pictured rooms full of cardboard containers, imagined months, years of looking and listening. Not to mention transcribing, arguing over transcriptions, identifying voices, authenticating statements.

She'd clamped down hard, ruled the time capsules inadmissible. Pressman had glared at her with blazing hatred. Worse, Wickham had been smarmy, as if she were his confederate.

After that, the summations had been an anticlimax, a boring rehearsal for the return to the courtroom. With all the public pressure even Joe Iapalucci agreed that her decision should be given tomorrow in open court.

Tomorrow the trial would end; tomorrow she could start being herself again. At least she'd begun mending things with Leonard. After tomorrow they could see each other freely, talk about the trial, talk about anything at all. Tomorrow she'd give her decision from the bench, the final word on *Bishop* v. *D'Arcy*. She'd face them all, litigants, lawyers, the crowd in her courtroom, the larger crowd outside, the press, the pundits. Adding a small footnote of her own to the law of the land.

Flora was coming out of the pantry, smiling, eyes wide.

"Judge! Did you see? Are you surprised?"

Before Pax could fathom what she was talking about, Flora was turning, hurrying to the far end of the big living room, switching on the terrace lights.

"Judge Ford," she said urgently, "look."

Pax looked. Blinked. And felt as if giant hands had gripped her shoulders, shaken her till she couldn't breathe.

The greenhouse was whole. Its glass was intact, gleaming. Its metal framework was straight. No sign of the rubble, the ugly mess that had been there this morning.

Dazzled, she sat down on the hall bench.

"How?" she said to Flora. "What happened?"

Without waiting for an answer, she was up, through the living room, out the terrace doors, staring, bringing the miracle closer.

It's bigger, she thought. I'm sure it's bigger than before.

Opening the door, she saw heavenly order. Tools in a row, shining, even the trowel she'd used to destroy. Books in place on their shelf. Plants, dewy from watering, a row of mauve orchids in bloom, seed trays showing tiny green sprouts. Her broken terra cotta pots had vanished. Now there were new ones, neatly stacked. Even her denim apron was hanging from its hook. With the skyline behind it, stars starting in the sky, the greenhouse was more fantastic than ever, fit for the world's great gardeners, Gertrude Jekyll, David Austin, Vita Sackville-West.

Pax felt gloriously reprieved. As if a terrible error had been erased, her childish, destructive actions forgiven. As if, like the greenhouse, she'd been restored, too.

Touching one of the smooth pots, admiring the ancient shape, the rich earth color, she felt her eyes grow moist. This was the kind of miracle she felt in her favorite garden daydream, that everything could bloom all at once instead of in sequence, snowdrops, crocus, forsythia, bleeding heart, roses, astilbe, lilies, mums, Montauk daisies.

"What?" she said to Flora. "How?"

"Mr. Scholer."

"Mr. Scholer? When?"

"All day today. Judge, he must have given the men downstairs a small fortune, the super, the back elevator men. He brought up a whole crew of men this morning as soon as you left for work."

Pax was only half listening, thinking, darling Mr. Scholer, wonderful Mr. Scholer. Who obviously hadn't gone to Washington. Who'd come to spend the day on her terrace instead.

"You're not cross I let them in? He couldn't wait to set things right. The men cleaned up everything, took the mess away, brought more men, the builders. By noon it was all together, by five they were washing down the glass. And then still more men brought the new things, all the plants, tools, books. By six it was as you see, perfect."

Perfect, Pax agreed, wanting to laugh and cry both at the same time. Grown-ups didn't get surprises like this. Only children, from Santa Claus. Leonard was Santa Claus, coming a day late, proving he loved her. If he didn't, he'd never have planned it, managed it. If Rosa meant anything at all to him, he'd never have done it.

"He must love you, Judge," Flora said, as if she could hear Pax think.

"Yes," Pax said.

Still, there was Rosa.

Could she ever stop remembering about Rosa?

"There's something more I have to tell you," Flora was saying. "About your trial."

Pax felt her shoulders slump, felt all the weight of tomorrow burden her again.

"Let's go in the kitchen while you tell me," she said. "Let's make me a tray, scrambled eggs, toast, a big pot of coffee. I have to write notes for tomorrow. But I'll do it where I can look at my new greenhouse."

Flora was already reaching for eggs, butter, a gleaming pan.

"Judge," she said, "my cousin? Who works on Park Avenue? Where those people live, those Bishops?"

The sizzling butter should have been making her hungry. But it was only making her queasy.

"Cecil called me. He couldn't wait to tell me, for you, Judge. The other night, middle of the night, Mrs. Bishop came down to his basement."

But I can't listen to this, Pax thought, dizzy. I don't want to listen. It's like when someone on a jury sneaks off to look at a crime scene, makes a mistrial because he thinks he's smarter than the police, brings some news back to the jury that never got put into evidence, messing up everything.

"Judge, Cecil said she was quite mad. In her bathrobe. Tearing open packages down there, throwing things all around. One package had a music box, she got up and danced to the tune, in bare feet, Judge. They were all presents for a little girl, dresses, dolls, everything. She was getting rid of them. Cecil was scared he'd be in trouble."

Don't tell me any more, Pax thought. It's hearsay, inadmissible, I can't do one thing about it.

But of course there the picture was, firmly lodged in her brain. Ba Bishop in bare feet throwing out good things, new things for a little girl, middle of the night. Not even a startling picture. The woman was so uptight it was easy to believe she could lose her temper, her control. The trial had been so hard for her, it was easy to believe she'd changed her mind about Caitlin.

"Flora," Pax began.

God, it was *worse* than a juror investigating on his own. It was like the moment in a trial when she'd have to strike something from the record, instruct the jury to forget a piece of testimony. They'd heard it. They couldn't unhear it. It was theirs forever, bound to affect their decision. And this was hers forever, waiting to affect hers.

"Flora," she said, "I know you mean well. But don't tell me any more. I can't listen to what your cousin told you, what he said he saw. I can only deal with evidence that comes properly into my courtroom. If your cousin wants to testify, that might be different."

"Testify? Oh, Judge, he would hate that. He would worry about his job."

"I know you want to help," Pax said. "But we finished everything this afternoon. All that's left now is my decision."

Suddenly the house phone buzzed, like a giant bee.

Leonard? Here? Now?

Hope rose in Pax's heart like a gas flame suddenly turned up, blue and orange, full force.

Oh, she thought, I want to tell him the greenhouse is the first prize, the last straw, a marvel. I want to tell him so much, ask him so much, I want to be with him so damned much.

Unbidden, she felt the worries crowd back while she waited for Flora to answer the phone.

She still couldn't properly talk about the trial, not yet. And Leonard couldn't properly talk about the screening panel's executive session.

Judge, lawyer.

Ridiculous, impossible.

All right, she could properly tell him she adored the greenhouse. The least she could do to make up for smashing things, not being judicial at all. She could hold him, kiss him, welcome him back with all her heart.

"It's Judge Macario," Flora said. "Isn't that nice? You can talk to her about your case, another judge."

Rosa?

Flora was already in the foyer poised to open the door. And Pax was already adjusting to disappointment, not so easy.

"When did she build it, Flora?" Pax heard from the foyer. "A whole little house of glass? And filled with flowers!"

Pax moved then, toward the living room, toward her visitor.

Tonight Rosa wasn't wearing bright scarlet or brilliant yellow.

She had on worn jeans, white sneakers, a white T-shirt that did its best for her tawny skin, her round, bountiful breasts. She looked all of sixteen.

"Pax, it's so beautiful, your garden, the little glass house!"

Pax wanted to turn, walk away. What right had Rosa to look sixteen?

"A present," she said, more sharply than she intended. "From Leonard."

Rosa's joyous expression didn't change at all, Pax noted. Something had happened to her. Pax knew her every expression, had known forever. Rosa was excited about something, too excited to worry about Leonard. Even so soon after Mami dying, something had dazzled her beyond anything a man could do for her. She was turning her back on the terrace, coming closer. Good news practically announced itself from the way she held her head high, clasped her hands together against those beautiful breasts.

"I need to talk to you."

More talk, Pax thought, suddenly shot through with impatience. How many words could she hear in one day?

Go away, she wanted to say. Before you make me say things I'll be sorry about later on. Before my supposed judicial temperament blows sky high!

"More trouble, Rosa? You need more help from me?"

Rosa's tan skin didn't show a blush easily. But now the blush that came to her cheeks, washed down her lovely neck, was plain to see.

Blotched, red, she looked older, not so beautiful.

"No," she said. "Not this time. There are two things I have to tell you, Pax. Because we're friends, old friends."

She paused, looked concerned.

"Before she died, Mami told me about Alden."

Pax felt herself go on guard, face blank, body still.

"She told me so I would know you deserved happiness, Pax. But she had no idea what it could mean now, with your trial. A gay husband wouldn't matter: we've got gay judges, a Gay and Lesbian Judges Association. But the failure to disclose? In a trial so concerned with gay issues? You're presiding over a trial involving gay custody. D'Arcy is a gay dancer."

Was this what was making Rosa so happy? The chance for once to warn *her*, advise *her*?

Something odd was happening in Pax's head. She saw pictures behind her eyelids, the way she saw printed words she'd read once in books. Herself holding Rosa's hand as they walked into Marymount. Herself coaching Rosa for college interviews, for the Kaplan LSAT cram course.

Stop it, Pax told herself. Take Rosa's speech as given. Her mother meant well. Rosa means well, too, she remembers those times, too. Besides, she's right. Secrets are stupid. They never stay secret, someone always knows, tells.

She firmly shut the picture book in her head, stood up.

Now, even looking up at Rosa, she felt tall.

"You're quite right," she said. "But I've thought about it a lot, Rosa. No one's going to know what to do with the news. Does it prejudice me against gays? Or for them? A good lawyer could argue either way. I could argue it either way."

Only I'd hate to have to, she kept thinking. I'd hate to go public with something so damned private.

"It's a mess, Pax," Rosa was saying. "Like everything else in this trial. Anyway, I said two things. This is the other."

She paused, smiled.

Pax felt her dizziness, her nausea, come back in full force. What next? What would Rosa throw at her now?

"I had a call from Barry Scott Williams at home this afternoon. He said he was letting a rabbit out of a hat because he wanted to tell me himself. I can expect a call from the governor's office after the weekend. His chief counsel will telephone. Barry wanted to congratulate me, let me know before anyone else did."

Now she looked gloriously beautiful again.

"I came through the panel, Pax. I'm going to be the next Appellate Division judge."

Each word was a stinging burn, making her pull back, want to cry out.

Bishop, Pax thought. A formidable enemy, a power on the screening panel. Not fair. That call belongs to me. I know more law than Rosa. I have years more service, a better right.

"Of course you know more law," Rosa was saying, as if she'd spoken aloud. "Of course you have a better right. But it's my turn, Pax, mine and people like me. I stand for something you don't, you can't, something that belongs out front now. Justice can't just be done, everybody knows the old saying, it has to be *seen* to be done. I can do that, Pax. I'm a good judge, I run a tight courtroom, I know plenty about the law. Mostly thanks to you, if that helps."

Pax felt her wounds dull down, ache like old bruises. Rosa was right. She'd figured it out. Years ago judges could be old white men and nobody complained. Now things were different. The city wasn't a melting pot anymore. More like a big salad, every piece separate, distinct, even though it was all mixed together. There were big pressures on the panel. Rosa was an idea whose time had come.

Pax took a good, deep breath.

"I guess," she said, "it's your time, Rosa. Your day, your year. Happy New Year."

Now Rosa was glowing again.

"Think, Pax. I'm just going to be thirty-six. Some woman is on the Connecticut high court who's thirty-nine, I've even beaten her!"

Pax put her hands together so they'd stop trembling, looked up with blurring eyes at Rosa, tall, stunning.

All she could see was a small girl in black braids, a Catholic school uniform, navy blue jumper, white blouse.

Rosa can't help it, she thought. I had too much. She had too little. I'll get the next vacancy, or the next, I know it, everyone knows it. And look at what I made here, this girl, this beauty. Thirty-six, sitting with all those old folks. She'll wake them all up. She'll make everyone in Manhattan and the Bronx pay attention.

"You were glad for me so often, Pax. Be glad now. I never meant to take anything from you, not your reputation, Leonard, anything. Forgive me my sins, Pax. They're not as big as you may think, I promise you."

The house phone was buzzing again, Pax could hear it even in the living room.

Flora was back again, smiling. "This time it *is* Mr. Scholer," she said. "He's coming right up."

"That's fine," Pax said.

And, oh, it was fine.

Leonard, my love, she thought. Your eye may wander. But your timing is beyond reproach. At least let Rosa see she hasn't won everything.

Would she stay? Or vanish? Ah, the flaming spirit of the conquistadors seemed to be burning low in Rosa Macario.

"I'm out of here," she said. "By the back door. Call you over the weekend. Think about Alden. And we'll talk, right?"

"We'll talk," Pax said.

In a moment the front door, Flora's footsteps, then Leonard's heavier ones. Pax stood straight, took a deep, deep breath. She heard his voice before she saw him.

"Hey, what do you think?" he called all the way from the foyer.

Leonard, rumpled as ever, the same as ever, smiling as if he'd never left her side.

"Didn't they do a job?"

He was waving at the greenhouse, thrilled with himself, like a two-year-old showing off a tall tower of blocks.

"It couldn't be more beautiful," Pax said softly. "It's marvelous, Len. It was a marvelous thing to do."

He reached for her, pulled her toward him. She gave him a quick kiss, then pushed him gently away.

"Listen, now. Come and sit. Before anything else, I have to tell you something."

He released her, frowned.

"I have a little news for you, too."

He's on that screening panel, Pax thought. He wants to tell me about Rosa's promotion before I hear it from anyone else, wants to cushion it for me.

She took his warm, rough hand, pulled him down on the deep sofa, sat very, very close.

"Me first. There's something I want to finish telling you about, so you have the whole story."

"Ah," Leonard said. "A deep, dark secret?"

"Leonard, listen. I told you Bishop was threatening me about Alden. I never said how it really was. But he had a lover, Leonard. I found out at his funeral."

Leonard was staring.

"The man came, told me, right here in this room. He said Alden hadn't wanted to hurt me. Unfortunately, this man did want to. Alden was dead, I didn't need to know at all. He told me to hurt me, and he did."

"Jesus, Pax," Leonard said.

"I felt so stupid," Pax said. "So cheated. I'd never dreamed. But he was dead. I couldn't exactly ask him about it."

Leonard's arms were going around her again. She could feel their strength, breathe in his warm, healthy smell.

"Sweetheart," he said, "it can't have been easy learning like that. But it hasn't held you back, made you angry. It hasn't harmed you, Pax."

He released her, stood up abruptly.

"I had something somewhat unflattering to confess myself, a more recent secret. But I think I'll forget about it if that's all right with you. I wouldn't worry any more about either problem if I were you."

"My worry," Pax said, "is the trial. It *is* something prejudicial. It *is* a guilty secret for the judge in a gay custody trial."

Leonard was frowning, starting to pace.

"All right," he said, "then disclose. You first, before anyone else does. Make it part of your decision, whatever that is. No sin, no crime, Pax. Argue it, like a lawyer, do it fast."

Oh, God, Pax thought. What have I been doing without him? What would I do without him?

"Now," he said, "you've heard about the App Div? That it's Rosa?"

"Only just," Pax said. "I understand it. I'm a little rueful about it, Leonard."

"It wasn't Bishop, he stayed out. But by the time they argued, digested that big speech of hers, I think they were afraid not to choose her. Your turn will come, Pax. As sure as anything in this world, your turn will come."

He took both her hands in his.

"Anyway, it's not your past that interests me. It's your future. Please, can we get married now? Or anyway, when the trial's finished? Make this a really new year? Of course, it's only fair I tell you some news before you make up your mind."

Pax began to laugh.

Because he was funny and darling and she'd missed him so terribly and here he was, back again.

Because he wasn't Rosa's, he was hers, he was saying so.

Because she wanted to marry him so, wanted him in her bed and out of it.

She coughed, choked, then couldn't stop laughing. Leonard was holding her, shaking her, telling her to quit it, be still, or he'd never propose to her again as long as he lived.

When she finally quieted, he kissed her lightly.

"Now, you listen," he said. "I've made up my mind about something I've thought about for a long, long time."

He looked so earnest, so serious, all the laughter went out of her.

"I'm going to quit Kistel," he said. "Resign my partnership. Leave the firm."

Oh, my God, Pax thought, is that all?

And then wondered if Leonard, darling Leonard, had felt the same about her news. That nothing, however awful, meant anything to him because he loved her, because whatever he told her, she loved him.

"I've been struggling over it because we're not doing so well. It's a little like leaving a sinking ship. But the place fascinates me less and less, the teaching, the television, more and more."

I'd better concentrate, Pax thought. I'd better listen.

"The fees from your trial will go a long way," he was saying. "The firm will always have my name. But I don't want it to have all my energy. Legal education for lay people is booming. The law's getting more complex. We have more lawyers, more lawsuits. Everything in the world winds up in court, everyone's watching trials on live television from every courtroom in the country. I'm a good teacher, Pax, a good explainer. There are a million books I'd like to write, really explaining to people which lawyers are good and which are charlatans, which statutes work and which should be changed, much, much more. What do you think?"

"Leonard, why would I think anything about your work but what you think? It'll be a lot easier for me as a trial judge if I'm not married to Kistel, Scholer, Pressman, Trager and Rosenstein. I don't have to recuse myself from your cases."

"I take it that's yes," Leonard said.

He was slapping his pockets, digging into them like a man who'd put something away and couldn't lay his hands on it.

He had put something away, Pax saw.

He was taking it out of an inside pocket. A blue box, Tiffany blue. And handing it to her.

Pax looked at him, then at the box. She pulled off the top, found a smaller velvet box, opened that. And saw the largest amethyst she'd ever seen in all her life except once, briefly, in this same place, with this same man.

The amethyst was the color of pink and blue sky at sunrise, of irises, lavender, lilac, violets. He'd said she should wear amethysts, long ago. To match her eyes. Could her eyes possibly be a color like this?

"Put it on, Pax. I've kept it a long time. It'll have to last you a long, long time. No more two-million-dollar fees. Just love and kisses. Don't smash up your greenhouse again, understand?"

"Poor Leonard," Pax said. "Riches to rags."

She took his face, his nice, craggy, smiling face, in both her hands.

"There's something else that hasn't happened for a long, long time. Let's go to bed, Leonard. Damn the trial. Damn being lawyer, judge."

In her bedroom she felt as if they were newly met and long married at the same time.

He was as hungry as a very young man, as gentle as a practiced one.

She was as eager as a courtesan, as knowing as a beloved wife. They were one, the same, judge, lawyer, man, woman, and when he knelt over her, kissed her throat, her eyelids, her breasts, they were love itself.

And then, after, Leonard was heavy in her arms, smiling as he slept.

21

PAX

PAX AWAKENED AS SUDDENLY AS IF A COURT OFFICER HAD just proclaimed, "All rise!"

The big windows were pitch black, the air chill. A moment after five o'clock. In four hours a real court officer would make that proclamation. And she'd give her decision from the bench, no writing, no waiting. The custody trial, for better or worse, would be over.

Excitement, fear sent a shiver through her.

She glanced at Leonard, still lost in sleep. Seeing him, bulky, familiar, so wonderfully welcome in her bed, the room felt suddenly warmed, all fear vanished.

How often, she wondered, do dreams come true for grown-ups? For real people with real problems? How many people have a marvelous person to cherish and depend on, too? Not a perfect person, but marvelous anyway. I'm lucky, so lucky.

She patted Leonard's broad back lightly, feeling his warmth, his peaceful stillness.

Then she edged out of bed, searched in the closet for her coziest robe and slippers, turned the cold door handle and slipped out to the terrace.

Frost? No, light snow everywhere. Shivering, she made for the greenhouse, its glass crusted over so it glowed like pearl in the pale moonlight.

Inside, Pax curled against the plump cushions of the wicker chair, put her feet on the stool she kept for reaching the top shelves.

Then she leaned back, shut her eyes, let pictures crowd into her head. Leonard, asleep in her bed. She'd never relinquish that picture again. Rosa, finally wearing a black robe, sitting with four other judges on the carved mahogany bench of the Appellate Division courtroom. My God, maybe in time to comment on whatever decision Pax made today! Though that wasn't likely. Custody decisions were seldom appealed. They were usually left to the trial judge, actually hearing the evidence, making the right decision.

And what was it, the right decision?

Yesterday in her chambers the lawyers had summed up.

Pressman had made as forceful and noisy an argument as if he'd been in open court playing to the reporters. He'd emphasized that Johnny California had intended D'Arcy to have the child. He'd provide familiar surroundings, continuity, absolute devotion.

Wickham had spoken with more awareness of the smaller forum, quietly, flatly. Pax had even felt somehow that his heart wasn't in his words. Mrs. Bishop, he said, would rescue Caitlin from a wildly abnormal life, a desperate round of pleasure seeking. Caitlin's own aunt, she was a blood relation who'd desperately wanted the child since she was born.

All right, then, which one, Tom D'Arcy, Barbara Bishop, would operate in Caitlin's best interests? Couldn't the child prosper with either? Be happy with both?

Try it from another angle, Pax ordered herself now. Think what happens if you make the wrong decision. Picture the disasters that could follow, track what could happen as a result of what you say today in your courtroom.

D'Arcy could get Caitlin and sicken with AIDS, give it to

the child through blood from a cut finger, saliva from a kiss; who knew how the disease was really transmitted? Caitlin could die years before she was supposed to. Or Ba Bishop could succumb to deep depression, spend her days in some institution. Tal Bishop could remain a potent enemy.

Already there'd been one disaster in the trial, an event by no means in the best interests of one set of children. Sean's wife was a widow, his kids fatherless. Who could guess how many more disasters could be ahead?

Pax felt her heart thicken, grow heavy.

Stop, she ordered herself. Things don't always turn out badly. Think of the letter Selma made you take the time to read before you left downtown.

A simple one-pager, handwritten. From a divorced woman Pax's committee had worked with for months. Whose lawyer had taken a hefty retainer, then taken her to dinner, and to bed. Two months later she was pregnant, told him so. He'd immediately returned her file, though not her money, stopped taking her calls, returned her letters unopened. Pax had sent two women lawyers on the committee into action. They'd pestered the Bar Association's Grievance Committee till the man submitted to a blood test, then brought a paternity suit while they lobbied to have his license revoked. The letter was to thank Pax for her support, and for the baby who'd just arrived. All the family she'd ever need, the woman said.

Was D'Arcy all the family Caitlin would ever need?

Pax reached out her hand, touched a pale green hyacinth shoot just emerging from its brown bulb. A little spike of hope, of struggle toward the light. It felt surprisingly strong, sturdy against her fingertip.

I'm struggling, Pax thought. But I'll get through, I'll reach the right place.

There were good possibilities, happy pictures she could conjure up. Caitlin hugging Tom D'Arcy. And D'Arcy, healthy, strong, holding her high in the air, teaching her to

be a beautiful ballerina. Ba Bishop, softened, strengthened by
caring for a child, finding peace, giving more, doing more
than ever for her Huguenot children, too. Sean's strong,
lovely Mary Catherine raising his kids to be good cops and
court officers like their father, or good lawyers and judges,
why not?

Pax sat straight.

Tom D'Arcy is a man, she thought. Strong, tough,
tender, loving. As fatherly as any man could be. Since Alden
died I *have* let that horrible episode with his lover color my
feelings about gays. I was wrong. That man was a bastard. But
he'd be a bastard gay or straight, the way that perjurer of a
witness is a bastard dying or not. I've learned something
from this trial.

She stood up, began pacing the warm little room as if
she'd caught the habit from Leonard.

When that didn't help, she stopped, filled the little electric kettle she kept in the greenhouse at the tiny sink,
switched it on, got out the tin box of tea, a cup, a spoon.

A few moments later, cup steaming, fragrant, in her hand,
she was back in the chair. One or two sips seemed to clear her
head. Of course, she'd remember this trial all her days. It was
too entwined with memories of Leonard, Rosa, Will, ever to
forget.

Now she had to finish it off, make the decision that would
turn the trial itself into a memory. An indelible memory certainly. But only a memory.

There was pearly light in the greenhouse now. The sun
was coming up, lightening the misted panes, making orderly
shadows of the terrace railing, sending glitter over the snowy
flower beds.

Tom D'Arcy, Barbara Bishop.

For a very little girl, a dashing, peripatetic life teeming
with excitement, intense love? Or a settled existence perhaps
a little short on loving but long on stability, order, normality?

At least, Pax thought, what better place to make the right

decision than in this remade greenhouse, this gift of love and promise?

At seven, with Leonard still sleeping, a call from Will.

He'd be at the courthouse, to wave at her, bolster her up. And he had something to tell her, take her mind off, he said.

Debo was pregnant.

That was one good reason he wanted a job, a paying job. Debo kept saying her father would take care of things. But Will didn't want Leonard taking care of things.

Pregnant, Pax thought, her mind actually off the trial, for a miracle. Twenty-four, a baby himself, and having a baby! And she herself, Grandmother, Grandma, Granny, Gram, imagine.

"Will," she said staunchly, "I'd call that great news."

"So do we, in spite of arguing. It does bring up a few problems. But it's basically all right, Mom. We just have to work out all the details ourselves."

In spite of her whirling mind, good, sound advice filled Pax's head. Law school more vital than ever now. A bigger apartment, a special place for the baby. More words of wisdom, many more, tingled on the tip of her tongue.

"Of course," she said succinctly. "You have to work it all out yourselves. When, Will?"

"About seven and a half months from now, I'd say. Plenty of time."

Plenty of time to finish first-year law, finish it well. Leonard would have something to say, he'd say it this time, with a baby to consider. He'd be thrilled about a baby, a grandchild! And my God, so would she, a grandchild she'd be young enough to enjoy, ten when she was sixty, twenty when she was seventy. A little luck and she'd be at her grandchild's wedding, maybe even make it to a great-grandchild!

If I can keep Will going just two more years, she thought, till he really understands what he's proposing to throw away.

She could easily imagine Will, too, a snowy-haired judge,

robed in black, presiding sternly in a courtroom of his own. But wait. Will was Alden's son. Alden had denied his real feelings, married her, lived a lie. Why would she want Will to do that? Be a lawyer, a judge, when he wanted something else so much? No one could deny feelings forever without blowing some kind of cork. She couldn't deny how much she needed Leonard. Rosa couldn't deny her own hungry drive to the top. Barbara Bishop couldn't deny how horribly she wanted to be free of raising a child; she'd gone down to a dark basement in the middle of the night to correct a mistake she'd made about herself.

I might have blown something dreadful in some other homosexual case, Pax thought. If I hadn't corrected a mistaken idea I had for a long time, I might have made a real judicial mess, never had a hope of promotion.

"Mom," Will said suddenly, "maybe this isn't the morning to ask you, even the right day, but what the hell. What's with you and Leonard? You're supposed to be a big decision-maker. So why aren't you deciding things? Wouldn't you like to be a wife before you're a grandmother?"

Instantly Pax felt shy, small, as if she were the child, he the parent.

She looked down at Leonard, curled into one of her big pillows, taking far more than his share of the bed, as comfortably settled as if their fiftieth anniversary were about to come up.

Growing up, she remembered, is protecting the innocence of your parents. Parent or child, Will doesn't need to know Leonard's here.

"Just like you," she said. "We're working it out. I want to finish the trial. I haven't had a chance to think about myself, let alone about a wedding."

"Nothing to think about," Will said, sounding relieved, happy. "We come up some Sunday morning, maybe get that gorgeous Judge Macario to preside, and everybody drinks champagne on the terrace after. Easy! Better still, we all crowd into your greenhouse."

No, Pax thought. Not that gorgeous Judge Macario. She doesn't put a foot in my greenhouse. Joe Iapalucci, maybe. He probably does terrific wedding ceremonies, lots of jokes, sentiment, prayerful good wishes.

"I've got to go," she said. "Kiss Debo, say I love her. I'll go up the minute the trial's finished and kiss her myself. Take care of her, Will, make her take care of herself. And now wish me luck. I'll look for you in court."

Coffee.

Formal best wishes from Flora.

A speedy ride downtown in Leonard's big car. More crowds, more cops. Her chambers. Getting a polite kiss from Tim, giving a warm one to Selma, rattling back downstairs in the judges' elevator to her robing room.

Hooking her robe, brushing down its silk, looking in the mirror at her smooth hair, her pale face.

And then, and then, walking into the pandemonium of her courtroom with everyone standing up, focusing their eyes on her.

Pax kept still for a moment.

Her time, her place. Her show, her calling.

At their table the Bishops, faces set, eyes down. And Scotty Wickham, neat navy suit, posture perfect, chin high. At the other table Tom D'Arcy, worn-looking, handsome, head up, too, but still as a stone. And Pressman in one of his shark-skins, huddled into himself, tapping his foot on the floor.

Behind them the crowd, an entity of its own, rustling, whispering. They were all hoping she'd do something they'd always remember, be able to talk about for a long, long time.

In front, poised with her big pad, her chalks, Caro Hansen, gazing intently at her, only at her.

And far, far back a glimpse of Will, crowded by his neighbors, leaning forward so she could see him.

And all the men and women of the press crowding the doorways, juggling the cameras she wouldn't allow them to use inside the courtroom, clutching their pads and pencils, waiting for what she would say.

Someone was holding up a sign at the back of the room, forbidden, but somehow there. Queer Nation. Another gay group? They were sprouting up everywhere.

And far, far back, leaning against the wall, Leonard, her Leonard, gazing only at her.

Pax sat down, sat straight, clasped her hands so tightly Leonard's enormous ring bit into her finger.

She waited another moment for quiet, then another beat longer.

"We come now," she said, "to the end of a trial. If there were jury members they would be retiring now to consider their verdict. But this is a child custody case, and the decision falls entirely to me."

The rustling vanished. People grew still, stared up at her. Had she ever felt so many eyes on her, ever known such attention?

Like walking over a swollen and rushing river on a tightrope, no handholds, setting her feet carefully, extending her arms, balancing, fighting nerves, controlling fears so she could get safely across.

She took the first step.

"This is a country of laws. In this country judges rule according to those laws. We're dealing with a custody case. The single, simple standard in a custody case is that the outcome must be in the best interests of the child."

She felt the audience exhale as one, sensed that everyone from front to back was listening carefully.

Good Lord, Joe Iapalucci, standing near the side door! Was he as worried as that, coming down to watch what she did? She made herself look away from his worried face.

"This case has had an unusual amount of attention outside my courtroom. A great many people have expressed opinions on both sides. None of those people or their opinions matters here. What matters is that the attorneys for both litigants have been forceful and articulate, and that each one has made a full presentation of his client's point of view."

Rustling again, whispers, movement at the back of the room.

Pax glanced sideways. Pressman, shuffling his feet, shifting in his chair.

She knew she must lower her voice several degrees when she spoke again, as she always did when a crowd got restless, to force their attention.

"Because of the inordinate attention paid to this case, because we're dealing with a small child whose future can't begin too soon, I'm departing from my usual practice of reserving my opinion until it can be published. I'm going to give you my decision now, straight from the bench."

The courtroom went quiet as a cathedral.

And, strangely, Pax felt exhausted, drained, almost uninterested, as if she'd already said what she wanted to say, as if she only wanted to get everyone out, get some peace, time for herself.

God, it felt like months since she'd had time for herself. Had there ever been a time when she hadn't fretted about *Bishop* v. *D'Arcy?*

She sat straighter, lifted her chin.

"I award custody of Caitlin California to the person she knows and loves best, who in my judgment is most concerned with her best interests. Tom D'Arcy."

A beat of silence.

Then the courtroom erupted. Shouts, boos, applause, catcalls, a tidal wave of noise came crashing toward her.

Pax raised both her hands, sat still.

She'd stay still till they calmed down, what else? She couldn't shout them down. She wouldn't clear the courtroom. She'd come this far without doing that, she wasn't about to give up and do it now. The only gavel she owned was a decorative one someone had given her long ago. She didn't use it. Few judges actually used gavels anyway, and they certainly weren't her style.

When the clamor died a little, she began speaking again, just loud enough to be heard by careful listeners at the back.

"This case would have been difficult for any judge," she said. "For me it's had a special difficulty."

Still noisy but less so, still movement, but quieting.

"A special difficulty," she repeated, to accommodate the noise, control it till the audience was still again.

"I've said very little during this trial. Now I'm going to make a statement to add to the record."

They were hers again. Now she could tell them what she wanted them to know.

"I've been a widow for almost ten years. My husband was a gifted architect, a brilliant and creative person, and, I learned only after his death, a homosexual."

Ah, not a single sound in her courtroom.

"Judges make decisions based on the law. But the law isn't administered by machines, computers, tosses of a coin. It's administered by people who bring their own experience to their decisions. I believe that's what I'm doing now. I know from my own experience that a man's sexual persuasion doesn't harm the people he loves. I know from my own experience that a man's sexual persuasion can warm and help the people he loves. I think Mr. D'Arcy will be a fine parent for Caitlin, just as my husband was for our son."

Faces staring at her, bodies motionless.

Are you listening, Will? she asked silently. Do you understand I'm proud of your father, proud of you?

"No one would expect a judge with a particularly loving mother to be unfit to preside in a custody battle between a mother and father. No one would expect a judge who'd been divorced to be unfit to preside in a divorce case. Judges aren't handicapped by their experience. They're informed by it, warmed by it, made better judges because of it."

Was that getting across? She couldn't tell. Everyone was silent, they were all, at least, listening.

"In that belief I close this case and tell you that this court stands in recess."

Another moment of dead silence.

Then the courtroom actually seemed to blow up, break apart, burst.

Pax turned her head, looked down at Tom D'Arcy.

He was pale, paler every second, as if he was holding himself together, as if he'd lost hope and was only just finding it now, finding his own safe place again.

He looked up, met her eye. And then stood up, bowed, a deep, sweeping, theatrical bow, as if he were a fine courtier and she a great queen.

The doors were opening, the court officers waving to everyone, edging them toward the hall.

Pax knew she should turn, leave. But somehow she wanted to see everyone out, wait for Leonard, wait for Will to come to her.

She looked over at the Bishops. Both of them seemed planted in their chairs. Bishop's face was still, stony. But Barbara Bishop looked as relieved as D'Arcy, joyous, younger, clasping her hands like a girl.

I did right, Pax thought then.

I'm a good judge, whoever that panel chose, whatever the politics of promotion are. My father would approve. Justinian and Solomon and Holmes and Frankfurter would approve. I'm a good judge.

Suddenly Caro Hansen was just below her, waving something, a page from her book.

Pax glimpsed a portrait, herself in soft colored chalks, herself more beautiful than she was, had ever been.

"Judge," Caro Hansen was calling to her, breathless, urgent, "it's yours. It's for you."

Pax lost her, because Tim was there crowding her out, applauding, smiling, Selma panting just behind him, all smiles, too.

And then Leonard pushing hard for the front of the

courtroom, making for Pressman, giving him a great bear hug. And then, and then, coming forward, coming to her.

But wait! Her new court officer, Sean's replacement, was leaping between them to protect her, holding out his arms, yelling something.

Pax waved the officer back, reached out her hands for Leonard.

Then she was under his arm, swept almost off her feet toward the back, toward her robing room, alone, quiet, far away from everyone else in the world.

Sun beat into the room, so the motes of dust floated in its light. Heat came too, warm coziness, comfort.

Leonard was releasing her, looking down at her, smiling.

His hands were reaching for her collar, unhooking her robe, pushing it away from her shoulders so that it slipped to the floor in a whispering fold of black silk.

He pulled her close. Pax put back her head, went on tiptoe to kiss him.

Then, suddenly, surprisingly, he swept her up in his arms, tightened his hold, whirled her around as if he were Tom D'Arcy himself.

"What's the point," he said, "of loving a small, beautiful woman if you don't grab your chance, pick her up, carry her off?"

His arms were tight around her, his enormous ring bit into her finger again, just a little, just enough to remind her it was on her finger forever.

"And I want you to know," Leonard said, bending his face to hers, "I'm not kissing a judge. I'm kissing the most fantastic woman I ever saw in action."

How pleasant, how marvelous to be light, small, with a tall, vigorous man to take her up in his arms!

"You don't have to choose," Pax told him gently. "Kiss us both. Judge, woman, we both love you. You don't have to choose at all."

• A NOTE ON TYPE •

The typeface used in this book is a version of Baskerville, originally designed by John Baskerville (1706-1775) and considered to be one of the first "transitional" typefaces between the "old style" of the Continental humanist printers and the "modern" style of the nineteenth century. With a determination bordering on the eccentric to produce the finest possible printing, Baskerville set out at age forty-five and with no previous experience to become a type founder and printer (his first fourteen letters took him two years). Besides the letter forms, his innovations included an improved printing press, smoother paper, and better inks, all of which made Baskerville decidedly uncompetitive as a businessman. Franklin, Beaumarchais, and Bodini were among his admirers, but his typeface had to wait for the twentieth century to achieve its due.